22

FIRST SIGHTINGS

Edited by John Loughery

FIRST
SIGHTINGS

CONTEMPORARY STORIES OF
AMERICAN YOUTH

PERSEA BOOKS ▲ NEW YORK

For my students and colleagues, past and present,
at the Columbia Grammar and Preparatory School

and in memory of a fine teacher,
John Drugg (1945–1992)

Since this page cannot legibly accommodate all copyright notices,
pages 293–295 constitute an extension of the copyright page.

Copyright © 1993 by John Loughery

For information, please write to the publisher:
Persea Books, Inc.
60 Madison Avenue
New York, New York 10010

Library of Congress Cataloging-in-Publication Data
First sightings : stories of American youth / edited by John Loughery.
        p. cm.
    Summary: Presents twenty short stories, with protagonists aged three
to eighteen years old, by such authors as John Updike, Alice Walker,
Genaro Gonzales, and Carson McCullers.
    ISBN 0-89255-186-0 : $29.95. — ISBN0-89255-187-9 : $11.95
    1. Short stories, American. [1. Short stories.] I. Loughery, John.
PZ5.F517 1993   92-37209
[Fic]—dc20   CIP
AC

Designed by REM Studio, Inc.
Printed on acid-free, recycled paper.
Printed and bound by The Haddon Craftsmen, Scranton, Pennsylvania.
Jacket and cover printed by Lynn Art, New York, New York.

First Edition

CONTENTS

ACKNOWLEDGMENTS

My thanks to those people who provided encouragement or suggested stories and authors for this book: Mary Allen, Karen Braziller, Linda Crowley, Paula Deitz, Stewart Galanor, Tom Gatch, Kevin Lally, Virginia Loughery, Frederick Morgan, Thomas Orefice, Maria Soares, Mark Speyer, Lillian Zietz.

INTRODUCTION:
IMAGES OF CHILDHOOD
AND ADOLESCENCE

In an age of child movie stars and teen magazines, of Dr. Spock's counsel on potty training and Dr. Ruth's on adolescent sex, of million-dollar ad campaigns aimed at the under-twelve set and an elaborate, highly specialized, endlessly debated education system, it can be hard to realize that there was a time in Western culture when the idea of childhood—not to mention adolescence—did not exist. Walk about in the early Renaissance rooms of any art museum and you can feel this great divide in human history most dramatically: among paintings of knights on parade and ceremonial occasions at court, we come upon images of children, decorative features of the scene much like the castle turrets or the boar on the spit, often just to the side of the center of the action. But they aren't children as we know them, and we wonder what life must have been like for these young people depicted on canvas as miniature adults, mirror images of their elders—same clothes, same expressions, same interests—reduced (sometimes) to more plausible proportions. Look further back, to paintings before the mid–1400s, and with the obvious exception of the Christ Child, children are entirely absent.

The reasons, according to historians, for this slight attention to life prior to adulthood are rooted in the harsh physical realities of their day. Infant mortality being what it was, it didn't make sense for adults to become preoccupied with the specialness of childhood itself: it was a period for one's offspring to get through, to survive. When the child was weaned, he mingled, worked, and played with his elders. The needs of society for farmers, warriors, and leaders demanded a quick entrance into the earnest world of action or responsibility, less time for a gradual initiation into the ways of one's parents and class. (How many readers of Shakespeare recall that Henry V was sixteen when he first led his father's troops into battle against Hotspur? That Joan of Arc was seventeen when she raised the siege of Orleans? That in Juliet's time the legal age for a girl to marry was twelve, for a boy fourteen?) And in any case, how could childhood be set apart from adolescence, and adolescence from adulthood, before the age of separate bedrooms, of more discrete living quarters of any kind? The medieval home left no room, literally, for the margin of inexperience or innocence about sex and childbearing, illness and adult anxiety, that we associate with youth. As always, good parents loved their sons and daughters and tended to their needs, but the world worked against any notion of childhood as a stage of life with special problems that called for particular study; that would have to wait for a time of greater leisure, privacy, longevity, and safety.

It was a long time in coming, too. As Philippe Ariès notes in *Centuries of Childhood,* his classic study of the development of family and school life in Europe, it wasn't until the seventeenth century that children ceased to be outfitted as little adults and acquired their own style of dress. Moreover, Ariès writes, the more subtle age distinctions didn't come about for another several generations: even in the eighteenth century, childhood and adolescence were still confused, with the Latin terms *puer* and *adolscens* being used interchangeably in schools. Yet, when the changes came, they came quickly and in a random, dynamic, overlapping form. Treatises on childrearing, education, and pediatric medicine proliferated. (The first English-language book on pediatrics had appeared in 1545, written by a doctor who wisely offered his volume "here to do them good that have most need, that is to say children.") People were ready, as a large bourgeois class and family life as we know it took shape, to give thought to topics that had formerly been ignored. A play like *Romeo and Juliet,* linking tragic love and generational conflict, would probably not have found a large audience much before 1595—not, at least, if its author dramatized as approvingly as Shakespeare did a stunning moment like Juliet's Act III questioning of her nurse's views and her decision to strike out on her own. And, as always, the visual arts offer a guide to the past: Dutch painting throughout the 1600s is an anecdotal feast of juvenile imagery, from Jan Steen's hellraisers to the more pliable children of Gerard ter Borch and Nicholas Maes. They topple plates at the dinner table or dangle from their mothers' laps waiting to have their bottoms wiped—a theme to unnerve a medieval painter—or, in the better households, stand quietly by mother's side at the window, but one way or another, they are *there,* present, a noticeable part of life.

Not everyone was pleased with the newfound interest in children or in the direction that some of that interest took. The great debate in the late 1600s was over the question of "coddling"—the Dutch were thought to be particularly guilty of this—and many words were written and sermons preached questioning just how much affection and playtime was good for a child. There were those who advised that the old benign neglect had its advantages, others who worried that self-discipline would be slow to develop if children were given too much freedom to romp and riot, and many who believed that the view of children as amusing creatures who shouldn't be dealt with too severely overlooked the crucial need for guidance and molding. In any case, whatever view prevailed in a given society, such matters were deemed important, and there was no turning back. More children were living to adulthood, less was expected of them before puberty, and modern "issues" were being defined. Barbara Kaye Greenleaf rightly observes in her history of childhood that it is not exactly a coincidence that the mid–1700s saw pediatrics established as a specialized branch of medicine, the beginning of government attention to child labor abuses (though their object of concern in England was limited to children under the age of eight), the publication of the first magazines for young readers, and—in 1762—the raging controversy of *Émile*. Jean-Jacques Rousseau's strange, angry book on the menace of "civilized" control and the strength of natural goodness excited a ferocious debate. Yet for all its idiosyncrasies, *Émile* could at least be said (even by its critics) to have called attention in a transforming way to the special nature of life before adulthood, of the need to learn about children and reflect on the process of their education. It was a subject on which Rousseau could be blunt and eloquent as few other writers before him had been: "Nature wants children to be children before they are men . . . Childhood has ways of seeing, thinking, and feeling peculiar to itself; nothing can be more foolish than to substitute our ways for them."

With the nineteenth century, the interest in childhood and young adulthood seemed to turn from a large social concern to something approaching an obsession. The Victorians had indeed done some reflecting on the nature of children, as Rousseau advised, but they weren't entirely happy with what they felt they knew. Celebration of home and hearth, the triumph of middle-class mores and civilized control, demanded a popular imagery that securely fixed each family member's place in the scheme of things. In the paintings of the Victorian Age, and even more so in the drawings and lithographs in contemporary periodicals, the authority of the father, the virtue of the mother, and the docility of good children were vigorously reaffirmed. So, too, novelists found fertile material in the little ones, and depictions of sweet souls struggling to be good citizens filled the three-volume novels of the day. There appeared to be no limit to the public appetite for manifestations of this cult of innocence, leaving us to wonder about the extent of the nineteenth-century fear of the dark, unruly ways of children, and, worse yet, sexuality and adolescent rebellion. Of course, the good of all this exaggerated attention was the focus it provided on abuses, on society's real affronts to innocence—dumping-ground orphanages, barbaric schoolmasters, the cruelty of child labor—

and the awakening of conscience that writers like Charles Dickens and reformers like Lord Shaftesbury brought about.

Yet, to modern sensibilities, there's something not quite right with the whole Victorian angle on the subject. Oliver Twist and Little Dorrit (not to mention the unctuous Little Nell), Tiny Tim and Dombey's son, Jane Eyre's friend Helen Burns and Father Time—all these children of Dickens or Brontë or Hardy are insufferable kids, no more lifelike and interesting than the time-honored stock heroes and syrupy endings those great writers rejected in their development of adult characters and serious plots. Nineteenth-century literature on both sides of the Atlantic is studded with these youthful paragons of meekness and duty. Today's reader accepts them as a sorry but inevitable part of the whole package—the package being the "bright book of life" in its golden age—rather than as portraits of children that mean anything to us. Not that there weren't some brilliant exceptions: in England, George Eliot's *The Mill on the Floss* and Thackeray's *Vanity Fair* (the feisty Maggie Tulliver and the cleverly selfish Becky Sharp would have shocked the life out of Dickens's little girls), the story of Dickens's own Pip in *Great Expectations*, and preeminently, in America, *Huckleberry Finn* by Mark Twain.

The appearance of Twain's novel in 1885, much like the publication of J. D. Salinger's *Catcher in the Rye* sixty-six years later, is a milestone in the history of the perception of young people. It can be argued that Twain's boys, Huck or Tom Sawyer, have been brought to life and shaped for social and symbolic purposes as much as Dickens's waifs and are naughty in the same self-conscious way that Oliver and Nell are nice, but the fact remains that the spirit of rebellion and adventure they personify has hardly diminished a century later. Certainly the adult audience of the time had an inkling of the threat to propriety implicit in depicting youthful experience in so freewheeling a manner. Though *Huckleberry Finn* made no great stir when it first came out—in contrast to *Tom Sawyer* nine years earlier—it was banned from a number of libraries, both urban and smalltown, as a potentially damaging influence on impressionable young minds. One critic sniffed that the book was "destitute of a single redeeming quality"—just the sort of defensiveness that usually marks the demise of an old order. For

Twain recognized, by way of this extraordinary novel, that Western culture was ready—if not precisely in 1885—to see the child or adolescent as a critic of adult values, as a force in the world less in need of guidance than attention, respect, and elbowroom. Even more importantly, the time had come for the young to narrate their own tales. "You don't know about me, without you have a read a book by the name of *The Adventures of Tom Sawyer*," Huck tells us, but rest assured that Twain will let him speak for himself from here on in, even to the point of bad grammar and uninhibited colloquialisms. Youth has been given its own voice. The idea of the fragile empty vessel was soon to be as dead as the medieval concept of the miniature adult.

Twain's descendants are a diverse group. F. Scott Fitzgerald, André Gide, Thomas Mann, Alberto Moravia, Richard Wright, and Vladimir Nabokov (among so many others) charted aspects of childhood and adolescence, both social and sexual, that had rarely if ever been dealt with before in imaginative literature; the initiation stories of Stephen Dedalus, Nick Adams, Philip Carey, and Paul Morel, like those of the young women of Willa Cather, Elizabeth Bowen, and Jean Stafford, were told with an insight and literary power that collectively changed the way youth was perceived. Filmmakers and playwrights from the thirties on were quick to follow the writers' lead. Nor was the study of childhood in the modern age a matter for artists alone anymore. After Freud, John Dewey, and the Progressive Era sociologists, and later Melanie Klein and Jean Piaget, the rise of a theoretically based concern with child development took on a life of its own. And, at an equally fast pace, midcentury in America saw children and teenagers established as a lucrative and definable market, an outlet for the ever-costlier products of an affluent, manic consumer culture. Our society sees its children as integral to the process of buying and selling goods, of keeping the economy going—the magazines and their ads, the videos and video games, the TV programs and commercials, the "TOYS 'R US" empire all fuel the engine.

In the last years of the twentieth century, we seem to be approaching another turning point. The recognition of the extent of child abuse in our midst, the complexities of learning problems, and the trauma of widespread divorce has made us more sensitive in some ways to the needs of children and adolescents. But other signs are extremely discouraging. Specialists, media inquiries, and well-meant slots of "quality time" don't suffice to cope with intractable emotional realities. Schools are allowed to become places of "savage inequalities," in the sobering phrase of Jonathan Kozol. Literacy levels continue to decline. Confused messages about sex, drugs, and authority abound. Neil Postman argues in *The Disappearance of Childhood* that we are on the verge of effacing what took four centuries to create. Television, he and others have suggested, has forced upon young people an experience of the world that isn't natural to their years and that exploits and commodifies their desires and identities.

It is just this idea of the young as types, consumers, and products themselves that the best modern fiction writers oppose. The stories in this collection come in many forms and many moods. Some are third-person narratives, others are told in the first person; some work largely through plot, others by tone of voice, by stark or reverberant images, or unstated currents of feeling. Yet, amusing or horrifying, narrated in the confusing present or recollected long after the fact, they all present the reader with conflicts, choices, and questions that real people are likely to face. That, fortunately, is the business of contemporary fiction: not marketing and exploitation, but reality, drama, and insight.

First Sightings is largely an anthology of postwar fiction. These stories were published in America between 1959 and 1991, with one exception. (Carson McCullers's "Wunderkind," written when McCullers was barely out of her teens herself, appeared in 1936.) They are arranged in an approximate chronological order of the ages of the children or adolescents who are the central figures in the narrative. (In the first story, it might well be argued that the father is the main character rather than his daughter, but in all of the other stories the young person is front-and-center.) Updike's little girl in "Should Wizard Hit Mommy?" is almost four, Gina Berriault's rural protagonist in "The Stone Boy" is nine, and Ernest Gaines's harried young man in "The Sky Is Gray" is eight. What these three children have in common—a daughter of a white middle-class suburban couple, an affable child whose experience of life is defined by farm chores and hunting rifles, and a poor black boy from the South of the 1950s—is just that attribute which all of us had in common in our earliest years: a passivity in the face of the power and guidance of adults, a sure sense that the terms of the world were theirs to set, not ours.

Seen in that light, the three stories that begin *First Sightings* are about manipulation, and the children have naturally (given their ages) limited insight into their situations. An atmosphere of vulnerability in the face of authority seemed the best starting point for a book that aims to tell its own tale through the selection and arrangement of the stories. That tale is about coming of age in the United States in the twentieth century, or certain key aspects of that experience. From Updike's Jo, full of energy and trust and waiting to be lulled to sleep by Daddy's fables, to Ethan Canin's protagonist just out of high school and cowed by the pressure of responsibility and commitment, the individual's tenuous journey to adulthood is one everyone knows, or can remember.

The next few stories deal with awakening perceptions— awareness and the first questionings of the world and one's place in it that often occur between nine and thirteen, often in rebellion. Genaro Gonzalez's nine-year-old in "Too Much His Father's Son" poignantly struggles to do right by his mother and father and by himself as a marriage breaks apart and everyone takes sides. At ten, Barbara Kingsolver's protagonist in "Rose-Johnny" is made well aware of the need to take sides as she tries to understand her rural community's ostracism of a woman she's befriended. Like Scout in *To Kill a Mockingbird*, Georgeann is curious, observant, and agreeably tough-minded about what's important to her. Like Huck, she is more alert to unfairness than anyone else around her, and she quickly learns the consequences of a sense of justice. Nathan, the boy in Michael Chabon's "The Little Knife," is the central figure of five stories in *A Model World* (1990) in which that character ages from ten to sixteen. In this, the first story of Chabon's chronicle, Nathan confronts the news of his parents' impending divorce with grief, confusion, and guilt. "The Kind of Light That Shines on Texas" by Reginald McKnight tells a dramatic story of racial violence in a school setting and offers us a portrait of an intelligent twelve-year-old black boy coming to terms not only with white hatred and condescension, but with his own ambivalent feelings toward his black schoolmates. And with Philip Roth's "The Conversion of the Jews," we finally have outright rebellion, part comic and part tragic; Ozzie Freedman has examined the adult world and is ready, in his own peculiar fashion, to fight its pettiness and its lies.

Adolescence, particularly as it has developed in the last twenty years, brings its own problems and pleasures. One difficulty in America is that parents don't assume the roles they used to. Donna Reed and Ozzie Nelson are long gone, replaced by single mothers with boyfriends and drinking problems. This is the predicament that bedevils Lynne Sharon Schwartz's droll thirteen-year-old Jodie in "Over the Hill" and, at a later age and in a different way, Shane in Bill Barich's "Hard to Be Good." The trouble for Schwartz's character is her divorced mother's rowdy social life, while Barich's appealing young man has to find his way as the child of the children of Haight-Ashbury, a now-older generation that has never quite known what to do with the offspring it brought into the world. As the girl in "Over the Hill" asks, "If grownups don't act their age who is going to keep any kind of order in the world?" Good question, even if it sees things from only one limited, needy perspective.

In "A Girl's Story," Toni Cade Bambara describes with her usual sharp eye and lack of sentimentality the onset of puberty for one black girl whose grandmother wrongly assumes she is better informed and more sexually active than she is. Richard McCann writes in "My Mother's Clothes: The School of Beauty and Shame" about the difficulty in early adolescence of coming to terms with gender roles and one's sexuality in a hostile atmosphere—a subject, given society's attitudes toward homosexuality, that was seldom raised before the 1970s and seldom treated as perceptively as it is in McCann's story. Carson McCullers's brilliant pianist in "Wunderkind" experiences, at fourteen, the special pressure that comes with great talent and high expectations, while Molly, the protagonist of Joy Williams's eerie story "The Skater," anticipates her imminent separation from her parents as she makes the admissions rounds of several New England boarding schools.

This is a break that Molly alternately needs and dreads. The possibilities of an existence away from home beckon—and, naturally, frighten as well.

The intricacies of social life and social pressures, made especially complex when set against the demands of a different cultural background, are the focus of the stories by Gish Jen and Helena María Viramontes. Jen's character, a Chinese-American eighth-grader, feels that it is high time that she had a boyfriend and finds that necessary attachment in the person of a Japanese-American classmate—a source of trouble on many fronts. Viramontes's Naomi groans beneath the indignity of having to drag along her younger sister as a chaperone wherever she goes. Somewhere between the designations of *girl* and *woman*, these two characters (one humorous and one angry) test uncertain boundaries.

In the last stories of this collection, two of the best-known American authors of short fiction—Joyce Carol Oates and Alice Walker—and two excellent writers who began to publish in the late 1980s—Melanie Rae Thon and Ethan Canin—evoke that time in late adolescence and early adulthood when childhood is far behind but few of the issues that trouble their characters have been resolved or even rendered more manageable. If Viramontes's young woman, caught in a biological as well as a cultural crossfire, is torn between her new physical urges and her kid's sense of play, Thon's Iona Moon experiences the nastier truth of sexual double standards and class distinction. If McKnight's sixth-grader is just beginning to grapple with the question of black identity, Walker's older scholarship student—a poor black Southerner accepted by virtue of her gifts into the white world of privilege and ease—has traveled much further down that road. She is ready to understand the need to reconcile the two worlds, both of which will try to define her. Joyce Carol Oates writes with haunting power of emotional breakdown and collapse; Canin, of the awareness that adulthood has somehow actually arrived. Just out of high school, Jack in "Lies" can't quite see how his future seems to be setting itself up so quickly, driving him as he does his car, "like a rocket" along a trajectory that won't allow for other choices, new adventures. Yet the choices really are Jack's to make, now, at eighteen, and that fact makes all the difference.

△

"Of all the characteristics in which the medieval age differs from the modern," the historian Barbara Tuchman once wrote, "none is so striking as the comparative absence of interest in children." That our society is interested in children is obvious; the toy and video industries are multi-billion-dollar businesses. That we haven't always done well by them where it counts—that their perceptions and experiences are varied, not generic, that their dilemmas require thoughtful responses—should also be obvious. With great skill and honesty, the writers in this book analyze, dramatize, and celebrate a time of life that is inherently fascinating and complex and has always been in danger of being subordinated to the wants of those with the power, and never more so than today.

JOHN LOUGHERY
New York, 1992

FIRST SIGHTINGS

John Updike

SHOULD WIZARD
HIT MOMMY?

In the evenings and for Saturday naps like today's, Jack told his daughter Jo a story out of his head. This custom, begun when she was two, was itself now nearly two years old, and his head felt empty. Each new story was a slight variation of a basic tale: a small creature, usually named Roger (Roger Fish, Roger Squirrel, Roger Chipmunk), had some problem and went with it to the wise old owl. The owl told him to go to the wizard, and the wizard performed a magic spell that solved the problem, demanding in payment a number of pennies greater than the number Roger Creature had but in the same breath directing the animal to a place where the extra pennies could be found. Then Roger was so happy he played many games with other creatures, and went home to his mother just in time to hear the train whistle that brought his daddy home from Boston. Jack described their supper, and the story was over. Working his way through this scheme was especially fatiguing on Saturday, because Jo never fell asleep in naps any more, and knowing this made the rite seem futile.

The little girl (not so little any more; the bumps her feet made under the covers were halfway down the bed, their big double bed that they let her be in for naps and when she was sick) had at last arranged herself, and from the way her fat face deep in the pillow shone in the sunlight sifting through the drawn shades, it did not seem fantastic that something magic would occur, and she would take her nap like an infant of two. Her brother, Bobby, was two, and already asleep with his bottle. Jack asked, "Who shall the story be about today?"

"Roger . . ." Jo squeezed her eyes shut and smiled to be thinking she was thinking. Her eyes opened, her mother's blue. "Skunk," she said firmly.

A new animal; they must talk about skunks at nursery school. Having a fresh hero momentarily stirred Jack to creative enthusiasm. "All right," he said. "Once upon a time, in the deep dark woods, there was a tiny little creature name of Roger Skunk. And he smelled very bad—"

"Yes," Jo said.

"He smelled so bad none of the other little woodland creatures would play with him." Jo looked at him solemnly; she hadn't foreseen this. "Whenever he would go out to play," Jack continued with zest, remembering certain humiliations of his own childhood, "all of the other tiny animals would cry, 'Uh-oh, here comes Roger Stinky Skunk,' and they would run away, and Roger Skunk would stand there all alone, and two little round tears would fall from his eyes." The corners of Jo's mouth drooped down and her lower lip bent forward as he traced with a forefinger along the side of her nose the course of one of Roger Skunk's tears.

"Won't he see the owl?" she asked in a high and faintly roughened voice.

Sitting on the bed beside her, Jack felt the covers tug as her legs switched tensely. He was pleased with this moment—he was telling her something true, something she must know—and had no wish to hurry on. But downstairs a chair scraped, and he realized

2

he must get down to help Clare paint the living-room woodwork.

"Well, he walked along very sadly and came to a very big tree, and in the tiptop of the tree was an enormous wise old owl."

"Good."

" 'Mr. Owl,' Roger Skunk said, 'all the other little animals run away from me because I smell so bad.' 'So you do,' the owl said. 'Very, very bad.' 'What can I do?' Roger Skunk said, and he cried very hard.'

"The wizard, the wizard," Jo shouted, and sat right up, and a Little Golden Book spilled from the bed.

"Now, Jo. Daddy's telling the story. Do you want to tell Daddy the story?"

"No. You me."

"Then lie down and be sleepy."

Her head relapsed onto the pillow and she said, "Out of your head."

"Well. The owl thought and thought. At last he said, 'Why don't you go see the wizard?' "

"Daddy?"

"What?"

"Are magic spells *real?*" This was a new phase, just this last month, a reality phase. When he told her spiders eat bugs, she turned to her mother and asked, "Do they *really?*" and when Clare told her God was in the sky and all around them, she turned to her father and insisted, with a sly yet eager smile, "Is He *really?*"

"They're real in stories," Jack answered curtly. She had made him miss a beat in the narrative. "The owl said, 'Go through the dark woods, under the apple trees, into the swamp, over the crick—' "

"What's a crick?"

"A little river. 'Over the crick, and there will be the wizard's house.' And that's the way Roger Skunk went, and pretty soon he came to a little white house, and he rapped on the door." Jack rapped on the window sill, and under the covers Jo's tall figure clenched in an infantile thrill. "And then a tiny little old man came out, with a long white beard and a pointed blue hat, and said, 'Eh? Whatzis? Whatcher want? You smell awful.' " The wizard's voice was one of Jack's own favorite effects; he did it by scrunching up his face and somehow whining through his eyes, which felt for the interval rheumy. He felt being an old man suited him.

" 'I know it,' Roger Skunk said, 'and all the little animals run away from me. The enormous wise owl said you could help me.'

" 'Eh? Well, maybe. Come on in. Don't git too close.' Now, inside, Jo, there were all these magic things, all jumbled together in a big dusty heap, because the wizard did not have any cleaning lady."

"Why?"

"Why? Because he was a wizard, and a very old man."

"Will he die?"

"No. Wizards don't die. Well, he rummaged around and found an old stick called a magic wand and asked Roger Skunk what he wanted to smell like. Roger thought and thought and said, 'Roses.' "

"Yes. Good," Jo said smugly.

Jack fixed her with a trancelike gaze and chanted in the wizard's elderly irritable voice:

"Abracadabry, hocus-poo,
Roger Skunk, how do you do,
Roses, boses, pull an ear,
Roger Skunk, you never fear:
          Bingo!' "

He paused as a rapt expression widened out from his daughter's nostrils, forcing her eyebrows up and her lower lip down in a wide noiseless grin, an expression in which Jack was startled to recognize his wife feigning pleasure at cocktail parties. "And all of a sudden," he whispered, "the whole inside of the wizard's house was full of the smell of—*roses!* 'Roses!' Roger Fish cried. And the wizard said, very cranky, 'That'll be seven pennies.' "

"Daddy."

"What?"

"Roger *Skunk*. You said Roger Fish."

"Yes. Skunk."

"You said Roger *Fish*. Wasn't that silly?"

"Very silly of your stupid old daddy. Where was I? Well, you know about the pennies."

"Say it."

"O.K. Roger Skunk said, 'But all I have is four pennies,' and he began to cry." Jo made the crying face again, but this time without a trace of sincerity. This annoyed Jack. Downstairs some more furniture rumbled. Clare shouldn't move heavy things; she was six months' pregnant. It would be their third.

"So the wizard said, 'Oh, very well. Go to the end of the lane and turn around three times and look down the magic well and there you will find three pennies. Hurry up.' So Roger Skunk went to the end of the lane and turned around three times and there in the magic well were *three pennies!* So he took them back to the wizard and was very happy and ran out into the woods and all the other little animals gathered around him because he smelled so good. And they played tag, baseball, football, basketball, lacrosse, hockey, soccer, and pick-up-sticks."

"What's pick-up-sticks?"

"It's a game you play with sticks."

"Like the wizard's magic wand?"

"Kind of. And they played games and laughed all afternoon and then it began to get dark and they all ran home to their mommies."

Jo was starting to fuss with her hands and look out of the window, at the crack of day that showed under the shade. She thought the story was all over. Jack didn't like women when they took anything for granted; he liked them apprehensive, hanging on his words. "Now, Jo, are you listening?"

"Yes."

"Because this is very interesting. Roger Skunk's mommy said, 'What's that awful smell?' "

"Wha-at?"

"And Roger Skunk said, 'It's me, Mommy. I smell like roses.' And she said, 'Who made you smell like that?' And he said, 'The wizard,' and she said, 'Well, of all the nerve. You come with me and we're going right back to that very awful wizard.' "

Jo sat up, her hands dabbling in the air with genuine fright.

"But Daddy, then he said about the other little aminals run *away!*" Her hands skittered off, into the underbrush.

"All right. He said, 'But Mommy, all the other little animals run away,' and she said, 'I don't care. You smelled the way a little skunk should have and I'm going to take you right back to that wizard,' and she took an umbrella and went back with Roger Skunk and hit that wizard right over the head."

"No," Jo said, and put her hand out to touch his lips, yet even in her agitation did not quite dare to stop the source of truth. Inspiration came to her. "Then the wizard hit *her* on the head and did not change that little skunk back."

"No," he said. "The wizard said 'O.K.' and Roger Skunk did not smell of roses any more. He smelled very bad again."

"But the other little amum—*oh!*—amum—"

"Joanne. It's Daddy's story. Shall Daddy not tell you any more stories?" Her broad face looked at him through sifted light, astounded. "This is what happened, then. Roger Skunk and his mommy went home and they heard *Woo-oo, woooo-oo* and it was the choo-choo train bringing Daddy Skunk home from Boston. And they had lima beans, pork chops, celery, liver, mashed potatoes, and Pie-Oh-My for dessert. And when Roger Skunk was in bed Mommy Skunk came up and hugged him and said he smelled like her little baby skunk again and she loved him very much. And that's the end of the story."

"But Daddy."

"What?"

"Then did the other little ani-mals run away?"

"No, because eventually they got used to the way he was and did not mind it at all."

"What's evenshiladee?"

"In a little while."

"That was a stupid mommy."

"It was *not*," he said with rare emphasis, and believed, from her expression, that she realized he was defending his own mother to her, or something as odd. "Now I want you to put your big heavy head in the pillow and have a good long nap." He adjusted the shade so not even a crack of day showed, and tiptoed to the door, in the pretense that she was already asleep. But when he turned, she was crouching on top of the covers and staring at him. "Hey. Get under the covers and fall faaast asleep. Bobby's asleep."

She stood up and bounced gingerly on the springs. "Daddy."

"What?"

"Tomorrow, I want you to tell me the story that that wizard took that magic wand and hit that mommy"—her plump arms chopped fiercely—"right over the head."

"No. That's not the story. The point is that the little skunk loved his mommy more than he loved aaalll the other little animals and she knew what was right."

"No. Tomorrow you say he hit that mommy. Do it." She kicked her legs up and sat down on the bed with a great heave and complaint of springs, as she had done hundreds of times before, except that this time she did not laugh. "Say it, Daddy."

"Well, we'll see. Now at least have a rest. Stay on the bed. You're a good girl."

He closed the door and went downstairs. Clare had spread the newspapers and opened the paint can and, wearing an old shirt of his on top of her maternity smock, was stroking the chair rail with a dipped brush. Above him footsteps vibrated and he called, "*Joanne.* Shall I come up there and spank you?" The footsteps hesitated.

"That was a long story," Clare said.

"The poor kid," he answered, and with utter weariness watched his wife labor. The woodwork, a cage of moldings and rails and baseboards all around them, was half old tan and half new ivory and he felt caught in an ugly middle position, and though he as well felt his wife's presence in the cage with him, he did not want to speak with her, work with her, touch her, anything.

Gina Berriault

THE STONE BOY

Arnold drew his overalls and raveling gray sweater over his naked body. In the other narrow bed his brother Eugene went on sleeping, undisturbed by the alarm clock's rusty ring. Arnold, watching his brother sleeping, felt a peculiar dismay; he was nine, six years younger than Eugie, and in their waking hours it was he who was subordinate. To dispel emphatically his uneasy advantage over his sleeping brother, he threw himself on the hump of Eugie's body.

"Get up! Get up!" he cried.

Arnold felt his brother twist away and saw the blankets lifted in a great wind, and, all in an instant, he was lying on his back under the covers with only his face showing, like a baby, and Eugie was sprawled on top of him.

"Whasa matter with you?" asked Eugie in sleepy anger, his face hanging close.

"Get up," Arnold repeated. "You said you'd pick peas with me."

Stupidly, Eugie gazed around the room to see if morning had come into it yet. Arnold began to laugh derisively, making soft, snorting noises, and was thrown off the bed. He got up from the floor and went down the stairs, the laughter continuing, like hiccups, against his will. But when he opened the staircase door and entered the parlor, he hunched up his shoulders and was quiet because his parents slept in the bedroom downstairs.

Arnold lifted his .22–caliber rifle from the rack on the kitchen wall. It was an old lever-action that his father had given him because nobody else used it anymore. On their way down to the garden he and Eugie would go by the lake, and if there were any ducks on it he'd take a shot at them. Standing on the stool before the cupboard, he searched on the top shelf in the confusion of medicines and ointments for man and beast and found a small yellow box of .22 cartridges. Then he sat down on the stool and began to load his gun.

It was cold in the kitchen so early, but later in the day, when his mother canned the peas, the heat from the wood stove would be almost unbearable. Yesterday she had finished preserving the huckleberries that the family had picked along the mountain, and before that she had canned all the cherries his father had brought from the warehouse in Corinth. Sometimes, on these summer days, Arnold would deliberately come out from the shade where he was playing and make himself as uncomfortable as his mother was in the kitchen by standing in the sun until the sweat ran down his body.

Eugie came clomping down the stairs and into the kitchen, his head drooping with sleepiness. From his perch on the stool Arnold watched Eugie slip on his green knit cap. Eugie didn't really need a cap; he hadn't had a haircut in a long time and his brown curls grew thick and matted, close around his ears and down his neck, tapering there to a small whorl. Eugie passed his left hand through his hair before he set his cap down with his right. The very way he slipped his cap on was an announcement of his status; almost everything he did was a reminder that he was eldest—first he, then Nora, then Arnold—and called attention to how tall he was, almost as tall as his father, how long his legs were, how small he was in the hips, and what a neat dip above his buttocks his thick-soled logger's boots gave him. Arnold never tired of watching Eugie offer silent praise unto himself. He wondered, as he sat enthralled, if when he got to be Eugie's age he would still be undersized and his hair still straight.

Eugie eyed the gun. "Don't you know this ain't duck season?" he asked gruffly, as if he were the sheriff.

"No, I don't know," Arnold sniggered.

Eugie picked up the tin washtub for the peas, unbolted the door with his free hand and kicked it open. Then, lifting the tub to his head, he went clomping down the back steps. Arnold followed, closing the door behind him.

The sky was faintly gray, almost white. The mountains behind the farm made the sun climb a long way to show itself. Several miles to the south, where the range opened up, hung an orange mist, but the valley in which the farm lay was still cold and colorless.

Eugie opened the gate to the yard and the boys passed between the barn and the row of chicken houses, their feet stirring up the carpet of brown feathers dropped by the molting chickens. They paused before going down the slope to the lake. A fluky morning wind ran among the shocks of wheat that covered the slope. It sent a shimmer northward across the lake, gently moving the rushes that formed an island in the center. Killdeer, their white markings flashing, skimmed the water, crying their shrill, sweet cry. And there at the south end of the lake were four wild ducks, swimming out from the willows into open water.

Arnold followed Eugie down the slope, stealing, as his brother did, from one shock of wheat to another. Eugie paused before climbing through the wire fence that divided the wheat field from the marshy pasture around the lake. They were screened from the ducks by the willows along the lake's edge.

"If you hit your duck, you want me to go in after it?" Eugie said.

"If you want," Arnold said.

Eugie lowered his eyelids, leaving slits of mocking blue. "You'd drown 'fore you got to it, them legs of yours are so puny," he said.

He shoved the tub under the fence and, pressing down the center wire, climbed through into the pasture.

Arnold pressed down the bottom wire, thrust a leg through and leaned forward to bring the other leg after. His rifle caught on the wire and he jerked at it. The air was rocked by the sound of the shot. Feeling foolish, he lifted his face, baring it to an expected shower of derision from his brother. But Eugie did not turn around. Instead, from his crouching position, he fell to his knees and then pitched forward onto his face. The ducks rose up crying from the lake, cleared the mountain background and beat away northward across the pale sky.

Arnold squatted beside his brother. Eugie seemed to be climbing the earth, as if the earth ran up and down, and when he found he couldn't scale it he lay still.

"Eugie?"

Then Arnold saw it, under the tendril of hair at the nape of the neck—a slow rising of bright blood. It had an obnoxious movement, like that of a parasite.

"Hey, Eugie," he said again. He was feeling the same discomfort he had felt when he had watched Eugie sleeping; his brother didn't know that he was lying face down in the pasture.

Again he said, "Hey, Eugie," an anxious nudge in his voice. But Eugie was as still as the morning around them.

Arnold set his rifle down on the ground and stood up. He picked up the tub and, dragging it behind him, walked along by the willows to the garden fence and climbed through. He went down on his knees among the tangled vines. The pods were cold with the night, but his hands were strange to him, and not until some time had passed did he realize that the pods were numbing his fingers. He picked from the top of the vine first, then lifted the vine to look underneath for pods, and moved on to the next.

II

It was a warmth on his back, like a large hand laid firmly there, that made him raise his head. Way up the slope the gray farmhouse was struck by the sun. While his head had been bent the land had grown bright around him.

When he got up his legs were so stiff that he had to go down on his knees again to ease the pain. Then, walking sideways, he dragged the tub, half full of peas, up the slope.

The kitchen was warm now; a fire was roaring in the stove with a closed-up, rushing sound. His mother was spooning eggs from a pot of boiling water and putting them into a bowl. Her short brown hair was uncombed and fell forward across her eyes as she bent her head. Nora was lifting a frying pan full of trout from the stove, holding the handle with a dish towel. His father had just come in from bringing the cows from the north pasture to the barn, and was sitting on the stool, unbuttoning his red plaid Mackinaw.

"Did you boys fill the tub?" his mother asked.

"They ought of by now," his father said. "They went out of the house an hour ago. Eugie woke me up comin' downstairs. I heard you shootin'—did you get a duck?"

"No," Arnold said. They would want to know why Eugie wasn't coming in for breakfast, he thought. "Eugie's dead," he told them.

They stared at him. The pitch crackled in the stove.

"You kids playin' a joke?" his father asked.

"Where's Eugene?" his mother asked scoldingly. She wanted, Arnold knew, to see his eyes, and when he had glanced at her she put the bowl and spoon down on the stove and walked past him. His father stood up and went out the door after her. Nora followed them with little skipping steps, as if afraid to be left behind.

Arnold went into the barn, down along the foddering passage past the cows waiting to be milked, and climbed into the loft. After a few minutes he heard a terrifying sound coming toward the house. His parents and Nora were returning from the willows, and sounds sharp as knives were rising from his mother's breast and carrying over the sloping fields. In a short while he heard his father go down the back steps, slam the car door and drive away.

Arnold lay still as a fugitive, listening to the cows eating close by. If his parents never called him, he thought, he would stay up in the loft forever, out of the way. In the night he would sneak down for a drink of water from the faucet over the trough and for whatever food they left for him by the barn.

The rattle of his father's car as it turned down the lane recalled him to the present. He heard the voices of his Uncle Andy and Aunt Alice as they and his father went past the barn to the lake. He could feel the morning growing heavier with sun. Someone, probably Nora, had let the chickens out of their coops and they were cackling in the yard.

After a while, a car, followed by another car, turned down the road off the highway. The cars drew to a stop and he heard the voices of strange men. The men also went past the barn and down to the lake. The sheriff's men and the undertakers, whom his father must have phoned from Uncle Andy's house, had arrived from Corinth. Then he heard everybody come back and heard the cars turn around and leave.

"Arnold!" It was his father calling from the yard.

He climbed down the ladder and went out into the sun, picking wisps of hay from his overalls.

Corinth, nine miles away, was the county seat. Arnold sat in the front seat of the old Ford between his father, who was driving, and Uncle Andy; no one spoke. Uncle Andy was his mother's brother, and he had been fond of Eugie because Eugie had resembled him. Andy had taken Eugie hunting and had given him a knife and a lot of things, and now Andy, his eyes narrowed, sat tall and stiff beside Arnold.

Arnold's father parked the car before the courthouse. It was a two-story brick building with a lamp on each side of the bottom step. They went up the wide stone steps, Arnold and his father going first, and entered the darkly paneled hallway. The shirt-sleeved man in the sheriff's office said that the sheriff was at Carlson's Parlor examining the boy who was shot.

Andy went off to get the sheriff while Arnold and his father waited on a bench in the corridor. Arnold felt his father watching him, and he lifted his eyes with painful casualness to the announcement, on the opposite wall, of the Corinth County Annual Rodeo, and then to the clock with its loudly clucking pendulum. After he had come down from the loft his father and Uncle Andy had stood in the yard with him and asked him to tell them everything, and he had explained to them how the gun had caught on the wire. But when they had asked him why he hadn't run back to the house to tell his parents, he had had no answer—all he could say was that he had gone down into the garden to pick the peas. His father had stared at him in a pale, puzzled way, and it was then that he had felt his father and the others set their cold, turbulent silence against him. Arnold shifted on the bench, his only feeling a small one of compunction imposed by his father's eyes.

At a quarter past nine, Andy and the sheriff came in. They all went into the sheriff's private office, and Arnold was sent forward to sit in the chair by the sheriff's desk; his father and Andy sat down on the bench against the wall.

The sheriff lumped down into his swivel chair and swung toward Arnold. He was an old man with white hair like wheat stubble. His restless green eyes made him seem not to be in his office but to be hurrying and bobbing around somewhere else.

"What did you say your name was?" the sheriff asked.

"Arnold," he replied, but he could not remember telling the sheriff his name before.

"What were you doing with a .22, Arnold?"

"It's mine," he said.

"Okay. What were you going to shoot?"

"Some ducks," he relied.

"Out of season?"

He nodded.

"That's bad," said the sheriff. "Were you and your brother good friends?"

What did he mean—good friends? Eugie was his brother. That was different from a friend, Arnold thought. A best friend was your own age, but Eugie was almost a man. Eugie had had a way of looking at him, slyly and mockingly and yet confidentially, that had summed up how they both felt about being brothers. Arnold had wanted to be with Eugie more than with anybody else, but he couldn't say they had been good friends.

"Did they ever quarrel?" the sheriff asked his father.

14

"Not that I know," his father replied. "It seemed to me that Arnold cared a lot for Eugie."

"Did you?" the sheriff asked Arnold.

If it seemed so to his father, then it was so. Arnold nodded.

"Were you mad at him this morning?"

"No."

"How did you happen to shoot him?"

"We was crawlin' through the fence."

"Yes?"

"An' the gun got caught on the wire."

"Seems the hammer must of caught," his father put in.

"All right, that's what happened," said the sheriff. "But what I want you to tell me is this. Why didn't you go back to the house and tell your father right away? Why did you go and pick peas for an hour?"

Arnold gazed over his shoulder at his father, expecting his father to have an answer for this also. But his father's eyes, larger and even lighter blue than usual, were fixed upon him curiously. Arnold picked at a callus in his right palm. It seemed odd now that he had not run back to the house and wakened his father, but he could not remember why he had not. They were all waiting for him to answer.

"I come down to pick peas," he said.

"Didn't you think," asked the sheriff, stepping carefully from word to word, "that it was more important for you to go tell your parents what happened?"

"The sun was gonna come up," Arnold said.

"What's that got to do with it?"

"It's better to pick peas while they're cool."

The sheriff swung away from him, laid both hands flat on his desk. "Well, all I can say is," he said across to Arnold's father and Uncle Andy, "he's either a moron or he's so reasonable that he's way ahead of us." He gave a challenging snort. "It's come to my notice that the most reasonable guys are mean ones. They don't feel nothing."

15

For a moment the three men sat still. Then the sheriff lifted his hand like a man taking an oath. "Take him home," he said.

"You don't want him?" Andy asked.

"Not now," replied the sheriff. "Maybe in a few years."

Arnold's father stood up. He held his hat against his chest. "The gun ain't his no more," he said wanly.

Arnold went first through the hallway, hearing behind him the heels of his father and Uncle Andy striking the floorboards. He went down the steps ahead of them and climbed into the back seat of the car. Andy paused as he was getting into the front seat and gazed back at Arnold, and Arnold saw that his uncle's eyes had absorbed the knowingness from the sheriff's eyes. Andy and his father and the sheriff had discovered what made him go down into the garden. It was because he was cruel, the sheriff had said, and didn't care about his brother. Arnold lowered his eyelids meekly against his uncle's stare.

The rest of the day he did his tasks around the farm, keeping apart from the family. At evening, when he saw his father stomp tiredly into the house, Arnold did not put down his hammer and leave the chicken coop he was repairing. He was afraid that they did not want him to eat supper with them. But in a few minutes another fear that they would go to the trouble of calling him and that he would be made conspicuous by his tardiness made him follow his father into the house. As he went through the kitchen he saw the jars of peas standing in rows on the workbench, a reproach to him.

No one spoke at supper, and his mother, who sat next to him, leaned her head in her hand all through the meal, curving her fingers over her eyes so as not to see him. They were finishing their small, silent supper when the visitors began to arrive, knocking hard on the back door. The men were coming from their farms now that it was growing dark and they could not work anymore.

Old Man Matthews, gray and stocky, came first, with his two sons, Orion, the elder, and Clint, who was Eugie's age. As the callers entered the parlor where the family ate, Arnold sat down in a rocking chair. Even as he had been undecided before supper whether to remain outside or take his place at the table, he now thought that he should go upstairs, and yet he stayed to avoid being conspicuous by his absence. If he stayed, he thought, as he always stayed and listened when visitors came, they would see that he was only Arnold and not the person the sheriff thought he was. He sat with his arms crossed and his hands tucked into his armpits and did not lift his eyes.

The Matthews men had hardly settled down around the table, after Arnold's mother and Nora cleared away the dishes, when another car rattled down the road and someone else rapped on the back door. This time it was Sullivan, a spare and sandy man, so nimble of gesture and expression that Arnold had never been able to catch more than a few of his meanings. Sullivan, in dusty jeans, sat down in another rocker, shot out his skinny legs and began to talk in his fast way, recalling everything that Eugene had ever said to him. The other men interrupted to tell of occasions they remembered, and after a time Clint's young voice, hoarse like Eugene's had been, broke in to tell about the time Eugene had beat him in a wrestling match.

Out in the kitchen the voices of Orion's wife and of Mrs. Sullivan mingled with Nora's voice but not, Arnold noticed, his mother's. Then dry little Mr. Cram came, leaving large Mrs. Cram in the kitchen, and there was no chair left for Mr. Cram to sit in. No one asked Arnold to get up and he was unable to rise. He knew that the story had got around to them during the day about how he had gone and picked peas after he had shot his brother, and he knew that although they were talking only about Eugie they were thinking about him, and if he got up, if he moved even his foot, they would all be alerted. Then Uncle Andy arrived and leaned his tall, lanky body against the doorjamb, and there were two men standing.

Presently Arnold was aware that the talk had stopped. He knew without looking up that the men were watching him.

"Not a tear in his eye," said Andy, and Arnold knew that his uncle had gestured the men to attention.

"He don't give a hoot, is that how it goes?" asked Sullivan.

"He's a reasonable fellow," Andy explained. "That's what the sheriff said. It's us who ain't reasonable. If we'd of shot our brother, we'd of come runnin' back to the house, cryin' like a baby. Well, we'd of been unreasonable. What would of been the use of actin' like that? If your brother is shot dead, he's shot dead. What's the use of gettin' emotional about it? The thing to do is go down to the garden and pick peas. Am I right?"

The men around the room shifted their heavy, satisfying weight of unreasonableness.

Matthews' son Orion said, "If I'd of done what he done, Pa would've hung my pelt by the side of that big coyote's in the barn."

Arnold sat in the rocker until the last man filed out. While his family was out in the kitchen bidding the callers good night and the cars were driving away down the dirt lane to the highway, he picked up one of the kerosene lamps and slipped quickly up the stairs. In his room he undressed by lamplight, although he and Eugie had always undressed in the dark, and not until he was lying in his bed did he blow out the flame. He felt nothing, not any grief. There was only the same immense silence and crawling inside of him; it was the way the house and fields felt under a merciless sun.

He awoke suddenly. He knew that his father was out in the yard, closing the doors of the chicken houses. The sound that had awakened him was the step of his father as he got up from the rocker and went down the back steps. And he knew that his mother was awake in her bed.

Throwing off the covers, he rose swiftly, went down the stairs and across the dark parlor to his parents' room. He rapped on the door.

"Mother?"

From the closed room her voice rose to him, a seeking a retreating voice. "Yes?"

"Mother?" he asked insistently. He had expected her to realize that he wanted to go down on his knees by her bed and tell her that Eugie was dead. She did not know it yet, nobody knew it, and yet she was sitting up in bed, waiting to be told, waiting for him to confirm her dread. He had expected her to tell him to come in, to allow him to dig his head into her blankets and tell her about the terror he had felt when he had knelt beside Eugie. He had come to clasp her in his arms and, in his terror, to pommel her breasts with his head. He put his hand upon the knob.

"Go back to bed, Arnold," she called sharply.

But he waited.

"Go back! Is night when you get afraid?"

At first he did not understand. Then, silently, he left the door and for a stricken moment stood by the rocker. Outside everything was still. The fences, the shocks of wheat seen through the window before him were so still it was as if they moved and breathed in the daytime and had fallen silent with the lateness of the hour. It was a silence that seemed to observe his father, a figure moving alone around the yard, his lantern casting a circle of light by his feet. In a few minutes his father would enter the dark house, the lantern still lighting his way.

Arnold was suddenly aware that he was naked. He had thrown off his blankets and come down the stairs to tell his mother how he felt about Eugie, but she had refused to listen to him and his nakedness had become unpardonable. At once he went back up the stairs, fleeing from his father's lantern.

At breakfast he kept his eyelids lowered as if to deny the night. Nora, sitting at his left, did not pass the pitcher of milk to him and he did not ask for it. He would never again, he vowed, ask them for anything, and he ate his fried eggs and potatoes only because everybody ate meals—the cattle ate, and the cats; it was customary for everybody to eat.

"Nora, you gonna keep that pitcher for yourself?" his father asked.

Nora lowered her head unsurely.

"Pass it on to Arnold," his father said.

Nora put her hands in her lap.

His father picked up the metal pitcher and set it down at Arnold's plate.

Arnold, pretending to be deaf to the discord, did not glance up, but relief rained over his shoulders at the thought that his parents recognized him again. They must have lain awake after his father had come in from the yard: had they realized together why he had come down the stairs and knocked at their door?

"Bessie's missin' this morning," his father called out to his mother, who had gone into the kitchen. "She went up the mountain last night and had her calf, most likely. Somebody's got to go up and find her 'fore the coyotes get the calf."

That had been Eugie's job, Arnold thought. Eugie would climb the cattle trails in search of a newborn calf and come down the mountain carrying the calf across his back, with the cow running behind him, mooing in alarm.

Arnold ate the few more forkfuls of his breakfast, put his hands on the edge of the table and pushed back his chair. If he went for the calf he'd be away from the farm all morning. He could switch the cow down the mountain slowly, and the calf would run along at its mother's side.

When he passed through the kitchen, his mother was setting a kettle of water on the stove. "Where you going?" she asked awkwardly.

"Up to get the calf," he replied, averting his face.

"Arnold?"

At the door he paused reluctantly, his back to her, knowing that she was seeking him out, as his father was doing.

"Was you knocking at my door last night?"

He looked over his shoulder at her, his eyes narrow.

"What'd you want?" she asked humbly.

"I didn't want nothing," he said flatly.

Then he went out the door and down the back steps, his legs trembling from the fright his answer gave him.

Ernest J. Gaines

THE SKY IS GRAY

1

Go'n be coming in a few minutes. Coming round that bend down there full speed. And I'm go'n get out my handkerchief and wave it down, and we go'n get on it and go.

I keep on looking for it, but Mama don't look that way no more. She's looking down the road where we just come from. It's a long old road, and far 's you can see you don't see nothing but gravel. You got dry weeds on both sides, and you got trees on both sides, and fences on both sides, too. And you got cows in the pastures and they standing close together. And when we was coming out here to catch the bus I seen the smoke coming out of the cows's noses.

I look at my mama and I know what she's thinking. I been with Mama so much, just me and her, I know what she's thinking all the time. Right now it's home—Auntie and them. She's thinking if they got enough wood—if she left enough there to keep them warm till we get back. She's thinking if it go'n rain and if any of them go'n have to go out in the rain. She's thinking 'bout the hog— if he go'n get out, and if Ty and Val be able to get him back in. She always worry like that when she leaves the house. She don't worry too much if she leave me there with the smaller ones, 'cause she know I'm go'n look after them and look after Auntie and everything else. I'm the oldest and she say I'm the man.

I look at my mama and I love my mama. She's wearing that black coat and that black hat and she's looking sad. I love my mama and I want put my arm round her and tell her. But I'm not supposed to do that. She say that's weakness and that's crybaby stuff, and she don't want no crybaby round her. She don't want you to be scared, either. 'Cause Ty's scared of ghosts and she's always whipping him. I'm scared of the dark, too, but I make 'tend I ain't. I make 'tend I ain't 'cause I'm the oldest, and I got to set a good sample for the rest. I can't ever be scared and I can't ever cry. And that's why I never said nothing 'bout my teeth. It's been hurting me and hurting me close to a month now, but I never said it, I didn't say it 'cause I didn't want act like a crybaby, and 'cause I know we didn't have enough money to go have it pulled. But, Lord, it been hurting me. And look like it wouldn't start till at night when you was trying to get yourself little sleep. Then soon 's you shut your eyes—ummm-ummm, Lord, look like it go right down to your heartstring.

"Hurting, hanh?" Ty'd say.

I'd shake my head, but I wouldn't open my mouth for nothing. You open your mouth and let that wind in, and it almost kill you.

I'd just lay there and listen to them snore. Ty there, right 'side me, and Auntie and Val over by the fireplace. Val younger than me and Ty, and he sleeps with Auntie. Mama sleeps round the other side with Louis and Walker.

I'd just lay there and listen to them, and listen to that wind out there, and listen to that fire in the fireplace. Sometimes it'd stop long enough to let me get little rest. Sometimes it just hurt, hurt, hurt. Lord, have mercy.

2

Auntie knowed it was hurting me. I didn't tell nobody but Ty, 'cause we buddies and he ain't go'n tell nobody. But some kind of way Auntie found out. When she asked me, I told her no, nothing was wrong. But she knowed it all the time. She told me to mash up a piece of aspirin and wrap it in some cotton and jugg it down in that hole. I did it, but it didn't do no good. It stopped for a little while, and started right back again. Auntie wanted to tell Mama, but I told her, "Uh-uh." 'Cause I knowed we didn't have any money, and it just was go'n make her mad again. So Auntie told Monsieur Bayonne, and Monsieur Bayonne came over to the house and told me to kneel down 'side him on the fireplace. He put his finger in his mouth and made the Sign of the Cross on my jaw. The tip of Monsieur Bayonne's finger is some hard, 'cause he's always playing on that guitar. If we sit outside at night we can always hear Monsieur Bayonne playing on his guitar. Sometimes we leave him out there playing on the guitar.

Monsieur Bayonne made the Sign of the Cross over and over on my jaw, but that didn't do no good. Even when he prayed and told me to pray some, too, that tooth still hurt me.

"How you feeling?" he say.

"Same," I say.

He kept on praying and making the Sign of the Cross and I kept on praying, too.

"Still hurting?" he say.

"Yes, sir."

Monsieur Bayonne mashed harder and harder on my jaw. He mashed so hard he almost pushed me over on Ty. But then he stopped.

"What kind of prayers you praying, boy?" he say.

"Baptist," I say.

"Well, I'll be—no wonder that tooth still killing him. I'm

going one way and he pulling the other. Boy, don't you know any Catholic prayers?"

"I know 'Hail Mary,' " I say.

"Then you better start saying it."

"Yes, sir."

He started mashing on my jaw again, and I could hear him praying at the same time. And, sure enough, after while it stopped hurting me.

Me and Ty went outside where Monsieur Bayonne's two hounds was and we started playing with them. "Let's go hunting," Ty say. "All right," I say; and we went on back in the pasture. Soon the hounds got on a trail, and me and Ty followed them all 'cross the pasture and then back in the woods, too. And then they cornered this little old rabbit and killed him, and me and Ty made them get back, and we picked up the rabbit and started on back home. But my tooth had started hurting me again. It was hurting me plenty now, but I wouldn't tell Monsieur Bayonne. That night I didn't sleep a bit, and first thing in the morning Auntie told me to go back and let Monsieur Bayonne pray over me some more. Monsieur Bayonne was in his kitchen making coffee when I got there. Soon's he seen me he knowed what was wrong.

"All right, kneel down there 'side that stove," he say. "And this time make sure you pray Catholic. I don't know nothing 'bout that Baptist, and I don't want know nothing 'bout him."

3

Last night Mama say, "Tomorrow we going to town."

"It ain't hurting me no more," I say. "I can eat anything on it."

"Tomorrow we going to town," she say.

And after she finished eating, she got up and went to bed. She always go to bed early now. 'Fore Daddy went in the Army, she used to stay up late. All of us sitting out on the gallery or round the fire. But now, look like soon's she finish eating she go to bed.

This morning when I woke up, her and Auntie was standing

'fore the fireplace. She say: "Enough to get there and get back. Dollar and a half to have it pulled. Twenty-five for me to go, twenty-five for him. Twenty-five for me to come back, twenty-five for him. Fifty cents left. Guess I get little piece of salt meat with that."

"Sure can use it," Auntie say. "White beans and no salt meat ain't white beans."

"I do the best I can," Mama say.

They was quiet after that, and I made 'tend I was still asleep.

"James, hit the floor," Auntie say.

I still made 'tend I was asleep. I didn't want them to know I was listening.

"All right," Auntie say, shaking me by the shoulder. "Come on. Today's the day."

I pushed the cover down to get out, and Ty grabbed it and pulled it back.

"You, too, Ty," Auntie say.

"I ain't getting no teef pulled," Ty say.

"Don't mean it ain't time to get up," Auntie say. "Hit it, Ty."

Ty got up grumbling.

"James, you hurry up and get in your clothes and eat your food," Auntie say. "What time y'all coming back?" she say to Mama.

"That 'leven o'clock bus," Mama say. "Got to get back in that field this evening."

"Get a move on you, James," Auntie say.

I went in the kitchen and washed my face, then I ate my breakfast. I was having bread and syrup. The bread was warm and hard and tasted good. And I tried to make it last a long time.

Ty came back there grumbling and mad at me.

"Got to get up," he say. "I ain't having no teefes pulled. What I got to be getting up for?"

Ty poured some syrup in his pan and got a piece of bread. He didn't wash his hands, neither his face, and I could see that white stuff in his eyes.

25

"You the one getting your teef pulled," he say. "What I got to get up for. I bet if I was getting a teef pulled, you wouldn't be getting up. Shucks; syrup again. I'm getting tired of this old syrup. Syrup, syrup, syrup. I'm go'n take with the sugar diabetes. I want me some bacon sometime.''

"Go out in the field and work and you can have your bacon," Auntie say. She stood in the middle door looking at Ty. "You better be glad you got syrup. Some people ain't got that—hard 's time is."

"Shucks," Ty say. "How can I be strong."

"I don't know too much 'bout your strength," Auntie say; "but I know where you go'n be hot at, you keep that grumbling up. James, get a move on you; your mama waiting."

I ate my last piece of bread and went in the front room. Mama was standing 'fore the fireplace warming her hands. I put on my coat and my cap, and we left the house.

4

I look down there again, but it still ain't coming. I almost say, "It ain't coming yet," but I keep my mouth shut. 'Cause that's something else she don't like. She don't like for you to say something just for nothing. She can see it ain't coming, I can see it ain't coming, so why say it ain't coming. I don't say it, I turn and look at the river that's back of us. It's so cold the smoke's just raising up from the water. I see a bunch of pool-doos not too far out—just on the other side the lilies. I'm wondering if you can eat pool-doos. I ain't too sure, 'cause I ain't never ate none. But I done ate owls and blackbirds, and I done ate redbirds, too. I didn't want kill the redbirds, but she made me kill them. They had two of them back there. One in my trap, one in Ty's trap. Me and Ty was go'n play with them and let them go, but she made me kill them 'cause we needed the food.

"I can't," I say. "I can't."

"Here," she say. "Take it."

"I can't," I say. "I can't. I can't kill him, Mama, please."

"Here," she say. "Take this fork, James."

"Please, Mama, I can't kill him," I say.

I could tell she was go'n hit me. I jerked back, but I didn't jerk back soon enough.

"Take it," she say.

I took it and reached in for him, but he kept on hopping to the back.

"I can't, Mama," I say. The water just kept on running down my face. "I can't," I say.

"Get him out of there," she say.

I reached in for him and he kept on hopping to the back. Then I reached in farther, and he pecked me on the hand.

"I can't, Mama," I say.

She slapped me again.

I reached in again, but he kept on hopping out my way. Then he hopped to one side and I reached there. The fork got him on the leg and I heard his leg pop. I pulled my hand out 'cause I had hurt him.

"Give it here," she say, and jerked the fork out my hand.

She reached in and got the little bird right in the neck. I heard the fork go in his neck, and I heard it go in the ground. She brought him out and helt him right in front of me.

"That's one," she say. She shook him off and gived me the fork. "Get the other one."

"I can't, Mama," I say. "I'll do anything, but don't make me do that."

She went to the corner of the fence and broke the biggest switch over there she could find. I knelt 'side the trap, crying.

"Get him out of there," she say.

"I can't, Mama."

She started hitting me 'cross the back. I went down on the ground, crying.

"Get him," she say.

"Octavia?" Auntie say.

'Cause she had come out of the house and she was standing by the tree looking at us.

"Get him out of there," Mama say.

"Octavia," Auntie say, "explain to him. Explain to him. Just don't beat him. Explain to him."

But she hit me and hit me and hit me.

I'm still young—I ain't no more than eight; but I know now; I know why I had to do it. (They was so little, though. They was so little. I 'member how I picked the feathers off them and cleaned them and helt them over the fire. Then we all ate them. Ain't had but a little bitty piece each, but we all had a little bitty piece, and everybody just looked at me 'cause they was so proud.) Suppose she had to go away? That's why I had to do it. Suppose she had to go away like Daddy went away? Then who was go'n look after us? They had to be somebody left to carry on. I didn't know it then, but I know it now. Auntie and Monsieur Bayonne talked to me and made me see.

5

Time I see it I get out my handkerchief and start waving. It's still 'way down there, but I keep waving anyhow. Then it come up and stop and me and Mama get on. Mama tell me go sit in the back while she pay. I do like she say, and the people look at me. When I pass the little sign that say "White" and "Colored," I start looking for a seat. I just see one of them back there, but I don't take it, 'cause I want my mama to sit down herself. She comes in the back and sit down, and I lean on the seat. They got seats in the front, but I know I can't sit there, 'cause I have to sit back of the sign. Anyhow, I don't want sit there if my mama go'n sit back here.

They got a lady sitting 'side my mama and she looks at me and smiles little bit. I smile back, but I don't open my mouth, 'cause the wind'll get in and make that tooth ache. The lady take out a pack of gum and reach me a slice, but I shake my head. The lady just can't understand why a little boy'll turn down gum, and she reach me a slice again. This time I point to my jaw. The lady understands and smiles little bit, and I smile little bit, but I don't open my mouth, though.

They got a girl sitting 'cross from me. She got on a red over-coat and her hair's plaited in one big plait. First, I make 'tend I don't see her over there, but then I start looking at her little bit. She make 'tend she don't see me, either, but I catch her looking that way. She got a cold, and every now and then she h'ist that little handkerchief to her nose. She ought to blow it, but she don't. Must think she's too much a lady or something.

Every time she h'ist that little handkerchief, the lady 'side her say something in her ear. She shakes her head and lays her hands in her lap again. Then I catch her kind of looking where I'm at. I smile at her little bit. But think she'll smile back? Uh-uh. She just turn up her little old nose and turn her head. Well, I show her both of us can turn us head. I turn mine too and look out at the river.

The river is gray. The sky is gray. They have pool-doos on the water. The water is wavy, and the pool-doos go up and down. The bus go round a turn, and you got plenty trees hiding the river. Then the bus go round another turn, and I can see the river again.

I look toward the front where all the white people sitting. Then I look at that little old gal again. I don't look right at her, 'cause I don't want all them people to know I love her. I just look at her little bit, like I'm looking out that window over there. But she knows I'm looking that way, and she kind of look at me, too. The lady sitting 'side her catch her this time, and she leans over and says something in her ear.

"I don't love him nothing," that little old gal says out loud.

Everybody back there hear her mouth, and all of them look at us and laugh.

"I don't love you, either," I say. "So you don't have to turn up your nose, Miss."

"You the one looking," she say.

"I wasn't looking at you," I say. "I was looking out that window, there."

"Out that window, my foot," she say. "I seen you. Everytime I turned round you was looking at me."

"You must of been looking yourself if you seen me all them times," I say.

"Shucks," she say, "I got me all kind of boyfriends."

"I got girlfriends, too," I say.

"Well, I just don't want you getting your hopes up," she say.

29

I don't say no more to that little old gal 'cause I don't want have to bust her in the mouth. I lean on the seat where Mama sitting, and I don't even look that way no more. When we get to

Bayonne, she jugg her little old tongue out at me. I make 'tend I'm go'n hit her, and she duck down 'side her mama. And all the people laugh at us again.

6

Me and Mama get off and start walking in town. Bayonne is a little bitty town. Baton Rouge is a hundred times bigger than Bayonne. I went to Baton Rouge once—me, Ty, Mama, and Daddy. But that was 'way back yonder, 'fore Daddy went in the Army. I wonder when we go'n see him again. I wonder when. Look like he ain't ever coming back home. . . . Even the pavement all cracked in Bayonne. Got grass shooting right out the sidewalk. Got weeds in the ditch, too; just like they got at home.

It's some cold in Bayonne. Look like it's colder than it is home. The wind blows in my face, and I feel that stuff running down my nose. I sniff. Mama says use that handkerchief. I blow my nose and put it back.

We pass a school and I see them white children playing in the yard. Big old red school, and them children just running and playing. Then we pass a café, and I see a bunch of people in there eating. I wish I was in there 'cause I'm cold. Mama tells me keep my eyes in front where they belong.

We pass stores that's got dummies, and we pass another café, and then we pass a shoe shop, and that bald-head man in there fixing on a shoe. I look at him and I butt into that white lady, and Mama jerks me in front and tells me stay there.

We come up to the courthouse, and I see the flag waving there. This flag ain't like the one we got at school. This one here ain't got but a handful of stars. One at school got a big pile of stars—one for every state. We pass it and we turn and there it is—the dentist office. Me and Mama go in, and they got people sitting everywhere you look. They even got a little boy in there younger than me.

Me and Mama sit on that bench, and a white lady come in there and ask me what my name is. Mama tells her and the white lady goes on back. Then I hear somebody hollering in there. Soon 's that little boy hear him hollering, he starts hollering, too.

30

His mama pats him and pats him, trying to make him hush up, but he ain't thinking 'bout his mama.

The man that was hollering in there comes out holding his jaw. He is a big old man and he's wearing overalls and a jumper.

"Got it, hanh?" another man asks him.

The man shakes his head—don't want open his mouth.

"Man, I thought they was killing you in there," the other man says. "Hollering like a pig under a gate."

The man don't say nothing. He just heads for the door, and the other man follows him.

"John Lee," the white lady says. "John Lee Williams."

The little boy juggs his head down in his mama's lap and holler more now. His mama tells him go with the nurse, but he ain't thinking 'bout his mama. His mama tells him again, but he don't even hear her. His mama picks him up and takes him in there, and even when the white lady shuts the door I can still hear little old John Lee.

"I often wonder why the Lord let a child like that suffer," a lady says to my mama. The lady's sitting right in front of us on another bench. She's got on a white dress and a black sweater. She must be a nurse or something herself, I reckon.

"Not us to question," a man says.

"Sometimes I don't know if we shouldn't," the lady says.

"I know definitely we shouldn't," the man says. The man looks like a preacher. He's big and fat and he's got on a black suit. He's got a gold chain, too.

"Why?" the lady says.

"Why anything?" the preacher says.

"Yes," the lady says. "Why anything?"

"Not us to question," the preacher says.

The lady looks at the preacher a little while and looks at Mama again.

"And look like it's the poor who suffers the most," she says. "I don't understand it."

"Best not to even try," the preacher says. "He works in mysterious ways—wonders to perform."

31

Right then little John Lee bust out hollering, and everybody turn they head to listen.

"He's not a good dentist," the lady says. "Dr. Robillard is much better. But more expensive. That's why most of the colored people come here. The white people go to Dr. Robillard. Y'all from Bayonne?"

"Down the river," my mama says. And that's all she go'n say, 'cause she don't talk much. But the lady keeps on looking at her, and so she says, "Near Morgan."

"I see," the lady says.

7

"That's the trouble with the black people in this country today," somebody else says. This one here's sitting on the same side me and Mama's sitting, and he is kind of sitting in front of that preacher. He looks like a teacher or somebody that goes to college. He's got on a suit, and he's got a book that he's been reading. "We don't question is exactly our problem," he says. "We should question and question and question—question everything."

The preacher just looks at him a long time. He done put a toothpick or something in his mouth, and he just keeps on turning it and turning it. You can see he don't like that boy with that book.

"Maybe you can explain what you mean," he says.

"I said what I meant," the boy says. "Question everything. Every stripe, every star, every word spoken. Everything."

"It 'pears to me that this young lady and I was talking 'bout God, young man," the preacher says.

"Question Him, too," the boy says.

"Wait," the preacher says. "Wait now."

"You heard me right," the boy says. "His existence as well as everything else. Everything."

The preacher just looks across the room at the boy. You can see he's getting madder and madder. But mad or no mad, the boy ain't thinking 'bout him. He looks at that preacher just 's hard 's the preacher looks at him.

"Is this what they coming to?" the preacher says. "Is this what we educating them for?"

"You're not educating me," the boy says. "I wash dishes at

32

night so that I can go to school in the day. So even the words you
spoke need questioning."

The preacher just looks at him and shakes his head.

"When I come in this room and seen you there with your book,
I said to myself, 'There's an intelligent man.' How wrong a person
can be."

"Show me one reason to believe in the existence of a God," the
boy says.

"My heart tells me," the preacher says.

" 'My heart tells me,' " the boy says. " 'My heart tells me.'
Sure, 'My heart tells me.' And as long as you listen to what your
heart tells you, you will have only what the white man gives you
and nothing more. Me, I don't listen to my heart. The purpose of
the heart is to pump blood throughout the body, and nothing else."

"Who's your paw, boy?" the preacher says.

"Why?"

"Who is he?"

"He's dead."

"And your mom?"

"She's in Charity Hospital with pneumonia. Half killed herself, working for nothing."

"And 'cause he's dead and she's sick, you mad at the world?"

"I'm not mad at the world. I'm questioning the world. I'm
questioning it with cold logic, sir. What do words like Freedom,
Liberty, God, White, Colored mean? I want to know. That's why
you are sending us to school, to read and to ask questions. And
because we ask these questions, you call us mad. No sir, it is not us
who are mad."

"You keep saying 'us'?"

" 'Us.' Yes—us. I'm not alone."

The preacher just shakes his head. Then he looks at everybody
in the room—everybody. Some of the people look down at the
floor, keep from looking at him. I kind of look 'way myself, but
soon 's I know he done turn his head, I look that way again.

"I'm sorry for you," he says to the boy.

33

"Why?" the boy says. "Why not be sorry for yourself? Why
are you so much better off than I am? Why aren't you sorry for
these other people in here? Why not be sorry for the lady who had

to drag her child into the dentist office? Why not be sorry for the lady sitting on that bench over there? Be sorry for them. Not for me. Some way or the other I'm going to make it."

"No, I'm sorry for you," the preacher says.

"Of course, of course," the boy says, nodding his head. "You're sorry for me because I rock that pillar you're leaning on."

"You can't ever rock the pillar I'm leaning on, young man. It's stronger than anything man can ever do."

"You believe in God because a man told you to believe in God," the boy says. "A white man told you to believe in God. And why? To keep you ignorant so he can keep his feet on your neck."

"So now we the ignorant?" the preacher says.

"Yes," the boy says. "Yes." And he opens his book again.

The preacher just looks at him sitting there. The boy done forgot all about him. Everybody else make 'tend they done forgot the squabble, too.

Then I see that preacher getting up real slow. Preacher's a great big old man and he got to brace himself to get up. He comes over where the boy is sitting. He just stands there a little while looking down at him, but the boy don't raise his head.

"Get up, boy," preacher says.

The boy looks up at him, then he shuts his book real slow and stands up. Preacher just hauls back and hit him in the face. The boy falls back 'gainst the wall, but he straightens himself up and looks right back at that preacher.

"You forgot the other cheek," he says.

The preacher hauls back and hit him again on the other side. But this time the boy braces himself and don't fall.

"That hasn't changed a thing," he says.

The preacher just looks at the boy. The preacher's breathing real hard like he just run up a big hill. The boy sits down and opens his book again.

"I feel sorry for you," the preacher says. "I never felt so sorry for a man before."

34

The boy makes 'tend he don't even hear that preacher. He keeps on reading his book. The preacher goes back and gets his hat off the chair.

"Excuse me," he says to us. "I'll come back some other time. Y'all, please excuse me."

And he looks at the boy and goes out the room. The boy h'ist his hand up to his mouth one time to wipe 'way some blood. All the rest of the time he keeps on reading. And nobody else in there say a word.

8

Little John Lee and his mama come out the dentist office, and the nurse calls somebody else in. Then little bit later they come out, and the nurse calls another name. But fast 's she calls somebody in there, somebody else comes in the place where we sitting, and the room stays full.

The people coming in now, all of them wearing big coats. One of them says something 'bout sleeting, another one says he hope not. Another one says he think it ain't nothing but rain. 'Cause, he says, rain can get awful cold this time of year.

All round the room they talking. Some of them talking to people right by them, some of them talking to people clear 'cross the room, some of them talking to anybody'll listen. It's a little bitty room, no bigger than us kitchen, and I can see everybody in there. The little old room's full of smoke, 'cause you got two old men smoking pipes over by that side door. I think I feel my tooth thumping me some, and I hold my breath and wait. I wait and wait, but it don't thump me no more. Thank God for that.

I feel like going to sleep, and I lean back 'gainst the wall. But I'm scared to go to sleep. Scared 'cause the nurse might call my name and I won't hear her. And Mama might go to sleep, too, and she'll be mad if neither one of us heard the nurse.

I look up at Mama. I love my mama. I love my mama. And when cotton come I'm go'n get her a new coat. And I ain't go'n get a black one, either. I think I'm go'n get her a red one.

"They got some books over there," I say. "Want read one of them?"

Mama looks at the books, but she don't answer me.

35

"You got yourself a little man there," the lady says.

Mama don't say nothing to the lady, but she must've smiled, 'cause I seen the lady smiling back. The lady looks at me a little while, like she's feeling sorry for me.

"You sure got that preacher out here in a hurry," she says to that boy.

The boy looks up at her and looks in his book again. When I grow up I want to be just like him. I want clothes like that and I want keep a book with me, too.

"You really don't believe in God?" the lady says.

"No," he says.

"But why?" the lady says.

"Because the wind is pink," he says.

"What?" the lady says.

The boy don't answer her no more. He just reads in his book.

"Talking 'bout the wind is pink," that old lady says. She's sitting on the same bench with the boy and she's trying to look in his face. The boy makes 'tend the old lady ain't even there. He just keeps on reading. "Wind is pink," she says again. "Eh, Lord, what children go'n be saying next?"

The lady 'cross from us bust out laughing.

"That's a good one," she says. "The wind is pink. Yes sir, that's a good one."

"Don't you believe the wind is pink?" the boy says. He keeps his head down in the book.

"Course I believe it, honey," the lady says. "Course I do." She looks at us and winks her eye. "And what color is grass, honey?"

"Grass? Grass is black."

She bust out laughing again. The boy looks at her.

"Don't you believe grass is black?" he says.

The lady quits her laughing and looks at him. Everybody else looking at him, too. The place quiet, quiet.

"Grass is green, honey," the lady says. "It was green yesterday, it's green today, and it's go'n be green tomorrow."

"How do you know it's green?"

"I know because I know."

"You don't know it's green," the boy says. "You believe it's green because someone told you it was green. If someone had told you it was black you'd believe it was black."

"It's green," the lady says. "I know green when I see green."

"Prove it's green," the boy says.

"Sure, now," the lady says. "Don't tell me it's coming to that."

"It's coming to just that," the boy says. "Words mean nothing. One means no more than the other."

"That's what it all coming to?" that old lady says. That old lady got on a turban and she got on two sweaters. She got a green sweater under a black sweater. I can see the green sweater 'cause some of the buttons on the other sweater's missing.

"Yes ma'am," the boy says. "Words mean nothing. Action is the only thing. Doing. That's the only thing."

"Other words, you want the Lord to come down here and show Hisself to you?" she says.

"Exactly, ma'am," he says.

"You don't mean that, I'm sure?" she says.

"I do, ma'am," he says.

"Done, Jesus," the old lady says, shaking her head.

"I didn't go 'long with that preacher at first," the other lady says; "but now—I don't know. When a person say the grass is black, he's either a lunatic or something's wrong."

"Prove to me that it's green," the boy says.

"It's green because the people say it's green."

"Those same people say we're citizens of these United States," the boy says.

"I think I'm a citizen," the lady says.

"Citizens have certain rights," the boy says. "Name me one right that you have. One right, granted by the Constitution, that you can exercise in Bayonne."

The lady don't answer him. She just looks at him like she don't know what he's talking 'bout. I know I don't.

"Things changing," she says.

"Things are changing because some black men have begun to think with their brains and not their hearts," the boy says.

"You trying to say these people don't believe in God?"

37

"I'm sure some of them do. Maybe most of them do. But they don't believe that God is going to touch these white people's hearts and change things tomorrow. Things change through action. By no other way."

Everybody sit quiet and look at the boy. Nobody says a thing. Then the lady 'cross the room from me and Mama just shakes her head.

"Let's hope that not all your generation feel the same way you do," she says.

"Think what you please, it doesn't matter," the boy says. "But it will be men who listen to their heads and not their hearts who will see that your children have a better chance than you had."

"Let's hope they ain't all like you, though," the old lady says. "Done forgot the heart absolutely."

"Yes ma'am, I hope they aren't all like me," the boy says. "Unfortunately, I was born too late to believe in your God. Let's hope that the ones who come after will have your faith—if not in your God, then in something else, something definitely that they can lean on. I haven't anything. For me, the wind is pink, the grass is black."

9

The nurse comes in the room where we all sitting and waiting and says the doctor won't take no more patients till one o'clock this evening. My mama jumps up off the bench and goes up to the white lady.

"Nurse, I have to go back in the field this evening," she says.

"The doctor is treating his last patient now," the nurse says. "One o'clock this evening."

"Can I at least speak to the doctor?" my mama asks.

"I'm his nurse," the lady says.

"My little boy's sick," my mama says. "Right now his tooth almost killing him."

The nurse looks at me. She's trying to make up her mind if to let me come in. I look at her real pitiful. The tooth ain't hurting me at all, but Mama say it is, so I make 'tend for her sake.

"This evening," the nurse says, and goes on back in the office.

"Don't feel 'jected, honey," the lady says to Mama. "I been round them a long time—they take you when they want to. If you was white, that's something else; but we the wrong color."

Mama don't say nothing to the lady, and me and her go outside and stand 'gainst the wall. It's cold out there. I can feel that wind going through my coat. Some of the other people come out of the room and go up the street. Me and Mama stand there a little while and we start walking. I don't know where we going. When we come to the other street we just stand there.

"You don't have to make water, do you?" Mama says.

"No, ma'am," I say.

We go on up the street. Walking real slow. I can tell Mama don't know where she's going. When we come to a store we stand there and look at the dummies. I look at a little boy wearing a brown overcoat. He's got on brown shoes, too. I look at my old shoes and look at his'n again. You wait till summer, I say.

Me and Mama walk away. We come up to another store and we stop and look at them dummies, too. Then we go on again. We pass a café where the white people in there eating. Mama tells me keep my eyes in front where they belong, but I can't help from seeing them people eat. My stomach starts to growling 'cause I'm hungry. When I see people eating, I get hungry; when I see a coat, I get cold.

A man whistles at my mama when we go by a filling station. She makes 'tend she don't even see him. I look back and I feel like hitting him in the mouth. If I was bigger, I say; if I was bigger, you'd see.

We keep on going. I'm getting colder and colder, but I don't say nothing. I feel that stuff running down my nose and I sniff.

"That rag," Mama says.

I get it out and wipe my nose. I'm getting cold all over now— my face, my hands, my feet, everything. We pass another little café, but this'n for white people, too, and we can't go in there, either. So we just walk. I'm so cold now I'm 'bout ready to say it.

If I knowed where we was going I wouldn't be so cold, but I don't know where we going. We go, we go, we go. We walk clean out of Bayonne. Then we cross the street and we come back. Same thing I seen when I got off the bus this morning. Same old trees, same old walk, same old weeds, same old cracked pave—same old everything.

I sniff again.

"That rag," Mama says.

I wipe my nose real fast and jugg that handkerchief back in my pocket 'fore my hand gets too cold. I raise my head and I can see David's hardware store. When we come up to it, we go in. I don't know why, but I'm glad.

It's warm in there. It's so warm in there you don't ever want to leave. I look for the heater, and I see it over by them barrels. Three white men standing round the heater talking in Creole. One of them comes over to see what my mama want.

"Got any axe handles?" she says.

Me, Mama and the white man start to the back, but Mama stops me when we come up to the heater. She and the white man go on. I hold my hands over the heater and look at them. They go all the way to the back, and I see the white man pointing to the axe handles 'gainst the wall. Mama takes one of them and shakes it like she's trying to figure how much it weighs. Then she rubs her hand over it from one end to the other end. She turns it over and looks at the other side, then she shakes it again, and shakes her head and puts it back. She gets another one and she does it just like she did the first one, then she shakes her head. Then she gets a brown one and do it that, too. But she don't like this one, either. Then she gets another one, but 'fore she shakes it or anything, she looks at me. Look like she's trying to say something to me, but I don't know what it is. All I know is I done got warm now and I'm feeling right smart better. Mama shakes this axe handle just like she did the others, and shakes her head and says something to the white man. The white man just looks at his pile of axe handles, and when Mama pass him to come to the front, the white man just scratch his head and follows her. She tells me come on and we go on out and start walking again.

We walk and walk, and no time at all I'm cold again. Look like

I'm colder now 'cause I can still remember how good it was back there. My stomach growls and I suck it in to keep Mama from hearing it. She's walking right 'side me, and it growls so loud you can hear it a mile. But Mama don't say a word.

10

When we come up to the courthouse, I look at the clock. It's got quarter to twelve. Mean we got another hour and a quarter to be out here in the cold. We go and stand 'side a building. Something hits my cap and I look up at the sky. Sleet's falling.

I look at Mama standing there. I want stand close 'side her, but she don't like that. She say that's crybaby stuff. She say you got to stand for yourself, by yourself.

"Let's go back to that office," she says.

We cross the street. When we get to the dentist office I try to open the door, but I can't. I twist and twist, but I can't. Mama pushes me to the side and she twist the knob, but she can't open the door, either. She turns 'way from the door. I look at her, but I don't move and I don't say nothing. I done seen her like this before and I'm scared of her.

"You hungry?" she says. She says it like she's mad at me, like I'm the cause of everything.

"No, ma'am," I say.

"You want eat and walk back, or you rather don't eat and ride?"

"I ain't hungry," I say.

I ain't just hungry, but I'm cold, too. I'm so hungry and cold I want to cry. And look like I'm getting colder and colder. My feet done got numb. I try to work my toes, but I don't even feel them. Look like I'm go'n die. Look like I'm go'n stand right here and freeze to death. I think 'bout home. I think 'bout Val and Auntie and Ty and Louis and Walker. It's 'bout twelve o'clock and I know they eating dinner now. I can hear Ty making jokes. He done forgot 'bout getting up early this morning and right now he's probably making jokes. Always trying to make somebody laugh. I wish I was right there listening to him. Give anything in the world if I was home round the fire.

"Come on," Mama says.

We start walking again. My feet so numb I can't hardly feel them. We turn the corner and go on back up the street. The clock on the courthouse starts hitting for twelve.

The sleet's coming down plenty now. They hit the pave and bounce like rice. Oh, Lord; oh, Lord, I pray. Don't let me die, don't let me die; don't let me die, Lord.

11

Now I know where we going. We going back of town where the colored people eat. I don't care if I don't eat. I been hungry before. I can stand it. But I can't stand the cold.

I can see we go'n have a long walk. It's 'bout a mile down there. But I don't mind. I know when I get there I'm go'n warm myself. I think I can hold out. My hands numb in my pockets and my feet numb, too, but if I keep moving I can hold out. Just don't stop no more, that's all.

The sky's gray. The sleet keeps on falling. Falling like rain now—plenty, plenty. You can hear it hitting the pave. You can see it bouncing. Sometimes it bounces two times 'fore it settles.

We keep on going. We don't say nothing. We just keep on going, keep on going.

I wonder what Mama's thinking. I hope she ain't mad at me. When summer come I'm go'n pick plenty cotton and get her a coat. I'm go'n get her a red one.

I hope they'd make it summer all the time. I'd be glad if it was summer all the time—but it ain't. We got to have winter, too. Lord, I hate the winter. I guess everybody hate the winter.

I don't sniff this time. I get out my handkerchief and wipe my nose. My hands's so cold I can hardly hold the handkerchief.

I think we getting close, but we ain't there yet. I wonder where everybody is. Can't see a soul but us. Look like we the only two people moving round today. Must be too cold for the rest of the people to move round in.

I can hear my teeth. I hope they don't knock together too hard and make that bad one hurt. Lord, that's all I need, for that bad one to start off.

I hear a church bell somewhere. But today ain't Sunday. They must be ringing for a funeral or something.

I wonder what they doing at home. They must be eating. Monsieur Bayonne might be there with his guitar. One day Ty played with Monsieur Bayonne's guitar and broke one of the strings. Monsieur Bayonne was some mad with Ty. He say Ty wasn't go'n ever 'mount to nothing. Ty can go just like Monsieur Bayonne when he ain't there. Ty can make everybody laugh when he starts to mocking Monsieur Bayonne.

I used to like to be with Mama and Daddy. We used to be happy. But they took him in the Army. Now, nobody happy no more. . . . I be glad when Daddy comes home.

Monsieur Bayonne say it wasn't fair for them to take Daddy and give Mama nothing and give us nothing. Auntie say, "Shhh, Etienne. Don't let them hear you talk like that." Monsieur Bayonne say, "It's God truth. What they giving his children? They have to walk three and a half miles to school hot or cold. That's anything to give for a paw? She's got to work in the field rain or shine just to make ends meet. That's anything to give for a husband?" Auntie say, "Shhh, Etienne, shhh." "Yes, you right," Monsieur Bayonne say. "Best don't say it in front of them now. But one day they go'n find out. One day." "Yes, I suppose so," Auntie say. "Then what, Rose Mary?" Monsieur Bayonne say. "I don't know, Etienne," Auntie say. "All we can do is us job, and leave everything else in His hand . . ."

We getting closer, now. We getting closer. I can even see the railroad tracks.

We cross the tracks, and now I see the café. Just to get in there, I say. Just to get in there. Already I'm starting to feel little better.

12

We go in. Ahh, it's good. I look for the heater; there 'gainst the wall. One of them little brown ones. I just stand there 'and hold my hands over it. I can't open my hands too wide 'cause they almost froze.

Mama's standing right 'side me. She done unbuttoned her coat. Smoke rises out of the coat, and the coat smells like a wet dog.

I move to the side so Mama can have more room. She opens out her hands and rubs them together. I rub mine together, too, 'cause this keep them from hurting. If you let them warm too fast, they hurt you sure. But if you let them warm just little bit at a time, and you keep rubbing them, they be all right every time.

They got just two more people in the café. A lady back of the counter, and a man on this side of the counter. They been watching us ever since we come in.

Mama gets out the handkerchief and count up the money. Both of us know how much money she's got there. Three dollars. No, she ain't got three dollars, 'cause she had to pay us way up here. She ain't got but two dollars and a half left. Dollar and a half to get my tooth pulled, and fifty cents for us to go back on, and fifty cents worth of salt meat.

She stirs the money round with her finger. Most of the money is change 'cause I can hear it rubbing together. She stirs it and stirs it. Then she looks at the door. It's still sleeting. I can hear it hitting 'gainst the wall like rice.

"I ain't hungry, Mama," I say.

"Got to pay them something for they heat," she says.

She takes a quarter out the handkerchief and ties the handkerchief up again. She looks over her shoulder at the people, but she still don't move. I hope she don't spend the money. I don't want her spending it on me. I'm hungry, I'm almost starving I'm so hungry, but I don't want her spending the money on me.

She flips the quarter over like she's thinking. She's must be thinking 'bout us walking back home. Lord, I sure don't want walk home. If I thought it'd do any good to say something, I'd say it. But Mama makes up her own mind 'bout things.

She turns 'way from the heater right fast, like she better hurry up and spend the quarter 'fore she change her mind. I watch her go toward the counter. The man and the lady look at her, too. She tells the lady something and the lady walks away. The man keeps on looking at her. Her back's turned to the man, and she don't even know he's standing there.

The lady puts some cakes and a glass of milk on the counter. Then she pours up a cup of coffee and sets it 'side the other stuff. Mama pays her for the things and comes on back where I'm standing. She tells me sit down at the table 'gainst the wall.

The milk and the cakes's for me; the coffee's for Mama. I eat slow and I look at her. She's looking outside at the sleet. She's looking real sad. I say to myself, I'm go'n make all this up one day. You see, one day, I'm go'n make all this up. I want say it now; I want tell her how I feel right now; but Mama don't like for us to talk like that.

"I can't eat all this," I say.

They ain't got but just three little old cakes there. I'm so hungry right now, the Lord knows I can eat a hundred times three, but I want my mama to have one.

Mama don't even look my way. She knows I'm hungry, she knows I want it. I let it stay there a little while, then I get it and eat it. I eat just on my front teeth, though, 'cause if cake touch that back tooth I know what'll happen. Thank God it ain't hurt me at all today.

After I finish eating I see the man go to the juke box. He drops a nickel in it, then he just stand there a little while looking at the record. Mama tells me keep my eyes in front where they belong. I turn my head like she say, but then I hear the man coming toward us.

"Dance, pretty?" he says.

Mama gets up to dance with him. But 'fore you know it, she done grabbed the little man in the collar and done heaved him 'side the wall. He hit the wall so hard he stop the juke box from playing.

"Some pimp," the lady back of the counter says. "Some pimp."

45

The little man jumps up off the floor and starts toward my mama. 'Fore you know it, Mama done sprung open her knife and she's waiting for him.

"Come on," she says. "Come on. I'll gut you from your neighbo to your throat. Come on."

I go up to the little man to hit him, but Mama makes me come and stand 'side her. The little man looks at me and Mama and goes on back to the counter.

"Some pimp," the lady back of the counter says. "Some pimp." She starts laughing and pointing at the little man. "Yes sir, you a pimp, all right. Yes sir-ree."

13

"Fasten that coat, let's go," Mama says.

"You don't have to leave," the lady says.

Mama don't answer the lady, and we right out in the cold again. I'm warm right now—my hands, my ears, my feet—but I know this ain't go'n last too long. It done sleet so much now you got ice everywhere you look.

We cross the railroad tracks, and soon's we do, I get cold. That wind goes through this little old coat like it ain't even there. I got on a shirt and a sweater under the coat, but that wind don't pay them no mind. I look up and I can see we got a long way to go. I wonder if we go'n make it 'fore I get too cold.

We cross over to walk on the sidewalk. They got just one sidewalk back here, and it's over there.

After we go just a little piece, I smell bread cooking. I look, then I see a baker shop. When we get closer, I can smell it more better. I shut my eyes and make 'tend I'm eating. But I keep them shut too long and I butt up 'gainst a telephone post. Mama grabs me and see if I'm hurt. I ain't bleeding or nothing and she turns me loose.

I can feel I'm getting colder and colder, and I look up to see how far we still got to go. Uptown is 'way up yonder. A half mile more, I reckon. I try to think of something. They say think and you won't get cold. I think of that poem, "Annabel Lee." I ain't been to school in so long—this bad weather—I reckon they done passed "Annabel Lee" by now. But passed it or not, I'm sure Miss

Walker go'n make me recite it when I get there. That woman don't never forget nothing. I ain't never seen nobody like that in my life.

I'm still getting cold. "Annabel Lee" or no "Annabel Lee," I'm still getting cold. But I can see we getting closer. We getting there gradually.

Soon 's we turn the corner, I see a little old white lady up in front of us. She's the only lady on the street. She's all in black and she's got a long black rag over her head.

"Stop," she says.

Me and Mama stop and look at her. She must be crazy to be out in all this bad weather. Ain't got but a few other people out there, and all of them's men.

"Y'all done ate?" she says.

"Just finish," Mama says.

"Y'all must be cold then?" she says.

"We headed for the dentist," Mama says. "We'll warm up when we get there."

"What dentist?" the old lady says. "Mr. Bassett?"

"Yes, ma'am," Mama says.

"Come on in," the old lady says. "I'll telephone him and tell him y'all coming."

Me and Mama follow the old lady in the store. It's a little bitty store, and it don't have much in there. The old lady takes off her head rag and folds it up.

"Helena?" somebody calls from the back.

"Yes, Alnest?" the old lady says.

"Did you see them?"

"They're here. Standing beside me."

"Good. Now you can stay inside."

The old lady looks at Mama. Mama's waiting to hear what she brought us in here for. I'm waiting for that, too.

"I saw y'all each time you went by," she says. "I came out to catch you, but you were gone."

"We went back of town," Mama says.

"Did you eat?"

"Yes, ma'am."

The old lady looks at Mama a long time, like she's thinking

47

Mama might be just saying that. Mama looks right back at her. The old lady looks at me to see what I have to say. I don't say nothing. I sure ain't going 'gainst my mama.

"There's food in the kitchen," she says to Mama. "I've been keeping it warm."

Mama turns right around and starts for the door.

"Just a minute," the old lady says. Mama stops. "The boy'll have to work for it. It isn't free."

"We don't take no handout," Mama says.

"I'm not handing out anything," the old lady says. "I need my garbage moved to the front. Ernest has a bad cold and can't go out there."

"James'll move it for you," Mama says.

"Not unless you eat," the old lady says. "I'm old, but I have my pride, too, you know."

Mama can see she ain't go'n beat this old lady down, so she just shakes her head.

"All right," the old lady says. "Come into the kitchen."

She leads the way with that rag in her hand. The kitchen is a little bitty little old thing, too. The table and the stove just 'bout fill it up. They got a little room to the side. Somebody in there laying 'cross the bed—'cause I can see one of his feet. Must be the person she was talking to: Ernest or Alnest—something like that.

"Sit down," the old lady says to Mama. "Not you," she says to me. "You have to move the cans."

"Helena?" the man says in the other room.

"Yes, Alnest?" the old lady says.

"Are you going out there again?"

"I must show the boy where the garbage is, Alnest," the old lady says.

"Keep that shawl over your head," the old man says.

"You don't have to remind me, Alnest. Come, boy," the old lady says.

We go out in the yard. Little old back yard ain't no bigger than the store or the kitchen. But it can sleet here just like it can sleet in any big back yard. And 'fore you know it, I'm trembling.

"There," the old lady says, pointing to the cans. I pick up one of the cans and set it right back down. The can's so light, I'm go'n see what's inside of it.

"Here," the old lady says. "Leave that can alone."

I look back at her standing there in the door. She's got that black rag wrapped round her shoulders, and she's pointing one of her little old fingers at me.

"Pick it up and carry it to the front," she says. I go by her with the can, and she's looking at me all the time. I'm sure the can's empty. I'm sure she could've carried it herself—maybe both of them at the same time. "Set it on the sidewalk by the door and come back for the other one," she says.

I go and come back, and Mama looks at me when I pass her. I get the other can and take it to the front. It don't feel a bit heavier than that first one. I tell myself I ain't go'n be nobody's fool, and I'm go'n look inside this can to see just what I been hauling. First, I look up the street, then down the street. Nobody coming. Then I look over my shoulder toward the door. That little old lady done slipped up there quiet 's mouse, watching me again. Look like she knowed what I was go'n do.

"Ehh, Lord," she says. "Children, children. Come in here, boy, and go wash your hands."

I follow her in the kitchen. She points toward the bathroom, and I go in there and wash up. Little bitty old bathroom, but it's clean, clean. I don't use any of her towels; I wipe my hands on my pants legs.

When I come back in the kitchen, the old lady done dished up the food. Rice, gravy, meat—and she even got some lettuce and tomato in a saucer. She even got a glass of milk and a piece of cake there, too. It looks so good, I almost start eating 'fore I say my blessing.

"Helena?" the old man says.

"Yes, Alnest?"

"Are they eating?."

"Yes," she says.

"Good," he says. "Now you'll stay inside."

The old lady goes in there where he is and I can hear them talking. I look at Mama. She's eating slow like she's thinking. I wonder what's the matter now. I reckon she's thinking 'bout home.

The old lady comes back in the kitchen.

"I talked to Dr. Bassett's nurse," she says. "Dr. Bassett will take you as soon as you get there."

"Thank you, ma'am," Mama says.

"Perfectly all right," the old lady says. "Which one is it?"

Mama nods toward me. The old lady looks at me real sad. I look sad, too.

"You're not afraid, are you?" she says.

"No, ma'am," I say.

"That's a good boy," the old lady says. "Nothing to be afraid of. Dr. Bassett will not hurt you."

When me and Mama get through eating, we thank the old lady again.

"Helena, are they leaving?" the old man says.

"Yes, Alnest."

"Tell them I say good-bye."

"They can hear you, Alnest."

"Good-bye both mother and son," the old man says. "And may God be with you."

Me and Mama tell the old man good-bye, and we follow the old lady in the front room. Mama opens the door to go out, but she stops and comes back in the store.

"You sell salt meat?" she says.

"Yes."

"Give me two bits' worth."

"That isn't very much salt meat," the old lady says.

"That's all I have," Mama says.

The old lady goes back of the counter and cuts a big piece off the chunk. Then she wraps it up and puts it in a paper bag.

"Two bits," she says.

"That looks like awful lot of meat for a quarter," Mama says.

"Two bits," the old lady says. "I've been selling salt meat behind this counter twenty-five years. I think I know what I'm doing."

"You got a scale there," Mama says.

"What?" the old lady says.

"Weigh it," Mama says.

"What?" the old lady says. "Are you telling me how to run my business?"

"Thanks very much for the food," Mama says.

"Just a'minute," the old lady says.

"James," Mama says to me. I move toward the door.

"Just one minute, I said," the old lady says.

Me and Mama stop again and look at her. The old lady takes the meat out of the bag and unwraps it and cuts 'bout half of it off. Then she wraps it up again and juggs it back in the bag and gives the bag to Mama. Mama lays the quarter on the counter.

"Your kindness will never be forgotten," she says. "James," she says to me.

We go out, and the old lady comes to the door to look at us. After we go a little piece I look back, and she's still there watching us.

The sleet's coming down heavy, heavy now, and I turn up my coat collar to keep my neck warm. My mama tells me turn it right back down.

"You not a bum," she says. "You a man."

Genaro Gonzalez

▼

TOO MUCH

HIS FATHER'S SON

△

▼

In the whorl of the argument, without warning, Arturo's mother confronted her husband point-blank: "Is it another woman?"

"For heaven's sake, Carmela, not in front of—"

"Nine is old enough to know. You owe both of us that much."

Sitting in the room, Arturo could not help but overhear. Usually he could dissimulate with little effort—being a constant chaperon on his cousin Anita's dates had made him a master at fading into the background. But at that moment he was struggling hard to control a discomfort even more trying than those his cousin and her boyfriends put him through.

The argument had already lasted an hour and, emotionally, his mother had carried its brunt. Trying to keep her voice in check was taking more out of her than if she had simply vented her tension.

His father, though, lay fully clothed in bed, shirt half-buttoned and hands locked under his head. From his closed eyes and placid breathing, one would have thought that her frustration was simply lulling him into a more profound relaxation. Only an occasional gleam from those perfect white teeth told Arturo he was still listening, and even then with bemused detachment.

"Is it another woman, Raul?"

His father batted open his eyes only to look away, as though the accusation did not even merit the dignity of a defense. His gaze caught Arturo and tried to lock him into the masculine intimacy they often shared, an unspoken complicity between father and son. But at that instant he simply aggravated Arturo's shame.

"Who is she, Raul?"

His smile made it clear that if there were another woman, he was not saying. "You tell me. You're the one who made her up."

Arturo had seen that smile in all its shadings—sometimes with disarming candor, but more often full of arrogance. When he wished, those teeth could take on such a natural luster that whoever saw it felt invigorated. In those moments his smile became a gift of pearls.

Yet other times, he had but to curl his lips and those same teeth turned into a sadistic show of strength. Well aware of his power over others, he seemed indifferent as to whether the end effect exalted or belittled.

Out of nowhere, perhaps to add to the confusion, he ordered. "Bring Abuelo's belt, Arturo."

Instead of strapping it on, he pretended to admire what had once been his own father's gun belt. The holster was gone, but a bullet that had remained rusted inside a middle clasp added a certain authority. The hand-tooled leather, a rich dark brown, had delicate etching now too smooth to decipher. Grandfather Edelmiro had been a large, mean-looking man in life, and Arturo still remembered the day his father received the belt. He had strapped it on for only a moment, over his own belt. Later that day Arturo opened the closet for a closer inspection and had

53

come upon his father, piercing another notch for his smaller waist.

His mother continued to confront his father, who idly looped the belt, grabbed it at opposite ends, and began whapping it with a solemn force. At first the rhythmic slaps disconcerted her, until she turned their tension into punctuations for her own argument. Suddenly the belt cracked so violently that Arturo thought the ancient cartridge had fired. He startled, as much from the noise as from the discovery that his father's legendary control had snapped. For an instant both parents, suddenly realizing how far things had gone, appeared paralyzed.

No, his father would never strike her, he was sure of that. But nobody had ever pushed him that far, least of all his mother, whose own strength had always been her patience.

He wondered why his eyes were suddenly brimming. Perhaps trespassing into the unknown terrified him, or perhaps he was ashamed of his father's indifference. That confusion—crying without knowing why—frightened him even more.

"See, Carmela? Now you've got the boy blubbering."

He was hoping to hide his weakness from his father, and the unmasking only added to the disgrace. Desperate to save face, he yelled, "I'm leaving!"

As always, his father turned the threat in his favor. "That's good, son. Wait outside and let me handle this."

"I'm going to Papa Grande's house!"

Arturo had never been that close to his mother's family, and that made his decision all the more surprising. But if his father felt betrayed he did not show it. "Fine, then. You're on your own."

It took him a while to catch his father's sarcasm and his own unthinking blunder: He did not know the way to his grandparents' house. He had walked there only once—last Sunday—and that time his mother had disoriented him with a different route from the one his father took.

But now, standing there facing his father, he had no choice. Rushing out the kitchen door he ran across the back yard, expecting at any moment to be stopped in his tracks. When his arms brushed against a clothesline, he almost tripped as if his father had lassoed him with his belt. Not until he reached the alley did he realize he had been hoping his father would indeed stop him, even with a word.

He crossed the alley into an abandoned lot. There he matted down a patch of grass and weeds reaching his waist and settled in, so as to give his heart time to hush. He sat for a long time, wondering whether to gather his thoughts or let them scramble until nothing mattered.

From Doña Chole's house came the blare of Mexican radio station, every song sandwiched by the frenzied assault of two announcers. Farther away, David's father continued working on his pet project, a coop and flypen for his game cocks: four or five swift whacks into wood . . . silence . . . then another volley. For a while he lost himself in that hammering, which imparted meaning to the day. If he listened closer he could hear the cursing and singing that gave the neighborhood life. Only his own home remained absolutely still.

Soon the sun began to get in his eyes whenever he looked homeward. A cool breeze was blowing at his back, but as he hunkered in the weeds a sun-toasted aroma penetrated his corduroy shirt.

Someone was coming up the path, making soft lashing sounds in the weeds; something told him that someone was Fela the *curandera*. His intuition seemed so certain that when he finally dared peek he immediately dove back into his hiding place, wondering whether to congratulate or curse himself.

A part of him scrambled for a rational explanation: Who else could it be? Fela the healer was the only grown-up unconcerned about snakes in the undergrowth. More than anyone else she had cut a swath through the weeds in her daily forages for herbs. Yet, another side of him was forced to side with the barrio lore—that she had special powers, that she appeared and disappeared at will, that she could think your thoughts before they occurred to you.

The brushing got closer, so he lay very still, trying to imitate his father's self-discipline. When the rustling suddenly stopped, he swore the waft of his corduroy shirt had given him away.

A voice called out: "Since when do little boys live in the wild?"

His heart began beating wildly, but her tone carried enough teasing that he half-raised his head.

"You're hiding from someone?"

All at once, he remembered why he was there, not in words but through a clear image of his father sprawled across the bed, amused, almost bored. He answered her question with a nod, afraid that if he spoke his rage might leap out and injure them both.

"You did something bad?"

He managed a hoarse, determined vow: "I'm going to smash my father's teeth."

He expected the violence in his words to stun her, but instead she disarmed him with a kind smile. "Whatever for? He has such nice teeth. Some day yours will look just like his."

For a moment, in place of the familiar habit of his own body, he experienced an undefined numbness, followed by the fascinated terror of someone who had inherited a gleaming crown with awesome responsibilities. He stood speechless, repulsed yet tempted by the corrupting thought of turning into his father.

"Anyway," she added, "before you know it he'll be old and toothless like me."

She picked a row of burrs clinging to her faded dress, then said as she left, "And tell your mother she's in my thoughts and prayers." Watching her walk away, he tried without success to retrace the route he and his mother had taken to her house during their secret visit last Sunday.

That Sunday morning, while his mother talked to her in the living room, he had sat on a wicker chair on Fela's porch, entertained by Cuco, an ancient caged parrot with colored semicircles under his eyes. Arturo was feeding him chili from a nearby plant to make him talk. "Say it," he urged between bribes: *"Chinga tu madre"*—screw your mother. But the chili only agitated Cuco's whistling.

"Come on, you stupid bird. *Chinga tu madre.*"

Suddenly there was a raucous squawk. "Screw your padre instead!"

As he wheeled about and felt the blood rush to his face, Fela was already raising her arms in innocence. "Who says he's stupid? That's an exotic bilingual bird you're talking to."

From there, he and his mother had gone to his grandparents'

house. Her route through alleys and unfenced backyards led him to ask, "How do you know all these shortcuts?"

She paused to dry her forehead on her sleeve, and for the first time in days he saw her smile. "I grew up in this barrio. This is where I used to play."

When he tried to imagine her his age, he too smiled.

When they arrived they had to wait until his grandfather Marcelo finished his radlonevela. After hearing where they had been and why, he shook his head. "I knew your marriage would come to this. But going to Fela was a mistake. If he finds out, he'll claim you're trying to win him back through witchcraft."

"I had to know if he's seeing another woman."

"And what if he is?"

Arturo had never seen her as serene and as serious as when she answered, "Then he's not worth winning back."

"But a *curandera* . . . Why not see a priest?"

Arturo's grandmother took her side. "What for, Marcelo? He'd only give her your advice: Accept him as your cross in life."

"I wouldn't in this case. An unfaithful husband is one thing, an arrogant SOB is another. Still, a priest could say a few prayers in your behalf."

"Fela offered to do that herself."

His grandmother added, "And no doubt offered good advice."

His mother's fist clenched his own. "Yes," she said, and her firmness made it obvious that that was the last word.

His grandfather, deep in thought, held his breath without taking his eyes off him. Then he closed his eyes and exhaled a stale rush of cigarette smoke, as if unclouding his thoughts. "I've always said your father was a prick."

"Now, Marcelo. Don't turn him against his own father."

"Mama's right. None of this is Arturo's fault. He's going through enough as it is."

"True. But I still wouldn't give a kilo of crap for the whole de la O family, starting with Edelmiro."

"May he rest in peace," said his grandmother.

His grandfather stood. "Not if there's a devil down below."

"Marcelo! He was your compadre."

"I had as much choice in the matter as the boy had in being his grandson." He turned to Arturo's mother. "Remember, if there's a falling out, don't ask that family for anything. Your place is here."

His grandmother added, "And of course that includes Arturo. He's as much a part as the rest of us."

His grandfather had simply said. "Let's hope he's not too much his father's son."

By now the late afternoon sun was slanting long, slender shadows his way, but he was determined to spend the night there if need be. He began counting in cycles of hundreds to keep his uncertainty in check.

Suddenly the rear screen door opened and his father leaned against it, his belt slung over his chest and shoulder like a bandoliered and battle-weary warrior.

"Arturo, come inside." Whenever he wanted to conceal something from the neighbors, he used that phrase.

He slowly stood but held his ground, as much from stubbornness as dread.

"It's all right, son." He sounded final yet forgiving, like asking who had put down a castle uprising, regained control, and had decided to pardon the traitors.

Arturo blinked but once, but his pounding heart made even something that small seem a life-and-death concession.

Then his mother appeared alongside his father, and for an instant, framed by the doorway, their pose reminded him of their newlywed portrait in the living room: his hands at his sides, her own clasped in front, both heads slightly tilted as if about to rest on each other's shoulder. In that eye blink of an interval before she stepped outside, he felt like an outsider looking in.

She was halfway between him and the house when his father said, "Your mother's bringing you back."

He could not believe her betrayal. After all that, she had surrendered and was bringing him in as well. He wanted to cry out at her for having put him through so much. But a deeper part understood he shared the blame, for not helping her; for being too much his father's son.

"I forgot the way," he said. Although she was quite close he could not tell whether she heard—much less accepted—his timid apology. He managed his first step homeward when she blocked his path, gently took his hand, and guided him in the opposite direction.

He heard, or perhaps only imagined, his father: "Come back." He tugged her arm in case she had not heard. She tightened her grasp to show that she had. Then, intuiting his dilemma, she paused, saying nothing but still gazing away from the house. He realized, then and there, that the wait was for him alone. Her own decision had already been made.

Unable to walk back or away, he felt like the only living thing in the open. Then his father called out, "Son," and he knew it was his last call. His spine shivered as though a weapon had been sighted at his back, and he imagined his father removing from his belt the cartridge reserved for the family traitor.

There was no way of telling how long he braced himself for whatever was coming, until he finally realized that the moment of reckoning was already behind him. It was then that he felt his father's defeat in his own blood. With it came the glorious fear of a fugitive burning his bridges into the unknown, or a believer orphaned from a false faith. And in that all-or-nothing instant that took so little doing and needed even less understanding, his all-powerful father evaporated into the myth he had always been.

He felt a flesh-and-blood grasp that both offered and drew strength. He began to walk away, knowing there was no turning back.

Barbara Kingsolver

ROSE-JOHNNY

Rose-Johnny wore a man's haircut and terrified little children, although I will never believe that was her intention. For her own part she inspired in us only curiosity. It was our mothers who took this fascination and wrung it, through daily admonitions, into the most irresistible kind of horror. She was like the old wells, covered with ancient rotting boards and overgrown with weeds, that waited behind the barns to swallow us down: our mothers warned us time and again not to go near them, and still were certain that we did.

My own mother was not one of those who had a great deal to say about her, but Walnut Knobs was a small enough town so that a person did not need to be told things directly. When I had my first good look at her, at close range, I was ten years old. I fully understood the importance of the encounter.

What mattered to me at the time, though, was that it was something my sister had not done before me. She was five years older, and as a consequence there was hardly an achievement in my life, nor even an article of clothing, that had not first been Mary Etta's. But, because of the circumstances of my meeting Rose-Johnny, I couldn't tell a living soul about it, and so for nearly a year I carried the secret torment of a great power that can't be used. My agitation was not relieved but made worse when I told the story to myself, over and over again.

She was not, as we always heard, half man and half woman, something akin to the pagan creatures whose naked torsos are inserted in various shocking ways into parts of animal bodies. In fact, I was astonished by her ordinariness. It is true that she wore Red Wing boots like my father. And also there was something not quite womanly in her face, but maybe any woman's face would look the same with that haircut. Her hair was coal black, cut flat across the top of her round head, so that when she looked down I could see a faint pale spot right on top where the scalp almost surfaced.

But the rest of her looked exactly like anybody's mother in a big flowered dress without a waistline and with two faded spots in front, where her bosom rubbed over the counter when she reached across to make change or wipe away the dust.

People say there is a reason for every important thing that happens. I was sent to the feed store, where I spoke to Rose-Johnny and passed a quarter from my hand into hers, because it was haying time. And because I was small for my age. I was not too small to help with tobacco setting in the spring, in fact I was better at it than Mary Etta, who complained about the stains on her hands, but I was not yet big enough to throw a bale of hay onto the flatbed. It was the time of year when Daddy complained about not having boys. Mama said that at least he oughtn't to bother going into town for the chicken mash that day because Georgeann could do it on her way home from school.

Mama told me to ask Aunt Minnie to please ma'am give me

61

a ride home. "Ask her nice to stop off at Lester Wall's store so you can run in with this quarter and get five pound of laying mash."

I put the quarter in my pocket, keeping my eye out to make certain Mary Etta understood what I had been asked to do. Mary Etta had once told me that I was no better than the bugs that suck on potato vines, and that the family was going to starve to death because of my laziness. It was one of the summer days when we were on our knees in the garden picking off bugs and dropping them into cans of coal oil. She couldn't go into town with Aunt Minnie to look at dress patterns until we finished with the potato bugs. What she said, exactly, was that if I couldn't work any harder than that, then she might just as well throw *me* into a can of coal oil. Later she told me she hadn't meant it, but I intended to remember it nonetheless.

Aunt Minnie taught the first grade and had a 1951 Dodge. That is how she referred to her car whenever she spoke of it. It was the newest automobile belonging to anyone related to us, although some of the Wilcox cousins had once come down to visit from Knoxville in a Ford they were said to have bought the same year it was made. But I saw that car and did not find it nearly as impressive as Aunt Minnie's, which was white and immense and shone like glass. She paid a boy to polish it every other Saturday.

On the day she took me to Wall's, she waited in the car while I went inside with my fist tight around the quarter. I had never been in the store before, and although I had passed by it many times and knew what could be bought there, I had never imagined what a wonderful combination of warm, sweet smells of mash and animals and seed corn it would contain. The dust lay white and thin on everything like a bridal veil. Rose-Johnny was in the back with a water can, leaning over into one of the chick tubs. The steel rang with the sound of confined baby birds, and a light bulb shining up from inside the tub made her face glow white. Mr. Wall, Rose-Johnny's Pa, was in the front of the store talking to two men about a horse. He didn't notice me as I crept up to the counter. It was Rose-Johnny who came forward to the cash register.

"And what for you, missy?"

She is exactly like anybody's mama, was all I could think, and I wanted to reach and touch her flowered dress. The two men were looking at me.

"My mama needs five pound of laying mash and here's a quarter for it." I clicked the coin quickly onto the counter.

"Yes, ma'am." She smiled at me, but her boots made heavy, tired sounds on the floor. She made her way slowly, like a duck in water, over to the row of wooden bins that stood against the wall. She scooped the mash into a paper bag and weighed it, then shoved the scoop back into the bin. A little cloud of dust rose out of the mash up into the window. I watched her from the counter.

"Don't your mama know she's wasting good money on chicken mash? Any fool chicken will eat corn." I jumped when the man spoke. It was one of the two, and they were standing so close behind me I would have had to look right straight up to see their faces. Mr. Wall was gone.

"No sir, they need mash," I said to the man's boots.

"What's that?" It was the taller man doing the talking.

"They need mash," I said louder. "To lay good sturdy eggs for selling. A little mash mixed in with the corn. Mama says it's got oster shells in it."

"Is that a fact," he said. "Did you hear that, Rose-Johnny?" he called out. "This child says you put oster shells in that mash. Is that right?"

When Rose-Johnny came back to the cash register she was moon-eyed. She made quick motions with her hands and pushed the bag at me as if she didn't know how to talk.

"Do you catch them osters yourself, Rose-Johnny? Up at Jackson Crick?" The man was laughing. The other man was quiet.

Rose-Johnny looked all around and up at the ceiling. She scratched at her short hair, fast and hard, like a dog with ticks.

When the two men were gone I stood on my toes and leaned over the counter as far as I could. "Do you catch the osters yourself?"

She hooked her eyes right into mine, the way the bit goes into the mule's mouth and fits just so, one way and no other. Her eyes were the palest blue of any I had ever seen. Then she threw back her head and laughed so hard I could see the wide, flat bottoms of her back teeth, and I wasn't afraid of her.

When I left the store, the two men were still outside. Their boots scuffed on the front-porch floorboards, and the shorter one spoke.

"Child, how much did you pay that woman for the chicken mash?"

"A quarter," I told him.

He put a quarter in my hand. "You take this here, and go home and tell your daddy something. Tell him not never to send his little girls to Wall's feed store. Tell him to send his boys if he has to, but not his little girls." His hat was off, and his hair lay back in wet orange strips. A clean line separated the white top of his forehead from the red-burned hide of his face. In this way, it was like my father's face.

"No, sir, I can't tell him, because all my daddy's got is girls."

"That's George Bowles's child, Bud," the tall man said. "He's just got the two girls."

"Then tell him to come for hisself," Bud said. His eyes had the sun in them, and looked like a pair of new pennies.

Aunt Minnie didn't see the man give me the quarter because she was looking at herself in the side-view mirror of the Dodge. Aunt Minnie was older than Mama, but everyone mistook her for the younger because of the way she fixed herself up. And, of course, Mama was married. Mama said if Aunt Minnie ever found a man she would act her age.

When I climbed in the car she was pulling gray hairs out of her part. She said it was teaching school that caused them, but early gray ran in my mama's family.

She jumped when I slammed the car door. "All set?"

"Yes, ma'am," I said. She put her little purple hat back on her head and slowly pushed the long pin through it. I shuddered as she started up the car.

Aunt Minnie laughed. "Somebody walked over your grave."

"I don't have a grave," I said. "I'm not dead."

"No, you most certainly are not. That's just what they say

when a person shivers like that." She smiled. I liked Aunt Minnie most of the time.

"I don't think they mean your real grave, with you in it," she said after a minute. "I think it means the place where your grave is going to be someday."

I thought about this for a while. I tried to picture the place, but could not. Then I thought about the two men outside Wall's store. I asked Aunt Minnie why it was all right for boys to do some things that girls couldn't.

"Oh, there's all kinds of reasons," she said. "Like what kinds of things, do you mean?"

"Like going into Wall's feed store."

"Who told you that?"

"Somebody."

Aunt Minnie didn't say anything.

Then I said, "It's because of Rose-Johnny, isn't it?"

Aunt Minnie raised her chin just a tiny bit. She might have been checking her lipstick in the mirror, or she might have been saying yes.

"Why?" I asked.

"Why what?"

"Why because of Rose-Johnny?"

"I can't tell you that, Georgeann."

"Why can't you tell me?" I whined. "Tell me."

The car rumbled over a cattle grate. When we came to the crossing, Aunt Minnie stepped on the brake so hard we both flopped forward. She looked at me. "Georgeann, Rose-Johnny is a Lebanese. That's all I'm going to tell you. You'll understand better when you're older."

When I got home I put the laying mash in the henhouse. The hens were already roosting high above my head, clucking softly into their feathers and shifting back and forth on their feet. I collected the eggs as I did every day, and took them into the house. I hadn't yet decided what to do about the quarter, and so I held on to it until dinnertime.

65

Mary Etta was late coming down, and even though she had washed and changed she looked pale as a haunt from helping with the haying all day. She didn't speak and she hardly ate.

"Here, girls, both of you, eat up these potatoes," Mama said after a while. "There's not but just a little bit left. Something to grow on."

"I don't need none then," Mary Etta said. "I've done growed all I'm going to grow."

"Don't talk back to your mama," Daddy said.

"I'm not talking back. It's the truth." Mary Etta looked at Mama. "Well, it is."

"Eat a little bite, Mary Etta. Just because you're in the same dresses for a year don't mean you're not going to grow no more."

"I'm as big as you are, Mama."

"All right then." Mama scraped the mashed potatoes onto my plate. "I expect now you'll be telling me you don't want to grow no more either," she said to me.

"No, ma'am, I won't," I said. But I was distressed, and looked sideways at the pink shirtwaist I had looked forward to inheriting along with the grown-up shape that would have to be worn inside it. Now it appeared that I was condemned to my present clothes and potato-shaped body; keeping these forever seemed to me far more likely than the possibility of having clothes that, like the Wilcox automobile, had never before been owned. I ate my potatoes quietly. Dinner was almost over when Daddy asked if I had remembered to get the laying mash.

"Yes, sir. I put it in the henhouse." I hesitated. "And here's the quarter back. Mr. Wall gave me the mash for nothing."

"Why did he do that?" Mama asked.

Mary Etta was staring like the dead. Even her hair looked tired, slumped over the back of her chair like a long black shadow.

"I helped him out," I said. "Rose-Johnny wasn't there, she was sick, and Mr. Wall said if I would help him clean out the bins and dust the shelves and water the chicks, then it wouldn't cost me for the laying mash."

"And Aunt Minnie waited while you did all that?"

"She didn't mind," I said. "She had some magazines to look at."

It was the first important lie I had told in my life, and I was thrilled with its power. Every member of my family believed I had brought home the laying mash in exchange for honest work.

I was also astonished at how my story, once I had begun it, wouldn't finish. "He wants me to come back and help him again the next time we need something," I said.

"I don't reckon you let on like we couldn't pay for the mash?" Daddy asked sternly.

"No, sir. I put the quarter right up there on the counter. But he said he needed the help. Rose-Johnny's real sick."

He looked at me like he knew. Like he had found the hole in the coop where the black snake was getting in. But he just said, "All right. You can go, if Aunt Minnie don't mind waiting for you."

"You don't have to say a thing to her about it," I said. "I can walk home the same as I do every day. Five pound of mash isn't nothing to carry."

"We'll see," Mama said.

That night I believed I would burst. For a long time after Mary Etta fell asleep I twisted in my blankets and told the story over to myself, both the true and false versions. I talked to my doll, Miss Regina. She was a big doll, a birthday present from my Grandma and Grandpa Bowles, with a tiny wire crown and lovely long blond curls.

"Rose-Johnny isn't really sick," I told Miss Regina. "She's a Lebanese."

I looked up the word in Aunt Minnie's Bible dictionary after school. I pretended to be looking up St. John the Baptist but then turned over in a hurry to the L's while she was washing her chalkboards. My heart thumped when I found it, but I read the passage quickly, several times over, and found it empty. It said the Lebanese were a seafaring people who built great ships from cedar trees. I couldn't believe that even when I was older I would be able, as Aunt Minnie promised, to connect this with what I had seen of Rose-Johnny. Nevertheless, I resolved to understand. The following week I went back to the store, confident that my lie would continue to carry its own weight.

△_____

Rose-Johnny recognized me. "Five pounds of laying mash," she said, and this time I followed her to the feed bins. There were flecks of white dust in her hair.

"Is it true you come from over the sea?" I asked her quietly as she bent over with the scoop.

She laughed and rolled her eyes. "A lot of them says I come from the moon," she said, and I was afraid she was going to be struck dumb and animal-eyed as she was the time before. But, when she finished weighing the bag, she just said, "I was born in Slate Holler, and that's as far from here as I ever been or will be."

"Is that where you get the osters from?" I asked, looking into the mash and trying to pick out which of the colored flecks they might be.

Rose-Johnny looked at me for a long time, and then suddenly laughed her big laugh. "Why, honey child, don't you know? Osters comes from the sea."

She rang up twenty-five cents on the register, but I didn't look at her.

"That was all, wasn't it?"

I leaned over the counter and tried to put tears in my eyes, but they wouldn't come. "I can't pay," I said. "My daddy said to ask you if I could do some work for it. Clean up or something."

"Your daddy said to ask me that? Well, bless your heart," she said. "Let me see if we can't find something for you to do. Bless your little heart, child, what's your name?"

"Georgeann," I told her.

"I'm Rose-Johnny," she said, and I did not say that I knew it, that like every other child I had known it since the first time I saw her in town, when I was five or six, and had to ask Mama if it was a man or a lady.

"Pleased to meet you," I said.

We kept it between the two of us: I came in every week to help with the pullets and the feed, and took home my mash. We did not tell Mr. Wall, although it seemed it would not have mattered one whit to him. Mr. Wall was in the store so seldom that he might not have known I was there. He kept to himself in the apartment at the back where he and Rose-Johnny lived.

It was she who ran the store, kept the accounts, and did the orders. She showed me how to feed and water the pullets and ducklings and pull out the sick ones. Later I learned how to weigh out packages of seed and to mix the different kinds of mash. There were lists nailed to the wall telling how much cracked corn and oats and grit to put in. I followed the recipes with enormous care, adding tiny amounts at a time to the bag on the hanging scales until the needle touched the right number. Although she was patient with me, I felt slow next to Rose-Johnny, who never had to look at the lists and used the scales only to check herself. It seemed to me she knew how to do more things than anyone I had ever known, woman or man.

She also knew the names of all the customers, although she rarely spoke to them. Sometimes such a change came over her when the men were there that it wasn't clear to me whether she was pretending or had really lost the capacity to speak. But afterward she would tell me their names and everything about them. Once she told me about Ed Charney, Sr. and Bud Mattox, the two men I had seen the first day I was in the store. According to Rose-Johnny, Ed had an old red mule he was in the habit of mistreating. "But even so," she said, "Ed's mule don't have it as bad as Bud's wife." I never knew how she acquired this knowledge.

When she said "Bud Mattox," I remembered his penny-colored eyes and connected him then with all the Mattox boys at school. It had never occurred to me that eyes could run in families, like early gray.

Occasionally a group of black-skinned children came to the store, always after hours. Rose-Johnny opened up for them. She called each child by name, and asked after their families and the health of their mother's laying hens.

The oldest one, whose name was Cleota, was shaped like Mary Etta. Her hair was straight and pointed, and smelled to me like citronella candles. The younger girls had plaits that curved out from their heads like so many handles. Several of them wore dresses made from the same bolt of cloth, but they were not sisters. Rose-Johnny filled a separate order for each child.

I watched, but didn't speak. The skin on their heels and palms was creased, and as light as my own. Once, after they had left, I asked Rose-Johnny why they only came into the store when it was closed.

"People's got their ways," she said, stoking up the wood stove for the night. Then she told me all their names again, starting with

Cleota and working down. She looked me in the eye. "When you see them in town, you speak. Do you hear? By *name*. I don't care who is watching."

I was allowed to spend half an hour or more with Rose-Johnny nearly every day after school, so long as I did not neglect my chores at home. Sometimes on days that were rainy or cold Aunt Minnie would pick me up, but I preferred to walk. By myself, without Mary Etta to hurry me up.

As far as I know, my parents believed I was helping Mr. Wall because of Rose-Johnny's illness. They had no opportunity to learn otherwise, though I worried that someday Aunt Minnie would come inside the store to fetch me, instead of just honking, or that Daddy would have to go to Wall's for something and see for himself that Rose-Johnny was fit and well. Come springtime he would be needing to buy tobacco seed.

It was soon after Christmas when I became consumed with a desire to confess. I felt the lies down inside me like cold, dirty potatoes in a root cellar, beginning to sprout and crowd. At night I told Miss Regina of my dishonesty and the things that were likely to happen to me because of it. In so doing, there were several times I nearly confessed by accident to Mary Etta.

"Who's going to wring your neck?" she wanted to know, coming into the room one night when I thought she was downstairs washing the supper dishes.

"Nobody," I said, clutching Miss Regina to my pillow. I pretended to be asleep. I could hear Mary Etta starting to brush her hair. Every night before she went to bed she sat with her dress hiked up and her head hung over between her knees, brushing her hair all the way down to the floor. This improved the circulation to the hair, she told me, and would prevent it turning. Mary Etta was already beginning to get white hairs.

70

"Is it because Mama let you watch Daddy kill the cockerels? Did it scare you to see them jump around like that with their necks broke?"

"I'm not scared," I murmured, but I wanted so badly to tell the truth that I started to cry. I knew, for certain, that something bad was going to happen. I believe I also knew it would happen to my sister, instead of me.

"Nobody's going to hurt you," Mary Etta said. She smoothed my bangs and laid my pigtails down flat on top of the quilt. "Give me Miss Regina and let me put her up for you now, so you won't get her hair all messed up."

I let her have the doll. "I'm not scared about the cockerels, Mary Etta. I promise." With my finger, under the covers, I traced a cross over my heart.

When Rose-Johnny fell ill I was sick with guilt. When I first saw Mr. Wall behind the counter instead of Rose-Johnny, so help me God, I prayed this would be the day Aunt Minnie would come inside to get me. Immediately after, I felt sure God would kill me for my wickedness. I pictured myself falling dead beside the oat bin. I begged Mr. Wall to let me see her.

"Go on back, littl'un. She told me you'd be coming in," he said.

I had never been in the apartment before. There was little in it beyond the necessary things and a few old photographs on the walls, all of the same woman. The rooms were cold and felt infused with sickness and an odor I incorrectly believed to be medicine. Because my father didn't drink, I had never before encountered the smell of whiskey.

Rose-Johnny was propped on the pillows in a lifeless flannel gown. Her face changed when she saw me, and I remembered the way her face was lit by the light bulb in the chick tub, the first time I saw her. With fresh guilt I threw myself on her bosom.

"I'm sorry. I could have paid for the mash. I didn't mean to make you sick." Through my sobs I heard accusing needly wheezing sounds in Rose-Johnny's chest. She breathed with a great pulling effort.

"Child, don't talk foolish."

71

As weeks passed and Rose-Johnny didn't improve, it became clear that my lie was prophetic. Without Rose-Johnny to run the store,

Mr. Wall badly needed my help. He seemed mystified by his inventory and was rendered helpless by any unusual demand from a customer. It was March, the busiest time for the store. I had turned eleven, one week before Mary Etta turned sixteen. These seven days out of each year, during which she was only four years older, I considered to be God's greatest gifts to me.

The afternoon my father would come in to buy the vegetable garden and tobacco seed was an event I had rehearsed endlessly in my mind. When it finally did transpire, Mr. Wall's confusion gave such complete respectability to my long-standing lie that I didn't need to say a word myself in support of it. I waited on him with dignity, precisely weighing out his tobacco seed, and even recommended to him the white runner beans that Mr. Wall had accidentally overstocked, and which my father did not buy.

Later on that same afternoon, after the winter light had come slanting through the dusty windows and I was alone in the store cleaning up, Cleota and the other children came pecking at the glass. I let them in. When I had filled all the orders Cleota unwrapped their coins, knotted all together into a blue handkerchief. I counted, and counted again. It was not the right amount, not even half.

"That's what Miss Rose-Johnny ast us for it," Cleota said. "Same as always." The smaller children—Venise, Anita, Little-Roy, James—shuffled and elbowed each other like fighting cocks, paying no attention. Cleota gazed at me calmly, steadily. Her eyebrows were two perfect arches.

"I thank you very much," I said, and put the coins in their proper places in the cash drawer.

During that week I also discovered an epidemic of chick droop in the pullets. I had to pull Mr. Wall over by the hand to make him look. There were more sick ones than well.

"It's because it's so cold in the store," I told him. "They can't keep warm. Can't we make it warmer in here?"

Mr. Wall shrugged at the wood stove, helpless. He could never keep a fire going for long, the way Rose-Johnny could.

"We have to try. The one light bulb isn't enough," I said. The chicks were huddled around the bulb just the way the men would collect around the stove in the mornings to say howdy-do to Mr.

Wall and warm up their hands on the way to work. Except the chicks were more ruthless: they climbed and shoved, and the healthy ones pecked at the eyes and feet of the sick ones, making them bleed.

I had not noticed before what a very old man Mr. Wall was. As he stared down at the light, I saw that his eyes were covered with a film. "How do we fix them up?" he asked me.

"We can't. We've got to take the sick ones out so they won't all get it. Rose-Johnny puts them in that tub over there. We give them water and keep them warm, but it don't do any good. They've got to die."

He looked so sad I stood and patted his old freckled hand.

I spent much more time than before at the store, but no longer enjoyed it particularly. Working in the shadow of Rose-Johnny's expertise, I had been a secret witness to a wondrous ritual of counting, weighing, and tending. Together we created little packages that sailed out like ships to all parts of the county, giving rise to gardens and barnyard life in places I had never even seen. I felt superior to my schoolmates, knowing that I had had a hand in the creation of their families' poultry flocks and their mothers' kitchen gardens. By contrast, Mr. Wall's bewilderment was pathetic and only increased my guilt. But each day I was able to spend a little time in the back rooms with Rose-Johnny.

There were rumors about her illness, both before and after the fact. It did not occur to me that I might have been the source of some of the earlier rumors. But, if I didn't think of this, it was because Walnut Knobs was overrun with tales of Rose-Johnny, and not because I didn't take notice of the stories. I did.

The tales that troubled me most were those about Rose-Johnny's daddy. I had heard many adults say that he was responsible for her misfortune, which I presumed to mean her short hair. But it was also said that he was a colored man, and this I knew to be untrue. Aunt Minnie, when I pressed her, would offer nothing more than that if it were up to her I wouldn't go near either one of them, advice which I ignored. I was coming to understand that I would not hear the truth about Rose-Johnny from Aunt Minnie or anyone else. I knew, in a manner that went beyond the meanings of words I could not understand, that she was no more masculine than my mother or aunt, and no more lesbian than Lebanese. Rose-Johnny was simply herself, and alone.

And yet she was such a capable woman that I couldn't believe she would be sick for very long. But as the warm weather came she grew sluggish and pale. Her slow, difficult breathing frightened me. I brought my schoolbooks and read to her from the foot of the bed. Sometimes the rather ordinary adventures of the boy in my reader would make her laugh aloud until she choked. Other times she fell asleep while I read, but then would make me read those parts over again.

She worried about the store. Frequently she would ask about Mr. Wall and the customers, and how he was managing. "He does all right," I always said. But eventually my eagerness to avoid the burden of further lies, along with the considerable force of my pride, led me to confess that I had to tell him nearly everything. "He forgets something awful," I told her.

Rose-Johnny smiled. "He used to be as smart as anything, and taught me. Now I've done taught you, and you him again." She was lying back on the pillows with her eyes closed and her plump hands folded on her stomach.

"But he's a nice man," I said. I listened to her breathing. "He don't hurt you, does he? Your pa?"

Nothing moved except her eyelids. They opened and let the blue eyes out at me. I looked down and traced my finger over the triangles of the flying-geese patch on the quilt. I whispered, "Does he make you cut off your hair?"

Rose-Johnny's eyes were so pale they were almost white, like ice with water running underneath. "He cuts it with a butcher knife. Sometimes he chases me all the way down to the river." She laughed a hissing laugh like a boy, and she had the same look the yearling calves get when they are cornered and jump the corral and run to the woods and won't be butchered. I understood then that Rose-Johnny, too, knew the power of a lie.

It was the youngest Mattox boy who started the fight at school on the Monday after Easter. He was older than me, and a boy, so nobody believed he would hit me, but when he started the name calling I called them right back, and he threw me down on the ground. The girls screamed and ran to get the teacher, but by the time she arrived I had a bloody nose and had bitten his arm wonderfully hard.

Miss Althea gave me her handkerchief for my nose and dragged Roy Mattox inside to see the principal. All the other children stood in a circle, looking at me.

"It isn't true, what he said," I told them. "And not about Rose-Johnny either. She isn't a pervert. I love her."

"Pervert," one of the boys said.

I marveled at the sight of my own blood soaking through the handkerchief. "I love her," I said.

I did not get to see Rose-Johnny that day. The door of Wall's store was locked. I could see Mr. Wall through the window, though, so I banged on the glass with the flats of my hands until he came. He had the strong medicine smell on his breath.

"Not today, littl'un." The skin under his eyes was dark blue.

"I need to see Rose-Johnny." I was irritated with Mr. Wall, and did not consider him important enough to prevent me from seeing her. But evidently he was.

"Not today," he said. "We're closed." He shut the door and locked it.

I shouted at him through the glass. "Tell her I hit a boy and bit his arm, that was calling her names. Tell her I fought with a boy, Mr. Wall."

The next day the door was open, but I didn't see him in the store. In the back, the apartment was dark except for the lamp by Rose-Johnny's bed. A small brown bottle and a glass stood just touching each other on the night table. Rose-Johnny looked asleep but made a snuffing sound when I climbed onto the bottom of the bed.

"Did your daddy tell you what I told him yesterday?"

She said nothing.

"Is your daddy sick?"

"My daddy's dead," she said suddenly, causing me to swallow a little gulp of air. She opened her eyes, then closed them again.

"Pa's all right, honey, just stepped out, I imagine." She stopped to breathe between every few words. "I didn't mean to give you a fright. Pa's not my daddy, he's my mama's daddy."

I was confused. "And your real daddy's dead?"

She nodded. "Long time."

"And your mama, what about her? Is she dead too?"

"Mm-hmm," she said, in the same lazy sort of way Mama would say it when she wasn't really listening.

"That her?" I pointed to the picture over the bed. The woman's shoulders were bare except for a dark lace shawl. She was looking backward toward you, over her shoulder.

Rose-Johnny looked up at the picture, and said yes it was.

"She's pretty," I said.

"People used to say I looked just like her." Rose-Johnny laughed a wheezy laugh, and coughed.

"Why did she die?"

Rose-Johnny shook her head. "I can't tell you that."

"Can you when I'm older?"

She didn't answer.

"Well then, if Mr. Wall isn't your daddy, then the colored man is your daddy," I said, mostly to myself.

She looked at me. "Is that what they say?"

I shrugged.

"Does no harm to me. Every man is some color," she said.

"Oh," I said.

"My daddy was white. After he died my mama loved another man and he was brown."

"What happened then?"

"What happened then," she said. "Then they had a sweet little baby Johnny." Her voice was more like singing than talking, and her eyes were so peacefully closed I was afraid they might not open again. Every time she breathed there was the sound of a hundred tiny birds chirping inside her chest.

"Where's he?"

"Mama's Rose and sweet little baby Johnny," she sang it like an old song. "Not nothing bad going to happen to them, not nobody going to take her babies." A silvery moth flew into the lamp and clicked against the inside of the lampshade. Rose-Johnny stretched out her hand toward the night table. "I want you to pour me some of that bottle."

I lifted the bottle carefully and poured the glass half full. "That your medicine?" I asked. No answer. I feared this would be another story without an end, without meaning. "Did somebody take your mama's babies?" I persisted.

"Took her man, is what they did, and hung him up from a tree." She sat up slowly on her elbows, and looked straight at me. "Do you know what lynched is?"

"Yes, ma'am," I said, although until that moment I had not been sure.

"People will tell you there's never been no lynchings north of where the rivers don't freeze over. But they done it. Do you know where Jackson Crick is, up there by Floyd's Mill?" I nodded. "They lynched him up there, and drowned her baby Johnny in Jackson Crick, and it was as froze as you're ever going to see it. They had to break a hole in the ice to do it." She would not stop looking right into me. "In that river. Poor little baby in that cold river. Poor Mama, what they did to Mama. And said they would do to me, when I got old enough."

She didn't drink the medicine I poured for her, but let it sit. I was afraid to hear any more, and afraid to leave. I watched the moth crawl up the outside of the lampshade.

And then, out of the clear blue, she sat up and said, "But they didn't do a thing to me!" The way she said it, she sounded more like she ought to be weighing out bags of mash than sick in bed. "Do you want to know what Mama did?"

I didn't say.

"I'll tell you what she did. She took her scissors and cut my hair right off, every bit of it. She said, 'From now on, I want you to be Rose and Johnny both.' And then she went down to the same hole in the crick where they put baby Johnny in."

I sat with Rose-Johnny for a long time. I patted the lumps in the covers where her knees were, and wiped my nose on my sleeve. "You'd better drink your medicine, Rose-Johnny," I said. "Drink up and get better now," I told her. "It's all over now."

It was the last time I saw Rose-Johnny. The next time I saw the store, more than a month later, it was locked and boarded up. Later on, the Londroski brothers took it over. Some people said she had died. Others thought she and Mr. Wall had gone to live somewhere up in the Blue Ridge, and opened a store there. This is the story I believed. In the years since, when passing through that part of the country, I have never failed to notice the Plymouth Rocks and Rhode Islands scratching in the yards, and the tomato vines tied up around the back doors.

I would like to stop here and say no more, but there are enough half-true stories in my past. This one will have to be heard to the end.

Whatever became of Rose-Johnny and her grandfather, I am certain that their going away had something to do with what happened on that same evening to Mary Etta. And I knew this to be my fault.

It was late when I got home. As I walked I turned Rose-Johnny's story over and over, like Grandpa Bowles's Indian penny with the head on both sides. You never could stop turning it over.

When I caught sight of Mama standing like somebody's ghost in the front doorway I thought she was going to thrash me, but she didn't. Instead she ran out into the yard and picked me up like she used to when I was a little girl, and carried me into the house.

"Where's Daddy?" I asked. It was suppertime, but there was no supper.

"Daddy's gone looking for you in the truck. He'll be back directly, when he don't find you."

"Why's he looking for me? What did I do?"

"Georgeann, some men tried to hurt Mary Etta. We don't know why they done it, but we was afraid they might try to hurt you."

"No, ma'am, nobody hurt me," I said quietly. "Did they kill her?" I asked.

"Oh Lordy no," Mama said, and hugged me. "She's all right. You can go upstairs and see her, but don't bother her if she don't want to be bothered."

Our room was dark, and Mary Etta was in bed crying. "Can I turn on the little light?" I asked. I wanted to see Mary Etta. I was afraid that some part of her might be missing.

"If you want to."

She was all there: arms, legs, hair. Her face was swollen, and there were marks on her neck.

"Don't stare at me," she said.

"I'm sorry." I looked around the room. Her dress was hanging over the chair. It was her best dress, the solid green linen with covered buttons and attached petticoat that had taken her all winter to make. It was red with dirt and torn nearly in half at the bodice.

"I'll fix your dress, Mary Etta. I can't sew as good as you, but I can mend," I said.

"Can't be mended," she said, but then tried to smile with her swollen mouth. "You can help me make another one."

"Who was it that done it?" I asked.

"I don't know." She rolled over and faced the wallpaper. "Some men. Three or four of them. Some of them might have been boys, I couldn't tell for sure. They had things over their faces."

"What kind of things?"

"I don't know. Just bandanners and things." She spoke quietly to the wall. "You know how the Mattoxes have those funny-colored eyes? I think some of them might of been Mattoxes. Don't tell, Georgeann. Promise."

I remembered the feeling of Roy Mattox's muscle in my teeth. I did not promise.

"Did you hit them?"

"No. I screamed. Mr. Dorsey come along the road."

"What did they say, before you screamed?"

"Nothing. They just kept saying, 'Are you the Bowles girl, are you the Bowles girl?' And they said nasty things."

"It was me they was looking for," I said. And no matter what anyone said, I would not believe otherwise. I took to my bed and would not eat or speak to anyone. My convalescence was longer than Mary Etta's. It was during that time that I found my sister's sewing scissors and cut off all my hair and all of Miss Regina's. I said that my name was George-Etta, not Georgeann, and I called my doll Rose-Johnny.

For the most part, my family tolerated my distress. My mother retrimmed my hair as neatly as she could, but there was little that could be done. Every time I looked in the mirror I was startled and secretly pleased to see that I looked exactly like a little boy. Mama said that when I went back to school I would have to do the explaining for myself. Aunt Minnie said I was going through a stage and oughtn't to be pampered.

But there was only a month left of school, and my father let Mary Etta and me stay home to help set tobacco. By the end of the summer my hair had grown out sufficiently so that no explanations were needed. Miss Regina's hair, of course, never grew back.

Michael Chabon

THE LITTLE KNIFE

One Saturday in that last, interminable summer before his parents separated and the Washington Senators baseball team was expunged forever from the face of the earth, the Shapiros went to Nags Head, North Carolina, where Nathan, without planning to, perpetrated a great hoax. They drove down I-95, through the Commonwealth of Virginia, to a place called the Sandpiper—a ragged, charming oval of motel cottages painted white and green as the Atlantic, and managed by a kind, astonishingly fat old man named Colonel Larue, who smoked cherry cigars and would, if asked, play catch or keep-away. Outside his office, in the weedy gravel, stood an old red-and-radium-white Coke machine, which dispensed bottles from a vertical glass door that sighed when you opened it, and which reminded Nathan of the Automat his grandmother had taken him to once in New York City. The sight of the faded machine and of the whole Sandpiper—like that of the Automat—filled Nathan with a happy sadness, or, really, a sad happiness; he was not too young, at ten, to have developed a sense of nostalgia.

There were children in every cottage—with all manner of floats, pails, paddles, trucks, and flying objects—and his younger brother Ricky, to Nathan's envy, immediately fell in with a gang of piratical little boys with water pistols, who were always reproducing fart sounds and giggling chaotically when their mothers employed certain ordinary words such as "hot dog" and "rubber." The Shapiros went to the ocean every summer, and at the beginning of this trip, as on all those that had preceded it, Nathan and his brother got along better than they usually did, their mother broke out almost immediately in a feathery red heat rash, and their father lay pale and motionless in the sun, like a monument, and always forgot to take off his wristwatch when he went into the sea. Nathan had brought a stack of James Bond books and his colored pencils; there were board games—he and his father were in the middle of their Strat-O-Matic baseball playoffs—and miniature boxes of cereal; the family ate out every single night. But when they were halfway through the slow, dazzling week—which was as far as they were to get—Nathan began to experience an unfamiliar longing: He wanted to go home.

He awoke very early on Wednesday morning, went into the cottage's small kitchen, where the floor was sticky and the table rocked and trembled, and chose the last of the desirable cereals from the Variety pack, leaving for Ricky only those papery, sour brands with the scientific names—the sort that their grandparents liked. As he began to eat, Nathan heard, from the big bedroom down the hall, the unmistakable, increasingly familiar sound of his father burying his mother under a heap of scorn and ridicule. It was, oddly, a soft and pleading sound. Lately, the conversation and actions of Dr. Shapiro's family seemed to disappoint him terribly. His left hand was always flying up to smack his sad and outraged forehead, so hard that Nathan often thought he could hear his father's wedding ring crack against his skull. When they'd played their baseball game the day before—Nathan's Baltimore Bonfires against his father's Brooklyn Eagles—every decision Nathan made led to a disaster, and his father pointed out each unwise substitution and foolish attempt to steal in this new tone of miserable sarcasm, so that Nathan had spent the afternoon apologizing, and, finally, crying. Now he listened for his mother's voice, for the note of chastened shame.

The bedroom door slammed, and Mrs. Shapiro came out into the kitchen. She was in her bathrobe, a wild, sleepless smile on her face.

"Good morning, honey," she said, then hummed to herself as she boiled water and made a cup of instant coffee. Her spoon tinkled gaily against the cup.

"Where are you going, Mom?" said Nathan. She had taken up her coffee and was heading for the sliding glass door that led out of the kitchen and down to the beach.

"See you, honey," she sang.

"Mom!" said Nathan. He stood up—afraid, absurdly, that she might be leaving for good, because she seemed so happy. After a few seconds he heard her whistling, and he went to the door and pressed his face against the wire screen. His mother had a Disney whistle, melodious and full, like a Scotsman's as he walks across a meadow in a brilliant kilt. She paced briskly along the ramshackle slat-and-wire fence, back and forth through the beach grass, drinking from the huge white mug of coffee and whistling heartily into the breeze; her red hair rose from her head and trailed like a defiant banner. He watched her observe the sunrise—it was going to be a perfect, breezy day—then continued to watch as she set her coffee on the ground, removed her bathrobe, and, in her bathing suit, began to engage in a long series of yoga exercises—a new fad of hers—as though she were playing statues all alone. Nathan was soon lost, with the fervor of a young scientist, in contemplation of his pretty, whistling mother rolling around on the ground.

"Oh, how can she?" said Dr. Shapiro.

"Yes," said Nathan, gravely, before he blushed and whirled around to find his father, in pajamas, staring out at Mrs. Shapiro. His smile was angry and clenched, but in his eyes was the same look of bleak surprise, of betrayal, that had been there when Nathan took out Johnny Sain, a slugging pitcher, and the pinch-hitter,

Enos Slaughter, immediately went down on strikes. There were a hundred new things that interested Nathan's mother—bonsai, the Zuni, yoga, real estate—and although Dr. Shapiro had always been a liberal, generous, encouraging man (as Nathan had heard his mother say to a friend), and had at first happily helped her to purchase the necessary manuals, supplies, and coffee-table books, lately each new fad seemed to come as a blow to him—a going astray, a false step.

"How can she?" he said again, shaking his big bearded head.

"She says it's really good for you," said Nathan.

His father smiled down on his son ruefully, and tapped him once on the head. Then he turned and went to the refrigerator, hitching up his pajama bottoms. They were the ones patterned with a blue stripe and red chevrons—the ones that Nathan always imagined were the sort worn by the awkward, doomed elephant in the Groucho Marx joke.

Later that day, as they made egg-salad sandwiches to carry down to the beach, Dr. and Mrs. Shapiro fought bitterly, for the fifth time since their arrival. In the cottage's kitchen was a knife—a small, new, foreign knife, which Mrs. Shapiro admired. As she used it to slice neat little horseshoes of celery, she praised it again. "Such a good little knife," she said. "Why don't you just take it?" said Dr. Shapiro. The air in the kitchen was suddenly full of sharp, caramel smoke, and Dr. Shapiro ran to unplug the toaster.

"That would be stealing," said Nathan's mother, ignoring her husband's motions of alarm and the fact that their lunch was on fire. "We are not taking this knife, Martin."

"Give it to me." Dr. Shapiro held out his hand, palm up.

"I'm not going to let you—make me—dishonest anymore!" said his mother. She seemed to struggle, at first, not to finish the sentence she had begun, but in the end she turned, put her face right up to his, and cried out boldly. After her outburst, both adults turned to look, with a simultaneity that was almost funny, at their sons. Nathan hadn't the faintest notion of what his mother was talking about.

"Don't steal, Dad," Ricky said.

"I only wanted it to extract the piece of toast," said their father. He was looking at their mother again. "God damn it." He turned and went out of the kitchen.

Her knuckles white around the handle of the knife, their mother freed the toast and began scraping the burnt surfaces into the sink. Because their father had said "God damn," Ricky wiggled his eyebrows and smiled at Nathan. At the slamming of the bedroom door, Nathan clambered up suddenly from the rickety kitchen table as though he had found an insect crawling on his leg.

"Kill it!" said Ricky. "What is it?"

"What is it?" said his mother. She scanned Nathan's body quickly, one hand half raised to swat.

"Nothing," said Nathan. He took off his glasses. "I'm going for a walk."

When he got to the edge of the water, he turned to look toward the Sandpiper. At that time in Nags Head there were few hotels and no condominiums, and it seemed to Nathan that their little ring of cottages stood alone, like Stonehenge, in the middle of a giant wasteland. He set off down the beach, watching his feet print and following the script left in the sand by the birds for which the motel was named. He passed a sand castle, then a heart drawn with a stick enclosing the names Jimmy and Beth. Sometimes his heels sank deeply into the sand, and he noticed the odd marks this would leave—a pair of wide dimples. He discovered that he could walk entirely on his heels, and his trail became two lines of big periods. If he took short steps, it looked as though a creature—a bird with two peg legs—had come to fish along the shore.

He lurched a long way in this fashion, watching his feet, and nearly forgot his parents' quarrel. But when at last he grew bored with walking on his heels and turned to go back, he saw that his mother and father had also decided to take a walk, and that they were, in fact, coming toward him—clasping hands, letting go, clasping hands again. Nathan ran to meet them, and they parted to let him walk between them. They all continued down the beach, stooping to pick up shells, glass, dead crabs, twine, and all the colored or smelly things that Nathan had failed to take note of before. At first his parents exclaimed with him over these discoveries, and his father took each striped seashell into his hands, to keep it safe, until there were two dozen and they jingled there like money. But after a while they seemed to lose interest, and Nathan found himself walking a few feet ahead of them, stooping alone, glumly dusting his toes with sand as he tried to eavesdrop on their careless and incomprehensible conversation.

"Never again," his mother said at last.

Dr. Shapiro let the shells fall. He rubbed his hands together and then stared at them as though waking from a dream in which he had been holding a fortune in gold. Straightening up so quickly that his head spun, Nathan let out a cry and pointed down at the sand beneath their feet, among the scattered shells. "Look at those weird tracks!" he cried.

They all looked down.

Speculation on the nature of the beast that went toeless down the shore went on for several minutes, and although Nathan was delighted at first, he soon began to feel embarrassed and, obscurely, frightened by the ease with which he had deceived his parents. His treachery was almost exposed when Ricky, carrying a long stick and wearing a riot of Magic Marker tattoos on his face and all down his arms, ran over to find out what was happening. The little boy immediately tipped back onto his heels, and would have taken a few steps like that had Nathan not grabbed him by the elbow and dragged him aside.

"Why do you have a dog on your face?" said Nathan.

"It's a jaguar," said Ricky.

Nathan bent to whisper into his brother's ear. "I'm tricking Mom and Dad," he said.

"Good," said Ricky.

"They think there's some kind of weird creature on the beach."

Ricky pushed Nathan away and then surveyed their mother and father, who were talking again, quietly, as though they were trying not to alarm their sons. "It can't be real," said Nathan's father.

Ricky's skin under the crude tattoos was tanned, his hair looked stiff and ragged from going unwashed and sea-tangled, and as he regarded their parents he held his skinny stick like a javelin at his side. "They're dumb," he said flatly.

Dr. Shapiro approached, stepping gingerly across the mysterious tracks, and then knelt beside his sons. His face was red, though not from the sun, and he seemed to have trouble looking directly at the boys. Nathan began to cry before his father even spoke.

"Boys," he said. He looked away, then back, and bit his lip. "I'm afraid—I'm sorry. We're going to go home. Your mom and I—don't feel very well. We don't seem to be well."

"No! No! It was Nathan!" said Ricky, laying down his spear and throwing himself into his father's arms. "It wasn't me. Make *him* go home."

Nathan, summoning up his courage, decided to admit that the curious trail of the crippled animal was his, and he said, "I'm responsible."

"Oh, no!" cried both his parents together, startling him. His mother rushed over and fell to her knees, and they took Nathan into their arms and said that it was never, never him, and they ruffled his hair with their fingers, as though he had done something they could love him for.

After they came back from dinner, the Shapiros, save Nathan, went down to the sea for a final, sad promenade. At the restaurant, Ricky had pleaded with his parents to stay through the end of the week—they had not even been to see the monument at Kitty Hawk, the Birthplace of Aviation. For Ricky's sake, Nathan had also tried to persuade them, but his heart wasn't in it—he himself wanted so badly to go home—and the four of them had all ended up crying and chewing their food in the brass-and-rope dining room of the Port O' Call; even Dr. Shapiro had shed a tear. They were going to leave that night. Nathan's family now stood, in sweatshirts, by the sliding glass door, his parents straining to adopt hard and impatient looks, and Nathan saw that they felt guilty about leaving him behind in the cottage.

"I'll pack my stuff," he said. "Just go." For a moment his stomach tightened with angry, secret glee as his mother and father, sighing, turned their backs on him and obeyed his small command. Then he was alone in the kitchen again, for the second time that day, and he wished that he had gone to look at the ocean, and he hated his parents, uncertainly, for leaving him behind. He got up and walked into the bedroom that he and Ricky had shared. There, in the twilight that fell in orange shafts through the open window, the tangle of their clothes and bedsheets, their scattered toys and books, the surfaces of the broken dresser and twin headboards seemed dusted with a film of radiant sand, as though the tide had washed across them and withdrawn, and the room was strewn with the seashells they had found. Nathan, after emptying his shoebox of baseball cards into his suitcase, went slowly around the room and harvested the shells with careful sweeps of his trembling hand. Bearing the shoebox back into the kitchen, he collected the few stray shards of salt-white and green beach glass that lay in a pile beside the electric can opener, and then added a hollow pink crab's leg in whose claw Ricky had fixed a colored pencil. When Nathan saw the little knife in the drainboard by the sink, he hesitated only a moment before dropping it into the box, where it swam, frozen, like a model shark in a museum diorama of life beneath the sea. Nathan chuckled. As clearly as if he were remembering them, he foresaw his mother's accusation, his father's enraged denial, and with an unhappy chuckle he foresaw, recalled, and fondly began to preserve all the discord for which, in his wildly preserving imagination, he was and would always be responsible.

Reginald McKnight

THE KIND OF LIGHT
THAT SHINES
ON TEXAS

I never liked Marvin Pruitt. Never liked him, never knew him, even though there were only three of us in the class. Three black kids. In our school there were fourteen classrooms of thirty-odd white kids (in '66, they considered Chicanos provisionally white) and three or four black kids. Primary school in primary colors. Neat division. Alphabetized. They didn't stick us in the back, or arrange us by degrees of hue, apartheidlike. This was real integration, a ten-to-one ratio as tidy as upper-class landscaping. If it all worked, you could have ten white kids all to yourself. They could talk to you, get the feel of you, scrutinize you bone deep if they wanted to. They seldom wanted to, and that was fine with me for two reasons. The first was that their scrutiny was irritating. How do you comb your hair—why do you comb your hair—may I please touch your hair—were the kinds of questions they asked. This is no way to feel at home. The second reason was Marvin. He embarrassed me. He smelled bad, was at least two grades behind, was hostile, dark-skinned, homely, close-mouthed. I feared him for his size, pitied him for his dress, watched him all the time. Marveled at him, mystified, astonished, uneasy.

He had the habit of spitting on his right arm, juicing it down till it would glisten. He would start in immediately after taking his seat when we'd finished with the Pledge of Allegiance, "The Yellow Rose of Texas," "The Eyes of Texas Are upon You," and "Mistress Shady." Marvin would rub his spit-flecked arm with his left hand, rub and roll as if polishing an ebony pool cue. Then he would rest his head in the crook of his arm, sniffing, huffing deep like black-jacket boys huff bagsful of acrylics. After ten minutes or so, his eyes would close, heavy. He would sleep till recess. Mrs. Wickham would let him.

There was one other black kid in our class. A girl they called Ah-so. I never learned what she did to earn this name. There was nothing Asian about this big-shouldered girl. She was the tallest, heaviest kid in school. She was quiet, but I don't think any one of us was subtle or sophisticated enough to nickname our classmates according to any but physical attributes. Fat kids were called Porky or Butterball, skinny ones were called Stick or Ichabod. Ah-so was big, thick, and African. She would impassively sit, sullen, silent as Marvin. She wore the same dark blue pleated skirt every day, the same ruffled white blouse every day. Her skin always shone as if worked by Marvin's palms and fingers. I never spoke one word to her, nor she to me.

Of the three of us, Mrs. Wickham called only on Ah-so and me. Ah-so never answered one question, correctly or incorrectly, so far as I can recall. She wasn't stupid. When asked to read aloud she read well, seldom stumbling over long words, reading with humor and expression. But when Wickham asked her about Farmer Brown and how many cows, or the capital of Vermont, or the date of this war or that, Ah-so never spoke. Not one word. But you always felt she could have answered those questions if she'd wanted to. I sensed no tension, embarrassment, or anger in Ah-so's reticence. She simply refused to speak. There was something unshakable about her, some core so impenetrably solid, you got the feeling that if you stood too close to her she could eat your thoughts like a black star eats light. I didn't despise Ah-so as I despised Marvin. There was nothing malevolent about her. She sat like a great icon in the back of the classroom, tranquil, guarded, sealed up, watchful. She was close to sixteen, and it was my guess she'd given up on school. Perhaps she was just obliging the wishes of her family, sticking it out till the law could no longer reach her.

There were at least half a dozen older kids in our class. Besides Marvin and Ah-so there was Oakley, who sat behind me, whispering threats into my ear; Varna Willard with the large breasts; Eddie Limon, who played bass for a high school rock band; and Lawrence Ridderbeck, who everyone said had a kid and a wife. You couldn't expect me to know anything about Texan educational practices of the 1960s, so I never knew why there were so many older kids in my sixth-grade class. After all, I was just a boy and had transferred into the school around midyear. My father, an air force sergeant, had been sent to Viet Nam. The air force sent my mother, my sister, Claire, and me to Connolly Air Force Base, which during the war housed "unaccompanied wives." I'd been to so many different schools in my short life that I ceased wondering about their differences. All I knew about the Texas schools is that they weren't afraid to flunk you.

Yet though I was only twelve then, I had a good idea why Wickham never once called on Marvin, why she let him snooze in the crook of his polished arm. I knew why she would press her lips together, and narrow her eyes at me whenever I correctly answered a question, rare as that was. I know why she badgered Ah-so with questions everyone knew Ah-so would never even consider answering. Wickham didn't like us. She wasn't gross about it, but it was clear she didn't want us around. She would prove her dislike day after day with little stories and jokes. "I just want to share with you all," she would say, "a little riddle my daughter told me at the supper table the other day. Now, where do you go when you injure your knee?" Then one, two, or all three of her pets would say for the rest of us, "We don't know, Miz Wickham," in that skin-chilling way suck-asses speak, "where?" "Why, to Africa," Wickham would say, "where the knee grows."

The thirty-odd white kids would laugh, and I would look across the room at Marvin. He'd be asleep. I would glance back at Ah-so. She'd be sitting still as a projected image, staring down at her desk. I, myself, would smile at Wickham's stupid jokes, sometimes fake a laugh. I tried to show her that at least one of us was alive and alert, even though her jokes hurt. I sucked ass, too, I suppose. But I wanted her to understand more than anything that I was not like her other nigra children, that I was worthy of more than the non-attention and the negative attention she paid Marvin and Ah-so. I hated her, but never showed it. No one could safely contradict that woman. She knew all kinds of tricks to demean, control, and punish you. And she could swing her two-foot paddle as fluidly as a big-league slugger swings a bat. You didn't speak in Wickham's class unless she spoke to you first. You didn't chew gum, or wear "hood" hair. You didn't drag your feet, curse, pass notes, hold hands with the opposite sex. Most especially, you didn't say anything bad about the Aggies, Governor Connolly, LBJ, Sam Houston, or Waco. You did the forbidden and she would get you. It was that simple.

She never got me, though. Never gave her reason to. But she could have invented reasons. She did a lot of that. I can't be sure, but I used to think she pitied me because my father was in Viet Nam and my uncle A.J. had recently died there. Whenever she would tell one of her racist jokes, she would always glance at me, preface the joke with, "Now don't you nigra children take offense. This is all in fun, you know. I just want to share with you all something Coach Gilchrest told me th'other day." She would tell her joke, and glance at me again. I'd giggle, feeling a little queasy. "I'm half Irish," she would chuckle, "and you should hear some of those Irish jokes." She never told any, and I never really expected her to. I just did my Tom-thing. I kept my shoes shined, my desk neat, answered her questions as best I could, never brought gum to school, never cursed, never slept in class. I wanted to show her we were not all the same.

I tried to show them all, all thirty-odd, that I was different. It worked to some degree, but not very well. When some article was stolen from someone's locker or desk, Marvin, not I, was the first accused. I'd be second. Neither Marvin, nor Ah-so nor I were ever chosen for certain classroom honors—"Pledge leader," "flag holder," "noise monitor," "paper passer-outer," but Mrs. Wickham once let me be "eraser duster." I was proud. I didn't even care about the cracks my fellow students made about my finally having turned the right color. I had done something that Marvin, in the deeps of his never-ending sleep, couldn't even dream of doing. Jack Preston, a kid who sat in front of me, asked me one day at recess whether I was embarrassed about Marvin. "Can you believe that guy?" I said. "He's like a pig or something. Makes me sick."

"Does it make you ashamed to be colored?"

"No," I said, but I meant yes. Yes, if you insist on thinking us all the same. Yes, if his faults are mine, his weaknesses inherent in me.

"I'd be," said Jack.

I made no reply. I was ashamed. Ashamed for not defending Marvin and ashamed that Marvin even existed. But if it had occurred to me, I would have asked Jack whether he was ashamed of being white because of Oakley. Oakley, "Oak Tree," Kelvin "Oak Tree" Oakley. He was sixteen and proud of it. He made it clear to everyone, including Wickham, that his life's ambition was to stay in school one more year, till he'd be old enough to enlist in the army. "Them slopes got my brother," he would say. "I'mna sign up and git me a few slopes. Gonna kill them bastards deader'n shit." Oakley, so far as anyone knew, was and always had been the oldest kid in his family. But no one contradicted him. He would, as anyone would tell you, "snap yer neck jest as soon as look at you." Not a boy in class, excepting Marvin and myself, had been able to avoid Oakley's pink bellies, Texas titty twisters, moon pie punches, or worse. He didn't bother Marvin, I suppose, because Marvin was closer to his size and age, and because Marvin spent five sixths of the school day asleep. Marvin probably never crossed Oakley's mind. And to say that Oakley hadn't bothered me is not to say he had no intention of ever doing so. In fact, this haphazard sketch of hairy fingers, slash of eyebrow, explosion of acne, elbows, and crooked teeth, swore almost daily that he'd like to kill me.

93

Naturally, I feared him. Though we were about the same height, he outweighed me by no less than forty pounds. He talked, stood, smoked, and swore like a man. No one, except for Mrs.

Wickham, the principal, and the coach, ever laid a finger on him. And even Wickham knew that the hot lines she laid on him merely amused him. He would smile out at the classroom, goofy and bashful, as she laid down the two, five, or maximum ten strokes on him. Often he would wink, or surreptitiously flash us the thumb as Wickham worked on him. When she was finished, Oakley would walk so cool back to his seat you'd think he was on wheels. He'd slide into his chair, sniff the air, and say, "Somethin's burnin. Do y'all smell smoke? I swanee, I smell smoke and fahr back here." If he had made these cracks and never threatened me, I might have grown to admire Oakley, even liked him a little. But he hated me, and took every opportunity during the six-hour school day to make me aware of this. "Some Sambo's gittin his ass broke open one of these days," he'd mumble. "I wanna fight somebody. Need to keep in shape till I git to Nam."

I never said anything to him for the longest time. I pretended not to hear him, pretended not to notice his sour breath on my neck and ear. "Yep," he'd whisper. "Coonies keep y' in good shape for slope killin." Day in, day out, that's the kind of thing I'd pretend not to hear. But one day when the rain dropped down like lead balls, and the cold air made your skin look plucked, Oakley whispered to me, "My brother tells me it rains like this in Nam. Maybe I oughta go out at recess and break your ass open today. Nice and cool so you don't sweat. Nice and wet to clean up the blood." I said nothing for at least half a minute, then I turned half right and said, "Thought you said your brother was dead." Oakley, silent himself, for a time, poked me in the back with his pencil and hissed, "*Yer* dead." Wickham cut her eyes our way, and it was over.

It was hardest avoiding him in gym class. Especially when we played murderball. Oakley always aimed his throws at me. He threw with unblinking intensity, his teeth gritting, his neck veining, his face flushing, his black hair sweeping over one eye. He could throw hard, but the balls were squishy and harmless. In fact, I found his misses more intimidating than his hits. The balls would whizz by, thunder against the folded bleachers. They rattled as though a locomotive were passing through them. I would duck, dodge, leap as if he were throwing grenades. But he always hit me, sooner or later. And after a while I noticed that the other boys would avoid throwing at me, as if I belonged to Oakley.

One day, however, I was surprised to see that Oakley was throwing at everyone else but me. He was uncommonly accurate, too; kids were falling like tin cans. Since no one was throwing at me, I spent most of the game watching Oakley cut this one and that one down. Finally, he and I were the only ones left on the court. Try as he would, he couldn't hit me, nor I him. Coach Gilchrest blew his whistle and told Oakley and me to bring the red rubber balls to the equipment locker. I was relieved I'd escaped Oakley's stinging throws for once. I was feeling triumphant, full of myself. As Oakley and I approached Gilchrest, I thought about saying something friendly to Oakley: Good game, Oak Tree, I would say. Before I could speak, though, Gilchrest said, "All right boys, there's five minutes left in the period. Y'all are so good, looks like, you're gonna have to play like men. No boundaries, no catch outs, and you gotta hit your opponent three times in order to win. Got me?"

We nodded.

"And you're gonna use these," said Gilchrest, pointing to three volleyballs at his feet. "And you better believe they're pumped full. Oates, you start at that end of the court. Oak Tree, you're at th'other end. Just like usual, I'll set the balls at mid-court, and when I blow my whistle I want y'all to haul your cheeks to the middle and th'ow for all you're worth. Got me?" Gilchrest nodded at our nods, then added, "Remember, no boundaries, right?"

I at my end, Oakley at his, Gilchrest blew his whistle. I was faster than Oakley and scooped up a ball before he'd covered three quarters of his side. I aimed, threw, and popped him right on the knee. "One-zip!" I heard Gilchrest shout. The ball bounced off his knee and shot right back into my hands. I hurried my throw and missed. Oakley bent down, clutched the two remaining balls. I remember being amazed that he could palm each ball, run full out, and throw left-handed or right-handed without a shade of awkwardness. I spun, ran, but one of Oakley's throws glanced off the back of my head. "One-one!" hollered Gilchrest. I fell and spun on

95

my ass as the other ball came sailing at me. I caught it. "He's out!" I yelled. Gilchrest's voice boomed, "No catch outs. Three hits. Three hits." I leapt to my feet as Oakley scrambled across the floor for another ball. I chased him down, leapt, and heaved the ball hard as he drew himself erect. The ball hit him dead in the face, and he went down flat. He rolled around, cupping his hands over his nose. Gilchrest sped to his side, helped him to his feet, asked him whether he was OK. Blood flowed from Oakley's nose, dripped in startlingly bright spots on the floor, his shoes, Gilchrest's shirt. The coach removed Oakley's T-shirt and pressed it against the big kid's nose to stanch the bleeding. As they walked past me toward the office I mumbled an apology to Oakley, but couldn't catch his reply. "You watch your filthy mouth, boy," said Gilchrest to Oakley.

The locker room was unnaturally quiet as I stepped into its steamy atmosphere. Eyes clicked in my direction, looked away. After I was out of my shorts, had my towel wrapped around me, my shower kit in hand, Jack Preston and Brian Nailor approached me. Preston's hair was combed slick and plastic-looking. Nailor's stood up like frozen flames. Nailor smiled at me with his big teeth and pale eyes. He poked my arm with a finger. "You fucked up," he said.

"I tried to apologize."

"Won't do you no good," said Preston.

"I swanee," said Nailor.

"It's part of the game," I said. "It was an accident. Wasn't my idea to use volleyballs."

"Don't matter," Preston said. "He's jest lookin for an excuse to fight you."

"I never done nothing to him."

"Don't matter," said Nailor. "He don't like you."

"Brian's right, Clint. He'd jest as soon kill you as look at you."

"I never done nothing to him."

"Look," said Preston, "I know him pretty good. And jest between you and me, it's 'cause you're a city boy—"

"Whadda you mean? I've never—"

"He don't like your clothes—"

"And he don't like the fancy way you talk in class."

"What fancy—"

"I'm tellin him, if you don't mind, Brian."

"Tell him then."

"He don't like the way you say 'tennis shoes' instead of sneakers. He don't like coloreds. A whole bunch a things, really."

"I never done nothing to him. He's got no reason—"

"*And*," said Nailor, grinning, "*and*, he says you're a stuck-up rich kid." Nailor's eyes had crow's-feet, bags beneath them. They were a man's eyes.

"My dad's a sergeant," I said.

"You chicken to fight him?" said Nailor.

"Yeah, Clint, don't be chicken. Jest go on and git it over with. He's whupped pert near ever'body else in the class. It ain't so bad."

"Might as well, Oates."

"Yeah, yer pretty skinny, but yer jest about his height. Jest git 'im in a headlock and don't let go."

"Goddamn," I said, "he's got no reason to—"

Their eyes shot right and I looked over my shoulder. Oakley stood at his locker, turning its tumblers. From where I stood I could see that a piece of cotton was wedged up one of his nostrils, and he already had the makings of a good shiner. His acne burned red like a fresh abrasion. He snapped the locker open and kicked his shoes off without sitting. Then he pulled off his shorts, revealing two paddle stripes on his ass. They were fresh red bars speckled with white, the white speckles being the reverse impression of the paddle's suction holes. He must not have watched his filthy mouth while in Gilchrest's presence. Behind me, I heard Preston and Nailor pad to their lockers.

Oakley spoke without turning around. "Somebody's gonna git his skinny black ass kicked, right today, right after school." He said it softly. He slipped his jock off, turned around. I looked away. Out the corner of my eye I saw him stride off, his hairy nakedness a weapon clearing the younger boys from his path. Just before he rounded the corner of the shower stalls, I threw my toilet kit to the floor and stammered, "I—I never did nothing to you, Oakley." He stopped, turned, stepped closer to me, wrapping his towel around himself. Sweat streamed down my rib cage. It felt like ice water. "You wanna go at it right now, boy?"

"I never did nothing to you." I felt tears in my eyes. I couldn't stop them even though I was blinking like mad. "Never."

He laughed. "You busted my nose, asshole."

"What about before? What'd I ever do to you?"

"See you after school, Coonie." Then he turned away, flashing his acne-spotted back like a semaphore. "Why?" I shouted. "Why you wanna fight me?" Oakley stopped and turned, folded his arms, leaned against a toilet stall. "Why you wanna fight *me*, Oakley?" I stepped over the bench. "What'd I do? Why me?" And then unconsciously, as if scratching, as if breathing, I walked toward Marvin, who stood a few feet from Oakley, combing his hair at the mirror. "Why not him?" I said. "How come you're after *me* and not *him?*" The room froze. Froze for a moment that was both evanescent and eternal, somewhere between an eye blink and a week in hell. No one moved, nothing happened; there was no sound at all. And then it was as if all of us at the same moment looked at Marvin. He just stood there, combing away, the only body in motion, I think. He combed his hair and combed it, as if seeing only his image, hearing only his comb scraping his scalp. I knew he'd heard me. There's no way he could not have heard me. But all he did was slide the comb into his pocket and walk out the door.

"I got no quarrel with Marvin," I heard Oakley say. I turned toward his voice, but he was already in the shower.

I was able to avoid Oakley at the end of the school day. I made my escape by asking Mrs. Wickham if I could go to the rest room.

" 'Rest room,' " Oakley mumbled. "It's a damn toilet, sissy."

"Clinton," said Mrs. Wickham. "Can you *not* wait till the bell rings? It's almost three o'clock."

"No ma'am," I said. "I won't make it."

"Well, I should make you wait just to teach you to be more mindful about . . . hygiene . . . uh, things." She sucked in her cheeks, squinted. "But I'm feeling charitable today. You may go." I immediately left the building, and got on the bus. "Ain't you a little early?" said the bus driver, swinging the door shut. "Just left the office," I said. The driver nodded, apparently not giving me a second thought. I had no idea why I'd told her I'd come from the office, or why she found it a satisfactory answer. Two minutes later the bus filled, rolled, and shook its way to Connolly Air Base. When I got home, my mother was sitting in the living room, smoking her Slims, watching her soap opera. She absently asked me how my day had gone and I told her fine. "Hear from Dad?" I said.

"No, but I'm sure he's fine." She always said that when we hadn't heard from him in a while. I suppose she thought I was worried about him, or that I felt vulnerable without him. It was neither. I just wanted to discuss something with my mother that we both cared about. If I spoke with her about things that happened at school, or on my weekends, she'd listen with half an ear, say something like, "Is that so?" or "You don't say?" I couldn't stand that sort of thing. But when I mentioned my father, she treated me a bit more like an adult, or at least someone who was worth listening to. I didn't want to feel like a boy that afternoon. As I turned from my mother and walked down the hall I thought about the day my father left for Viet Nam. Sharp in his uniform, sure behind his aviator specs, he slipped a cigar from his pocket and stuck it in mine. "Not till I get back," he said. "We'll have us one when we go fishing. Just you and me, out on the lake all day, smoking and casting and sitting. Don't let Mama see it. Put it in y'back pocket." He hugged me, shook my hand, and told me I was the man of the house now. He told me he was depending on me to take good care of my mother and sister. "Don't you let me down, now, hear?" And he tapped his thick finger on my chest. "You almost as big as me. Boy, you something else." I believed him when he told me those things. My heart swelled big enough to swallow my father, my mother, Claire. I loved, feared, and respected myself, my manhood. That day I could have put all of Waco, Texas, in my heart. And it wasn't till about three months later that I discovered I really wasn't the man of the house, that my mother and sister, as they always had, were taking care of me.

For a brief moment I considered telling my mother about what had happened at school that day, but for one thing, she was deep down in the halls of *General Hospital,* and never paid you much mind till it was over. For another thing, I just wasn't the kind of

99

person—I'm still not, really—to discuss my problems with any-one. Like my father I kept things to myself, talked about my problems only in retrospect. Since my father wasn't around I con-sciously wanted to be like him, doubly like him, I could say. I wanted to be the man of the house in some respect, even if it had to be in an inward way. I went to my room, changed my clothes, and laid out my homework. I couldn't focus on it. I thought about Marvin, what I'd said about him or done to him—I couldn't tell which. I'd done something to him, said something about him; said something about and done something to myself. *How come you're after me and not him?* I kept trying to tell myself I hadn't meant it that way. *That* way. I thought about approaching Marvin, tell-ing him what I really meant was that he was more Oakley's age and weight than I. I would tell him I meant I was no match for Oakley. *See, Marvin, what I meant was that he wants to fight a colored guy, but is afraid to fight you 'cause you could beat him.* But try as I did, I couldn't for a moment convince myself that Marvin would be-lieve me. I meant it *that* way and no other. Everybody heard. Everybody knew. That afternoon I forced myself to confront the notion that tomorrow I would probably have to fight both Oakley and Marvin. I'd have to be two men.

I rose from my desk and walked to the window. The light made my skin look orange, and I started thinking about what Wickham had told us once about light. She said that oranges and apples, leaves and flowers, the whole multicolored world, was not what it appeared to be. The colors we see, she said, look like they do only because of the light or ray that shines on them. "The color of the thing isn't what you see, but the light that's reflected off it." Then she shut out the lights and shone a white light lamp on a prism. We watched the pale splay of colors on the projector screen; some people oohed and aahed. Suddenly, she switched on a black light and the color of everything changed. The prism colors van-ished, Wickham's arms were purple, the buttons of her dress were as orange as hot coals, rather than the blue they had been only seconds before. We were all very quiet. "Nothing," she said, after a while, "is really what it appears to be." I didn't really understand then. But as I stood at the window, gazing at my orange skin, I wondered what kind of light I could shine on Marvin, Oakley, and me that would reveal us as the same.

I sat down and stared at my arms. They were dark brown again. I worked up a bit of saliva under my tongue and spat on my left arm. I spat again, then rubbed the spittle into it, polishing, working till my arm grew warm. As I spat, and rubbed, I wondered why Marvin did this weird, nasty thing to himself, day after day. Was he trying to rub away the black, or deepen it, doll it up? And if he did this weird nasty thing for a hundred years, would he spit-shine himself invisible, rolling away the eggplant skin, revealing the scarlet muscle, blue vein, pink and yellow tendon, white bone? Then disappear? Seen through, all colors, no colors. Spitting and rubbing. Is this the way you do it? I leaned forward, sniffed the arm. It smelled vaguely of mayonnaise. After an hour or so, I fell asleep.

I saw Oakley the second I stepped off the bus the next morning. He stood outside the gym in his usual black penny loafers, white socks, high-water jeans, T-shirt, and black jacket. Nailor stood with him, his big teeth spread across his bottom lip like playing cards. If there was anyone I felt like fighting, that day, it was Nailor. But I wanted to put off fighting for as long as I could. I stepped toward the gymnasium, thinking that I shouldn't run, but if I hurried I could beat Oakley to the door and secure myself near Gilchrest's office. But the moment I stepped into the gym, I felt Oakley's broad palm clap down on my shoulder. "Might as well stay out here, Coonie," he said. "I need me a little target practice." I turned to face him and he slapped me, one-two, with the back, then the palm of his hand, as I'd seen Bogart do to Peter Lorre in *The Maltese Falcon*. My heart went wild. I could scarcely breathe. I couldn't swallow.

"Call me a nigger," I said. I have no idea what made me say this. All I know is that it kept me from crying. "Call me a nigger, Oakley."

"Fuck you, ya black-ass slope." He slapped me again, scratching my eye. "I don't do what coonies tell me."

"Call me a nigger."

"Outside, Coonie."

"Call me one. Go ahead!"

He lifted his hand to slap me again, but before his arm could swing my way, Marvin Pruitt came from behind me and calmly pushed me aside. "Git out my way, boy," he said. And he slugged Oakley on the side of his head. Oakley stumbled back, stiff-legged. His eyes were big. Marvin hit him twice more, once again to the side of the head, once to the nose. Oakley went down and stayed down. Though blood was drawn, whistles blowing, fingers pointing, kids hollering, Marvin just stood there, staring at me with cool eyes. He spat on the ground, licked his lips, and just stared at me, till Coach Gilchrest and Mr. Calderon tackled him and violently carried him away. He never struggled, never took his eyes off me.

Nailor and Mrs. Wickham helped Oakley to his feet. His already fattened nose bled and swelled so that I had to look away. He looked around, bemused, walleyed, maybe scared. It was apparent he had no idea how bad he was hurt. He didn't blink. He didn't even touch his nose. He didn't look like he knew much of anything. He looked at me, looked me dead in the eye, in fact, but didn't seem to recognize me.

That morning, like all other mornings, we said the Pledge of Allegiance, sang "The Yellow Rose of Texas," "The Eyes of Texas Are upon You," and "Mistress Shady." The room stood strangely empty without Oakley, and without Marvin, but at the same time you could feel their presence more intensely somehow. I felt like I did when I'd walk into my mother's room and could smell my father's cigars or cologne. He was more palpable, in certain respects, than when there in actual flesh. For some reason, I turned to look at Ah-so, and just this once I let my eyes linger on her face. She had a very gentle-looking face, really. That surprised me. She must have felt my eyes on her because she glanced up at me for a second and smiled, white teeth, downcast eyes. Such a pretty smile. That surprised me too. She held it for a few seconds, then let it fade. She looked down at her desk, and sat still as a photograph.

Philip Roth

THE CONVERSION
OF THE JEWS

"You're a real one for opening your mouth in the first place," Itzie said. "What do you open your mouth all the time for?"

"I didn't bring it up, Itz, I didn't," Ozzie said.

"What do you care about Jesus Christ for anyway?"

"I didn't bring up Jesus Christ. He did. I didn't even know what he was talking about. Jesus is historical, he kept saying. Jesus is historical." Ozzie mimicked the monumental voice of Rabbi Binder.

"Jesus was a person that lived like you and me," Ozzie continued. "That's what Binder said—"

"Yeah?... So what! What do I give two cents whether he lived or not. And what do you gotta open your mouth!" Itzie Lieberman favored closed-mouthedness, especially when it came to Ozzie

Freedman's questions. Mrs. Freedman had to see Rabbi Binder twice before about Ozzie's questions and this Wednesday at four-thirty would be the third time. Itzie preferred to keep *his* mother in the kitchen; he settled for behind-the-back subtleties such as gestures, faces, snarls and other less delicate barnyard noises.

"He was a real person, Jesus, but he wasn't like God, and we don't believe he is God." Slowly, Ozzie was explaining Rabbi Binder's position to Itzie, who had been absent from Hebrew School the previous afternoon.

"The Catholics," Itzie said helpfully, "they believe in Jesus Christ, that he's God." Itzie Lieberman used "the Catholics" in its broadest sense—to include the Protestants.

Ozzie received Itzie's remark with a tiny head bob, as though it were a footnote, and went on. "His mother was Mary, and his father probably was Joseph," Ozzie said. "But the New Testament says his real father was God."

"His *real* father?"

"Yeah," Ozzie said, "that's the big thing, his father's supposed to be God."

"Bull."

"That's what Rabbi Binder says, that it's impossible—"

"Sure it's impossible. That stuff's all bull. To have a baby you gotta get laid," Itzie theologized. "Mary hadda get laid."

"That's what Binder says: 'The only way a woman can have a baby is to have intercourse with a man.'"

"He said *that*, Ozz?" For a moment it appeared that Itzie had put the theological question aside. "He said that, intercourse?" A little curled smile shaped itself in the lower half of Itzie's face like a pink mustache. "What you guys do, Ozz, you laugh or something?"

"I raised my hand."

"Yeah? Whatja say?"

"That's when I asked the question."

Itzie's face lit up. "Whatja ask about—intercourse?"

"No, I asked the question about God, how if He could create the heaven and earth in six days, and make all the animals and the fish and the light in six days—the light especially, that's what always gets me, that He could make the light. Making fish and animals, that's pretty good—"

"That's damn good." Itzie's appreciation was honest but unimaginative: it was as though God had just pitched a one-hitter.

"But making light . . . I mean when you think about it, it's really something," Ozzie said. "Anyway, I asked Binder if He could make all that in six days, and He could *pick* the six days he wanted right out of nowhere, why couldn't He let a woman have a baby without having intercourse."

"You said intercourse, Ozz, to Binder?"

"Yeah."

"Right in class?"

"Yeah."

Itzie smacked the side of his head.

"I mean, no kidding around," Ozzie said, "that'd really be nothing. After all that other stuff, that'd practically be nothing."

Itzie considered a moment. "What'd Binder say?"

"He started all over again explaining how Jesus was historical and how he lived like you and me but he wasn't God. So I said I under*stood* that. What I wanted to know was different."

What Ozzie wanted to know was always different. The first time he had wanted to know how Rabbi Binder could call the Jews "The Chosen People" if the Declaration of Independence claimed all men to be created equal. Rabbi Binder tried to distinguish for him between political equality and spiritual legitimacy, but what Ozzie wanted to know, he insisted vehemently, was different. That was the first time his mother had to come.

Then there was the plane crash. Fifty-eight people had been killed in a plane crash at La Guardia. In studying a casualty list in the newspaper his mother had discovered among the list of those dead eight Jewish names (his grandmother had nine but she counted Miller as a Jewish name); because of the eight she said the plane crash was "a tragedy." During free-discussion time on Wednesday Ozzie had brought to Rabbi Binder's attention this matter of "some of his relations" always picking out the Jewish names. Rabbi Binder had begun to explain cultural unity and some other things when Ozzie stood up at his seat and said that what he wanted to know was different. Rabbi Binder insisted that he sit down and it was then that Ozzie shouted that he wished all fifty-eight were Jews. That was the second time his mother came.

"And he kept explaining about Jesus being historical, and so I kept asking him. No kidding, Itz, he was trying to make me look stupid."

"So what he finally do?"

"Finally he starts screaming that I was deliberately simple-minded and a wise guy, and that my mother had to come, and this was the last time. And that I'd never get bar-mitzvahed if he could help it. Then, Itz, then he starts talking in that voice like a statue, real slow and deep, and he says that I better think over what I said about the Lord. He told me to go to his office and think it over." Ozzie leaned his body towards Itzie. "Itz, I thought it over for a solid hour, and now I'm convinced God could do it."

Ozzie had planned to confess his latest transgression to his mother as soon as she came home from work. But it was a Friday night in November and already dark, and when Mrs. Freedman came through the door she tossed off her coat, kissed Ozzie quickly on the face, and went to the kitchen table to light the three yellow candles, two for the Sabbath and one for Ozzie's father.

When his mother lit the candles she would move her two arms slowly towards her, dragging them through the air, as though persuading people whose minds were half made up. And her eyes would get glassy with tears. Even when his father was alive Ozzie remembered that her eyes had gotten glassy, so it didn't have anything to do with his dying. It had something to do with lighting the candles.

As she touched the flaming match to the unlit wick of a Sabbath candle, the phone rang, and Ozzie, standing only a foot from it, plucked it off the receiver and held it muffled to his chest. When his mother lit candles Ozzie felt there should be no noise; even breathing, if you could manage it, should be softened. Ozzie pressed the phone to his breast and watched his mother dragging whatever she was dragging, and he felt his own eyes get glassy. His mother was a round, tired, gray-haired penguin of a woman whose gray skin had begun to feel the tug of gravity and the weight of her own history. Even when she was dressed up she didn't look like a chosen person. But when she lit candles she looked like something better; like a woman who knew momentarily that God could do anything.

After a few mysterious minutes she was finished. Ozzie hung up the phone and walked to the kitchen table where she was beginning to lay the two places for the four-course Sabbath meal. He told her that she would have to see Rabbi Binder next Wednesday at four-thirty, and then he told her why. For the first time in their life together she hit Ozzie across the face with her hand.

All through the chopped liver and chicken soup part of the dinner Ozzie cried; he didn't have any appetite for the rest.

On Wednesday, in the largest of the three basement classrooms of the synagogue, Rabbi Marvin Binder, a tall, handsome, broad-shouldered man of thirty with thick strong-fibered black hair, removed his watch from his pocket and saw that it was four o'clock. At the rear of the room Yakov Blotnik, the seventy-one-year-old custodian, slowly polished the large window, mumbling to himself, unaware that it was four o'clock or six o'clock, Monday or Wednesday. To most of the students Yakov Blotnik's mumbling, along with his brown curly beard, scythe nose, and two heel-trailing black cats, made of him an object of wonder, a foreigner, a relic, towards whom they were alternately fearful and disrespectful. To Ozzie the mumbling had always seemed a monotonous, curious prayer; what made it curious was that old Blotnik had been mumbling so steadily for so many years, Ozzie suspected he had memorized the prayers and forgotten all about God.

"It is now free-discussion time," Rabbi Binder said. "Feel free to talk about any Jewish matter at all—religion, family, politics, sports—"

There was silence. It was a gusty, clouded November afternoon and it did not seem as though there ever was or could be a thing called baseball. So nobody this week said a word about that hero from the past, Hank Greenberg—which limited free discussion considerably.

And the soul-battering Ozzie Freedman had just received from Rabbi Binder had imposed its limitation. When it was Ozzie's turn to read aloud from the Hebrew book the rabbi had asked him petulantly why he didn't read more rapidly. He was showing no progress. Ozzie said he could read faster but that if he did he was sure not to understand what he was reading. Nevertheless, at the rabbi's repeated suggestion Ozzie tried, and showed a great talent, but in the midst of a long passage he stopped short and said he didn't understand a word he was reading, and started in again at a drag-footed pace. Then came the soul-battering.

Consequently when free-discussion time rolled around none of the students felt too free. The rabbi's invitation was answered only by the mumbling of feeble old Blotnik.

"Isn't there anything at all you would like to discuss?" Rabbi Binder asked again, looking at his watch. "No questions or comments?"

There was a small grumble from the third row. The rabbi requested that Ozzie rise and give the rest of the class the advantage of his thought.

Ozzie rose. "I forget it now," he said, and sat down in his place.

Rabbi Binder advanced a seat towards Ozzie and poised himself on the edge of the desk. It was Itzie's desk and the rabbi's frame only a dagger's-length away from his face snapped him to sitting attention.

"Stand up again, Oscar," Rabbi Binder said calmly, "and try to assemble your thoughts."

Ozzie stood up. All his classmates turned in their seats and watched as he gave an unconvincing scratch to his forehead.

"I can't assemble any," he announced, and plunked himself down.

"Stand up!" Rabbi Binder advanced from Itzie's desk to the one directly in front of Ozzie; when the rabbinical back was turned Itzie gave it five-fingers off the tip of his nose, causing a small titter in the room. Rabbi Binder was too absorbed in squelching Ozzie's nonsense once and for all to bother with titters. "Stand up, Oscar. What's your question about?"

Ozzie pulled a word out of the air. It was the handiest word. "Religion."

"Oh, now you remember?"

"Yes."

"What is it?"

Trapped, Ozzie blurted the first thing that came to him. "Why can't He make anything He wants to make!"

As Rabbi Binder prepared an answer, a final answer, Itzie, ten feet behind him, raised one finger on his left hand, gestured it meaningfully towards the rabbi's back, and brought the house down.

Binder twisted quickly to see what had happened and in the midst of the commotion Ozzie shouted into the rabbi's back what he couldn't have shouted to his face. It was a loud, toneless sound that had the timbre of something stored inside for about six days.

"You don't know! You don't know anything about God!"

The rabbi spun back towards Ozzie. "What?"

"You don't know—you don't—"

"Apologize, Oscar, apologize!" It was a threat.

"You don't—"

Rabbi Binder's hand flicked out at Ozzie's cheek. Perhaps it had only been meant to clamp the boy's mouth shut, but Ozzie ducked and the palm caught him squarely on the nose.

The blood came in a short, red spurt on to Ozzie's shirt front.

The next moment was all confusion. Ozzie screamed, "You bastard, you bastard!" and broke for the classroom door. Rabbi Binder lurched a step backwards, as though his own blood had started flowing violently in the opposite direction, then gave a clumsy lurch forward and bolted out the door after Ozzie. The class followed after the rabbi's huge blue-suited back, and before old Blotnik could turn from his window, the room was empty and everyone was headed full speed up the three flights leading to the roof.

If one should compare the light of day to the life of man: sunrise to birth; sunset—the dropping down over the edge—to death;

then as Ozzie Freedman wiggled through the trapdoor of the synagogue roof, his feet kicking backwards bronco-style at Rabbi Binder's outstretched arms—at that moment the day was fifty years old. As a rule, fifty or fifty-five reflects accurately the age of late afternoons in November, for it is in that month, during those hours, that one's awareness of light seems no longer a matter of seeing, but of hearing: light begins clicking away. In fact, as Ozzie locked shut the trapdoor in the rabbi's face, the sharp click of the bolt into the lock might momentarily have been mistaken for the sound of the heavier gray that had just throbbed through the sky.

With all his weight Ozzie kneeled on the locked door; any instant he was certain that Rabbi Binder's shoulder would fling it open, splintering the wood into shrapnel and catapulting his body into the sky. But the door did not move and below him he heard only the rumble of feet, first loud then dim, like thunder rolling away.

A question shot through his brain. "Can this be *me?*" For a thirteen-year-old who had just labeled his religious leader a bastard, twice, it was not an improper question. Louder and louder the question came to him—"Is it me? It is me?"—until he discovered himself no longer kneeling, but racing crazily towards the edge of the roof, his eyes crying, his throat screaming, and his arms flying everywhichway as though not his own.

"Is it me? Is it me ME ME ME ME! It has to be me—but is it!"

It is the question a thief must ask himself the night he jimmies open his first window, and it is said to be the question with which bridegrooms quiz themselves before the altar.

In the few wild seconds it took Ozzie's body to propel him to the edge of the roof, his self-examination began to grow fuzzy. Gazing down at the street, he became confused as to the problem beneath the question: was it, is-it-me-who-called-Binder-a-bastard? or, is-it-me-prancing-around-on-the-roof? However, the scene below settled all, for there is an instant in any action when whether it is you or somebody else is academic. The thief crams the money in his pockets and scoots out the window. The bridegroom signs the hotel register for two. And the boy on the roof finds a streetful of people gaping at him, necks stretched backwards, faces up, as though he were the ceiling of the Hayden Planetarium. Suddenly you know it's you.

"Oscar! Oscar Freedman!" A voice rose from the center of the crowd, a voice that, could it have been seen, would have looked like the writing on scroll. "Oscar Freedman, get down from there. Immediately!" Rabbi Binder was pointing one arm stiffly up at him; and at the end of that arm, one finger aimed menacingly. It was the attitude of a dictator, but one—the eyes confessed all—whose personal valet had spit neatly in his face.

Ozzie didn't answer. Only for a blink's length did he look towards Rabbi Binder. Instead his eyes began to fit together the world beneath him, to sort out people from places, friends from enemies, participants from spectators. In little jagged starlike clusters his friends stood around Rabbi Binder, who was still pointing. The topmost point on a star compounded not of angels but of five adolescent boys was Itzie. What a world it was, with those stars below, Rabbi Binder below . . . Ozzie, who a moment earlier hadn't been able to control his own body, started to feel the meaning of the word control: he felt Peace and he felt Power.

"Oscar Freedman, I'll give you three to come down."

Few dictators give their subjects three to do anything; but, as always, Rabbi Binder only looked dictatorial.

"Are you ready, Oscar?"

Ozzie nodded his head yes, although he had no intention in the world—the lower one or the celestial one he'd just entered—of coming down even if Rabbi Binder should give him a million.

"All right then," said Rabbi Binder. He ran a hand through his black Samson hair as though it were the gesture prescribed for uttering the first digit. Then, with his other hand cutting a circle out of the small piece of sky around him, he spoke. "One!"

There was no thunder. On the contrary, at that moment, as though "one" was the cue for which he had been waiting, the world's least thunderous person appeared on the synagogue steps. He did not so much come out the synagogue door as lean out, onto the darkening air. He clutched at the doorknob with one hand and looked up at the roof.

"Oy!"

Yakov Blotnik's old mind hobbled slowly, as if on crutches,

III

and though he couldn't decide precisely what the boy was doing on the roof, he knew it wasn't good—that is, it wasn't-good-for-the-Jews. For Yakov Blotnik life had fractionated itself simply: things were either good-for-the-Jews or no-good-for-the-Jews.

He smacked his free hand to his in-sucked cheek, gently. "Oy, Gut!" And then quickly as he was able, he jacked down his head and surveyed the street. There was Rabbi Binder (like a man at an auction with only three dollars in his pocket, he had just delivered a shaky "Two!"); there were the students, and that was all. So far it-wasn't-so-bad-for-the-Jews. But the boy had to come down immediately, before anybody saw. The problem: how to get the boy off the roof?

Anybody who has ever had a cat on the roof knows how to get him down. You call the fire department. Or first you call the operator and you ask her for the fire department. And the next thing there is great jamming of brakes and clanging of bells and shouting of instructions. And then the cat is off the roof. You do the same thing to get a boy off the roof.

That is, you do the same thing if you are Yakov Blotnik and you once had a cat on the roof.

When the engines, all four of them, arrived, Rabbi Binder had four times given Ozzie the count of three. The big hook-and-ladder swung around the corner and one of the firemen leaped from it, plunging headlong towards the yellow fire hydrant in front of the synagogue. With a huge wrench he began to unscrew the top nozzle. Rabbi Binder raced over to him and pulled at his shoulder.

"There's no fire . . ."

The fireman mumbled back over his shoulder and, heatedly, continued working at the nozzle.

"But there's no fire, there's no fire . . ." Binder shouted. When the fireman mumbled again, the rabbi grasped his face with both his hands and pointed it up at the roof.

To Ozzie it looked as though Rabbi Binder was trying to tug the fireman's head out of his body, like a cork from a bottle. He had to giggle at the picture they made: it was a family portrait—rabbi in black skullcap, fireman in red fire hat, and the little yellow hydrant squatting beside like a kid brother, bareheaded. From the edge of the roof Ozzie waved at the portrait, a one-handed, flapping, mocking wave; in doing it his right foot slipped from under him. Rabbi Binder covered his eyes with his hands.

Firemen work fast. Before Ozzie had even regained his balance, a big, round, yellowed net was being held on the synagogue lawn. The firemen who held it looked up at Ozzie with stern, feelingless faces.

One of the firemen turned his head towards Rabbi Binder. "What, is the kid nuts or something?"

Rabbi Binder unpeeled his hands from his eyes, slowly, painfully, as if they were tape. Then he checked: nothing on the sidewalk, no dents in the net.

"Is he gonna jump, or what?" the fireman shouted.

In a voice not at all like a statue, Rabbi Binder finally answered. "Yes. Yes, I think so . . . He's been threatening to . . ."

Threatening to? Why, the reason he was on the roof, Ozzie remembered, was to get away; he hadn't even thought about jumping. He had just run to get away, and the truth was that he hadn't really headed for the roof as much as he'd been chased there.

"What's his name, the kid?"

"Freedman," Rabbi Binder answered. "Oscar Freedman."

The fireman looked up at Ozzie. "What is it with you, Oscar? You gonna jump, or what?"

Ozzie did not answer. Frankly, the question had just arisen.

"Look, Oscar, if you're gonna jump, jump—and if you're not gonna jump, don't jump. But don't waste our time, willya?"

Ozzie looked at the fireman and then at Rabbi Binder. He wanted to see Rabbi Binder cover his eyes one more time.

"I'm going to jump."

And then he scampered around the edge of the roof to the corner, where there was no net below, and he flapped his arms at his sides, swishing the air and smacking his palms to his trousers on the downbeat. He began screaming like some kind of engine, "Wheeeee . . . wheeeeee," and leaning way out over the edge with the upper half of his body. The firemen whipped around to cover the ground with the net. Rabbi Binder mumbled a few words to Somebody and covered his eyes. Everything happened quickly, jerkily, as in a silent movie. The crowd, which had arrived with the fire engines, gave out a long, Fourth-of-July fireworks oooh-aahhh. In the excitement no one had paid the crowd much heed, except, of course, Yakov Blotnik, who swung from the doorknob counting heads. "Fier und tsvansik . . . finf and tsvantsik . . . Oy, Gut!" It wasn't like this with the cat.

Rabbi Binder peeked through his fingers, checked the sidewalk and net. Empty. But there was Ozzie racing to the other corner. The firemen raced with him but were unable to keep up. Whenever Ozzie wanted to he might jump and splatter himself upon the sidewalk, and by the time the firemen scooted to the spot all they could do with their net would be to cover the mess.

"Wheeeee . . . wheeeee . . ."

"Hey, Oscar," the winded fireman yelled. "What the hell is this, a game or something?"

"Wheeeee . . . wheeeee . . ."

"Hey, Oscar—"

But he was off now to the other corner, flapping his wings fiercely. Rabbi Binder couldn't take it any longer—the fire engines from nowhere, the screaming suicidal boy, the net. He fell to his knees, exhausted, and with his hands curled together in front of his chest like a little dome, he pleaded, "Oscar, stop it, Oscar. Don't jump, Oscar. Please come down . . . Please don't jump."

And further back in the crowd a single voice, a single young voice, shouted a lone word to the boy on the roof.

"Jump!"

It was Itzie. Ozzie momentarily stopped flapping.

"Go ahead, Ozz—jump!" Itzie broke off his point of the star and courageously, with the inspiration not of a wise-guy but of a disciple, stood alone. "Jump, Ozz, jump!"

Still on his knees, his hands still curled, Rabbi Binder twisted his body back. He looked at Itzie, then, agonizingly, back to Ozzie.

"OSCAR, DON'T JUMP! PLEASE, DON'T JUMP . . . please please . . ."

"Jump!" This time it wasn't Itzie but another point of the star. By the time Mrs. Freedman arrived to keep her four-thirty appointment with Rabbi Binder, the whole little upside down heaven was shouting and pleading for Ozzie to jump, and Rabbi

Binder no longer was pleading with him not to jump, but was crying into the dome of his hands.

Understandably Mrs. Freedman couldn't figure out what her son was doing on the roof. So she asked.

"Ozzie, my Ozzie, what are you doing? My Ozzie, what is it?"

Ozzie stopped wheeeeeing and slowed his arms down to a cruising flap, the kind birds use in soft winds, but he did not answer. He stood against the low, clouded, darkening sky—light clicked down swiftly now, as on a small gear—flapping softly and gazing down at the small bundle of a woman who was his mother.

"What are you doing, Ozzie?" She turned towards the kneeling Rabbi Binder and rushed so close that only a paper-thickness of dusk lay between her stomach and his shoulders.

"What is my baby doing?"

Rabbi Binder gaped up at her but he too was mute. All that moved was the dome of his hands; it shook back and forth like a weak pulse.

"Rabbi, get him down! He'll kill himself. Get him down, my only baby . . ."

"I can't," Rabbi Binder said, "I can't . . ." and he turned his handsome head towards the crowd of boys behind him. "It's them. Listen to them."

And for the first time Mrs. Freedman saw the crowd of boys, and she heard what they were yelling.

"He's doing it for them. He won't listen to me. It's them." Rabbi Binder spoke like one in a trance.

"For them?"

"Yes."

"Why for them?"

"They want him to . . ."

Mrs. Freedman raised her two arms upward as though she were conducting the sky. "For them he's doing it!" And then in a gesture older than pyramids, older than prophets and floods, her arms came slapping down to her sides. "A martyr I have. Look!" She tilted her head to the roof. Ozzie was still flapping softly. "My martyr."

"Oscar, come down, *please*," Rabbi Binder groaned.

In a startlingly even voice Mrs. Freedman called to the boy on the roof. "Ozzie, come down, Ozzie. Don't be a martyr, my baby."

As though it were a litany, Rabbi Binder repeated her words. "Don't be a martyr, my baby. Don't be a martyr."

"Gawhead, Ozz—*be* a Martin!" It was Itzie. "Be a Martin, be a Martin," and all the voices joined in singing for Martindom, whatever *it* was. "Be a Martin, be a Martin . . ."

Somehow when you're on a roof the darker it gets the less you can hear. All Ozzie knew was that two groups wanted two new things: his friends were spirited and musical about what they wanted; his mother and the rabbi were even-toned, chanting, about what they didn't want. The rabbi's voice was without tears now and so was his mother's.

The big net stared up at Ozzie like a sightless eye. The big, clouded sky pushed down. From beneath it looked like a gray corrugated board. Suddenly, looking up into that unsympathetic sky, Ozzie realized all the strangeness of what these people, his friends, were asking: they wanted him to jump, to kill himself; they were singing about it now—it made them that happy. And there was an even greater strangeness: Rabbi Binder was on his knees, trembling. If there was a question to be asked now it was not "Is it me?" but rather "Is it us? . . . Is it us?"

Being on the roof, it turned out, was a serious thing. If he jumped would the singing become dancing? Would it? What would jumping stop? Yearningly, Ozzie wished he could rip open the sky, plunge his hands through, and pull out the sun; and on the sun, like a coin, would be stamped JUMP or DON'T JUMP.

Ozzie's knees rocked and sagged a little under him as though they were setting him for a dive. His arms tightened, stiffened, froze, from shoulders to fingernails. He felt as if each part of his body were going to vote as to whether he should kill himself or not—and each part as though it were independent of *him*.

The light took an unexpected click down and the new darkness, like a gag, hushed the friends singing for this and the mother and rabbi chanting for that.

Ozzie stopped counting votes, and in a curiously high voice, like one who wasn't prepared for speech, he spoke.

"Mamma?"

"Yes, Oscar."

"Mamma, get down on your knees, like Rabbi Binder."

"Oscar—"

"Get down on your knees," he said, "or I'll jump."

Ozzie heard a whimper, then a quick rustling, and when he looked down where his mother had stood he saw the top of a head and beneath that a circle of dress. She was kneeling beside Rabbi Binder.

He spoke again. "Everybody kneel." There was the sound of everybody kneeling.

Ozzie looked around. With one hand he pointed towards the synagogue entrance. "Make *him* kneel."

There was a noise, not of kneeling, but of body-and-cloth stretching. Ozzie could hear Rabbi Binder saying in a gruff whisper, ". . . or he'll *kill* himself," and when next he looked there was Yakov Blotnik off the doorknob and for the first time in his life upon his knees in the Gentile posture of prayer.

As for the firemen—it is not as difficult as one might imagine to hold a net taut while you are kneeling.

Ozzie looked around again; and then he called to Rabbi Binder.

"Rabbi?"

"Yes, Oscar."

"Rabbi Binder, do you believe in God?"

"Yes."

"Do you believe God can do Anything?" Ozzie leaned his head out into the darkness. "Anything?"

"Oscar, I think—"

"Tell me you believe God can do Anything."

There was a second's hesitation. Then: "God can do Anything."

"Tell me you believe God can make a child without intercourse."

"He can."

"Tell me!"

"God," Rabbi Binder admitted, "can make a child without intercourse."

"Mamma, you tell me."

"God can make a child without intercourse," his mother said.

"Make *him* tell me." There was no doubt who *him* was.

In a few moments Ozzie heard an old comical voice say something to the increasing darkness about God.

Next, Ozzie made everybody say it. And then he made them all say they believed in Jesus Christ—first one at a time, then all together.

When the catechizing was through it was the beginning of evening. From the street it sounded as if the boy on the roof might have sighed.

"Ozzie?" A woman's voice dared to speak. "You'll come down now?"

There was no answer, but the woman waited, and when a voice finally did speak it was thin and crying, and exhausted as that of an old man who has just finished pulling the bells.

"Mamma, don't you see—you shouldn't hit me. He shouldn't hit me. You shouldn't hit me about God, Mamma. You should never hit anybody about God—"

"Ozzie, please come down now."

"Promise me, promise me you'll never hit anybody about God."

He had asked only his mother, but for some reason everyone kneeling in the street promised he would never hit anybody about God.

Once again there was silence.

"I can come down now, Mamma," the boy on the roof finally said. He turned his head both ways as though checking the traffic lights. "Now I can come down . . ."

And he did, right into the center of the yellow net that glowed in the evening's edge like an overgrown halo.

Lynne Sharon Schwartz

OVER THE HILL

I'm not sorry. I couldn't help it, the way she was acting with Pat. My mother, who is a draftsman (or draftsperson) in an architect's office, and Pat, who is an art teacher, somehow got the idea that they could make a lot of money on the side doing bartending at fancy parties. So they're taking a short course, one night a week. They both need the money. Pat is divorced also, and has two children to support.

Pat came over after supper with a shopping bag full of equipment, shakers and strainers and stirrers that she said she had picked up wholesale on the Bowery. "I felt like a bag lady," she said, "carrying this around all afternoon." My mother had stopped off at the liquor store on her way home from work. She lined up bottles on the table till our kitchen looked like a saloon. Then they put on their glasses and opened their notebooks, and practiced making these weird concoctions, Sloe Gin Fizzes, Sidecars, Sombreros, Margaritas, Harvey Wallbangers, etc.

I was sitting and watching them, but not really paying attention at first. What I couldn't get out of my mind for some reason were those pregnant women I saw on the street yesterday. I swear, practically every woman on the street was pregnant—every age, race, religion, and creed. Some were already pushing strollers with babies. There was one blond girl in a long floaty Indian dress and hanging earrings. I thought she looked something like my mother might have looked years ago, and she was holding hands with this neat-looking guy with a red beard and a yellow checked shirt. I wondered if he was the one who made her pregnant. I even tried to imagine them, but as usual I was unsuccessful. If I ever get pregnant I plan to stay indoors the entire time, not only because of the way I would look, which is reason enough, but more because a pregnant person is living evidence that she actually did that with a man. Even though my mother claims everyone does it, everyone doesn't have to go around advertising it.

I went into my mother's room late last night when she came home from her date with James Wertheim, her new boyfriend who is a lawyer. I wasn't exactly waiting up, I was going over my social studies for the midterm. I am too old to have a babysitter—I am a babysitter myself—but I do like to know she is there when I go to sleep. I mentioned about seeing all the pregnant women and she said, "Oh yes, that's nothing unusual. They hibernate in winter, then they come out in spring." Obviously she didn't get my point, which is that it is unusual to see them all in one day. Anyhow, from pregnancy we drifted on to the subject of abortion. My mother's opinion was that under certain circumstances abortion might be a good idea. "Try to understand, Jodie. What if it happened to you? I don't mean right now." She laughed a sort of awkward laugh. "But when you were, oh, eighteen or nineteen and going to college or something, and unprepared for it." She stopped in the middle of getting undressed and sat down on her bed. It was kind of funny but nice, her sitting there in her bra and panty hose in the middle of the night, talking so earnestly about this topic.

I told her that in my opinion abortion is basically murder. I don't see how you can get around that. "Anyhow," I said, "it couldn't happen to me."

My mother crossed her legs in the lotus position and smiled. She is rather small and has a youthful figure for her age, as you would need to have to get in that position. (She is thirty-four, over the hill, despite her appearance.) "What do you mean, it couldn't happen to you?" she said. "It could happen to anyone."

I suppose she ought to know, since it happened to her in her senior year of college. Sometimes she says I am the most important person in the world to her. Usually it's after she's gotten disgusted with some man she thought was great but then didn't call her, or who turned out on closer inspection to be not so great. My father has pretty much dropped out of our family group. He used to write me from New Mexico but I haven't had a letter in several months, not even for my birthday last Monday, although I understand the mail is very slow these days.

"It couldn't happen to me," I repeated. "It just wouldn't."

She tossed her head back and laughed in this special way she has—she sort of shakes her hair, which is short and naturally curly, and her big hoop earrings shake too. (We had our ears pierced together just a year ago for my twelfth birthday—she was scared to death, I had to hold her hand.) Then she patted my head like I was a baby that had made an extremely amusing statement, and said I better get to sleep since I had two midterms the next day. She even wanted to come and tuck me in but I reminded her I was a little old for that.

Well, to return to tonight, there they are, she and Pat, having themselves a fine time fooling around with their shakers and glasses like kids playing tea party, the way my mother used to do with me.

"I can't drink all this garbage," my mother announced. "No one drinks this stuff anymore. I'm going to make myself a nice martini and sip along as we work."

"I'll sample," said Pat. "I've always had an experimenting nature."

121

"Why do you have to practice making all those drinks if no one drinks them anymore?" I asked.

"We have to do what the teacher says," my mother answers.

She and Pat find this remark highly droll. They are old friends from high school and laugh at everything the other says as though they are a TV comedy team. It's true that Pat is a lot of fun to have around, as my mother says, but I get the impression she doesn't quite realize she is over the hill. She's very tall and has long auburn hair and wears fancy pants suits and silk shirts and scarves. She chain-smokes and laughs a lot and talks constantly, and she seems to bring out a silly streak in people around her. My mother is basically a more quiet type, and wears jeans with turtleneck sweaters and junk jewelry and clunky Frye boots. (She paid eighty-five dollars for those boots, incidentally, and bought me a fake pair for only thirty-two.)

"Now, do you serve this straight up or on the rocks?" Pat asks, holding up this shaker full of some yellowish stuff. Straight up means with no ice.

"Wait, I'll have to check my notes." In the midst of their giggling they had to keep putting on their glasses to check things in their notebooks. My mother wet the tip of her finger to turn the pages, which is another sign of age.

"On the rocks, it says. Wait, hold it, that's much too many rocks, Pat. Get some of those rocks out."

"I don't think there're too many."

"Come on," my mother says, "off with those rocks."

"I beg your pardon," Pat says, laughing. She is poking around at the ice cubes in the shaker with a long spoon, trying to get a few out. "You can't have too many rocks. I distinctly remember him saying that, Barbara."

"Like the Big Rock Candy Mountain," my mother says. " 'Oh, the buzzing of the bees in the cigarette trees,' " she starts to sing.

" 'Get a piece of the Rock,' " Pat sings.

" 'Rock of ages, cleft for thee. Let me hide—' " But my mother has to stop singing, as they are both collapsing with laughter and Pat's rocks are melting all over the kitchen table. At this point I opened my math book and tried to do some homework, though there was not much room left. Besides being wet, the table was cluttered with pink and yellow and grayish concoctions in different-shaped glasses. I forgot to mention that they were both helping themselves to everything in sight. They said they had to, to see if they were coming out right.

"Do you have to be so noisy?" I said. "I'm trying to concentrate."

"Oh, Jodie is disapproving again. Do you feel left out, Jodie?" my mother said. "Wait, I'm going to make you something you can drink. Something spectacular, just for you."

"I don't like that stuff. It smells bitter."

"This won't be bitter." She put her glasses on again and flipped around in her notebook, then she poured a little bit of some really pretty green stuff over a shaker of ice, added cream and sugar and a few other things, put a big silver shaker on top, and began to shake it up.

"Remember, he said to shake very vigorously, Barbara," said Pat.

My mother shook harder. She looked like she was doing some kind of tribal dance, jiggling that thing up and down, and her whole body and her hoop earrings jiggling along with it.

"Watch out for your rocks, they could fall out," Pat said. "Did you remember to put in Frothee?"

"What's Frothee?" I asked.

"Frothee," my mother told me, still dancing around, "is this wonderful milky-white substance that spurts out of a little plastic container. On the table there, see? It's a magic fluid that makes everything it gets into creamy and yummy." Pat is again going into fits of laughter.

"I don't see what's so hilarious about Frothee," I said.

"Oh, you will," said Pat. "You will."

Finally my mother finished shaking and poured this beautiful thick light-green drink with a nice creamy top into a cocktail glass. "Here, try this. It's called a Grasshopper. But take small sips."

"Will it be bitter?"

She sipped it herself and smiled and twinkled her eyes at me over the rim of the glass. "Why don't you risk it?" she said.

It smelled light and minty, so I tried it. It was fantastic, like mint ice cream, not bitter at all. I must say, about my mother, that when she makes an effort she can really do things well.

"Is it good?"

123

"Not too bad." I drank some more. It felt smooth going down, like a malted with a little sting.

"Now, Jodie," said Pat, "for our next act I am going to demonstrate the wonders of Frothee, on the rocks." She studied something in her notebook for a couple of minutes, then filled her shaker with rocks, poured from a couple of bottles, and held up the little plastic container. "I squeeze the container gently," she said in this funny accent, like a foreign magician, "I squirt in three or four drops, and abracadabra! Whoosh!" She began to shake the mixture very vigorously. Since she is so tall the whole kitchen seemed to shake with her.

I didn't want to interrupt her performance to tell her that when she squeezed the white stuff out it reminded me of those spitters I had been passing all day. Spitters are mostly old men with baggy pants and dangling shoelaces, but on occasion you will see boys in tight jeans and leather jackets doing it (who will probably grow up to be old men with baggy pants and dangling shoelaces). What they do is, they sort of jerk their heads back and make this choppy gurgling noise in their throats like a car engine trying to start in cold weather, then flip their heads forward and shoot the stuff sideways out of the corner of their mouths, if they have any decency left aiming it off the curb. If you are watching closely you can see the gob shoot out and land in the street, where it makes a splatter and then lies there in a sunburst pattern till a car or bus comes along and rides over it. Naturally this is not the most pleasant thing to see, especially first thing in the morning on the way to two midterms, and I had the good fortune to run into quite a few, both going and coming. What bothers me most about the spitters is that they have no self-control whatsoever. It is also called expectorating. My mother and I have this routine that began last year when we saw a funny sign about it in a bus terminal. Since then whenever we see a person doing it one of us whispers, Don't Expectorate if You Expect to Rate, and the other one answers, Don't Expect to Rate if You Expectorate. I realize it is extremely corny but for some it makes us crack up.

Anyhow, Pat was doing this flamenco-type dance as she shook the drink, and my mother was clicking her fingers and providing background music. It did come out very frothy, I must admit. I

124

think it was a Brandy Alexander. Needless to say, they went into ecstasies over the way it looked. When they calmed down I asked my mother if she would make me another Grasshopper, but she said no, one was quite enough.

"But I don't feel anything."

"Absolutely not. You're still a child. Do you want to get drunk?"

"You're the ones who are drunk. I really believe you two are drunk."

"Oh, Jodie, come on. I haven't even had the equivalent of two drinks. When have you ever seen me drunk? That child is so strict with me," she said to Pat.

"Well, you're both acting so silly," I said.

"What is wrong with having a little fun?"

So I shut my mouth and went back to the math homework.

Pat took off her glasses and laid them on the table, then leaned back in her chair and blew out a long puff of smoke at the ceiling. She suddenly seemed very tired, and she waved her arm in a tired way over the table full of half-empty glasses. "What are we going to do with all of this? It's a pity to waste all our efforts."

"Listen," my mother said. "I have an idea. I can call James and ask him if he wants to come over and drink some of it. Maybe he can bring that friend of his I told you about, Sam Larkin? The reporter. They live on the same block. You would like him, I think."

"Oh, I don't know. I'm not dressed or anything."

"You look fine, Pat. It'll be fun."

"Well, I don't know."

"Every encounter is not a major thing. Look, you don't have to marry the man. I'm only suggesting that they come over for a drink. Informal, friendly, no big deal."

"Oh, all right," Pat said. "I'll have to use your hairbrush, though. I left mine home."

So my mother went to the living room to phone James, and they arranged that he would ask Sam and call back in a few minutes to let her know. While she and Pat sat around waiting for his call this jittery feeling crept into the air, like they were two kids waiting for their first date. One of them would make a remark and laugh a little, then it would die down and the creepy silence would come back. To pass the time they sipped from the drinks lined up on the table, first one then another, as if it didn't matter which.

"What is he like, anyway?" Pat asked.

"Who, James or Sam?"

"James."

I took my homework into the living room and shut the door, because if there is one thing I cannot stand, it is to hear grown women sounding like the high-school seniors who have taken over our pizzeria. They are both revolting, but at least the seniors are going through a normal phase for their age. I could still hear everything through the door, though. My mother told her how intelligent, good-natured, witty, etc., James was. Prince Charming himself, except for the horse. "Still, he's very reserved about some things," she said. "His privacy is important to him. I get the message that I shouldn't push anything. Not that I want to. I feel the same way myself."

"How about in the rocks department?" Pat asked, and she laughed.

"Pat, honestly, you must be looped."

"You're blushing, Barbara. Well, how about Sam? What is he like?"

Since my mother had only seen Sam twice there wasn't much to say, fortunately, as I was becoming sicker and sicker. After all, they are supposed to be mothers, though you'd never know it. First they spend the whole evening fooling around and drinking, with no self-control whatsoever, then they arrange this date, which will probably turn out to be a drunken orgy, music and laughing and everything, and I will have to go to my room to avoid it, then Sam will take Pat home and James will want to stay over and my mother will feel funny about it because of me, but in the end she'll let him, and I'll hear them whispering in her room, and in the morning he'll be gone before I get up and my mother will have that bright rosy but slightly guilty look, eyeing me like she's thinking, I dare you to say one word about it, and I'll go to school feeling all alone in the world and to top it off I will most likely meet a few dozen spitters along the way, not to mention pregnant women, since spring is almost in full bloom.

So when the phone rang about ten minutes later I dashed to get it first. My mother had taken Pat into the bedroom to give her the hairbrush and show her the new Frye boots.

It was James. He made his usual awkward attempt to be friendly, then said, "Can I speak to your mother, please?"

"Oh, she went out to meet some people. She just left."

"That's funny. I was supposed to call her back and come over with a friend."

"Yes, well, she got another call meanwhile and rushed right out. I think she was tired of waiting. Sorry."

There was a long pause. "I see. My friend's line was tied up before. Will you tell her I called, please?"

My mother appeared then. "Is that for me, Jodie? I'm expecting a call."

"Okay, 'bye," I said. "See you," and I hung up fast. "It was just Jennifer about the math homework." Jennifer calls every other night about the math homework.

"Oh." She looked like she was shrinking right before my eyes, very small and sad. "Well, listen, don't tie up the phone. James might call. He might be coming over."

They went into the kitchen again. It was very quiet. I could hear the glasses clinking on the table every now and then. Pat said, "Did you know Lisa had an abortion?"

"No! How awful."

"It wasn't so bad. She had broken up with him weeks before."

"Still," said my mother. "I'm glad I never had to. I don't know if I could."

"You've never . . ."

"No. Just lucky. Also careful."

Long silence.

"What do you suppose happened to them?" Pat asked.

"I don't know."

"Maybe the signals got crossed or something. Why don't you try again."

"Oh, all right. I don't like to but I will." She came into the living room and dialed. I watched her. Her shoulders slumped as she wound the cord round and round her wrist like a bracelet. I got

127

a little scared, but it turned out to be a false alarm. "There's no answer," she told Pat back in the kitchen.

"Maybe he's on his way."

"I doubt it. He's not like that. He would have called first."

"Something must have happened."

"I'll wash out these shakers," my mother said. I heard water running for a few minutes, then silence again.

"I thought you and he were getting along so well," said Pat.

"So did I. You never know what they're thinking. They're so peculiar, all of them. Maybe he didn't like the idea of my asking him on the spur of the moment, or of asking Sam. Who the hell knows."

"There must have been a mix-up. Don't you think you ought to try once more?"

"Pat, I don't want to call again, all right? I'm going to make some coffee. I don't like those fancy drinks. I'm getting a headache."

"You're upset."

"No, it's nothing. I just thought it was different. . . . I'm sorry about Sam."

"Don't be silly. I never even met him. I'm sorry about . . ." Finally Pat said she'd help clean up. "We might as well throw all this in the sink, right?"

"Yes, go ahead. I'm certainly not going to drink it. Jodie," she called, "you should be going to bed, you have the dentist tomorrow." Then she said to Pat, "I wish I had never thought of calling, then this wouldn't have happened."

"Don't get so upset. He'll probably turn up tomorrow with some perfectly reasonable excuse."

"That's the whole trouble," my mother said. "They always have wonderful excuses."

They drank their coffee and finished cleaning up and Pat left. I kissed my mother good night and went to bed. She didn't look like she was in the mood for talking.

This incident is actually no big deal. I mean, James will call again sooner or later, I suppose, and then it will all come out. My mother will be furious, and when she's through yelling at me she'll calm down and explain for the twentieth time how she's not over the hill yet and wants some fun out of life, but don't I know I'm still the most important person to her. And I guess I will feel rotten. Still and all, a person has to make some effort to keep things under control and I'm glad I did, even if it was only for one night. Because with kids it's different, I mean, that is why they're kids, but if grownups don't act their age who is going to keep any kind of order in the world?

Toni Cade Bambara

A GIRL'S STORY

She was afraid to look at herself just yet. By the time I count to twenty, she decided, if the bleeding hasn't stopped . . . she went blank. She hoisted her hips higher toward the wall. Already her footprints were visible. Sweat prints on the wall, though she was shivering. She swung her feet away from the map she'd made with Dada Bibi, the map of Africa done in clay and acrylics. The bright colors of Mozambique distracted her for a moment. She pictured herself in one of the wraps Dada Bibi had made for them to dance in. Pictured herself in Africa talking another language in that warm, rich way Dada Bibi and the brother who tutored the little kids did. Peaceful, friendly, sharing.

Rae Ann swept through her head again for other possible remedies to her situation. For a nosebleed, you put your head way back and stuffed tissue up your nostrils. Once she'd seen her brother Horace plaster his whole set of keys on the back of the neck. The time he had the fight with Joe Lee and his nose bled. Well, she'd tried ice cubes on the neck, on the stomach, on the thighs. Had stuffed herself with tissue. Had put her hips atop a pile of sofa cushions. And still she was bleeding. And what was she going to do about M'Dear's towels? No one would miss the panties and skirt she'd bundled up in the bottom of the garbage. But she couldn't just disappear a towel, certainly not two. M'Dear always counted up the stacks of laundry before the Saturday put-away.

Rae Ann thought about Dada Bibi over at the Center. If the shiny-faced woman were here now with her, it wouldn't be so bad. She'd know exactly what to do. She would sit in the chair and examine Rae Ann's schoolbooks. Would talk calmly. Would help her. Would tell her there was nothing to worry about, that she was a good girl and was not being punished. Would give an explanation and make things right. But between the house and the Center she could bleed to death.

Between her bed and the toilet she'd already left many a trail. Had already ragged the green sponge a piece, scrubbing up after herself. If Horace came home, she could maybe ask him to run over to the Center. Cept he'd want to know what for. Besides, he didn't go round the Center any more since they jumped on his case so bad about joining the army. He didn't want to hear no more shit about the Vietnamese were his brothers and sisters, were fighting the same enemy as Black folks and was he crazy, stupid or what. And he surely wouldn't want to have to walk all the long way back alone with Dada Bibi in her long skirt and turban, trying to make conversation and getting all tongue-tied sliding around the cussin he always did, and everybody checking them out walking as they were toward his house and all. But maybe if she told him it was an emergency and cried hard, he wouldn't ask her nothing, would just go.

Yesterday Dada Bibi had hugged her hello and didn't even fuss where you been little sister and why ain't you been coming round, don't you want to know about your heritage, ain't you got no pride? Dada Bibi never said none of them things ever. She just hugged you and helped you do whatever it was you thought you came to do at the Center. Rae Ann had come to cut a dress for graduation. She'd be going to intermediate in the fall, and that was a big thing. And maybe she had come to hear about the African queens. Yesterday as they sewed, Dada Bibi told them about some African queen in the old days who kept putting off marriage cause she had to be a soldier and get the Europeans out the land and stop the slaving.

She liked the part where Dada Bibi would have the dude come over to propose umpteen times. Rae Ann could just see him knocking real polite on the screen door and everything. Not like Horace do, or like Pee Wee neither, the boy she was halfway liking but really couldn't say she respected any. They just stood on the corner and hollered for their women, who had better show up quick or later for their ass.

Dada Bibi would have the dude say, "Well, darling, another harvest has past and I now have twenty acres to work and have started building on the new house and the cattle have multiplied. When can we marry?" And then Dada Bibi would have the sister say, "My husband-to-be, there are enemies in the land, crushing our people, our traditions underfoot. We must raise an army and throw them out." And then the dude would go sell a cow or something and help organize the folks on the block to get guns and all. And the sister would get the blacksmith to make her this bad armor stuff. Course Gretchen got to interrupt the story to say the sister chumping the dude, taking his money to have her some boss jewelry made and what a fool he was. But the girls tell her to hush so they can hear the rest. Dada Bibi maintaining it's important to deal with how Gretchen seeing things go down. But no one really wants to give Gretchen's view a play.

Anyway, after many knocks on the screen door and raising of armies and battles, the two of them are old-timers. Then the sister finally says, "My husband-to-be, there is peace in the land now. The children are learning, the folks are working, the elders are happy, our people prosper. Let us get married on the new moon." Gretchen got to spoil it all saying what old folks like that need to get married for, too old to get down anyway. And Dada Bibi try to get the girls to talk that over. But they just tell Gretchen to shut her big mouth and stop hogging all the straight pins. Rae Ann liked to retell the stories to the kids on the block. She always included Gretchen's remarks and everybody's response, since they seemed, in her mind, so much a part of the story.

Rae Ann's legs were tiring. Her left foot was stinging, going to sleep. Her back hurt. And her throat was sore with tension. She looked up at the map and wondered if Dada Bibi had seen the whole trouble coming. When Rae Ann had stayed behind to clean up the sewing scraps, the woman had asked her if there was anything she wanted to talk about now she was getting to be such a young woman. And Rae Ann had hugged her arms across her chest and said, "No, ma'am," cause she figured she might have to hear one of them one-way talks like M'Dear do about not letting boys feel on your tits. But when she got ready to leave, Dada Bibi hugged her like she always did, even to the girls who squirmed out of her reach and would rather not even wave hello and goodbye, just come in and split at their leisure.

"My sister," she had said into her ear, gently releasing her with none of the embarrassed shove her relatives seemed to always punctuate their embraces with. "You're becoming a woman and that's no private thing. It concerns us all who love you. Let's talk sometimes?"

Rae Ann liked the way she always made it a question. Not like the teachers, who just flat-out told you you were going to talk, or rather they were going to talk at you. And not like M'Dear or Aunt Candy, who always just jumped right in talking without even a let's this or could we that.

Maybe Dada Bibi had seen something in her face, in her eyes. Or maybe there had been a telltale spot on the back of her jeans as early as yesterday. Rae Ann twisted her head around toward the pile of clothes on the back of her chair. Upside down her jeans were spotless. Well, then, she reasoned methodically, how did Dada Bibi know? But then who said she had known anything? "That ole plain-face bitch don't know nuthin" was Horace's word to the wise. But just the same, he hung around the bus stop on Tuesday nights, acting blasé like he didn't know Dada Bibi had Tuesday night classes at the college. Not that anybody would speak on this. Joe Lee had cracked and had his ass whipped for his trouble.

Rae Ann was smelling herself and not liking it. She'd already

133

counted three sets of twenties, which meant it was time to move. She rejected the notion of a bath. The last bath had only made it worse. Fore she could even get one foot good out the water, red spots were sliding off the side of the tub onto the tile. She exhaled deeply and tried to make a list in her head. New tissue, tight pants to hold it all in place, the last of the ice tray still in the sink on her twat. She closed her eyes and moaned. Her list was all out of order. She tried again. Check floors and tub. Put towels in bottom of garbage. Put garbage out. Scrape carrots and make salad. Secrete a roll of tissue in her closet for later. Get to the Center. She opened her eyes. What would she say?

Rae Ann pulled her legs down and swung off the bed. She checked to see that the newspaper was still in place before drawing the covers up. She stood and parted the flaps of her bathrobe. Last time she had moved too quickly and the oozing had started, a blob of syrupy brown slipping down the inside of her leg and she afraid to touch it, to stop it, just stood there like a simpleton till it reached her ankle, and then she fled into the bathroom too late. She was looking into the toilet as the water swirled away the first wad of tissue. What if the toilet stuffed up, backed up on the next flush? She could imagine M'Dear bellowing the roof down as the river of red overran the rim and spilled over onto the tiles, flooding the bathroom, splashing past the threshold and onto the hall linoleum.

"Get out the bathroom, willya damn it!"

She jumped and banged an elbow on the sink. She hadn't heard Horace come into the house. He usually announced his arrivals by singing, stamping, and doing a bump-de-bump against the furniture. Had thought she was all alone with her terror. Hadn't even locked the door and here she was with her pants down and the last clump of tissue shredding, sticky red.

"Come on now. I gotta shower fore M'Dear get home."

She was trapped. If she unhooked the roll of toilet paper to take into her room, he'd see that. And M'Dear would be in any minute and would come into her room to set her bags down and get her slippers. If she hid in the closet and squatted down behind the bundles of mothballed blankets . . .

"Hey," Horace was bamming on the door. "You okay?"

Something in her brother's voice startled her. Before she could stop herself she was brimming over and shivering hard.

"Rae Ann?" he called through the door. "Rachel?"

"Don't come in!" she screamed. "Don't come in."

The doorknob was being held in position, she could see that. It had stopped turning. And it seemed to her that he was holding his breath on his side of the door just like she was holding hers on hers.

"Hey," he whispered "you okay?" When she didn't answer, he let go of the knob. She watched it move back into place and then heard him walk away. She sat there hugging herself, trying to ease the chattering of her teeth. She leaned over to yank her washcloth off the hook. And then the smell gripped her. That smell was in everything. In her bed, her clothes, her breath. The smell of death. A dry, rank graveyard smell. The smell of her mother's sickroom years ago, so long ago all the memory that had survived was the smell and the off-yellow color from the lamp, a color she'd never ever seen again anywhere. A brown stain was smack in the middle of the washcloth. She flung it into the basin and ran the water.

"She in there crying."

Rae Ann's heart stopped. M'Dear was in the kitchen. Just behind the medicine cabinet, just behind the wall, they were talking about her. She jumped up and ran to the door.

"Don't be locking that door," the voice boomed through the wall. "We hear you in there."

"And we know what you been doin too," her brother's voice rang out. She wondered what happened to that something that was in his voice just minutes ago. Where had that brother gone to so quick? Maybe cause he was scared he sounded so nice. That time when Furman and his gang were after Pee Wee he had sounded like that. Up on the roof, scrunched between the pigeon coop and the chimney, Pee Wee revealed a voice Rae Ann had never known he had. Told her she was a nice girl and shouldn't mess around with guys like him, would have to be careful. Not at all the voice bragging on the handball court, Pee Wee mounting his motorbike, Pee Wee in the schoolyard smoking. Why did it take scarifying to bring out the voice?

"Horace just scared I may die in here and he won't be able to take his damn shower," she mumbled into the washcloth, gagging on the smell. She was too afraid to think anything else.

"You best get in here, Madame." The voice came at her through the mirror. Madame. She was freezing again. Madame never meant anything good. Madame, you best cut a switch. Madame, there's a letter here from school. Madame, where's the receipt from the telephone bill. Madame, do you think you too grown to mind.

Rae Ann swished around some mouthwash and rewrapped her bathrobe tight. She knew she was waddling, the minute she saw the way they looked at her, but she couldn't get herself together. Horace turned back to a plate in the icebox he was eating from. M'Dear was leaning up against the sink, her hat still on her head, the shopping bags leaning against her legs, her shoes not even unlaced.

"You had somebody in here?"

"No, ma'am."

"Ask her how come she in her bathrobe."

"You hush," the old woman warned, and Horace disappeared behind the icebox door.

"What you been doin?"

"Nothin."

"Don't tell me nothin when I'm trying to find out somethin. Miz Gladys run all the way up to the bus stop to tell me she seen you comin home from school way before three o'clock."

Rae Ann heard the pause, felt the pause on top of her head, weighing it down into her shoulders. She shrugged. She didn't know how to fill it and lift it.

"You play hookey from school today? Went somewhere with somebody?"

"No, ma'am."

M'Dear breathing in and out, the huffin-puffin getting wheezy. It was clear Rae Ann had better say something, cause there wouldn't be too many more questions, just a heavier pausing swelling, swelling to crush her.

"You cold or somethin?" A question that came out finally and lifted her from her knees. She didn't know why she was so grateful to hear it. She hadn't expected it. Was nodding yes while her mouth said no and smiling and fixing to cry all at the same time.

"Tears don't tell me a damn thing, Rachel Ann."

"Tears say a whole lot to me," Horace was telling the toaster, singing it lest the woman get on him again for butting in.

"I sure wish you'd go somewhere," Rae Ann said over her shoulder. It might be easier to talk with just her grandmother. Though she was still a blank as to what she could possibly say to take the hardness out of her grandmother's face. M'Dear's eyes shot from the boy to the girl to the boy then back again, her head swiveling, her eyes flashing, like she was on the trail of something and there was danger sure for somebody.

"M'Dear, I'm bleeding," she heard herself say, huddling smaller into her bathrobe, feeling an oozing on the inside of her leg.

The old woman's face looked red-hot and strangled, and for a minute the girl thought she was going to be slapped.

"Whatcha been doin?" she hissed through clenched teeth. Rae Ann backed up as a whole bunch of questions and accusations tumbled out of the woman's mouth ramming into her. "You been to the barbershop, haven't you? Let that filthy man go up inside you with a clothes hanger. You going to be your mama all over again. Why didn't you come to me? Who's the boy? Tell me his name quick. And you better not lie."

M'Dear had snatched up her pocketbook, not waiting on an answer in the meantime, and was heading out the door, waving Horace to come on. He burned his fingers pulling out the toast, eager for the adventure.

"I didn't do anything," Rae Ann screamed, racing to the door before it closed against the back of her brother. "I didn't do anything, I swear to God," her throat raspy, failing her, the words barely pushed out and audible.

"Ooooh," she heard echoing in the tiled hallway, the word hollow and cool, bouncing off the walls as the old woman shoved past the boy back into the kitchen. "Oh, my goodness," she said through her hands. And then Rae Ann felt the hands on her shoulders moist from the mouth coming right through the terry cloth. The hands giving slight pull, pat, tug but not a clear embrace. "Oh, Rachel Ann," the woman whispered, steering her gently down the hall. "Girl, why didn't you say so?" she said, helping her into bed.

Rae Ann bent her knees and eased herself down onto the newspapers. She watched the woman back out of the room, her hands smoothing her waistband, as though she were leaving the dishes to make a call or leaning up from the dough on the bread-board to shout across the air shaft to Miz Gladys. Smoothing the bulk that bunched up over the waistband, nervous.

"Be right back, sugar," still backing out the room. And Rae Ann glad she'd moved her sneakers out the doorway. That'd be all she needed, M'Dear falling over some sneakers.

"Hush your ugly mouth, cause you don't know what you talkin about," she heard in the kitchen just before the front door slammed. Was she going to get a doctor? Maybe she'd gone for Dada Bibi? That wasn't likely. I ain't studyin them folks over there, M'Dear and Miz Gladys like to say, sucking their teeth at the letters, flyers, posters, numerous papers that came into the block, the building, the house, explaining what the Center was about.

"I ain't nobody's African," Miz Gladys had said. "One hundred percent American and proud of it." And M'Dear had jerked her head in agreement, trashing the latest flyer Rae Ann had slipped onto the table.

Rae Ann had tried to push all they said up against other things in her head. Being American and being proud and they weren't the same in her head. When Dada Bibi talked about Harriet Tubman and them, she felt proud. She felt it in her neck and in her spine. When the brother who ran the program for the little kids talked about powerful white Americans robbing Africa and bombing Vietnam and doing ugly all over the world, causing hard times for Black folks and other colored people, she was glad not to be American. And when she watched the films about Africans fighting white folks so that hospitals and schools could be built for the kids, and the books about Fanny Lew somebody and Malcolm fighting for freedom, and the posters about the kids, kids littler than her even, studying and growing vegetables and all and the print saying how even kids were freedom fighters—she was proud not to be American. What she heard in school she pushed up against what was in her head. Then she started looking, just looking in the teacher's bloodshot eyes, looking at M'Dear's fat, looking at Dada Bibi's shiny skin, to decide just how she was going to arrange things in her head. It was simpler to watch than to listen.

"Ma Dear gone for the ambulance?" Horace in the doorway grinning, biting at the toast. "Old Freeny botch up the job? Next time I can take you to this nurse who—"

"Go to hell, nigger."

"Okay, okay," he said, closing his eyes and raising his hands like he wouldn't dream of pressing the magic number on nobody, would gladly take his pot of gold elsewhere. "But when that dead baby drops down and rips you open, don't yell for me to save ya. You'll bleed to death first."

Her sneaker missed his head by a fraction of an inch. And she sang real loud the Guinea-Bissau marching song the brother at the Center had taught her, to drown out his laughing. Her song ended as the door slammed. She eased into the mattress, not realizing she'd been tensed up and inches off the newspaper. Her body was sore with the clutching. She wanted to sleep, her eyes dry and stinging. She'd been afraid that if she blinked too long, she'd never open them again in life.

"To die for the people." Somebody in one of the films had said that. It had seemed okay to her at first. She tried to picture Pee Wee willing to die for the people. But all the pictures that came into her head about Pee Wee dying were mostly about Pee Wee and not the people. She tried to picture Horace standing up against the cops in the name of the kids, protecting Pee Wee maybe, or the other boys the pigs liked to beat up on. But it didn't exactly fit. She dreamed up another dude altogether. He looked a little like the brother in the film, only he was different cause he was hers. And he was blowing up police stations and running through the alleyways back of the projects, and she hiding him in her closet, sneaking him food from the kitchen. Was helping him load his guns to shoot the big businessmen with. And she was seeing him dragging through the streets, one leg shot off. And the President's special cops bending in the street to squeeze off the final bullet in his back. And she'd be holding his head in her lap, the blood trickling out of the side of his mouth, just like in the movies. But the pictures were no fun after a while.

139

So when Dada Bibi was rewinding, just looking at them, one at a time, but not pressing any discussion, Rae Ann'd said, "I want to live for the people." And Gretchen had said, "Right on." Wasn't nothin hip about dying. Then they started talking about what they could do with their lives to help Black people, to free Black people. And Gretchen said she didn't know if she'd feel like going to school long enough to teach, and she knew for sure she didn't feel like going back to the country so she couldn't see herself feeding nobody directly.

"Shit. I'm just here and ain't nobody gonna run no lame shit on me. Specially them teachers up at the school. Shit. That's the best I can do for the people, give them teachers hell. Shit," she added again, just to make clear no one had better ask her anything else about what she was prepared to do for her people.

"That's cool," said Dada Bibi, surprising them all. "Giving the teachers some static means you gotta hit them books, eat well, get plenty rest to keep the mind alert. Can't hit them with no lame shit, right?" She nodding to Gretchen.

"That's right," Gretchen said, her ass off her shoulders and her whole self trapped.

Rae Ann sniffled back a tear. She wasn't convinced she was really dying, but there was something righteous in the pain that came with thinking it. Something was wrong. She was being punished, that she knew. But she probably wasn't going to really die. She looked hard at the posters by the window, the wood carving she'd made for Kwanza on her desk, the map on the wall, the picture of Jesus on the closet she shared with her grandmother. She wasn't sure just who to make the promise to. So she simply addressed it to them all. If I can get through this time, she promised, I'm going to do something good. It left her dissatisfied, cold. To die for the people left her scared, mad, it wasn't fair. To live for the people left her confused, faintly inadequate. Was she up to it? And what?

"Here you go," M'Dear was saying, pitching the bag onto her bed. "Dinner be on in a minute."

What's wrong with me, she thought, M'Dear fraid to come in the room and get her slippers, fraid to come near me. What have

I done? She up-ended the bag and set everything out neatly. A plan. She had to think methodically and stop all this crying and confusion. I will read everything two times. Then I'll know what to do. She allowed herself a moist blink. She would find out what she had done and take her whipping. Then everything would be like before. M'Dear would come into the room again and set awhile talking while she changed her shoes. Dada Bibi would hug her again. But then Dada Bibi would hug her no matter what. She even hugged the dirty kids from Mason Street. And drank behind them too without even rinsing the cup. Either Dada Bibi had a powerful health to combat germs, she thought, ripping open the packages, or the woman was crazy.

Richard McCann

MY MOTHER'S CLOTHES: THE SCHOOL OF BEAUTY AND SHAME

He is troubled by any image of himself, suffers when he is named. He finds the perfection of a human relationship in this vacancy of the image: to abolish—in oneself, between oneself and others—adjectives; a relationship which adjectivizes is on the side of the image, on the side of domination, of death.

—ROLAND BARTHES, *Roland Barthes*

Like every corner house in Carroll Knolls, the corner house on our block was turned backward on its lot, a quirk introduced by the developer of the subdivision, who, having run short of money, sought variety without additional expense. The turned-around houses, as we kids called them, were not popular, perhaps because they seemed too public, their casement bedroom windows cranking open onto sunstruck asphalt streets. In actuality, however, it was the rest of the houses that were public, their picture windows offering dioramic glimpses of early-American sofas and Mediterranean-style pole lamps whose mottled globes hung like iridescent melons from wrought-iron chains. In order not to be seen walking across the living room to the kitchen in our pajamas, we had to close the venetian blinds. The corner house on our block was secretive, as though it had turned its back on all of us, whether in superiority or in shame, refusing to acknowledge even its own unkempt yard of yellowing zoysia grass. After its initial occupants moved away, the corner house remained vacant for months.

The spring I was in sixth grade, it was sold. When I came down the block from school, I saw a moving van parked at its curb. "Careful with that!" a woman was shouting at a mover as he unloaded a tiered end table from the truck. He stared at her in silence. The veneer had already been splintered from the table's edge, as though someone had nervously picked at it while watching TV. Then another mover walked from the truck carrying a child's bicycle, a wire basket bolted over its thick rear tire, brightly colored plastic streamers dangling from its handlebars.

The woman looked at me. "What have you got there? In your hand."

I was holding a scallop shell spray-painted gold, with imitation pearls glued along its edges. Mrs. Eidus, the art teacher who visited our class each Friday, had showed me how to make it.

"A hatpin tray," I said. "It's for my mother."

"It's real pretty." She glanced up the street as though trying to guess which house I belonged to. "I'm Mrs. Tyree," she said, "and I've got a boy about your age. His daddy's bringing him tonight in the new Plymouth. I bet you haven't sat in a new Plymouth."

"We have a Ford." I studied her housedress, tiny blue and purple flowers imprinted on thin cotton, a line of white buttons as large as Necco Wafers marching toward its basted hemline. She was the kind of mother my mother laughed at for cutting recipes out of *Woman's Day*. Staring from our picture window, my mother would sometimes watch the neighborhood mothers drag their folding chairs into a circle on someone's lawn. "There they go," she'd

143

say, "a regular meeting of the Daughters of the Eastern Star!" "They're hardly even *women*," she'd whisper to my father, "and their *clothes*." She'd criticize their appearance—their loud nylon scarves tied beneath their chins, their disintegrating figures stuffed into pedal pushers—until my father, worried that my brother, Davis, and I could hear, although laughing himself, would beg her, "Stop it, Maria, please stop; it isn't funny." But she wouldn't stop, not ever. "Not even thirty and they look like they belong to the DAR! They wear their pearls inside their bosoms in case the rope should break!" She was the oldest mother on the block but she was the most glamorous, sitting alone on the front lawn in her sleek kickpleated skirts and cashmere sweaters, reading her thick paperback novels, whose bindings had split. Her hair was lightly hennaed, so that when I saw her pillowcases piled atop the washer, they seemed dusted with powdery rouge. She had once lived in New York City.

After dinner, when it was dark, I joined the other children congregated beneath the streetlamp across from the turned-around house. Bucky Trueblood, an eighth-grader who had once twisted the stems off my brother's eyeglasses, was crouched in the center, describing his mother's naked body to us elementary school children gathered around him, our faces slightly upturned, as though searching for a distant constellation, or for the bats that Bucky said would fly into our hair. I sat at the edge, one half of my body within the circle of light, the other half lost to darkness. When Bucky described his mother's nipples, which he'd glimpsed when she bent to kiss him goodnight, everyone giggled; but when he described her genitals, which he'd seen by dropping his pencil on the floor and looking up her nightie while her feet were propped on a hassock as she watched TV, everyone huddled nervously together, as though listening to a ghost story that made them fear something dangerous in the nearby dark. "I don't believe you," someone said; "I'm telling you," Bucky said, *"that's what it looks like."*

I slowly moved outside the circle. Across the street a cream-colored Plymouth was parked at the curb. In a lighted bedroom window Mrs. Tyree was hanging café curtains. Behind the chain-link fence, within the low branches of a willow tree, the new child was standing in his yard. I could see his white T-shirt and the pale oval of his face, a face deprived of detail by darkness and distance. Behind him, at the open bedroom window, his mother slowly fiddled with a valance. Behind me the children sat spellbound beneath the light. Then Bucky jumped up and pointed in the new child's direction—"Hey, you, you want to hear something really *good?*"—and even before the others had a chance to spot him, he vanished as suddenly and completely as an imaginary playmate.

The next morning, as we waited at our bus stop, he loitered by the mailbox on the opposite corner, not crossing the street until the yellow school bus pulled up and flung open its door. Then he dashed aboard and sat down beside me. "I'm Denny," he said. Denny: a heavy, unbeautiful child, who, had his parents stayed in their native Kentucky, would have been a farm boy, but who in Carroll Knolls seemed to belong to no particular world at all, walking past the identical ranch houses in his overalls and Keds, his whitish-blond hair close-cropped all around except for the distinguishing, stigmatizing feature of a wave that crested perfectly just above his forehead, a wave that neither rose nor fell, a wave he trained with Hopalong Cassidy hair tonic, a wave he tended fussily, as though it were the only loveliness he allowed himself.

What in Carroll Knolls might have been described by someone not native to those parts—a visiting expert, say—as *beautiful,* capable of arousing terror and joy? The brick ramblers strung with multicolored Christmas lights? The occasional front-yard plaster Virgin entrapped within a chicken-wire grotto entwined with plastic roses? The spring Denny moved to Carroll Knolls, I begged my parents to take me to a nightclub, had begged so hard for months, in fact, that by summer they finally agreed to a Sunday matinee. Waiting in the back seat of our Country Squire, a red bow tie clipped to my collar, I watched our house float like a mirage behind the sprinkler's web of water. The front door opened, and a white dress fluttered within the mirage's ascending waves: slipping on her sunglasses, my mother emerged onto the concrete stoop, adjusted her shoulder strap, and teetered across the wet grass in new spectator shoes. Then my father stepped out and cut the sprinkler

145

off. We drove—the warm breeze inside the car sweetened by my mother's Shalimar—past ranch houses tethered to yards by chain-link fences; past the Silver Spring Volunteer Fire Department and Carroll Knolls Elementary School; past the Polar Bear Soft-Serv stand, its white stucco siding shimmery with mirror shards; past a bulldozed red-clay field where a weathered billboard advertised IF YOU LIVED HERE YOU'D BE HOME BY NOW, until we arrived at the border—a line of cinder-block discount liquor stores, a traffic light—of Washington, D.C. The light turned red. We stopped. The breeze died and the Shalimar fell from the air. Exhaust fumes mixed with the smell of hot tar. A drunk man stumbled into the crosswalk, followed by an old woman shielding herself from the sun with an orange umbrella, and two teen-aged boys dribbling a basketball back and forth between them. My mother put down her sun visor. "Lock your door," she said.

Then the light changed, releasing us into another country. The station wagon sailed down boulevards of Chinese elms and flowering Bradford pears, through hot, dense streets where black families sat on wooden chairs at curbs, along old streetcar tracks that caused the tires to shimmy and the car to swerve, onto Pennsylvania Avenue, past the White House, encircled by its fence of iron spears, and down Fourteenth Street, past the Treasury Building, until at last we reached the Neptune Room, a cocktail lounge in the basement of a shabbily elegant hotel.

Inside, the Neptune Room's walls were painted with garish mermaids reclining seductively on underwater rocks, and human frogmen who stared longingly through their diving helmets' glass masks at a loveliness they could not possess on dry earth. On stage, leaning against the baby grand piano, a *chanteuse* (as my mother called her) was singing of her grief, her wrists weighted with rhinestone bracelets, a single blue spotlight making her seem like one who lived, as did the mermaids, underwater.

I was transfixed. I clutched my Roy Rogers cocktail (the same as a Shirley Temple, but without the cheerful, girlish grenadine) tight in my fist. In the middle of "The Man I Love" I stood and struggled toward the stage.

I strayed into the spotlight's soft-blue underwater world. Close up, from within the light, the singer was a boozy, plump peroxide blonde in a tight black cocktail dress; but these indiscretions made her yet more lovely, for they showed what she had lost, just as her songs seemed to carry her backward into endless regret. When I got close to her, she extended one hand—red nails, a huge glass ring—and seized one of mine.

"Why, what kind of little sailor have we got here?" she asked the audience.

I stared through the border of blue light and into the room, where I saw my parents gesturing, although whether they were telling me to step closer to her microphone or to step farther away, I could not tell. The whole club was staring.

"Maybe he knows a song!" a man shouted from the back.

"Sing with me," she whispered. "What can you sing?"

I wanted to lift her microphone from its stand and bow deeply from the waist, as Judy Garland did on her weekly TV show. But I could not. As she began to sing, I stood voiceless, pressed against the protection of her black dress; or, more accurately, I stood beside her, silently lip-synching to myself. I do not recall what she sang, although I do recall a quick, farcical ending in which she falsettoed, like Betty Boop, "Gimme a Little Kiss, Will Ya, Huh?" and brushed my forehead with pursed red lips.

That summer, humidity enveloping the landfill subdivision, Denny, "the new kid," stood on the boundaries, while we neighborhood boys played War, a game in which someone stood on Stanley Allen's front porch and machine-gunned the rest of us, who one by one clutched our bellies, coughed as if choking on blood, and rolled in exquisite death throes down the grassy hill. When Stanley's father came up the walk from work, he ducked imaginary bullets. "Hi, Dad," Stanley would call, rising from the dead to greet him. Then we began the game again: whoever died best in the last round got to kill in the next. Later, after dusk, we'd smear the wings of balsa planes with glue, ignite them, and send them flaming through the dark on kamikaze missions. Long after the streets were deserted, we children sprawled beneath the corner streetlamp, praying our mothers would not call us—*"Time to come in!"*—back to our oven-like houses; and then sometimes Bucky, hoping to scare the elementary school kids, would lead his solemn procession of junior high "hoods" down the block, their penises hanging from their unzipped trousers.

Denny and I began to play together, first in secret, then visiting each other's houses almost daily, and by the end of the summer I imagined him to be my best friend. Our friendship was sealed by our shared dread of junior high school. Davis, who had just finished seventh grade, brought back reports of corridors so long that one could get lost in them, of gangs who fought to control the lunchroom and the bathrooms. The only safe place seemed to be the Health Room, where a pretty nurse let you lie down on a cot behind a folding screen. Denny told me about a movie he'd seen in which the children, all girls, did not have to go to school at all but were taught at home by a beautiful governess, who, upon coming to their rooms each morning, threw open their shutters so that sunlight fell like bolts of satin across their beds, whispered their pet names while kissing them, and combed their long hair with a silver brush. "She never got mad," said Denny, beating his fingers up and down through the air as though striking a keyboard, "except once when some old man told the girls they could never play piano again."

With my father at work in the Pentagon and my mother off driving the two-tone Welcome Wagon Chevy to new subdivisions, Denny and I spent whole days in the gloom of my living room, the picture window's venetian blinds closed against an August sun so fierce that it bleached the design from the carpet. Dreaming of fabulous prizes—sets of matching Samsonite luggage, French Provincial bedroom suites, Corvettes, jet flights to Hawaii—we watched Jan Murray's *Treasure Hunt* and Bob Barker's *Truth or Consequences* (a name that seemed strangely threatening). We watched *The Loretta Young Show*, worshipping yet critiquing her elaborate gowns. When *The Early Show* came on, we watched old Bette Davis, Gene Tierney, and Joan Crawford movies—*Dark Victory*, *Leave Her to Heaven*, *A Woman's Face*. Hoping to become their pen pals, we wrote long letters to fading movie stars, who in turn sent us autographed photos we traded between ourselves. We searched the house for secrets, like contraceptives, Kotex, and my mother's hidden supply of Hershey bars. And finally, Denny and

I, running to the front window every few minutes to make sure no one was coming unexpectedly up the sidewalk, inspected the secrets of my mother's dresser: her satin nightgowns and padded brassieres, folded atop pink drawer liners and scattered with loose sachet; her black mantilla, pressed inside a shroud of lilac tissue paper; her heart-shaped candy box, a flapper doll strapped to its lid with a ribbon, from which spilled galaxies of cocktail rings and cultured pearls. Small shrines to deeper intentions, private grottoes of yearning: her triangular cloisonné earrings, her brooch of enameled butterfly wings.

Because beauty's source was longing, it was infused with romantic sorrow; because beauty was defined as "feminine," and therefore as "other," it became hopelessly confused with my mother: Mother, who quickly sorted through new batches of photographs, throwing unflattering shots of herself directly into the fire before they could be seen. Mother, who dramatized herself, telling us and our playmates, "My name is Maria Dolores; in Spanish, that means 'Mother of Sorrows.'" Mother who had once wished to be a writer and who said, looking up briefly from whatever she was reading, "Books are my best friends." Mother, who read aloud from Whitman's *Leaves of Grass* and O'Neill's *Long Day's Journey Into Night* with a voice so grave I could not tell the difference between them. Mother, who lifted cut-glass vases and antique clocks from her obsessively dusted curio shelves to ask, "If this could talk, what story would it tell?"

And more, always more, for she was the only woman in our house, a "people-watcher," a "talker," a woman whose mysteries and moods seemed endless: Our Mother of the White Silk Gloves; Our Mother of the Veiled Hats; Our Mother of the Paper Lilacs; Our Mother of the Sighs and Heartaches; Our Mother of the Gorgeous Gypsy Earrings; Our Mother of the Late Movies and the Cigarettes; Our Mother whom I adored and who, in adoring, I ran from, knowing it "wrong" for a son to wish to be like his mother; Our Mother who wished to influence us, passing the best of herself along, yet who held the fear common to that era, the fear that by loving a son too intensely she would render him unfit—"Momma's boy," "tied to apron strings"—and who therefore alternately drew us close and sent us away, believing a son needed "male influence"

149

in large doses, that female influence was pernicious except as a final finishing, like manners; Our Mother of the Mixed Messages; Our Mother of Sudden Attentiveness; Our Mother of Sudden Distances; Our Mother of Anger; Our Mother of Apology. The simplest objects of her life, objects scattered accidentally about the house, became my shrines to beauty, my grottoes of romantic sorrow; her Revlon lipstick tubes, "Cherries in the Snow"; her Art Nouveau atomizers on the blue mirror top of her vanity; her pastel silk scarves knotted to a wire hanger in her closet; her white handkerchiefs blotted with red mouths. Voiceless objects; silences. The world halved with a cleaver: "masculine," "feminine." In these ways was the plainest ordinary love made complicated and grotesque. And in these ways was beauty, already confused with the "feminine," also confused with shame, for all these longings were secret, and to control me all my brother had to do was to threaten to expose that Denny and I were dressing ourselves in my mother's clothes.

Denny chose my mother's drabbest outfits, as though he were ruled by the deepest of modesties, or by his family's austere Methodism: a pink wraparound skirt from which the color had been laundered, its hem almost to his ankles; a sleeveless white cotton blouse with a Peter Pan collar; a small straw summer clutch. But he seemed to challenge his own primness, as though he dared it with his "effects": an undershirt worn over his head to approximate cascading hair; gummed holepunch reinforcements pasted to his fingernails so that his hands, palms up, might look like a woman's—flimsy crescent moons waxing above his fingertips.

He dressed slowly, hesitantly, but once dressed, he was a manic Proteus metamorphosizing into contradictory, half-realized forms, throwing his "long hair" back and balling it violently into a French twist; tapping his paper nails on the glass-topped vanity as though he were an important woman kept waiting at a cosmetics counter; stabbing his nails into the air as though he were an angry teacher assigning an hour of detention; touching his temple as though he were a shy schoolgirl tucking back a wisp of stray hair; resting his fingertips on the rim of his glass of Kool-Aid as though

150

he were an actress seated over an ornamental cocktail—a Pink Lady, say, or a Silver Slipper. Sometimes, in an orgy of jerky movement, his gestures overtaking him with greater and greater force, a dynamo of theatricality unleashed, he would hurl himself across the room like a mad girl having a fit, or like one possessed; or he would snatch the chenille spread from my parents' bed and drape it over his head to fashion for himself the long train of a bride. "Do you like it?" he'd ask anxiously, making me his mirror. "Does it look *real?*" He wanted, as did I, to become something he'd neither yet seen nor dreamed of, something he'd recognize the moment he saw it: himself. Yet he was constantly confounded, for no matter how much he adorned himself with scarves and jewelry, he could not understand that this was himself, as was also and at the same time the boy in overalls and Keds. He was split in two pieces—as who was not?—the blond wave cresting rigidly above his close-cropped hair.

"He makes me nervous," I heard my father tell my mother one night as I lay in bed. They were speaking about me. That morning I'd stood awkwardly on the front lawn—"Maybe you should go help your father," my mother had said—while he propped an extension ladder against the house, climbed up through the power lines he separated with his bare hands, and staggered across the pitched roof he was reshingling. When his hammer slid down the incline, catching on the gutter, I screamed, "You're falling!" Startled, he almost fell.

"He needs to spend more time with you," I heard my mother say.

I couldn't sleep. Out in the distance a mother was calling her child home. A screen door slammed. I heard cicadas, their chorus as steady and loud as the hum of a power line. *He needs to spend more time with you.* Didn't she know? Saturday mornings, when he stood in his rubber hip boots fishing off the shore of Triadelphia Reservoir, I was afraid of the slimy bottom and could not wade after him; for whatever reasons of his own—something as simple as shyness, perhaps—he could not come to get me. I sat in the parking lot drinking Tru-Ade and reading *Betty and Veronica*, wondering if Denny had walked alone to Wheaton Plaza, where the weekend manager of Port-o'-Call allowed us to Windex the illuminated glass shelves that held Lladro figurines, the porcelain ballerina's hands so realistic one could see tiny life and heart lines etched into her palms. *He needs to spend more time with you.* Was she planning to discontinue the long summer afternoons that she and I spent together when there were no new families for her to greet in her Welcome Wagon car? "I don't feel like being alone today," she'd say, inviting me to sit on their chenille bedspread and watch her model new clothes in her mirror. Behind her an oscillating fan fluttered nylons and scarves she'd heaped, discarded, on a chair. "Should I wear the red belt with this dress or the black one?" she'd ask, turning suddenly toward me and cinching her waist with her hands.

Afterward we would sit together at the rattan table on the screened-in porch, holding cocktail napkins around sweaty glasses of iced Russian tea and listening to big-band music on the Zenith.

"You look so pretty," I'd say. Sometimes she wore outfits I'd selected for her from her closet—pastel chiffon dresses, an apricot blouse with real mother-of-pearl buttons.

One afternoon she leaned over suddenly and shut off the radio. "You know you're going to leave me one day," she said. When I put my arms around her, smelling the dry carnation talc she wore in hot weather, she stood up and marched out of the room. When she returned, she was wearing Bermuda shorts and a plain cotton blouse. "Let's wait for your father on the stoop," she said.

Late that summer—the summer before he died—my father took me with him to Fort Benjamin Harrison, near Indianapolis, where, as a colonel in the U.S. Army Reserves, he did his annual tour of duty. On the propjet he drank bourbon and read newspapers while I made a souvenir packet for Denny: an airsickness bag, into which I placed the Chiclets given me by the stewardess to help pop my ears during take-off, and the laminated white card that showed the location of emergency exits. Fort Benjamin Harrison looked like Carroll Knolls: hundreds of acres of concrete and sun-scorched shrubbery inside a cyclone fence. Daytimes I waited for my father in the dining mess with the sons of other officers, drinking chocolate milk that came from a silver machine, and desultorily setting fires in ashtrays. When he came to collect me, I walked behind him—gold braid hung from his epaulets—while enlisted men saluted us and opened doors. At night, sitting in our BOQ room, he asked me questions about myself: "Are you looking forward to seventh grade?" "What do you think you'll want to be?" When these topics faltered—I stammered what I hoped were right answers—we watched TV, trying to pre-guess lines of dialogue on reruns of his favorite shows, *The Untouchables* and *Rawhide*. "That Della Street," he said as we watched *Perry Mason*, "is almost as pretty as your mother." On the last day, eager to make the trip memorable, he brought me a gift: a glassine envelope filled with punched IBM cards that told me my life story as his secretary had typed it into the office computer. Card One: *You live at 10406 Lillians Mill Court, Silver Spring, Maryland.* Card Two: *You are entering seventh grade.* Card Three: *Last year your teacher was Mrs. Dillard.* Card Four: *Your favorite color is blue.* Card Five: *You love the Kingston Trio.* Card Six: *You love basketball and football.* Card Seven: *Your favorite sport is swimming.*

Whose son did these cards describe? The address was correct, as was the teacher's name and the favorite color; and he'd remembered that one morning during breakfast I'd put a dime in the jukebox and played the Kingston Trio's song about "the man who never returned." But whose fiction was the rest? Had I, who played no sport other than kickball and Kitty-Kitty-Kick-the-Can, lied to him when he asked me about myself? Had he not heard from my mother the outcome of the previous summer's swim lessons? At the swim club a young man in black trunks had taught us, as we held hands, to dunk ourselves in water, surface, and then go down. When he had told her to let go of me, I had thrashed across the surface, violently afraid I'd sink. But perhaps I had not lied to him; perhaps he merely did not wish to see. It was my job, I felt, to reassure him that I was the son he imagined me to be, perhaps because the role of reassurer gave me power. In any case, I thanked him for the computer cards. I thanked him the way a father thanks a child for a well-intentioned gift he'll never use—a set of handkerchiefs, say, on which the embroidered swirls construct a monogram of no particular initial, and which thus might be used by anyone.

153

▼

As for me, when I dressed in my mother's clothes, I seldom moved at all: I held myself rigid before the mirror. The kind of beauty I'd seen practiced in movies and in fashion magazines was beauty attained by lacquered stasis, beauty attained by fixed poses— "ladylike stillness," the stillness of mannequins, the stillness of models "caught" in mid-gesture, the stillness of the passive moon around which active meteors orbited and burst. My costume was of the greatest solemnity: I dressed like the *chanteuse* in the Neptune Room, carefully shimmying my mother's black slip over my head so as not to stain it with Brylcreem, draping her black mantilla over my bare shoulders, clipping her rhinestone dangles to my ears. Had I at that time already seen the movie in which French women who had fraternized with German soldiers were made to shave their heads and walk through the streets, jeered by their fellow villagers? And if so, did I imagine myself to be one of the collaborators, or one of the villagers, taunting her from the curb? I ask because no matter how elaborate my costume, I made no effort to camouflage my crew cut or my male body.

How did I perceive myself in my mother's triple-mirrored vanity, its endless repetitions? I saw myself as doubled—both an image and he who studied it. I saw myself as beautiful, and guilty: the lipstick made my mouth seem the ripest rose, or a wound; the small rose on the black slip opened like my mother's heart disclosed, or like the Sacred Heart of Mary, aflame and pierced by arrows; the mantilla transformed me into a Mexican penitent or a Latin movie star, like Dolores Del Rio. The mirror was a silvery stream: on the far side, in a clearing, stood the woman who was icily immune from the boy's terror and contempt; on the close side, in the bedroom, stood the boy who feared and yet longed after her inviolability. (Perhaps, it occurs to me now, this doubleness is the source of drag queens' vulnerable ferocity.) Sometimes, when I saw that person in the mirror, I felt as though I had at last been lifted from that dull, locked room, with its mahogany bedroom suite and chalky blue walls. But other times, particularly when I saw Denny and me together, so that his reality shattered my fantasies, we seemed merely ludicrous and sadly comic, as though we were

▼

dressed in the garments of another species, like dogs in human clothes. I became aware of my spatulate hands, my scarred knees, my large feet; I became aware of the drooping, unfilled bodice of my slip. Like Denny, I could neither dispense with images nor take their flexibility as pleasure, for the idea of self I had learned and was learning still was that one was constructed by one's images— *"When boys cross their legs, they cross one ankle atop the knee"* —so that one finally sought the protection of believing in one's own image and, in believing in it as reality, condemned oneself to its poverty.

(That locked room. My mother's vanity; my father's highboy. If Denny and I, still in our costumes, had left that bedroom, its floor strewn with my mother's shoes and handbags, and gone through the darkened living room, out onto the sunstruck porch, down the sidewalk, and up the street, how would we have carried ourselves? Would we have walked boldly, chattering extravagantly back and forth between ourselves, like drag queens refusing to acknowledge the stares of contempt that are meant to halt them? Would we have walked humbly, with the calculated, impervious piety of the condemned walking barefoot to the public scaffold? Would we have walked simply, as deeply accustomed to the normalcy of our own strangeness as Siamese twins? Or would we have walked gravely, a solemn procession, like Bucky Trueblood's gang, their manhood hanging from their unzipped trousers?

(We were eleven years old. Why now, more than two decades later, do I wonder for the first time how we would have carried ourselves through a publicness we would have neither sought nor dared? I am six feet two inches tall; I weigh 198 pounds. Given my size, the question I am most often asked about my youth is "What football position did you play?" Overseas I am most commonly taken to be a German or a Swede. Right now, as I write this, I am wearing L. L. Bean khaki trousers, a Lacoste shirt, Weejuns: the anonymous American costume, although partaking of certain signs of class and education, and, most recently, partaking also of certain signs of sexual orientation, this costume having become the standard garb of the urban American gay man. Why do I tell you these things? Am I trying—not subtly—to inform us of my "maleness," to reassure us that I have "survived" without noticeable "complexes"? Or is this my urge, my constant urge, to complicate my portrait of myself to both of us, so that I might layer my selves like so many multicolored crinoline slips, each rustling as I walk? When the wind blows, lifting my skirt, I do not know which slip will be revealed.)

Sometimes, while Denny and I were dressing up, Davis would come home unexpectedly from the bowling alley, where he'd been hanging out since entering junior high. At the bowling alley he was courting the protection of Bucky's gang.

"Let me in!" he'd demand, banging fiercely on the bedroom door, behind which Denny and I were scurrying to wipe the makeup off our faces with Kleenex.

"We're not doing anything," I'd protest, buying time.

"Let me in this minute or I'll tell!"

Once in the room, Davis would police the wreckage we'd made, the emptied hatboxes, the scattered jewelry, the piled skirts and blouses. "You'd better clean this up right now," he'd warn. "You two make me *sick*."

Yet his scorn seemed modified by awe. When he helped us rehang the clothes in the closet and replace the jewelry in the candy box, a sullen accomplice destroying someone else's evidence, he sometimes handled the garments as though they were infused with something of himself, although at the precise moment when he seemed to find them loveliest, holding them close, he would cast them down.

After our dress-up sessions Denny would leave the house without good-byes. I was glad to see him go. We would not see each other for days, unless we met by accident; we never referred to what we'd done the last time we'd been together. We met like those who have murdered are said to meet, each tentatively and warily examining the other for signs of betrayal. But whom had we murdered? The boys who walked into that room? Or the women who briefly came to life within it? Perhaps this metaphor has outlived its meaning. Perhaps our shame derived not from our having killed but from our having created.

△

In early September, as Denny and I entered seventh grade, my father became ill. Over Labor Day weekend he was too tired to go fishing. On Monday his skin had vaguely yellowed; by Thursday he was severely jaundiced. On Friday he entered the hospital, his liver rapidly failing; Sunday he was dead. He died from acute hepatitis, possibly acquired while cleaning up after our sick dog, the doctor said. He was buried at Arlington National Cemetery, down the hill from the Tomb of the Unknown Soldier. After the twenty-one-gun salute, our mother pinned his colonel's insignia to our jacket lapels. I carried the flag from his coffin to the car. For two weeks I stayed home with my mother, helping her write thank-you notes on small white cards with black borders; one afternoon, as I was affixing postage to the square, plain envelopes, she looked at me across the dining room table. "You and Davis are all I have left," she said. She went into the kitchen and came back. "Tomorrow," she said, gathering up the note cards, "you'll have to go to school." Mornings I wandered the long corridors alone, separated from Denny by the fate of our last names, which had cast us into different homerooms and daily schedules. Lunchtimes we sat together in silence in the rear of the cafeteria. Afternoons, just before gym class, I went to the Health Room, where, lying on a cot, I'd imagine the Phys. Ed. coach calling my name from the class roll, and imagine my name, unclaimed, unanswered to, floating weightlessly away, like a balloon that one jumps to grab hold of but that is already out of reach. Then I'd hear the nurse dial the telephone. "He's sick again," she'd say. "Can you come pick him up?" At home I helped my mother empty my father's highboy. "No, we want to save that," she said when I folded his uniform into a huge brown bag that read GOODWILL INDUSTRIES; I wrapped it in a plastic dry-cleaner's bag and hung it in the hall closet.

After my father's death my relationship to my mother's things grew yet more complex, for as she retreated into her grief, she left behind only her mute objects as evidence of her life among us: objects that seemed as lonely and vulnerable as she was, objects that I longed to console, objects with which I longed to console myself—a tangled gold chain, thrown in frustration on the mantel; a wineglass, its rim stained with lipstick, left unwashed in the sink. Sometimes at night Davis and I heard her prop her pillow up against her bedroom wall, lean back heavily, and tune her radio to a call-in show: *"Nightcaps, what are you thinking at this late hour?"* Sunday evenings, in order to help her prepare for the next day's job hunt, I stood over her beneath the bare basement bulb, the same bulb that first illuminated my father's jaundice. I set her hair, slicking each wet strand with gel and rolling it, inventing gossip that seemed to draw us together, a beautician and his customer.

"You have such pretty hair," I'd say.

"At my age, don't you think I should cut it?" She was almost fifty.

"No, never."

That fall Denny and I were caught. One evening my mother noticed something out of place in her closet. (Perhaps now that she no longer shared it, she knew where every belt and scarf should have been.)

I was in my bedroom doing my French homework, dreaming of one day visiting Au Printemps, the store my teacher spoke of so excitedly as she played us the Edith Piaf records that she had brought back from France. In the mirror above my desk I saw my mother appear at my door.

"Get into the living room," she said. Her anger made her small, reflected body seem taut and dangerous.

In the living room Davis was watching TV with Uncle Joe, our father's brother, who sometimes came to take us fishing. Uncle Joe was lying in our father's La-Z-Boy recliner.

"There aren't going to be any secrets in this house," she said. "You've been in my closet. What were you doing there?"

"No, we weren't," I said. "We were watching TV all afternoon."

"*We?* Was Denny here with you? Don't you think I've heard about that? Were you and Denny going through my clothes? Were you wearing them?"

"No, Mom," I said.

"Don't lie!" She turned to Uncle Joe, who was staring at us. "Make him stop! He's lying to me!"

She slapped me. Although I was already taller than she, she slapped me over and over, slapped me across the room until I was backed against the TV. Davis was motionless, afraid. But Uncle Joe jumped up and stood between my mother and me, holding her until her rage turned to sobs. "I can't be both a mother and a father," she said to him. "I can't, I can't do it." I could not look at Uncle Joe, who, although he was protecting me, did not know I was lying.

She looked at me. "We'll discuss this later," she said. "Get out of my sight."

We never discussed it. Denny was outlawed. I believe, in fact, that it was I who suggested he never be allowed in our house again. I told my mother I hated him. I do not think I was lying when I said this. I truly hated him—hated him, I mean, for being me.

For two or three weeks Denny tried to speak with me at the bus stop, but whenever he approached, I busied myself with kids I barely knew. After a while Denny found a new best friend, Lee, a child despised by everyone, for Lee was "effeminate." His clothes were too fastidious; he often wore his cardigan over his shoulders, like an old woman feeling a chill. Sometimes, watching the street from our picture window, I'd see Lee walking toward Denny's house. "What a queer," I'd say to whoever might be listening. "He walks like a *girl*." Or sometimes, at the junior high school, I'd see him and Denny walking down the corridor, their shoulders pressed together as if they were telling each other secrets, or as if they were joined in mutual defense. Sometimes when I saw them, I turned quickly away, as though I'd forgotten something important in my locker. But when I felt brave enough to risk rejection, for I belonged to no group, I joined Bucky Trueblood's gang, sitting on the radiator in the main hall, and waited for Lee and Denny to pass us. As Lee and Denny got close, they stiffened and looked straight ahead.

"Faggots," I muttered.

I looked at Bucky, sitting in the middle of the radiator. As Lee and Denny passed, he leaned forward from the wall, accidentally disarranging the practiced severity of his clothes, his jeans puckering beneath his tooled belt, the breast pocket of his T-shirt drooping with the weight of a pack of Pall Malls. He whistled. Lee and Denny flinched. He whistled again. Then he leaned back, the hard lines of his body reasserting themselves, his left foot striking a steady beat on the tile floor with the silver V tap of his black loafer.

Carson McCullers

WUNDERKIND

She came into the living room, her music satchel plopping against her winter-stockinged legs and her other arm weighted down with schoolbooks, and stood for a moment listening to the sounds from the studio. A soft procession of piano chords and the tuning of a violin. Then Mister Bilderbach called out to her in his chunky, guttural tones:

"That you, Bienchen?"

As she jerked off her mittens she saw that her fingers were twitching to the motions of the fugue she had practiced that morning. "Yes," she answered. "It's me."

"I," the voice corrected. "Just a moment."

She could hear Mister Lafkowitz talking—his words spun out

in a silky, unintelligible hum. A voice almost like a woman's, she thought, compared to Mister Bilderbach's. Restlessness scattered her attention. She fumbled with her geometry book and *Le Voyage de Monsieur Perrichon* before putting them on the table. She sat down on the sofa and began to take her music from the satchel. Again she saw her hands—the quivering tendons that stretched down from her knuckles, the sore finger tip cupped with curled, dingy tape. The sight sharpened the fear that had begun to torment her for the past few months.

Noiselessly she mumbled a few phrases of encouragement to herself. A good lesson—a good lesson—like it used to be—Her lips closed as she heard the stolid sound of Mister Bilderbach's footsteps across the floor of the studio and the creaking of the door as it slid open.

For a moment she had the peculiar feeling that during most of the fifteen years of her life she had been looking at the face and shoulders that jutted from behind the door, in a silence disturbed only by the muted, blank plucking of a violin string. Mister Bilderbach. Her teacher, Mister Bilderbach. The quick eyes behind the horn-rimmed glasses; the light, thin hair and the narrow face beneath; the lips full and loose shut and the lower one pink and shining from the bites of his teeth; the forked veins in his temples throbbing plainly enough to be observed across the room.

"Aren't you a little early?" he asked, glancing at the clock on the mantelpiece that had pointed to five minutes of twelve for a month. "Josef's in here. We're running over a little sonatina by someone he knows."

"Good," she said, trying to smile. "I'll listen." She could see her fingers sinking powerless into a blur of piano keys. She felt tired—felt that if he looked at her much longer her hands might tremble.

He stood uncertain, halfway in the room. Sharply his teeth pushed down on his bright, swollen lip. "Hungry, Bienchen?" he asked. "There's some apple cake Anna made, and milk."

"I'll wait till afterward," she said. "Thanks."

"After you finish with a very fine lesson—eh?" His smile seemed to crumble at the corners.

There was a sound from behind him in the studio and Mister Lafkowitz pushed at the other panel of the door and stood beside him.

"Frances?" he said, smiling. "And how is the work coming now?"

Without meaning to, Mister Lafkowitz always made her feel clumsy and overgrown. He was such a small man himself, with a weary look when he was not holding his violin. His eyebrows curved high above his sallow, Jewish face as though asking a question, but the lids of his eyes drowsed languorous and indifferent. Today he seemed distracted. She watched him come into the room for no apparent purpose, holding his pearl-tipped bow in his still fingers, slowly gliding the white horsehair through a chalky piece of rosin. His eyes were sharp bright slits today and the linen handkerchief that flowed down from his collar darkened the shadows beneath them.

"I gather you're doing a lot now," smiled Mister Lafkowitz, although she had not yet answered the question.

She looked at Mister Bilderbach. He turned away. His heavy shoulders pushed the door open wide so that the late afternoon sun came through the window of the studio and shafted yellow over the dusty living room. Behind her teacher she could see the squat long piano, the window, and the bust of Brahms.

"No," she said to Mister Lafkowitz, "I'm doing terribly." Her thin fingers flipped at the pages of her music. "I don't know what's the matter," she said, looking at Mister Bilderbach's stooped muscular back that stood tense and listening.

Mister Lafkowitz smiled. "There are times, I suppose, when one—"

A harsh chord sounded from the piano. "Don't you think we'd better get on with this?" asked Mister Bilderbach.

"Immediately," said Mister Lafkowitz, giving the bow one more scrape before starting toward the door. She could see him pick up his violin from the top of the piano. He caught her eye and lowered the instrument. "You've seen the picture of Heime?"

163

Her fingers curled tight over the sharp corner of the satchel. "What picture?"

"One of Heime in the *Musical Courier* there on the table. Inside the top cover."

The sonatina began. Discordant yet somehow simple. Empty but with a sharp-cut style of its own. She reached for the magazine and opened it.

There Heime was—in the left-hand corner. Holding his violin with his fingers hooked down over the strings for a pizzicato. With his dark serge knickers strapped neatly beneath his knees, a sweater and rolled collar. It was a bad picture. Although it was snapped in profile his eyes were cut around toward the photographer and his finger looked as though it would pluck the wrong string. He seemed suffering to turn around toward the picture-taking apparatus. He was thinner—his stomach did not poke out now—but he hadn't changed much in six months.

Heime Israelsky, talented young violinist, snapped while at work in his teacher's studio on Riverside Drive. Young Master Israelsky, who will soon celebrate his fifteenth birthday, has been invited to play the Beethoven Concerto with—

That morning, after she had practiced from six until eight, her dad had made her sit down at the table with the family for breakfast. She hated breakfast; it gave her a sick feeling afterward. She would rather wait and get four chocolate bars with her twenty cents lunch money and munch them during school—bringing up little morsels from her pocket under cover of her handkerchief, stopping dead when the silver paper rattled. But this morning her dad had put a fried egg on her plate and she had known that if it burst—so that the slimy yellow oozed over the white—she would cry. And that had happened. The same feeling was upon her now. Gingerly she laid the magazine back on the table and closed her eyes.

The music in the studio seemed to be urging violently and clumsily for something that was not to be had. After a moment her thoughts drew back from Heime and the concerto and the picture—and hovered around the lesson once more. She slid over on the sofa until she could see plainly into the studio—the two of them playing, peering at the notations on the piano, lustfully drawing out all that was there.

She could not forget the memory of Mister Bilderbach's face as he had stared at her a moment ago. Her hands, still twitching unconsciously to the motions of the fugue, closed over her bony knees. Tired, she was. And with a circling, sinking away feeling like the one that often came to her just before she dropped off to sleep on the nights when she had over-practiced. Like those weary half-dreams that buzzed and carried her out into their own whirling space.

A *Wunderkind*—a *Wunderkind*—a *Wunderkind*. The syllables would come out rolling in the deep German way, roar against her ears and then fall to a murmur. Along with the faces circling, swelling out in distortion, diminishing to pale blobs—Mister Bilderbach, Mrs. Bilderbach, Heime, Mister Lafkowitz. Around and around in a circle revolving to the guttural *Wunderkind*. Mister Bilderbach looming large in the middle of the circle, his face urging—with the others around him.

Phrases of music seesawing crazily. Notes she had been practicing falling over each other like a handful of marbles dropped downstairs. Bach, Debussy, Prokofieff, Brahms—timed grotesquely to the far off throb of her tired body and the buzzing circle.

Sometimes—when she had not worked more than three hours or had stayed out from high school—the dreams were not so confused. The music soared clearly in her mind and quick, precise little memories would come back—clear as the sissy "Age of Innocence" picture Heime had given her after their joint concert was over.

A *Wunderkind*—a *Wunderkind*. That was what Mister Bilderbach had called her when, at twelve, she first came to him. Older pupils had repeated the word.

Not that he had ever said the word to her. "Bienchen—" (She had a plain American name but he never used it except when her mistakes were enormous.) "Bienchen," he would say, "I know it must be terrible. Carrying around all the time a head that thick. Poor Bienchen—"

Mister Bilderbach's father had been a Dutch violinist. His mother was from Prague. He had been born in this country and had spent his youth in Germany. So many times she wished she had not been born and brought up in just Cincinnati. How do you say *cheese* in German? Mister Bilderbach, what is Dutch for *I don't understand you?*

The first day she came to the studio. After she played the whole Second Hungarian Rhapsody from memory. The room graying with twilight. His face as he leaned over the piano.

"Now we begin all over," he said that first day. "It—playing music—is more than cleverness. If a twelve-year-old girl's fingers cover so many keys to a second—that means nothing."

He tapped his broad chest and his forehead with his stubby hand. "Here and here. You are old enough to understand that." He lighted a cigarette and gently blew the first exhalation above her head. "And work—work—work. We will start now with these Bach Inventions and these little Schumann pieces." His hands moved again—this time to jerk the cord of the lamp behind her and point to the music. "I will show you how I wish this practiced. Listen carefully now."

She had been at the piano for almost three hours and was very tired. His deep voice sounded as though it had been straying inside her for a long time. She wanted to reach out and touch his muscle-flexed finger that pointed out the phrases, wanted to feel the gleaming gold band ring and the strong hairy back of his hand.

She had lessons Tuesday after school and on Saturday afternoons. Often she stayed, when the Saturday lesson was finished, for dinner, and then spent the night and took the streetcar home the next morning. Mrs. Bilderbach liked her in her calm, almost dumb way. She was much different from her husband. She was quiet and fat and slow. When she wasn't in the kitchen, cooking the rich dishes that both of them loved, she seemed to spend all her time in their bed upstairs, reading magazines or just looking with a half-smile at nothing. When they had married in Germany she had been a *lieder* singer. She didn't sing any more (she said it was her throat). When he would call her in from the kitchen to listen to a pupil she would always smile and say that it was *gut*, very *gut*.

166

When Frances was thirteen it came to her one day that the Bilderbachs had no children. It seemed strange. Once she had been back in the kitchen with Mrs. Bilderbach when he had come striding in from the studio, tense with anger at some pupil who had annoyed him. His wife stood stirring the thick soup until his hand groped out and rested on her shoulder. Then she turned—stood placid—while he folded his arms about her and buried his sharp face in the white, nerveless flesh of her neck. They stood that way without moving. And then his face jerked back suddenly, the anger diminished to a quiet inexpressiveness, and he had returned to the studio.

After she had started with Mister Bilderbach and didn't have time to see anything of the people at high school, Heime had been the only friend of her own age. He was Mister Lafkowitz's pupil and would come with him to Mister Bilderbach's on evenings when she would be there. They would listen to their teachers' playing. And often they themselves went over chamber music together—Mozart sonatas or Bloch.

A *Wunderkind*—a *Wunderkind*.

Heime was a *Wunderkind*. He and she, then.

Heime had been playing the violin since he was four. He didn't have to go to school; Mister Lafkowitz's brother, who was crippled, used to teach him geometry and European history and French verbs in the afternoon. When he was thirteen he had as fine a technique as any violinist in Cincinnati—everyone said so. But playing the violin must be easier than the piano. She knew it must be.

Heime always seemed to smell of corduroy pants and the food he had eaten and rosin. Half the time, too, his hands were dirty around the knuckles and the cuffs of his shirts peeped out dingily from the sleeves of his sweater. She always watched his hands when he played—thin only at the joints with the hard little blobs of flesh bulging over the short-cut nails and the babyish-looking crease that showed so plainly in his bowing wrist.

In the dreams, as when she was awake, she could remember the concert only in a blur. She had not known it was unsuccessful for her until months after. True, the papers had praised Heime more than her. But he was much shorter than she. When they stood together on the stage he came only to her shoulders. And that made a difference with people, she knew. Also, there was the matter of the sonata they played together. The Bloch.

"No, no—I don't think that would be appropriate," Mis-

167

ter Bilderbach had said when the Bloch was suggested to end the programme. "Now that John Powell thing—the Sonate Virginianesque."

She hadn't understood then; she wanted it to be the Bloch as much as Mister Lafkowitz and Heime.

Mister Bilderbach had given in. Later, after the reviews had said she lacked the temperament for that type of music, after they called her playing thin and lacking in feeling, she felt cheated.

"That oie oie stuff," said Mister Bilderbach, crackling the newspapers at her. "Not for you, Bienchen. Leave all that to the Heimes and vitses and skys."

A *Wunderkind*. No matter what the papers said, that was what he had called her.

Why was it Heime had done so much better at the concert than she? At school sometimes, when she was supposed to be watching someone do a geometry problem on the blackboard, the question would twist knife-like inside her. She would worry about it in bed, and even sometimes when she was supposed to be concentrating at the piano. It wasn't just the Bloch and her not being Jewish—not entirely. It wasn't that Heime didn't have to go to school and had begun his training so early, either. It was—?

Once she thought she knew.

"Play the Fantasia and Fugue," Mister Bilderbach had demanded one evening a year ago—after he and Mister Lafkowitz had finished reading some music together.

The Bach, as she played, seemed to her well done. From the tail of her eye she could see the calm, pleased expression on Mister Bilderbach's face, see his hands rise climactically from the chair arms and then sink down loose and satisfied when the high points of the phrases had been passed successfully. She stood up from the piano when it was over, swallowing to loosen the bands that the music seemed to have drawn around her throat and chest. But—

"Frances—" Mister Lafkowitz had said then, suddenly, looking at her with his thin mouth curved and his eyes almost covered by their delicate lids. "Do you know how many children Bach had?"

She turned to him, puzzled. "A good many. Twenty some odd."

"Well then—" The corners of his smile etched themselves gently in his pale face. "He could not have been so cold—then."

Mister Bilderbach was not pleased; his guttural effulgence of German words had *Kind* in it somewhere. Mister Lafkowitz raised his eyebrows. She had caught the point easily enough, but she felt no deception in keeping her face blank and immature because that was the way Mister Bilderbach wanted her to look.

Yet such things had nothing to do with it. Nothing very much, at least, for she would grow older. Mister Bilderbach understood that, and even Mister Lafkowitz had not meant just what he said.

In the dreams Mister Bilderbach's face loomed out and contracted in the center of the whirling circle. The lip surging softly, the veins in his temples insisting.

But sometimes, before she slept, there were such clear memories; as when she pulled a hole in the heel of her stocking down, so that her shoe would hide it. "Bienchen, Bienchen!" And bringing Mrs. Bilderbach's work basket in and showing her how it should be darned and not gathered together in a lumpy heap.

And the time she graduated from Junior High.

"What you wear?" asked Mrs. Bilderbach the Sunday morning at breakfast when she told them about how they had practiced to march into the auditorium.

"An evening dress my cousin had last year."

"Ah—Bienchen!" he said, circling his warm coffee cup with his heavy hands, looking up at her with wrinkles around his laughing eyes. "I bet I know what Bienchen wants—"

He insisted. He would not believe her when she explained that she honestly didn't care at all.

"Like this, Anna," he said, pushing his napkin across the table and mincing to the other side of the room, swishing his hips, rolling up his eyes behind his horn-rimmed glasses.

The next Saturday afternoon, after her lessons, he took her to the department stores downtown. His thick fingers smoothed over the filmy nets and crackling taffetas that the saleswomen unwound from their bolts. He held colors to her face, cocking his head to one side, and selected pink. Shoes, he remembered too. He liked best some white kid pumps. They seemed a little like old ladies' shoes to her and the Red Cross label in the instep had a charity look. But it really didn't matter at all. When Mrs. Bilderbach began to cut out the dress and fit it to her with pins, he interrupted his lessons to stand by and suggest ruffles around the hips and neck and a fancy rosette on the shoulder. The music was coming along nicely then. Dresses and commencement and such made no difference.

Nothing mattered much except playing the music as it must be played, bringing out the thing that must be in her, practicing, practicing, playing so that Mister Bilderbach's face lost some of its urging look. Putting the thing into her music that Myra Hess had, and Yehudi Menuhin—even Heime!

What had begun to happen to her four months ago? The notes began springing out with a glib, dead intonation. Adolescence, she thought. Some kids played with promise—and worked and worked until, like her, the least little thing would start them crying, and worn out with trying to get the thing across—the longing thing they felt—something queer began to happen—But not she! She was like Heime. She had to be. She—

Once it was there for sure. And you didn't lose things like that. A *Wunderkind*. . . . A *Wunderkind*. . . . Of her he said it, rolling the words in the sure, deep German way. And in the dreams even deeper, more certain than ever. With his face looming out at her, and the longing phrases of music mixed in with the zooming, circling round, round, round—A *Wunderkind*. A *Wunderkind*. . . .

This afternoon Mister Bilderbach did not show Mister Lafkowitz to the front door, as he usually did. He stayed at the piano, softly pressing a solitary note. Listening, Frances watched the violinist wind his scarf about his pale throat.

"A good picture of Heime," she said, picking up her music. "I got a letter from him a couple of months ago—telling about hearing Schnabel and Huberman and about Carnegie Hall and things to eat at the Russian Tea Room."

To put off going into the studio a moment longer she waited until Mister Lafkowitz was ready to leave and then stood behind him as he opened the door. The frosty cold outside cut into the room. It was growing late and the air was seeped with the pale yellow of winter twilight. When the door swung to on its hinges, the house seemed darker and more silent than ever before she had known it to be.

As she went into the studio Mister Bilderbach got up from the piano and silently watched her settle herself at the keyboard.

"Well, Bienchen," he said, "this afternoon we are going to begin all over. Start from scratch. Forget the last few months."

He looked as though he were trying to act a part in a movie. His solid body swayed from toe to heel, he rubbed his hands together, and even smiled in a satisfied, movie way. Then suddenly he thrust this manner brusquely aside. His heavy shoulders slouched and he began to run through the stack of music she had brought in. "The Bach—no, not yet," he murmured. "The Beethoven? Yes. The Variation Sonata. Opus 26."

The keys of the piano hemmed her in—stiff and white and dead-seeming.

"Wait a minute," he said. He stood in the curve of the piano, elbows propped, and looked at her. "Today I expect something from you. Now this sonata—it's the first Beethoven sonata you ever worked on. Every note is under control—technically—you have nothing to cope with but the music. Only music now. That's all you think about."

He rustled through the pages of her volume until he found the place. Then he pulled his teaching chair halfway across the room, turned it around and seated himself, straddling the back with his legs.

For some reason, she knew, this position of his usually had a good effect on her performance. But today she felt that she would notice him from the corner of her eye and be disturbed. His back was stiffly tilted, his legs looked tense. The heavy volume before him seemed to balance dangerously on the chair back. "Now we begin," he said with a peremptory dart of his eyes in her direction.

Her hands rounded over the keys and then sank down. The first notes were too loud, the other phrases followed dryly.

Arrestingly his hand rose up from the score. "Wait! Think a minute what you're playing. How is this beginning marked?"

"An—andante."

"All right. Don't drag it into an *adagio* then. And play deeply into the keys. Don't snatch it off shallowly that way. A graceful, deep-toned *andante*—"

She tried again. Her hands seemed separate from the music that was in her.

"Listen," he interrupted. "Which of these variations dominates the whole?"

"The dirge," she answered.

"Then prepare for that. This is an *andante*—but it's not salon stuff as you just played it. Start out softly, *piano,* and make it swell out just before the arpeggio. Make it warm and dramatic. And down here—where it's marked *dolce* make the counter melody sing out. You know all that. We've gone over all that side of it before. Now play it. Feel it as Beethoven wrote it down. Feel that tragedy and restraint."

She could not stop looking at his hands. They seemed to rest tentatively on the music, ready to fly up as a stop signal as soon as she would begin, the gleaming flash of his ring calling her to halt. "Mister Bilderbach—maybe if I—if you let me play on through the first variation without stopping I could do better."

"I won't interrupt," he said.

Her pale face leaned over too close to the keys. She played through the first part, and, obeying a nod from him, began the second. There were no flaws that jarred on her, but the phrases shaped from her fingers before she had put into them the meaning that she felt.

When she had finished he looked up from the music and began to speak with dull bluntness: "I hardly heard those harmonic fillings in the right hand. And incidentally, this part was supposed to take on intensity, develop the foreshadowings that were supposed to be inherent in the first part. Go on with the next one, though."

She wanted to start it with subdued viciousness and progress to a feeling of deep, swollen sorrow. Her mind told her that. But her hands seemed to gum in the keys like limp macaroni and she could not imagine the music as it should be.

When the last note had stopped vibrating, he closed the book and deliberately got up from the chair. He was moving his lower jaw from side to side—and between his open lips she could glimpse the pink healthy lane to his throat and his strong, smoke-yellowed teeth. He laid the Beethoven gingerly on top of the rest of her music and propped his elbows on the smooth, black piano top once more. "No," he said simply, looking at her.

Her mouth began to quiver. "I can't help it. I—"

Suddenly he strained his lips into a smile. "Listen, Bienchen," he began in a new, forced voice. "You still play the Harmonious Blacksmith, don't you? I told you not to drop it from your repertoire."

"Yes," she said. "I practice it now and then."

His voice was the one he used for children. "It was among the first things we worked on together—remember. So strongly you used to play it—like a real blacksmith's daughter. You see, Bienchen, I know you so well—as if you were my own girl. I know what you have—I've heard you play so many things beautifully. You used to—"

He stopped in confusion and inhaled from his pulpy stub of cigarette. The smoke drowsed out from his pink lips and clung in a gray mist around the lank hair and childish forehead.

"Make it happy and simple," he said, switching on the lamp behind her and stepping back from the piano.

For a moment he stood just inside the bright circle the light made. Then impulsively he squatted down to the floor. "Vigorous," he said.

She could not stop looking at him, sitting on one heel with the other foot resting squarely before him for balance, the muscles of his strong thighs straining under the cloth of his trousers, his back straight, his elbows staunchly propped on his knees. "Simply now," he repeated with a gesture of his fleshy hands. "Think of the blacksmith—working out in the sunshine all day. Working easily and undisturbed."

She could not look down at the piano. The light brightened the hairs on the backs of his outspread hands, made the lenses of his glasses glitter.

"All of it," he urged. "Now!"

She felt that the marrows of her bones were hollow and there was no blood left in her. Her heart that had been springing against her chest all afternoon felt suddenly dead. She saw it gray and limp and shriveled at the edges like an oyster.

His face seemed to throb out in space before her, come closer with the lurching motion in the veins of his temples. In retreat, she looked down at the piano. Her lips shook like jelly and a surge of noiseless tears made the white keys blur in a watery line. "I can't," she whispered. "I don't know why, but I just can't—can't any more."

His tense body slackened and, holding his hand to his side, he pulled himself up. She clutched her music and hurried past him.

Her coat. The mittens and galoshes. The schoolbooks and the satchel he had given her on her birthday. All from the silent room that was hers. Quickly—before she would have to speak.

As she passed through the vestibule she could not help but see his hands—held out from his body that leaned against the studio door, relaxed and purposeless. The door shut to firmly. Dragging her books and satchel she stumbled down the stone steps, turned in the wrong direction, and hurried down the street that had become confused with noise and bicycles and the games of other children.

Joy Williams

THE SKATER

Annie and Tom and Molly are looking at boarding schools. Molly is the applicant, fourteen years old. Annie and Tom are the mom and dad. This is how they are referred to by the admissions directors. "Now if Mom and Dad would just make themselves comfortable while we steal Molly away for a moment . . ." Molly is stolen away and Tom and Annie drink coffee. There are brown donuts on a plate. Colored slides are slapped upon a screen showing children earnestly learning and growing and caring through the seasons. These things have been captured. Rather, it's clear that's what they're getting at. The children's faces blur in Tom's mind. And all those autumn leaves. All those laboratories and playing fields and bell towers.

It is winter and there is snow on the ground. They have flown in from California and rented a car. Their plan is to see seven New England boarding schools in five days. Icicles hang from the admissions building. Tom gazes at them. They are lovely and refractive. They are formed and then they vanish. Tom looks away.

Annie is sitting on the other side of the room, puzzling over a mathematics problem. There are sheets of problems all over the waiting room. The sheets are to keep parents and kids on their toes as they wait. The cold, algebraic problems are presented in little stories. Five times as many girls as boys are taking music lessons or trees are growing at different rates or ladies in a bridge club are lying about their age. The characters and situations are invented only to be exiled to measurement. Watching Annie search for solutions makes Tom's heart ache. He remembers a class he took once himself, almost twenty years ago, a class in myth. In mythical stories, it seems, there were two ways to disaster. One of the ways was to answer an unanswerable question. The other was to fail to answer an answerable question.

Down a corridor there are several shut doors and behind one is Molly. Molly is their living child. Tom and Annie's other child, Martha, has been dead a year. Martha was one year older than Molly. Now Molly is her age. Martha choked to death in her room on a piece of bread. It was early in the morning and she was getting ready for school. The radio was playing and two disc jockeys called the Breakfast Flakes chattered away between songs.

The weather is bad, the roads are slippery. From the backseat, Molly says, "He asked what my favorite ice cream was and I said, 'Quarterback Crunch.' Then he asked who was President of the United States when the school was founded and I said, 'No one.' Wasn't that good?"

"I hate trick questions," Annie says.

"Did you like the school?" Tom asks.

"Yeah," Molly says.

"What did you like best about it?"

"I liked the way our guide, you know, Peter, just walked right across the street that goes through the campus and the cars just stopped. You and Mom were kind of hanging back, looking both ways and all, but Peter and I just trucked right across."

Molly was chewing gum that smelled like oranges.
"Peter was cute," Molly says.

Tom and Annie and Molly sit around a small table in their motel room. Snow accumulates beyond the room's walls. Molly drinks cranberry juice from a box and Tom and Annie drink Scotch. They are nowhere. The brochure that the school sent them states that the school is located thirty-five miles from Boston. Nowhere! They are all exhausted and merely sit there, regarding their beverages. The television set is chained to the wall. This is indicative, Tom thinks, of considerable suspicion on the part of the management. There was also a four-dollar deposit on the room key. The management, when Tom checked in, was in the person of a child about Molly's age, a boy eating from a bag of potato chips and doing his homework.

"There's a kind of light that glows in the bottom of the water in an atomic reactor that exists nowhere else, do you know that?" the boy said to Tom.

"Is that right?" Tom said.

"Yeah," the boy said, and marked the book he was reading with his pencil. "I think that's right."

The motel room is darkly paneled and there is a picture of a moose between the two beds. The moose is knee-deep in a lake and he has raised his head to some sound, the sound of a hunter approaching, one would imagine. Water drips from his muzzle. The woods he gazes at are dark. Annie looks at the picture. The moose is preposterous and doomed. After a few moments, after she has finished her Scotch, Annie realizes she is waiting to hear the sound. She goes into the bathroom and washes her hands and face. The towel is thin. It smells as if it's been line-dried. It was her idea that Molly go away to school. She wants Molly to be free. She doesn't want her to be afraid. She fears that she is making her afraid, as she is afraid. Annie hears Molly and Tom talking in the other room and then she hears Molly laugh. She raises her fingers to the window frame and feels the cold air seeping in. She adjusts the lid to the toilet tank. It shifts slightly. She washes her hands again. She goes into the room and sits on one of the beds.

"What are you laughing about?" she says. She means to be offhand, but her words come out heavily.

"Did you see the size of that girl's radio in the dorm room we visited?" Molly says, laughing. "It was the biggest radio I'd ever seen. I told Daddy there was a real person lying in it, singing." Molly giggles. She pulls her turtleneck sweater up to just below her eyes.

Annie laughs, then she thinks she has laughed at something terrible, the idea of someone lying trapped and singing. She raises her hands to her mouth. She had not seen a radio large enough to hold anyone. She saw children in classes, in laboratories in some brightly painted basement. The children were dissecting sheep's eyes. "Every winter term in Biology you've got to dissect sheep's eyes," their guide said wearily. "The colors are really nice though." She saw sacks of laundry tumbled down a stairwell with names stenciled on them. Now she tries not to see a radio large enough to hold anyone singing.

At night, Tom drives in his dreams. He dreams of ice, of slick treachery. All night he fiercely holds the wheel and turns in the direction of the skid.

In the morning when he returns the key, the boy has been replaced by an old man with liver spots the size of quarters on his hands. Tom thinks of asking where the boy is, but then realizes he must be in school learning about eerie, deathly light. The bills the old man returns to Tom are soft as cloth.

In California, they live in a canyon. Martha's room is not situated with a glimpse of the ocean like some of the other rooms. It faces a rocky ledge where owls nest. The canyon is cold and full of small birds and bitter-smelling shrubs. The sun moves quickly through it. When the rocks are touched by the sun, they steam. All of Martha's things remain in her room—the radio, the posters and mirrors and books. It is a "guest" room now, although no one ever refers to it in that way. They refer to it as "Martha's room." But it has become a guest room, even though there are never any guests.

The rental car is blue and without distinction. It is a four-door sedan with automatic transmission and a poor turning circle. Martha would have been mortified by it. Martha had a boyfriend who, with his brothers, owned a monster truck. The Super Swamper tires were as tall as Martha, and all the driver of an ordinary car would see when it passed by was its colorful undercarriage with its huge shock and suspension coils, its long orange stabilizers. For hours on a Saturday they would wallow in sloughs and rumble and pitch across stony creek beds, and then they would wash and wax the truck or, as James, the boyfriend, would say, dazzle the hog. The truck's name was Bear. Tom and Annie didn't care for James, and they hated and feared Bear. Martha loved Bear. She wore a red and white peaked cap with MONSTER TRUCK stenciled on it. After Martha died, Molly put the cap on once or twice. She thought it would help her feel closer to Martha but it didn't. The sweatband smelled slightly of shampoo, but it was just a cap.

Tom pulls into the frozen field that is the parking lot for the Northwall School. The admissions office is very cold. The receptionist is wearing an old worn Chesterfield coat and a scarf. Someone is playing a hesitant and plaintive melody on a piano in one of the nearby rooms. They are shown the woodlot, the cafeteria, and the arts department, where people are hammering out their own silver bracelets. They are shown the language department, where a class is doing tarot card readings in French. They pass a room and hear a man's voice say, "Matter is a sort of blindness."

While Molly is being interviewed, Tom and Annie walk to the barn. The girls are beautiful in this school. The boys look a little dull. Two boys run past them, both wearing jeans and denim jackets. Their hair is short and their ears are red. They appear to be pretending that they are in a drama, that they are being filmed. They dart and feint. One stumbles into a building while the other crouches outside, tossing his head and scowling, throwing an imaginary knife from hand to hand.

179

Annie tries a door to the barn but it is latched from the inside. She walks around the barn in her high heels. The hem of her coat dangles. She wears gloves on her pale hands. Tom walks beside her, his own hands in his pockets. A flock of starlings fly overhead in an oddly tight formation. A hawk flies above them. The hawk will not fall upon them, clenched like this. If one would separate from the flock, then the hawk could fall.

"I don't know about this 'matter is a sort of blindness' place," Tom says. "It's not what I had in mind."

Annie laughs but she's not paying attention. She wants to get into the huge barn. She tugs at another door. Dirt smears the palms of her gloves. Then suddenly, the wanting leaves her face.

"Martha would like this school, wouldn't she," she says.

"We don't know, Annie," Tom says. "Please don't, Annie."

"I feel that I've lived my whole life in one corner of a room," Annie says. "That's the problem. It's just having always been in this one corner. And now I can't see anything. I don't even know the room, do you see what I'm saying?"

Tom nods but he doesn't see the room. The sadness in him has become his blood, his life flowing in him. There's no room for him.

In the admissions building, Molly sits in a wooden chair facing her interviewer, Miss Plum. Miss Plum teaches composition and cross-country skiing.

"You asked if I believe in *aluminum?*" Molly asks.

"Yes, dear. Uh-huh, I did," Miss Plum says.

"Well, I suppose I'd have to *believe* in it," Molly says.

Annie has a large cardboard file that holds compartmentalized information on the schools they're visiting. The rules and regulations for one school are put together in what is meant to look like an American passport. In the car's backseat, Molly flips through the book, annoyed.

"You can't do anything in this place!" she says. "The things on your walls have to be framed and you can only cover sixty percent of the wall space. You can't wear jeans." Molly gasps. "And you have to eat breakfast!" Molly tosses the small book onto the floor, on top of the ice scraper. She gazes glumly out the window at an orchard. She is sick of the cold. She is sick of discussing her "interests." White fields curve by. Her life is out there somewhere, fleeing from her while she is in the backseat of this stupid car. Her life is never going to be hers. She thinks of it raining, back home in the canyon, the rain falling upon the rain.

Her legs itch and her scalp itches. She has never been so bored. She thinks that the worst thing she has done so far in her life was to lie in a hot bath one night, smoking a cigarette and saying *I hate God.* That was the very worst thing. It's pathetic. She bangs her knees irritably against the front seat.

"You want to send me far enough away," she says to her parents. "I mean, it's the other side of the dumb continent. Maybe I don't even want to do this," she says.

She looks at the thick sky holding back snow. She doesn't hate God anymore. She doesn't even think about God. Anybody who would let a kid choke on a piece of bread . . .

The next school has chapel four times a week and an indoor hockey rink. In the chapel, two fir trees are held in wooden boxes. Wires attached to the ceiling hold them upright. It is several weeks before Christmas.

"When are you going to decorate them?" Molly asks Shirley, her guide. Shirley is handsome and rather horrible. The soles of her rubber boots are a bright, horrible orange. She looks at Molly.

"We don't decorate the trees in the chapel," she says.

Molly looks at the tree stumps bolted into the wooden boxes. Beads of sap pearl golden on the bark.

"This is a very old chapel," Shirley says. "See those pillars? They look like marble, but they're just pine, painted to look like marble." She isn't being friendly, she's just saying what she knows. They walk out of the chapel, Shirley soundlessly, on her horrible orange soles.

"Do you play hockey?" she asks.

"No," Molly says.

"Why not?"

"I like my teeth," Molly says.

"You *do,*" Shirley says in mock amazement. "Just kidding," she says. "I'm going to show you the hockey rink anyway. It's new. It's a big deal."

Molly sees Tom and Annie standing some distance away beneath a large tree draped with many strings of extinguished lights. Her mother's back is to her, but Tom sees her and waves.

Molly follows Shirley into the cold, odd air of the hockey rink.

No one is on the ice. The air seems distant, used up. On one wall is a big painting of a boy in a hockey uniform. He is in a graceful, easy posture, skating alone on bluish ice, skating toward the viewer, smiling. He isn't wearing a helmet. He has brown hair and wide golden eyes. Molly reads the plaque beneath the painting. His name is Jimmy Watkins and he had died six years before at the age of seventeen. His parents had built the rink and dedicated it to him.

Molly takes a deep breath. "My sister, Martha, knew him," she says.

"Oh yeah?" Shirley says with interest. "Did your sister go here?"

"Yes," Molly says. She frowns a little as she lies. Martha and Jimmy Watkins of course know each other. They know everything but they have secrets too.

The air is not like real air in here. Neither does the cold seem real. She looks at Jimmy Watkins, bigger than life, skating toward them on his black skates. It is not a very good painting. Molly thinks that those who love Jimmy Watkins must be disappointed in it.

"They were very good friends," Molly says.

"How come you didn't tell me before your sister went here?"

Molly shrugs. She feels happy, happier than she has in a long time. She has brought Martha back from the dead and put her in school. She has given her a room, friends, things she must do. It can go on and on. She has given her a kind of life, a place in death. She has freed her.

"Did she date him or what?" Shirley asks.

"It wasn't like that," Molly says. "It was better than that."

She doesn't want to go much further, not with this girl whom she dislikes, but she goes a little further.

"Martha knew Jimmy better than anybody," Molly says.

She thinks of Martha and Jimmy Watkins being together, telling each other secrets. They will like each other. They are seventeen and fourteen, living in the single moment that they have been gone.

Molly is with her parents in the car again on a winding road, going through the mountains. Tonight they will stay in an inn that Annie has read about and tomorrow they will visit the last school. Several large rocks, crusted with dirty ice, have slid upon the road. They are ringed with red cones and traffic moves slowly around them. The late low sun hotly strikes the windshield.

"Bear could handle those rocks," Molly says. "Bear would go right over them."

"Oh, that truck," Annie says.

"That truck is an ecological criminal," Tom says.

"Big Bad Bear," Molly says.

Annie shakes her head and sighs. Bear is innocent. Bear is only a machine, gleaming in a dark garage.

Molly can't see her parents' faces. She can't remember the way they looked when she was little. She can't remember what she and Martha last argued about. She wants to ask them about Martha. She wants to ask them if they are sending her so far away so that they can imagine Martha is just far away too. But she knows she will never ask such questions. There are secrets now. The dead have their secrets and the living have their secrets with the dead. This is the way it must be.

Molly has her things. And she sets them up each night in the room she's in. She lays a little scarf upon the bureau first, and then her things upon it. Painted combs for her hair, a little dish for her rings. They are the only guests at the inn. It is an old rambling structure on a lake. In a few days, the owner will be closing it down for the winter. It's too cold for such an old place in the winter, the owner says. He had planned to keep it open for skating on the lake when he first bought it and had even remodeled part of the cellar as a skate room. There is a bar down there, a wooden floor, and shelves of old skates in all sizes. Window glass runs the length of one wall just above ground level and there are spotlights that illuminate a portion of the lake. But winter isn't the season here. The pipes are too old and there are not enough guests.

"Is this the deepest lake in the state?" Annie asks. "I read that

183

somewhere, didn't I?" She has her guidebooks, which she examines each night. Everywhere she goes, she buys books.

"No," the inn's owner says. "It's not the deepest, but it's deep. You should take a look at that ice. It's beautiful ice."

He is a young man, balding, hopelessly proud of his ice. He lingers with them, having given them thick towels and new bars of soap. He offers them venison for supper, fresh bread and pie. He offers them his smooth, frozen lake.

"Do you want to skate?" Tom asks his wife and daughter. Molly shakes her head.

"No," Annie says. She takes a bottle of Scotch from her suitcase. "Are there any glasses?" she asks the man.

"I'm sorry," the man says, startled. He seems to blush. "They're all down in the skate room, on the bar." He gives a slight nod and walks away.

Tom goes down into the cellar for the glasses. The skates, their runners bright, are jumbled upon the shelves. The frozen lake glitters in the window. He pushes open the door and there it is, the ice. He steps out onto it. Annie, in their room, waits without taking off her coat, without looking at the bottle. Tom takes a few quick steps and then slides. He is wearing a suit and tie, his good shoes. It is a windy night and the trees clatter with the wind and the old inn's sign creaks on its chains. Tom slides across the ice, his hands pushed out, then he holds his hands behind his back, going back and forth in the space where the light is cast. There is no skill without the skates, he knows, and probably no grace without them either, but it is enough to be here under the black sky, cold and light and moving. He wants to be out here. He wants to be out here with Annie.

From a window, Molly sees her father on the ice. After a moment, she sees her mother moving toward him, not skating, but slipping forward, making her way. She sees their heavy awkward shapes embrace.

Molly sees them, already remembering it.

Gish Jen

WHAT MEANS SWITCH

There we are, nice Chinese family—father, mother, two born-here girls. Where should we live next? My parents slide the question back and forth like a cup of ginseng neither one wants to drink. Until finally it comes to them, what they really want is a milkshake (chocolate) and to go with it a house in Scarsdale. What else? The broker tries to hint: the neighborhood, she says. Moneyed. Many delis. Meaning rich and Jewish. But someone has sent my parents a list of the top ten schools nationwide (based on the opinion of selected educators and others) and so *many-deli* or not we nestle into a Dutch colonial on the Bronx River Parkway. The road's windy where we are, very charming; drivers miss their turns, plough up our flower beds, then want to use our telephone. "Of course," my mom tells them, like it's no big deal, we can replant.

We're the type to adjust. You know—the lady drivers weep, my mom gets out the Kleenex for them. We're a bit down the hill from the private plane set, in other words. Only in our dreams do our jacket zippers jam, what with all the lift tickets we have stapled to them, Killington on top of Sugarbush on top of Stowe, and we don't even know where the Virgin Islands are—although certain of us do know that virgins are like priests and nuns, which there were a lot more of in Yonkers, where we just moved from, than there are here.

This is my first understanding of class. In our old neighborhood everybody knew everything about virgins and non-virgins, not to say the technicalities of staying in-between. Or almost everybody, I should say; in Yonkers I was the laugh-along type. Here I'm an expert.

"You mean the man . . . ?" Pigtailed Barbara Gugelstein spits a mouthful of Coke back into her can. "That is *so* gross!"

Pretty soon I'm getting popular for a new girl, the only problem is Danielle Meyers, who wears blue mascara and has gone steady with two boys. "How do *you* know," she starts to ask, proceeding to edify us all with how she French-kissed one boyfriend and just regular-kissed another. ("Because, you know, he had braces.") We hear about his rubber bands, how once one popped right into her mouth. I begin to realize I need to find somebody to kiss too. But how?

Luckily, I just about then happen to tell Barbara Gugelstein I know karate. I don't know why I tell her this. My sister Callie's the liar in the family; ask anybody. I'm the one who doesn't see why we should have to hold our heads up. But for some reason I tell Barbara Gugelstein I can make my hands like steel by thinking hard. "I'm not supposed to tell anyone," I say.

The way she backs away, blinking, I could be the burning bush.

"I can't do bricks," I say—a bit of expectation management. "But I can do your arm if you want." I set my hand in chop position.

"Uhh, it's okay," she says. "I know you can, I saw it on TV last night."

That's when I recall that I too saw it on TV last night—in

fact, at her house. I rush on to tell her I know how to get pregnant with tea.

"With *tea?*"

"That's how they do it in China."

She agrees that China is an ancient and great civilization that ought to be known for more than spaghetti and gunpowder. I tell her I know Chinese. *"Be-yeh fa-foon,"* I say. *"Shee-veh. Ji nu."* Meaning, "Stop acting crazy. Rice gruel. Soy sauce." She's impressed. At lunch the next day, Danielle Meyers and Amy Weinstein and Barbara's crush, Andy Kaplan, are all impressed too. Scarsdale is a liberal town, not like Yonkers, where the Whitman Road Gang used to throw crabapple mash at my sister Callie and me and tell us it would make our eyes stick shut. Here we're like permanent exchange students. In another ten years, there'll be so many Orientals we'll turn into Asians; a Japanese grocery will buy out that one deli too many. But for now, the mid-sixties, what with civil rights on TV, we're not so much accepted as embraced. Especially by the Jewish part of town—which, it turns out, is not all of town at all. That's just an idea people have, Callie says, and lots of them could take us or leave us same as the Christians, who are nice too; I shouldn't generalize. So let me not generalize except to say that pretty soon I've been to so many bar and bas mitzvahs, I can almost say myself whether the kid chants like an angel or like a train conductor, maybe they could use him on the commuter line. At seder I know to forget the bricks, get a good pile of that mortar. Also I know what is schmaltz. I know that I am a goy. This is not why people like me, though. People like me because I do not need to use deodorant, as I demonstrate in the locker room before and after gym. Also, I can explain to them, for example, what is tofu (*der-voo*, we say at home). Their mothers invite me to taste-test their Chinese cooking.

"Very authentic." I try to be reassuring. After all, they're nice people, I like them. "De-lish." I have seconds. On the question of what we eat, though, I have to admit, "Well, no, it's different than that." I have thirds. "What my mom makes is home style, it's not in the cookbooks."

Not in the cookbooks! Everyone's jealous. Meanwhile, the big deal at home is when we have turkey pot pie. My sister Callie's the

187

one introduced them—Mrs. Wilder's, they come in this green-and-brown box—and when we have them, we both get suddenly interested in helping out in the kitchen. You know, we stand in front of the oven and help them bake. Twenty-five minutes. She and I have a deal, though, to keep it secret from school, as everybody else thinks they're gross. We think they're a big improvement over authentic Chinese home cooking. Oxtail soup—now that's gross. Stir-fried beef with tomatoes. One day I say, "You know, Ma, I have never seen a stir-fried tomato in any Chinese restaurant we have ever been in, ever."

"In China," she says, real lofty, "we consider tomatoes are a delicacy."

"Ma," I say. "Tomatoes are *Italian.*"

"No respect for elders." She wags her finger at me, but I can tell it's just to try and shame me into believing her. "I'm tell you, tomatoes *invented* in China."

"*Ma.*"

"Is true. Like noodles. Invented in China."

"That's not what they said in *school.*"

"In *China,*" my mother counters, "we also eat tomatoes uncooked, like apple. And in summertime we slice them, and put some sugar on top."

"Are you sure?"

My mom says of course she's sure, and in the end I give in, even though she once told me that China was such a long time ago, a lot of things she can hardly remember. She said sometimes she has trouble remembering her characters, that sometimes she'll be writing a letter, just writing along, and all of sudden she won't be sure if she should put four dots or three.

"So what do you do then?"

"Oh, I just make a little sloppy."

"You mean you *fudge?*"

She laughed then, but another time, when she was showing me how to write my name, and I said, just kidding, "Are you sure that's the right number of dots now?" she was hurt.

"I mean, of course you know," I said. "I mean, *oy.*"

Meanwhile, what *I* know is that in the eighth grade, what people want to hear does not include how Chinese people eat sliced tomatoes with sugar on top. For a gross fact, it just isn't gross enough. On the other hand, the fact that somewhere in China somebody eats or has eaten or once ate living monkey brains—now that's conversation.

"They have these special tables," I say, "kind of like a giant collar. With a hole in the middle, for the monkey's neck. They put the monkey in the collar, and then they cut off the top of its head."

"Whadda they use for cutting?"

I think. "Scalpels."

"*Scalpels?*" says Andy Kaplan.

"Kaplan, don't be dense," Barbara Gugelstein says. "The Chinese *invented* scalpels."

Once a friend said to me, You know, everybody is valued for something. She explained how some people resented being valued for their looks; others resented being valued for their money. Wasn't it still better to be beautiful and rich than ugly and poor, though? You should be just glad, she said, that you have something people value. It's like having a special talent, like being good at ice-skating, or opera-singing. She said, You could probably make a career out of it.

Here's the irony: I am.

Anyway. I am ad-libbing my way through eighth grade, as I've described. Until one bloomy spring day, I come in late to homeroom, and to my chagrin discover there's a new kid in class.

Chinese.

So what should I do, pretend to have to go to the girls' room, like Barbara Gugelstein the day Andy Kaplan took his I.D. back? I sit down; I am so cool I remind myself of Paul Newman. First thing I realize, though, is that no one looking at me is thinking of Paul Newman. The notes fly:

"*I* think he's cute."

"Who?" I write back. (I am still at an age, understand, when I believe a person can be saved by aplomb.)

"I don't think he talks English too good. Writes it either."

"Who?"

"They might have to put him behind a grade, so don't worry."

189

"He has a crush on you already, you could tell as soon as you walked in, he turned kind of orangish."

I hope I'm not turning orangish as I deal with my mail, I could use a secretary. The second round starts:

"What do you mean who? Don't be weird. Didn't you *see* him??? Straight back over your right shoulder!!!!"

I have to look; what else can I do? I think of certain tips I learned in Girl Scouts about poise. I cross my ankles. I hold a pen in my hand. I sit up as though I have a crown on my head. I swivel my head slowly, repeating to myself, *I* could be Miss America.

"Miss Mona Chang."

Horror raises its hoary head.

"Notes, please."

Mrs. Mandeville's policy is to read all notes aloud.

I try to consider what Miss America would do, and see myself, back straight, knees together, crying. Some inspiration. Cool Hand Luke, on the other hand, would, quick, eat the evidence. And why not? I should yawn as I stand up, and boom, the notes are gone. All that's left is to explain that it's an old Chinese reflex.

I shuffle up to the front of the room.

"One minute, please," Mrs. Mandeville says.

I wait, noticing how large and plastic her mouth is.

She unfolds a piece of paper.

And I, Miss Mona Chang, who got almost straight A's her whole life except in math and conduct, am about to start crying in front of everyone.

I am delivered out of hot Egypt by the bell. General pandemonium. Mrs. Mandeville still has her hand clamped on my shoulder, though. And the next thing I know, I'm holding the new boy's schedule. He's standing next to me like a big blank piece of paper. "This is Sherman," Mrs. Mandeville says.

"Hello," I say.

"Non how a," I say.

I'm glad Barbara Gugelstein isn't there to see my Chinese in action.

"*Ji nu*," I say. "*Shee-veh.*"

Later I find out that his mother asked if there were any other Orientals in our grade. She had him put in my class on purpose. For now, though, he looks at me as though I'm much stranger than anything else he's seen so far. Is this because he understands I'm saying "soy sauce rice gruel" to him or because he doesn't?

"Sher-man," he says finally.

I look at his schedule card. Sherman Matsumoto. What kind of name is that for a nice Chinese boy?

(Later on, people ask me how I can tell Chinese from Japanese. I shrug. You just kind of know, I say. *Oy!*)

Sherman's got the sort of looks I think of as pretty-boy. Monsignor-black hair (not monk-brown like mine), bouncy. Crayola eyebrows, one with a round bald spot in the middle of it, like a golf hole. I don't know how anybody can think of him as orangish; his skin looks white to me, with pink triangles hanging down the front of his cheeks like flags. Kind of delicate-looking, but the only truly uncool thing about him is that his spiral notebook has a picture of a kitty cat on it. A big white fluffy one, with a blue ribbon above each perky little ear. I get much opportunity to view this, as all the poor kid understands about life in junior high school is that he should follow me everywhere. It's embarrassing. On the other hand, he's obviously even more miserable than I am, so I try not to say anything. Give him a chance to adjust. We communicate by sign language, and by drawing pictures, which he's better at than I am; he puts in every last detail, even if it takes forever. I try to be patient.

A week of this. Finally I enlighten him. "You should get a new notebook."

His cheeks turn a shade of pink you mostly only see in hyacinths.

"Notebook." I point to his. I show him mine, which is psychedelic, with big purple and yellow stick-on flowers. I try to explain he should have one like this, only without the flowers. He nods enigmatically, and the next day brings me a notebook just like his, except that this cat sports pink bows instead of blue.

"Pret-ty," he says. "You."

He speaks English! I'm dumbfounded. Has he spoken it all this time? I consider: Pretty. You. What does that mean? Plus actually, he's said *plit-ty*, much as my parents would; I'm assuming he means pretty, but maybe he means pity. Pity. You.

"Jeez," I say finally.

"You are wel-come," he says.

I decorate the back of the notebook with stick-on flowers, and hold it so that these show when I walk through the halls. In class I mostly keep my book open. After all, the kid's so new; I think I really ought to have a heart. And for a livelong day nobody notices.

Then Barbara Gugelstein sidles up. "Matching notebooks, huh?"

I'm speechless.

"First comes love, then comes marriage, and then come chappies in a baby carriage."

"Barbara!"

"Get it?" she says. "Chinese Japs."

"Bar-*bra*," I say to get even.

"Just make sure he doesn't give you any *tea*," she says.

Are Sherman and I in love? Three days later, I hazard that we are. My thinking proceeds this way: I think he's cute, and I think he thinks I'm cute. On the other hand, we don't kiss and we don't exactly have fantastic conversations. Our talks *are* getting better, though. We started out, "This is a book." "Book." "This is a chair." "Chair." Advancing to, "What is this?" "This is a book." Now, for fun, he tests me.

"What is this?" he says.

"This is a book," I say, as if I'm the one who has to learn how to talk.

He claps. "Good!"

Meanwhile, people ask me all about him, I could be his press agent.

"No, he doesn't eat raw fish."

"No, his father wasn't a kamikaze pilot."

"No, he can't do karate."
"Are you sure?" somebody asks.

Indeed he doesn't know karate, but judo he does. I am hurt I'm not
the one to find this out; the guys know from gym class. They line
up to be flipped, he flips them all onto the floor, and after that he
doesn't eat lunch at the girls' table with me anymore. I'm more or
less glad. Meaning, when he was there, I never knew what to say.
Now that he's gone, though, I seem to be stuck at the "This is a
chair" level of conversation. Ancient Chinese eating habits have
lost their cachet; all I get are more and more questions about me
and Sherman. "I dunno," I'm saying all the time. *Are* we going
out? We do stuff, it's true. For example, I take him to the department stores, explain to him who shops in Alexander's, who shops
in Saks. I tell him my family's the type that shops in Alexander's.
He says he's sorry. In Saks he gets lost; either that, or else I'm the
lost one. (It's true I find him calmly waiting at the front door,
hands behind his back, like a guard.) I take him to the candy store.
I take him to the bagel store. Sherman is crazy about bagels. I
explain to him that Lender's is gross, he should get his bagels from
the bagel store. He says thank you.
"Are you going steady?" people want to know.
How can we go steady when he doesn't have an I.D. bracelet?
On the other hand, he brings me more presents than I think any
girl's ever gotten before. Oranges. Flowers. A little bag of bagels.
But what do they mean? Do they mean thank you, I enjoyed our
trip; do they mean I like you; do they mean I decided I liked the
Lender's better even if they are gross, you can have these? Sometimes I think he's acting on his mother's instructions. Also I know
at least a couple of the presents were supposed to go to our teachers. He told me that once and turned red. I figured it still might
mean something that he didn't throw them out.
More and more now, we joke. Like, instead of "I'm thinking,"
he always says, "I'm sinking," which we both think is so funny,
that all either one of us has to do is pretend to be drowning and the
other one cracks up. And he tells me things—for example, that
there are electric lights everywhere in Tokyo now.

"You mean you didn't have them before?"

"Everywhere now!" He's amazed too. "Since Olympics!"

"Olympics?"

"Nineteen sixty," he says proudly, and as proof, hums for me the Olympic theme song. "You know?"

"Sure," I say, and hum with him happily. We could be a picture on a UNICEF poster. The only problem is that I don't really understand what the Olympics have to do with the modernization of Japan, any more than I get this other story he tells me, about that hole in his left eyebrow, which is from some time his father accidentally hit him with a lit cigarette. When Sherman was a baby. His father was drunk, having been out carousing; his mother was very mad but didn't say anything, just cleaned the whole house. Then his father was so ashamed he bowed to ask her forgiveness.

"Your mother cleaned the house?"

Sherman nods solemnly.

"And your father *bowed?*" I find this more astounding than anything I ever thought to make up. "That is so weird," I tell him.

"Weird," he agrees. "This I no forget, forever. *Father* bow to *mother!*"

We shake our heads.

As for the things he asks me, they're not topics I ever discussed before. Do I like it here? Of course I like it here, I was born here, I say. Am I Jewish? Jewish! I laugh. *Oy!* Am I American? "Sure I'm American," I say. "Everybody who's born here is American, and also some people who convert from what they were before. You could become American." But he says no, he could never. "Sure you could," I say. "You only have to learn some rules and speeches."

"But I Japanese," he says.

"You could become American anyway," I say. "Like I *could* become Jewish, if I wanted to. I'd just have to switch, that's all."

"But you Catholic," he says.

I think maybe he doesn't get what means switch.

I introduce him to Mrs. Wilder's turkey pot pies. "Gross?" he asks. I say they are, but we like them anyway. "Don't tell any-

▼

body." He promises. We bake them, eat them. While we're eating, he's drawing me pictures.

"This American," he says, and he draws something that looks like John Wayne. "This Jewish," he says, and draws something that looks like the Wicked Witch of the West, only male.

"I don't think so," I say.

He's undeterred. "This Japanese," he says, and draws a fair rendition of himself. "This Chinese," he says, and draws what looks to be another fair rendition of himself.

"How can you tell them apart?"

"This way," he says, and he puts the picture of the Chinese so that it is looking at the pictures of the American and the Jew. The Japanese faces the wall. Then he draws another picture, of a Japanese flag, so that the Japanese has that to contemplate. "Chinese lost in department store," he says. "Japanese know how go." For fun, he then takes the Japanese flag and fastens it to the refrigerator door with magnets. "In school, in ceremony, we this way," he explains, and bows to the picture.

When my mother comes in, her face is so red that with the white wall behind her she looks a bit like the Japanese flag herself. Yet I get the feeling I better not say so. First she doesn't move. Then she snatches the flag off the refrigerator, so fast the magnets go flying. Two of them land on the stove. She crumples up the paper. She hisses at Sherman, *"This is the U.S. of A., do you hear me!"*

Sherman hears her.

"You call your mother right now, tell her come pick you up."

He understands perfectly. *I*, on the other hand, am stymied. How can two people who don't really speak English understand each other better than I can understand them? "But Ma," I say.

"Don't *Ma* me," she says.

Later on she explains that World War II was in China, too. "Hitler," I say. "Nazis. Volkswagens." I know the Japanese were on the wrong side, because they bombed Pearl Harbor. My mother explains about before that. The Napkin Massacre. *"Nan-king,"* she corrects me.

△_____

195

"Are you sure?" I say. "In school, they said the war was about putting the Jews in ovens."

"Also about ovens."

"About both?"

"Both."

"That's not what they said in school."

"Just forget about school."

Forget about school? "I thought we moved here for the schools."

"We moved here," she says, "for your education."

Sometimes I have no idea what she's talking about.

"I like Sherman," I say after a while.

"He's nice boy," she agrees.

Meaning what? I would ask, except that my dad's just come home, which means it's time to start talking about whether we should build a brick wall across the front of the lawn. Recently a car made it almost into our living room, which was so scary, the driver fainted and an ambulance had to come. "We should have discussion," my dad said after that. And so for about a week, every night we do.

"Are you just friends, or more than just friends?" Barbara Gugelstein is giving me the cross-ex.

"Maybe," I say.

"Come on," she says, "I told you *everything* about me and Andy."

"I actually *am* trying to tell Barbara everything about Sherman, but everything turns out to be nothing. Meaning, I can't locate the conversation in what I have to say. Sherman and I go places, we talk, one time my mother threw him out of the house because of World War II.

"I think we're just friends," I say.

"You think or you're sure?"

Now that I do less of the talking at lunch, I notice more what other people talk about—cheerleading, who likes who, this place in White Plains to get earrings. On none of these topics am I an expert. Of course, I'm still friends with Barbara Gugelstein, but I notice Danielle Meyers has spun away to other groups.

Barbara's analysis goes this way: To be popular, you have to have big boobs, a note from your mother that lets you use her Lord and Taylor credit card, and a boyfriend. On the other hand, what's so wrong with being unpopular? "We'll get them in the end," she says. It's what her dad tells her. "Like they'll turn out too dumb to do their own investing, and then they'll get killed in fees and then they'll have to move to towns where the schools stink. And my dad should know," she winds up. "He's a broker."

"I guess," I say.

But the next thing I know, I have a true crush on Sherman Matsumoto. *Mister* Judo, the guys call him now, with real respect; and the more they call him that, the more I don't care that he carries a notebook with a cat on it.

I sigh. "Sherman."

"I thought you were just friends," says Barbara Gugelstein.

"We were," I say mysteriously. This, I've noticed, is how Danielle Meyers talks; everything's secret, she only lets out so much, it's like she didn't grow up with everybody telling her she had to share.

And here's the funny thing: The more I intimate that Sherman and I are more than just friends, the more it seems we actually are. It's the old imagination giving reality a nudge. When I start to blush, he starts to blush; we reach a point where we can hardly talk at all.

"Well, there's first base with tongue, and first base without," I tell Barbara Gugelstein.

In fact, Sherman and I have brushed shoulders, which was equivalent to first base I was sure, maybe even second. I felt as though I'd turned into one huge shoulder; that's all I was, one huge shoulder. We not only didn't talk, we didn't breathe. But how can I tell Barbara Gugelstein that? So instead I say, "Well, there's second base and second base."

Danielle Meyers is my friend again. She says, "I know exactly what you mean," just to make Barbara Gugelstein feel bad.

"Like *what* do I mean?" I say.

Danielle Meyers can't answer.

"You know what I think?" I tell Barbara the next day. "I think Danielle's giving us a line."

Barbara pulls thoughtfully on one of her pigtails.

▼

If Sherman Matsumoto is never going to give me an I.D. to wear, he should at least get up the nerve to hold my hand. I don't think he sees this. I think of the story he told me about his parents, and in a synaptic firestorm realize we don't see the same things at all.

So one day, when we happen to brush shoulders again, I don't move away. He doesn't move away either. There we are. Like a pair of bleachers, pushed together but not quite matched up. After a while, I have to breathe, I can't help it. I breathe in such a way that our elbows start to touch too. We are in a crowd, waiting for a bus. I crane my neck to look at the sign that says where the bus is going; now our wrists are touching. Then it happens: He links his pinky around mine.

Is that holding hands? Later, in bed, I wonder all night. One finger, and not even the biggest one.

Sherman is leaving in a month. Already! I think, well, I suppose he will leave and we'll never even kiss. I guess that's all right. Just when I've resigned myself to it, though, we hold hands, all five fingers. Once when we are at the bagel shop, then again in my parents' kitchen. Then, when we are at the playground, he kisses the back of my hand.

He does it again not too long after that, in White Plains.

I invest in a bottle of mouthwash.

Instead of moving on, though, he kisses the back of my hand again. And again. I try raising my hand, hoping he'll make the jump from my hand to my cheek. It's like trying to wheedle an inchworm out the window. You know, *This way, this way.*

All over the world, people have their own cultures. That's what we learned in social studies.

If we never kiss, I'm not going to take it personally.

▼

It is the end of the school year. We've had parties. We've turned in our textbooks. Hooray! Outside the asphalt already steams if you spit on it. Sherman isn't leaving for another couple of days, though, and he comes to visit every morning, staying until the afternoon, when Callie comes home from her big-deal job as a bank teller. We drink Kool-Aid in the backyard and hold hands until they are sweaty and make smacking noises coming apart. He tells me how busy his parents are, getting ready for the move. His mother, particularly, is very tired. Mostly we are mournful.

The very last day we hold hands and do not let go. Our palms fill up with water like a blister. We do not care. We talk more than usual. How much airmail is to Japan, that kind of thing. Then suddenly he asks, will I marry him?

I'm only thirteen.

But when old? Sixteen?

If you come back to get me.

I come. Or you can come to Japan, be Japanese.

How can I be Japanese?

Like you become American. Switch.

He kisses me on the cheek, again and again and again.

His mother calls to say she's coming to get him. I cry. I tell him how I've saved every present he's ever given me—the ruler, the pencils, the bags from the bagels, all the flower petals. I even have the orange peels from the oranges.

All?

I put them in a jar.

I'd show him, except that we're not allowed to go upstairs to my room. Anyway, something about the orange peels seems to choke him up too. *Mister* Judo, but I've gotten him in a soft spot. We are going together to the bathroom to get some toilet paper to wipe our eyes when poor tired Mrs. Matsumoto, driving a shiny new station wagon, skids up onto our lawn.

"Very sorry!"

We race outside.

"Very sorry!"

Mrs. Matsumoto is so short that about all we can see of her is a green cotton sun hat, with a big brim. It's tied on. The brim is trembling.

I hope my mom's not going to start yelling about World War II.

"Is all right, no trouble," she says, materializing on the steps

199

behind me and Sherman. She's propped the screen door wide open; when I turn I see she's waving. "No trouble, no trouble!"

"No trouble, no trouble!" I echo, twirling a few times with relief.

Mrs. Matsumoto keeps apologizing; my mom keeps insisting she shouldn't feel bad, it was only some grass and a small tree. Crossing the lawn, she insists Mrs. Matsumoto get out of the car, even though it means trampling some lilies of the valley. She insists that Mrs. Matsumoto come in for a cup of tea. Then she will not talk about anything unless Mrs. Matsumoto sits down, and unless she lets my mom prepare her a small snack. The coming in and the tea and the sitting down are settled pretty quickly, but they negotiate ferociously over the small snack, which Mrs. Matsumoto will not eat unless she can call Mr. Matsumoto. She makes the mistake of linking Mr. Matsumoto with a reparation of some sort, which my mom will not hear of.

"Please!"

"No no no no."

Back and forth it goes: "No no no no." "No no no no." "No no no no." What kind of conversation is that? I look at Sherman, who shrugs. Finally Mr. Matsumoto calls on his own, wondering where his wife is. He comes over in a taxi. He's a heavy-browed businessman, friendly but brisk—not at all a type you could imagine bowing to a lady with a taste for tie-on sunhats. My mom invites him in as if it's an idea she just this moment thought of. And would he maybe have some tea and a small snack?

Sherman and I sneak back outside for another farewell, by the side of the house, behind the forsythia bushes. We hold hands. He kisses me on the cheek again, and then—just when I think he's finally going to kiss me on the lips—he kisses me on the neck.

Is this first base?

He does it more. Up and down, up and down. First it tickles, and then it doesn't. He has his eyes closed. I close my eyes too. He's hugging me. Up and down. Then down.

He's at my collarbone.

Still at my collarbone. Now his hand's on my ribs. So much for first base. More ribs. The idea of second base would probably make me nervous if he weren't on his way back to Japan and if I really thought we were going to get there. As it is, though, I'm not in much danger of wrecking my life on the shoals of passion; his unmoving hand feels more like a growth than a boyfriend. He has his whole face pressed to my neck skin so I can't tell his mouth from his nose. I think he may be licking me.

From indoors, a burst of adult laughter. My eyelids flutter. I start to try and wiggle such that his hand will maybe budge upward.

Do I mean for my top blouse button to come accidentally undone?

He clenches his jaw, and when he opens his eyes, they're fixed on that button like it's a gnat that's been bothering him for far too long. He mutters in Japanese. If later in life he were to describe this as a pivotal moment in his youth, I would not be surprised. Holding the material as far from my body as possible, he buttons the button. Somehow we've landed up too close to the bushes.

What to tell Barbara Gugelstein? She says, "Tell me what were his last words. He must have said something last."

"I don't want to talk about it."

"Maybe he said Good-bye?" she suggests. "Sayonara?" She means well.

"I don't want to talk about it."

"Aw, come on, I told you everything about . . ."

I say, "Because it's private, excuse me."

She stops, squints at me as though at a far-off face she's trying to make out. Then she nods and very lightly places her hand on my forearm.

The forsythia seemed to be stabbing us in the eyes. Sherman said, more or less, *You will need to study how to switch.*

And I said, *I think you should switch. The way you do everything is weird.*

201

And he said, *You just want to tell everything to your friends. You just want to have boyfriend to become popular.*

Then he flipped me. Two swift moves, and I went sprawling

through the air, a flailing confusion of soft human parts such as had no idea where the ground was.

It is the fall, and I am in high school, and still he hasn't written, so finally I write him.

I still have all your gifts, I write. *I don't talk so much as I used to. Although I am not exactly a mouse either. I don't care about being popular anymore. I swear. Are you happy to be back in Japan? I know I ruined everything. I was just trying to be entertaining. I miss you with all my heart, and hope I didn't ruin everything.*

He writes back, *You will never be Japanese.*

I throw all the orange peels out that day. Some of them, it turns out, were moldy anyway. I tell my mother I want to move to Chinatown.

"Chinatown!" she says.

I don't know why I suggested it.

"What's the matter?" she says. "Still boy-crazy? That Sherman?"

"No."

"Too much homework?"

I don't answer.

"Forget about school."

Later she tells me if I don't like school, I don't have to go every day. Some days I can stay home.

"Stay home?" In Yonkers, Callie and I used to stay home all the time, but that was because the schools there were *waste of time.*

"No good for a girl be too smart anyway."

For a long time I think about Sherman. But after a while I don't think about him so much as I just keep seeing myself flipped onto the ground, lying there shocked as the Matsumotos get ready to leave. My head has hit a rock; my brain aches as though it's been shoved to some new place in my skull. Otherwise I am okay. I see the forsythia, all those whippy branches, and can't believe how many leaves there are on a bush—every one green and perky and durably itself. And past them, real sky. I try to remember about

why the sky's blue, even though this one's gone the kind of inde-
scribable gray you associate with the insides of old shoes. I smell
grass. Probably I have grass stains all over my back. I hear my
mother calling through the back door, "Mon-a! Everyone leaving
now," and "Not coming to say good-bye?" I hear Mr. and Mrs.
Matsumoto bowing as they leave—or at least I hear the embarrassment in my mother's voice as they bow. I hear their car start.
I hear Mrs. Matsumoto directing Mr. Matsumoto how to back off
the lawn so as not to rip any more of it up. I feel the back of my
head for blood—just a little. I hear their chug-chug grow fainter
and fainter, until it has faded into the whuzz-whuzz of all the other
cars. I hear my mom singing, "*Mon*-a! *Mon*-a!" until my dad
comes home. Doors open and shut. I see myself standing up, brushing myself off so I'll have less explaining to do if she comes out to
look for me. Grass stains—just like I thought. I see myself walking
around the house, going over to have a look at our churned-up
yard. It looks pretty sad, two big brown tracks, right through the
irises and the lilies of the valley, and that was a new dogwood we'd
just planted. Lying there like that. I hear myself thinking about
my father, having to go dig it up all over again. Adjusting. I think
how we probably ought to put up that brick wall. And sure enough,
when I go inside, no one's thinking about me, or that little bit of
blood at the back of my head, or the grass stains. That's what
they're talking about—that wall. Again. My mom doesn't think
it'll do any good, but my dad thinks we should give it a try. Should
we or shouldn't we? How high? How thick? What will the neighbors
say? I plop myself down on a hard chair. And all I can think is, we
are the complete only family that has to worry about this. If I
could, I'd switch everything to be different. But since I can't, I
might as well sit here at the table for a while, discussing what
I know how to discuss. I nod and listen to the rest.

Helena María Viramontes

GROWING

The two walked down First Street hand in reluctant hand. The smaller of the two wore a thick, red sweater with a desperately loose button swinging like a pendulum. She carried her crayons, swinging her arm while humming *Jesus loves little boys and girls* to the speeding echo of the Saturday morning traffic and was totally oblivious to her older sister's wrath.

"My eye!" Naomi ground out the words from between her teeth. She turned to her youngest sister who seemed unconcerned and quite delighted at the prospect of another adventure. "Chaperone," she said with great disdain. "My EYE!" Lucía was chosen by Apá to be Naomi's chaperone and this infuriated her so much that she dragged her along impatiently, pulling and jerking at almost every step. She was fourteen, almost going on fifteen and she thought the idea of having to be watched by a young snot like Lucía was insulting to her maturity. She flicked her hair over her shoulder. "Goddamnit," she said finally, making sure that the words were low enough so that neither God nor Lucía would hear them.

There seemed to be no way out of this custom either. Her arguments were always the same and always turned into pleas. This morning was no different. Amá, Naomi said, exasperated but determined not to back out of this one, Amá, América is different. Here girls don't need chaperones. Mothers trust their daughters. As usual Amá turned to the kitchen sink or the icebox, shrugged her shoulders and said: You have to ask your father. Naomi's nostrils flexed in fury as she said, But Amá, it's so embarrassing. I'm too old for that; I am an adult. And as usual, Apá felt different and in his house, she had absolutely no other choice but to drag Lucía to a sock hop or church carnival or anywhere Apá was sure she would be found around boys. Lucía came along as a spy, a gnat, a pain in the neck.

Well, Naomi debated with herself; it wasn't Lucía's fault, really. She suddenly felt sympathy for the humming little girl who scrambled to keep up with her as they crossed the freeway overpass. She stopped and tugged Lucía's shorts up, and although her shoelaces were tied, Naomi retied them. No, it wasn't her fault after all, Naomi thought, and she patted her sister's soft light brown and almost blondish hair, it was Apá's. She slowed her pace as they continued their journey to Fierro's house. It was Apá who refused to trust her and she could not understand what she had done to make him so distrustful. *Tú eres mujer*, he thundered, and that was the end of any argument, any question, and the matter was closed because he said those three words as if they were a condemnation from the heavens and so she couldn't be trusted. Naomi tightened her grasp with the thought, shaking her head in disbelief.

"Really," she said out loud.

"Wait up. Wait," Lucía said, rushing behind her. "Well, would you hurry. Would you?" Naomi reconsidered: Lucía did have some fault in the matter after all, and she became irritated at once at Lucía's smile and the way her chaperone had of taking and

205

holding her hand. As they passed El Gallo, Lucía began fussing, grabbing onto her older sister's waist for reassurance and hung onto it.

"Stop it. Would you stop it?" She unglued her sister's grasp and continued pulling her along. "What's wrong with you?" she asked Lucía. I'll tell you what's wrong with you, she thought, as they waited at the corner of an intersection for the light to change: You have a big mouth. That's it. If it wasn't for Lucía's willingness to provide information, she would not have been grounded for three months. Three months, twelve Saturday nights, and two church bazaars later, Naomi still hadn't forgiven her youngest sister. When they crossed the street, a homely young man with a face full of acne honked at her tight purple pedal pushers. The two were startled by the honk.

"Go to hell," she yelled at the man in the blue-and-white Chevy. She indignantly continued her walk.

"Don't be mad, baby," he said, his car crawling across the street, then speeding off leaving tracks on the pavement, "You make me ache," he yelled, and he was gone.

"GO TO HELL, goddamn you!" she screamed at the top of her lungs forgetting for a moment that Lucía told everything to Apá. What a big mouth her youngest sister had, for christsakes. Three months.

Naomi stewed in anger when she thought of the Salesian Carnival and how she first made eye contact with a Letterman Senior whose eyes, she remembered with a soft smile, sparkled like crystals of brown sugar. She sighed as she recalled the excitement she experienced when she first became aware that he was following them from booth to booth. Joe's hair was greased back to a perfect sculptured ducktail and his dimples were deep. When he finally handed her a stuffed rabbit he had won pitching dimes, she knew she wanted him.

As they continued walking, Lucía waved to the Fruit Man. He slipped his teeth off and again, she was bewildered.

"Would you hurry up!" Naomi ordered Lucía as she had the night at the Carnival. Joe walked beside them and he took out a whole roll of tickets, trying to convince her to leave her youngest sister on the ferris wheel. "You could watch her from behind the gym," he had told her, and his eyes smiled pleasure. "Come on," he said, "have a little fun." They waited in the ferris wheel line of people. Finally:

"Stay on the ride," she instructed Lucía, making sure her sweater was buttoned. "And when it stops again, just give the man another ticket, okay?" Lucía said okay, excited at the prospect of highs and lows and her stomach wheezing in between. After Naomi saw her go up for the first time, she waved to her, then slipped away into the darkness and joined the other hungry couples behind the gym. Occasionally, she would open her eyes to see the lights of the ferris wheel spinning in the air with dizzy speed.

When Naomi returned to the ferris wheel, her hair undone, her lips still tingling from his newly stubbled cheeks, Lucía walked off and vomited. Lucía vomited the popcorn, a hot dog, some chocolate raisins, and a candied apple, and all Naomi knew was that she was definitely in trouble.

"It was the ferris wheel," Lucía said to Apá. "The wheel going like this over and over again." She circled her arms in the air and vomited again at the thought of it.

"Where was your sister?" Apá had asked, his voice rising.

"I don't know." Lucía replied, and Naomi knew she had just committed a major offense, and that Joe would never wait until her prison sentence was completed.

"Owww," Lucía said. "You're pulling too hard."

"You're a slowpoke, that's why," Naomi snarled back. They crossed the street and passed the rows of junkyards and the shells of cars which looked like abandoned skull heads. They passed Señora Nuñez's neat, wooden house and Naomi saw her peeking through the curtains of her window. They passed the "TU y YO," the one-room dirt pit of a liquor store where the men bought their beers and sat outside on the curb drinking quietly. When they reached Fourth Street, Naomi spotted the neighborhood kids playing stickball with a broomstick and a ball. Naomi recognized them right away and Tina waved to her from the pitcher's mound.

"Wanna play?" Lourdes yelled from center field. "Come on, have some fun."

"Can't," Naomi replied. "I can't." Kids, kids, she thought. My, my. It wasn't more than a few years ago that she played baseball with Eloy and the rest of them. But she was in high school now, too old now, and it was unbecoming of her. She was an adult.

"I'm tired," Lucía said. "I wanna ice cream."

"You got money?"

"No."

"Then shut up."

Lucía sat on the curb, hot and tired, and she began removing her sweater. Naomi decided to sit down next to her for a few minutes and watch the game. Anyway, she wasn't really in that much of a hurry to get to Fierro's. A few minutes wouldn't make much difference to someone who spent most of his time listening to the radio.

She counted them by names. They were all there. Fifteen of them and their ages varied just as much as their clothes. Pants, skirts, shorts were always too big and had to be tugged up constantly, and shirt sleeves rolled and unrolled, or socks mismatched with shoes that didn't fit. But the way they dressed presented no obstacle for scoring or yelling foul and she enjoyed the zealous abandonment with which they played. She knew that the only decision these kids possibly made was what to play next, and she wished to be younger.

Chano's team was up. The teams were oddly numbered. Chano had nine on his team because everybody wanted to be in a winning team. It was an unwritten law of stickball that anyone who wanted to play joined whatever team they preferred. Tina's team had the family faithful six. Of course numbers determined nothing. Naomi remembered once playing with Eloy and three of her cousins against ten kids, and still winning by three points.

Chano was at bat and everybody fanned out far and wide. He was a power hitter and Tina's team prepared for him. They couldn't afford a homerun now because Piri was on second, legs apart, waiting to rush home and score a crucial point. And Piri wanted to score it at all costs. It was important for him because his father sat outside the liquor store with a couple of his uncles and a couple of malt liquors watching the game.

"Steal the base!" his father yelled, "Run, menso!" But Piri hesitated. He was too afraid to take the risk. Tina pitched and Chano swung, missed, strike one.

"Batter, batter, swing!" Naomi yelled from the curb. She stood up to watch the action better.

"I wanna ice cream," Lucía said.

"Come on, Chano!" Piri yelled, bending his knees and resting his hands on them like a true baseball player. He spat, clapped his hands. "Come on."

"Ah, shut up, sissy." This came from Lourdes, Tina's younger sister. Naomi smiled at the rivals. "Can't you see you're making the pitcher nervous?" and she pushed him hard between the shoulder blades, then returned to her position in the outfield, holding her hand over her eyes to shield them from the sun. "Strike the batter out," she screamed at the top of her lungs. "Come on, strike the menso out!" Tina delivered another pitch, but not before going through the motions of a professional preparing for the perfect pitch. Naomi knew she was a much better pitcher than Tina. Strike two. Maybe not, and Lourdes let out such a taunting grito of joy that Piri's father called her a dog.

Chano was angry now, nervous and upset. He put his bat down, spat in his hands and rubbed them together, wiped the sides of his jeans, kicked the dirt for perfect footing.

"Get on with the game!" Naomi shouted impatiently. Chano swung a couple of times to test his swing. He swung so hard he caused Juan, Tina's brother and devoted catcher, to jump back.

"Hey baboso, watch out," he said. "You almost hit my coco." And he pointed to his forehead.

"Well, don't be so stupid," Chano replied, positioning himself once again. "Next time back off when I come to bat."

"Baboso," Juan repeated.

"Say it to my face," Chano said, breaking his stand and turning to Juan, "say it again so I could break this bat over your head."

"Ah, come on, Kiki," the shortstop yelled, "I gotta go home pretty soon."

"Let up," Tina demanded.

"Shut up, marrana," Piri said, turning to his father to make sure he heard. "Tinasana, cola de marrana, Tinasana, cola de marrana." Tina became so infuriated that she threw the ball directly to his stomach. Piri folded over in pain.

209

"No! No!" Sylvia yelled. "Don't get off the base or she'll tag you out!"

"It's a trick!" Miguel yelled from behind home plate.

"That's what you get!" This came from Lourdes. Piri did not move, and for a moment Naomi felt sorry for him, but giggled at the scene anyway.

"I heard the ice cream man." Lucía said.

"You're all right, Tina," Naomi yelled, laughing, "You're A-O-K." And with that compliment, Tina bowed, proud of her performance until everyone began shouting, "STOP WASTING TIME!" Tina was prepared. She pitched and Chano made the connection quick, hard, the ball rising high and flying over her head, Piri's, Lourdes', Naomi's and Lucía's, and landed inside the Chinese Cemetery.

"DON'T JUST STAND THERE!" Tina screamed at Lourdes, "Go get it, stupid!" After Lourdes broke out of her trance, she ran to the tall, chain-link fence which surrounded the cemetery, jumped on the fence and crawled up like a scrambling spider, her dress tearing with a rip roar.

"We saw your calzones, we saw your calzones," Lucía sang.

"Go! Lourdes, go!" Naomi jumped up and down in excitement, feeling like a player who although benched in the sidelines, was dying to get out there and help her team win. The kids blended into one huge noise, like an untuned orchestra, screaming and shouting Get the Ball, Run in Piri, Go Lourdes, Go throw the ball Chano pick up your feet throw the ballrunrunrunrunthrow the ball. "THROW the ball to me!!" Naomi waved and waved her arms. For that moment she forgot all about growing up, her period, her breasts that bounced with glee. All she wanted was an out on home base. To hell with being benched. "Throw it to me," she yelled.

In the meantime, Lourdes searched frantically for the ball, tip-toeing across the graves saying Excuse me, please excuse me, excuse me, until she found the ball peacefully buried behind a huge gray marble stone, and she yelled to no one in particular, CATCH IT, SOMEONE CATCH IT! She threw the ball up and over the fence and it landed near Lucía. Lucía was about to reach for the ball when Naomi picked it off the ground and threw it straight to Tina. Tina caught the ball, dropped it, picked it up, and was about to throw the ball to Juan at homeplate, when she realized that Juan had picked up the homeplate and ran, zig-zagging across the street while Piri and Chano ran after him. Chano was a much faster runner, but Piri insisted that he be the first to touch the base.

"I gotta touch it first," he kept repeating between pantings, "I gotta."

The kids on both teams grew wild with anger and encouragement. Seeing an opportunity, Tina ran as fast as her stocky legs could take her. Because Chano slowed down to let Piri touch the base first, Tina was able to reach him, and with one quick blow, she thundered OUT! She threw one last desperate throw to Juan so that he could tag Piri out, but she threw it so hard that it struck Piri right in the back of his head, and the blow forced him to stumble just within reach of Juan and homeplate.

"You're out!" Tina said, out of breath. "O-U-T, out."

"No fair!" Piri immediately screamed. "NO FAIR!" He stomped his feet in rage like Rumpelstiltskin. "You marrana, you marrana."

"Don't be such a baby," Piri's father said. "Take it like a man," he said as he opened another malt liquor with a can opener. But Piri continued stomping and screaming until his shouts were buried by the honk of an oncoming car and the kids obediently opened up like the Red Sea to let the car pass.

Naomi felt like a victor. She had helped, once again. Delighted, she giggled, laughed, laughed harder, suppressed her laughter into chuckles, then laughed again. Lucía sat quietly, to her surprise, and her eyes were heavy with sleep. She wiped them, looked at Naomi. "Vamos," Naomi said, offering her hand. By the end of the block, she lifted Lucía and laid her head on her shoulder. As Lucía fell asleep, Naomi wondered why things were always so complicated when you became older. Funny how the old want to be young and the young want to be old. Now that she was older, her obligations became heavier both at home and at school. There were too many demands on her, and no one showed her how to fulfill them, and wasn't it crazy? She cradled Lucía gently, kissed her cheek. They were almost at Fierro's now, and reading to him was just one more thing she dreaded doing, and one more thing she had no control over: it was another one of Apá's thunderous commands.

When she was Lucía's age, she hunted for lizards and played stickball with her cousins until her body began to bleed at twelve, and Eloy saw her in a different light. Under the house, he sucked her swelling nipples and became jealous. He no longer wanted to throw rocks at the cars on the freeway with her and she began to act different because everyone began treating her different and wasn't it crazy? She could no longer be herself and her father could no longer trust her because she was a woman. Fierro's gate hung on a hinge and she was almost afraid it would fall off when she opened it. She felt Lucía's warm, deep breath on her neck and it tickled her momentarily. Enjoy, she whispered to Lucía, enjoy being a young girl, because you will never enjoy being a woman.

Melanie Rae Thon

▼

IONA MOON

△

▼

Willy Hamilton never did like Iona Moon. He said country girls always had shit on their shoes and he could smell her after she'd been in his car. Jay Tyler said his choice of women was nobody's business, and if Willy didn't like it, he should keep his back doors locked.

Choice of women, Jay said that so nice. He thought Iona was a woman because the first night they were together he put his hand under her shirt and she didn't stop kissing him. He inched his fingers under her brassiere, like some five-legged animal, until his wrist was caught by the elastic and his hand was squished against her breast. She said, "Here, baby, let me help you," and she reached around behind her back and released the hooks. One hand on each breast, Jay Tyler whistled through his teeth. "Sweet

Jesus," he said, and unbuttoned her blouse, his fingers clumsy and stiff with the fear that she might change her mind. Jay Tyler had known plenty of girls, girls who let him do whatever he wanted as long as he could take what he was after without any assistance on their part, without ever saying, "Yes, Jay," the way Iona did, just a murmur, "yes," soft as snow on water.

In the moonlight, her skin was pale, her breasts small but warm, something a boy couldn't resist. Jay cupped them in his palms, touching the nipples with the very tips of his fingers, as if they were precious and alive, something separate from the girl, something that could still be frightened and disappear. He pressed his lips to the hard bones of Iona Moon's chest, rested his head in the hollow between her breasts and whispered words no boy had ever spoken to her.

He said, "Thank you, oh God, thank you." His voice was hushed and amazed, the voice of a drowning man just pulled from the river. As his mouth found her nipple, Jay Tyler closed his eyes tight, as if he wanted to be blind, and Iona Moon almost laughed to see his sweet face wrinkle that way; she couldn't help thinking of the newborn pigs, their little eyes glued shut, scrambling for a place at their mother's teats.

Iona supposed Willy Hamilton was right about her shoes, but she was past noticing it herself. Every morning, she got up early to milk the four cows. Mama had always done it before Iona and her brothers were awake. Even in the winter, Hannah Moon trudged to the barn while it was still dark, slogged through the mud and slush, wearing her rubber boots and Daddy's fur-lined coat that she could have wrapped around herself twice. The waves of blue snow across the fields fluttered, each drift a breast heaving, giving up its last breath.

Mama said she liked starting the day that way, in the lightless peace God made before he made the day, sitting with your cheek pressed against the cow's warm flank, your hands on her udder, understanding your pull has to be strong and steady but not too hard, knowing she likes you there and she feels grateful in the way cows do, so she makes a sleepy sound like a moan or a hum, the same sound Iona heard herself make at the edge of a dream.

△

Willy had a girl, Belinda Beller. She wore braces, and after gym class, Iona saw her stuff her bra with toilet paper. Willy and Belinda, Iona and Jay, parked down by the river in Willy's Chevy. Belinda kept saying, "No, honey, please, I don't want to." Jay panted over Iona, licking her neck, slipping his tongue as far in her ear as it would go; her bare back stuck to the vinyl seat, and Willy said, "I'm sorry." His voice was serious and small. "I'm sorry." He said it again, like a six-year-old who had killed his own gerbil by mistake.

Willy thought of his father handcuffing that boy who stole the floodlights from the funeral home. Willy was twelve and liked cruising with his dad, pretending they might get lucky and find some trouble. They caught up with the boy down by the old Miller Creek bridge. His white face rose like a moon above his dark clothes, his eyes enchanted to stone by the twin beams of the headlights.

Horton Hamilton climbed out of the patrol car, one hand on his hip. The thick fingers unsnapped the leather band that held the pistol safe in the holster. Willy's father said, "Don't you be gettin' any ideas of makin' like a jackrabbit, boy; I got a gun." He padded toward the skittery, long-legged kid, talking all the time, using the low rumble of his voice to hold the boy in one place, like a farmer trying to mesmerize a dog that's gone mad so he can put a bullet through its head.

Willy recognized the kid. His name was Matt Fry and he lived out west of town on the Kila Flats, a country boy. Horton Hamilton believed you could scare the mischief out of a child. He cuffed Matt Fry as if he were a grown man who'd done a lot worse. He said stealing those lights was no petty crime: they were worth a lot of money, enough to make the theft a felony even though Matt Fry was only fifteen years old.

A policeman didn't get much action in White Falls, Idaho, so Horton Hamilton took what business he had seriously. He'd drawn his gun any number of times, or put his hand on it at least, but he'd had cause to shoot only once in nineteen years, and that was to kill a badger that had taken up residence on poor Mrs. Griswold's porch and refused to be driven away by more peaceable means.

Fear of God, fear of the devil, that was good for a boy, but

△_____

215

Willy heard later that Matt Fry's parents had had enough of his shenanigans and that a felony was the limit, the very limit. They told the county judge they'd lost control of their boy and it would be best for everyone to lock him up and set him straight. Until then, Willy didn't know that if you did a bad enough thing, your parents could decide they didn't want you anymore.

When Matt Fry came back from the boys' home, he smelled like he forgot sometimes and pissed his own pants; he didn't look at you if you saw him on the street and said, "Hey." His parents still wouldn't let him come home and he slept in a burned-out barn down in the gully. People said Matt Fry got caught fighting his first day at the state home. They threw him in the hole for eighteen days, all by himself, without any light, and when they dragged him out he was like this: lame in one foot, mumbling syllables that didn't add up to words, skinny as a coyote at the end of winter.

Willy stopped pawing at Belinda and sat with his hands in his lap until she leaned over to peck his cheek and say, "It's all right now, honey." Iona Moon had no sympathy for Belinda Beller's point of view. What sense was there in saving everything up for some special occasion that might not ever come? How do you hold a boy back if it feels good when he slides his knee between your legs? How do you say *no* when his tongue in your ear makes you arch your back and grab his hair?

Willy liked nice girls, girls who accidentally brushed their hands against a guy's crotch, girls who wiggled their butts when they walked past you in the hall, threw their shoulders back and almost closed their eyes when they said hello. Girls who could pull you right up to the edge and still always, always say no.

Iona thought, you hang on to something too long, you start to think it's worth more than it is. She was never that way on account of having three brothers and being the youngest. When she was nine, her oldest brother gave her a penny to dance for him. Before long, they made it regular. Night after night Iona twirled around the barn for Leon, spun in the circle of light from the lantern hanging off the rafter. Dale and Rafe started coming too; she earned three cents a night from her brothers and saved every penny till she had more than four dollars. Later they gave her nickels for lifting her shirt and letting them touch the buds that weren't breasts yet. And one time, when Leon and Iona were alone in the loft, he paid her a dime for lying down and letting him rub against her. She was scared, all that grunting and groaning, and when she looked down she saw that his little prick wasn't little anymore: it was swollen and dark and she yelled, "You're hurting yourself." He clamped his dirty hand over her mouth and hissed. Finally he made a terrible sound, like the wail a cow makes when her calf is halfway out of her; his mouth twisted and his face turned red, as if Iona had choked him. But she hadn't; her arms were flung straight out from her sides; her hands clutched fistfuls of straw. Leon collapsed on his sister like a dead man, and she lay there wondering how she was going to explain to Mama and Daddy that she'd killed him. He crushed the breath out of her; sweat from his face trickled onto hers, and she felt something damp and sticky soaking through her jeans. When she tried to wriggle out from under him, he sprang back to life. He pinched her face with one hand. Squeezing her cheeks with his big fingers, he said, "Don't you ever tell, Iona. Mama will hate you if you ever tell."

After that her brothers stopped paying her to dance for them, and Leon made Rafe and Dale cut their thumbs with his hunting knife and swear by their own blood that they'd never tell anyone what they did in the barn that year.

You can't make my brothers do much of anything unless you force them to swear in blood, Iona thought.

One morning after a storm, she tramped out to the barn to do her milking. The wind howled, cutting through her jeans. Snow had drifted against the door; she bent over and dug like a dog. The first stall was empty. She ran to the next, shining her flashlight in every corner, trying to believe a cow could hide in a shadow like a cat, but she knew, even as she ran in circles, she knew that all four cows were out in the fields, that her brothers had just assumed an animal will head for shelter on its own. They didn't know cows the way Iona and her mama did. A cow's hardly any smarter than a chicken; a cow has half the brains of a pig; a cow's like an over-

217

grown child, like the Wilkerson boy, who grew tall and fat but never got smart.

She heard them. As she ran across the fields, stumbling in the snow, falling on her face more than once and snorting ice through her nose, she heard them crying like old women. The four of them huddled together, standing up past their knees in the drifts. Snow had piled in ridges down their backs; they hadn't moved all night. They let out that sound, that awful wail, as if their souls were being torn out of them. Iona had to whip them with her belt to get them going; that's how cows are: they'll drop to their knees and freeze to death with their eyes wide open and the barn door barely a hundred feet in front of them.

Later, Iona took Mama her aspirin and hot milk, sat on the edge of her bed and moaned like the cows, closing her eyes and stretching her mouth wide as it would go. Mama breathed deep with laughter, holding her stomach; the milk sloshed in the cup and Iona had to hold it. Mama had a bad time holding on to things. Her fingers were stiff and twisted, and that winter, her knees swelled up so big she couldn't walk.

Iona Moon told Jay Tyler how it was in the winter on the Kila Flats, how the wind had nothing to stand in its way, how the water froze in the pipes and you had to use the outhouse, how you held it just as long as you could because the snow didn't fall, it blew straight in your face; splinters of ice pierced your skin and you could go blind or lose your way just walking to that little hut twenty-five yards behind the house. She told him she kept a thunder mug under her bed in case she had to pee in the night. But she didn't tell him her mama had to use a bedpan all the time, and Iona was the one who slid it under her bony butt because Mama said it wasn't right for the man you love to see you that way.

Mama knew Iona had a guy. She made Iona tell her that Jay Tyler was on the diving team in the summer. He could fly off the high board backward, do two somersaults and half a twist; he seemed to open the water with his hands, and his body made a sound like a flat stone you spin sideways so it cuts without a splash: blurp, that's all. Mama worked the rest of it out of Iona too. Jay's father was a dentist with a pointed gray beard and no hair. Jay was going to college so he could come back to White Falls and go into business with his dad. Iona said it as if she was proud, but Mama shook her head and blinked hard at her gnarled hands, trying to make something go away. She said, "If I was a strong woman, Iona, I'd lock you in this house till you got over that boy. I'd rather have you hate me than see your heart be broke."

"Jay's not like that," Iona said.

"Every boy's like that in the end. Dentists don't marry the daughters of potato farmers. He'll be lookin' for a girl with an education." She didn't talk that way to be mean. Iona knew Mama loved her more than anyone alive.

Willy thought that just listening to Jay Tyler and his father might be dangerous, a bad thing that made his stomach thump like a second heart. Horton Hamilton had raised his son to believe there was one way that was right and one way that was wrong and nothing, absolutely nothing, in between. Willy said, "What if someone steals food because he's hungry?" And his father said, "Stealing's wrong." Willy said, "If a man's dying, if he feels his whole body filling up with pain, would the Lord blame him for taking his own life?" Horton Hamilton rubbed his chin. "The Lord would *forgive* him, Willy, because that's the good Lord's way, but no man has the right to choose his time of death, or any other man's time of death." Willy thought he had him now: "Why do you carry a gun?" His father said his gun was to warn and to wound, but only if there was no other way. He liked talking better.

Willy remembered the way his father talked to Matt Fry. He saw Matt Fry hobbling down the middle of the street, his head bobbing, his pants crusted with dirt, smelling of piss. He thought maybe Matt Fry would have been better off if his father had shot him dead at Miller Creek. And he bowed his head with the shame of letting himself think it.

Jay Tyler's dad wanted to be a lawyer but became a dentist like his own father instead. He taught Jay to argue both sides of every question with equal passion. When Willy told him there was one right and one wrong and all you had to do was look in the Bible to see which was which, Andrew Johnson Tyler scratched his bald head and said, "Well, Willy, I tell you, it's hard for a *medical man* to believe in God." Willy couldn't figure out why, but there was something about the way Dr. Tyler said "medical man," some secret reverence, that made Willy afraid to question him.

Jay's mother floated across the veranda, her footsteps so soft that Willy glanced at her feet to be sure they touched wood. The folds of her speckled dress fell forward and back; Willy saw the outline of her thighs and had to look away. "All this talk, all this talk," she said. "How about some lemonade? I'm so dry I could choke." Everything about her was pale: her cheeks, flushed from the heat; the sweep of yellow hair, wound in a bun but not too tight; a few blond tendrils swirling at the nape of her neck, damp with her own sweat; the white dress with tiny pink roses, cut low in front so that when she leaned forward and said, "Why don't you help me, Willy," he saw the curve of her breasts.

In the kitchen she brushed his hair from his eyes, touched his hand, almost as if she didn't mean to do it, but he knew. He scurried out to the porch with the lemonade on a tray, ice rattling against glass. From the cool shadows of the house, he swore he heard a woman holding her laughter in her throat.

Willy lost his way on the Kila Flats. All those dirt roads looked the same. Jay told him: "Turn left, turn right, take another right at the fork"; he sent Willy halfway around the county so he'd have time in the backseat with Iona Moon, time to unhook her bra, time to unzip his pants. Willy kept looking in the rearview mirror; he'd dropped Belinda Beller off hours ago. He imagined his father cruising Main and Woodvale Park, looking for him. He imagined his mother at the window, parting the drapes with one hand, pressing her nose to the glass. She worried. She saw a metal bumper twisted around a tree, a wheel spinning a foot above the ground, headlights blasting into the black woods. She washed the blood off the faces of the four teenagers, combed their hair, dabbed their bruises with flesh-colored powder, painted their blue lips a fresh, bright pink.

That was back in '57, but she saw their open eyes and surprised mouths every time Willy was late. "Forgive me, Lord, for not trusting you. I know my thoughts are a curse. I know he's safe with you, Lord, and he's a good boy, a careful boy, but I can't help my worrying, Lord: he's my only son. I love my girls, but he's special, you see, in that way." She unlaced her fingers and hissed, "I'll thrash his hide when he walks in that door." She said it out loud because God only listened to prayers and silence. He was too busy to pay attention to all the clatter of words spoken in ordinary tones.

Jay said, "Shit, Willy, you took the wrong turn back there. I told you *right* at the fork." And Willy said he did go right, and Jay answered, "We'd be in front of Iona's house if you went right." There was something in Jay's voice, a creak or a gurgle in the throat, that gave him away. Willy slammed the brakes; his Chevy did a quarter spin that threw Jay and Iona against the door. "What the hell?" said Jay.

"Get out," Willy said.

"What?"

"You heard me. Get out of my car."

Jay zipped his pants and opened the door; Iona started to climb out after him. "Just Jay," Willy said, and he got out too. The front window was cracked open enough for Iona to hear Willy say, "You're gonna get me grounded because you wanna fool around with that little slut." Jay shoved Willy over the hood of the car, and Iona watched the dust curl in the streams of yellow light, waiting for the blow. But Jay didn't hit him; he held him there, leaning on top of him, ten seconds, twenty; and when he let Willy up, Jay clapped him on the shoulder, said, "Sorry, buddy, I'll make it up to you."

Jay stood on the diving board, lean and tan, unbeatable. Willy was almost as good, some days better; but next to Jay he was pale and scrawny, unconvincing. Jay rolled off the balls of his feet, muscles flexing from his calves to his thighs. He threw an easy one first, a single somersault in lay-out position. As he opened up above the water, Iona gasped, expecting him to swoop back into the air.

Willy did the same dive, nearly as well. All day they went on

221

this way, first one, then the other; Jay led Willy by a point and a half; the rest of the field dropped by ten.

Jay saved the backward double somersault with a twist for last. He climbed the ladder slowly, as if he had to think about the dive rung by rung. His buttocks bunched up tight, clenched like fists. On the board, he rolled his shoulders, shook his hands, his feet. He strutted to the end, raised his arms, and spun on his toes. Every muscle frozen, he grit his teeth and leaped, clamped his knees to his chest and heaved head over heel, once, twice, opened up and twisted, his limbs straight as a drill.

But in that last moment, Jay Tyler's concentration snapped. By some fluke, some sudden weakness, his knees bent and his feet slapped the water.

Iona thought she'd see Jay spit with disgust as he gripped the gutter of the pool, but he came up grinning, flashing his straight, white teeth, his father's best work. Willy offered his hand. "I threw it too hard, buddy," Jay said. Buddy. Iona stood outside the chain-link fence; she barely heard it, but it made her think of that dusty road; stars flung in the cool black sky by a careless hand; Willy pinned to the hood of the car; and Jay saying: *Sorry, buddy, I'll make it up to you.* Only this way, Willy would never know. It was just like Jay not to give a damn about blame or forgiveness.

Willy's dive was easier, two somersaults without a twist, but flawless. He crept ahead of Jay and no one else touched their scores. They sauntered to the bathhouse with their arms around each other's shoulders, knowing they'd won the day.

Standing in the dappled light beneath an oak, Jay Tyler's mother hugged Willy and Jay, and his father pumped their hands. Willy wished his parents could have seen him, this day above all others, but his father was on duty; and old lady Griswold had died, so his mother was busy making her look prettier than she ever was.

Iona Moon shuffled toward them, head down, eyes on the ground. Willy nudged Jay. In a single motion, graceful as the dive he almost hit, Jay turned, smiled, winked, and flicked his wrist near his thigh, a wave that said everything: go away, Iona; can't you see I'm with *my parents?* Willy felt the empty pit of his stomach, a throb of blood in his temples that made him dizzy, as if he were the one shooed away, as if he slunk in the shadows and disappeared behind the thick trunk of the tired tree, its limbs drooping with their own weight.

He was ashamed, like the small boy squinting under the fluorescent lights of the bathroom. His mother stripped his flannel pajamas off him with quick, hard strokes and said, "You're *soaked*, Willy; you're absolutely *drowned*."

Upstairs the air was still and hot, but Hannah Moon couldn't stand the noise of the fan and told Iona, no, please, don't turn it on. Iona said, "I'm going to town tonight, Mama. You want anything?"

"Why don't you just stay here and read to me till I fall asleep? What are you planning in town?"

"Nothing, nothing at all in particular. I get this desire, you know. It's so dark out here at night, just our little lights and the black fields and the blacker hills. I want to see a whole blaze of lights, all the streetlamps going on at once, all the houses burning—like something's about to happen. You have to believe something's going to happen."

"Don't you go looking for him," Mama said. "Don't you go looking for that boy. I know he hasn't called you once since school got out. Bad enough what he did, but don't you go making it worse by being a fool."

"He's nothing to me, Mama. You want a treat or something, maybe a magazine?"

"Take a dollar from my jewelry box and get me as much chocolate as that'll buy. And don't you tell your daddy, promise?"

"Promise."

"He thinks it's not good for me; I think I've got to have some pleasure."

Daddy sat on the porch with Leon and Rafe and Dale. They rocked in the great silence of men, each with his pipe, each with the same tilt of the head as if a single thought wove through their minds. A breeze high in the pines made the tops sway so the limbs rubbed up against one another. The sound they made was less than a breath, a whisper in a dream or the last thing your mother said before she kissed you good night. You were too small to understand the words, but you knew from her voice that you were loved and safe; the kiss on your forehead was a whisper too, a promise no one could keep.

Iona buzzed up and down Main, feeling strong riding up high in the cab of Daddy's red truck, looking down on cars and rumbling over potholes too fast. Daddy kept a coil of rope, a hacksaw and a rifle in the back behind the seat. She had no intention, no intention at all, but she swung down Willow Glen Road, past Jay Tyler's house. She honked her horn at imaginary children in the street, stomped on her brakes and laid rubber to avoid a cat that wasn't there; but all that noise didn't lure anyone out of the Tyler house, and no lights popped on upstairs or down. In the green light of dusk, the house looked gray and cool, a huge lifeless thing waiting to crumble.

She sped toward Seventh, Willy Hamilton's street. She might just happen to roll by, and maybe in the course of conversation she'd say, "Are the Tylers out of town?" Not that she cared; she was only mildly curious. "The house looks absolutely deserted," she'd say. "I don't know why anyone would want to live in that big old thing."

Sure enough, Willy stood in the driveway, hosing down his sky-blue Chevrolet. Iona leaned out the window. "Hey, Willy," she said. He wrinkled up his forehead and didn't say anything. Iona was undaunted. "You wanna go get an ice cream with me?" she said. The spray from the hose made a clear arc before it spattered on the cement and trickled toward the gutter in thick muddy rivulets.

Willy was feeling sorry for her in a way. But he still didn't like her, and he didn't think he could stand the smell of her truck. He told himself to be brave; it wouldn't last long, and it was such a small thing to do, such a small, kind gesture; then he felt very proud, overcome with the realization that he was going to do this good thing.

He was still thinking how generous he was when they finished their cones and Iona jolted out along the river road instead of heading toward his house. He said, "Where are you going?" And she said, "The river." He told her he needed to get home; it was almost dark. Iona said, "I know." He told her he meant it, but his voice was feeble, and she kept plowing through the haze of dusk, faster and faster, till the whole seat was shaking.

She swerved down to the bank of the river, where all the kids came to park; but it was too early for that, so they were alone. Willy stared at the water, at the beer bottles bobbing near the shore, and the torn-off limb of a tree being dragged downstream. "I'm sorry about Jay," he said.

"Why're you sorry? He's not dead."

"He didn't treat you right."

Iona slid across the seat so her thigh pressed against Willy's thigh. "Would you treat me right?" she said. He tried to inch away, but there was nowhere to go. Iona's hand rested on his knee, then started moving up his leg, real slow. Willy swatted it away. "You still think I'm a slut?" Iona said. She touched his thigh again, lightly, higher than before. "I'm not a slut, Willy; I'm just more *generous* than most girls you know." She clutched his wrist and tried to pull his closed hand to her breast. "Don't be afraid," she said. "You won't be fingering Kleenex when you get a grip on my titties." Willy looked so confused that Iona blew a snort of laughter out her nose, right in his face. "You don't know, do you, sweetheart? You don't know Belinda Beller's boobs are made of paper."

"I don't want to hear you say her name," Willy said.

"Fine," said Iona, breathing in his ear, "I don't wanna talk about her either."

Willy felt the pressure in his crotch, his penis rising against his will. He thought of his mother putting lipstick and rouge on old Mrs. Griswold after she died, but even that didn't help this time.

Iona Moon pounced on top of him, kissing his mouth and locking the door at the same time. She fumbled with his belt, clawed at his zipper. He mumbled *no*, but she smothered the word, swallowed it up in her own mouth.

When Willy wrestled his sisters, his father told him to be careful: The strong have to look out for the weak, he said. It didn't matter that his sisters were older. Even if they jumped him two at a time, Willy was the one who had to go easy. He wasn't strong enough to win a fight without hurting them, without kicking and wrenching and taking a few blind swings, so he had to hold back. Most times he was lucky just to get away.

Willy clamped Iona's arms, but she twisted free. "You know you want it, Willy," she said. "Everybody wants it." But he

225

didn't, not like this, not with Iona Moon. She bit at his lips and his ears, sharp little nips; her fingers between his legs cupped his balls dangerously tight.

With his hands on her shoulders, he shoved her back, flung her against the dashboard so hard it stunned her, and he had time to unlock the door, leap, and flee. But he didn't get far before he heard the unmistakable sputter of tires in mud, an engine revving, going nowhere. Slowing to a trot, he listened: Rock it, he thought, first to reverse, first to reverse.

He heard her grind through the gears, imagined her slamming the stick, stamping the clutch, thought that by now tears streamed down her hot cheeks. Finally he heard the engine idle down, a pitiful, defeated sound in the near darkness.

Slowly he turned, knowing what he had to do, hearing his father's voice: *A gentleman always helps a lady in distress.* She's no lady. *Who are you to judge?*

He found small dead branches and laid them under the tires in two-foot rows. One steady push, his feet braced against a tree, one more, almost, third time's charm, and the front tires caught the sticks, spun, spat up mud all the way to his mouth, and heaved the truck backward onto solid ground. He wiped his hands on his jeans and clumped toward the road.

"Hey," said Iona, "don't you want a ride?" He kept marching. "Hey, Willy, get in. I won't bite." She pulled up right beside him. "It'll take you more than an hour to get home. Your mama will skin you. Now get in. I won't lay a hand on you." He didn't dare look at her. His face felt swollen, about to explode. "What I did before, I didn't mean anything by it. I never would have tried anything if I thought you wouldn't like it. Willy?" He glanced up at her; she seemed no bigger than a child, hanging on to that huge steering wheel. "Willy, I got a gun. Right here behind the seat, I got my daddy's gun." *Don't you be gettin' any ideas of makin' like a jackrabbit, boy.* Willy didn't know if Iona meant it as a warning or a threat, but he knew there was nothing real behind her words, no reason not to get in the truck, no reason except his pride, and that seemed like a small thing when he weighed it against the five-mile trek along the winding road, his mother's pinched face, and the spot of grease from her nose on the windowpane.

White Falls sat in a hollow, a fearful cluster of lights drawn up in a circle for the night, a town closed in on itself. Iona said, "I almost died once. My brother Leon and I started back from town in a storm that turned to a blizzard. Everything was white, like there was nothing in the world besides us and the inside of this truck. Leon drove straight into a six-foot drift; it looked just the same as the sky and the road. We had to get out and walk, or sit there and freeze like the damn cows. We stumbled, breaking the wind with our hands; then we crawled because the gusts were less wild near the ground. I saw the shadows of houses wavering in the snow, right in front of us, but they were never there. A sheet of ice built up around my cheek and chin, and I kept stopping to shatter it with my fist, but it took too long; Leon said, leave it, it will stop the wind. I thought they'd find me that way, the girl in glass, and they'd keep me frozen in a special truck, take me from town to town along with the nineteen-inch man and the two-headed calf. But Leon, Leon never thought for a minute we were going to die on that road. When I dropped to my belly and said I was warm now, he swatted my butt. Not this way, he said, not this way, God. And then I wondered if he'd whispered it or if I heard what he was thinking. Leon talking to God, I thought; that was more of a miracle than surviving, and I scrambled back to my knees and lunged forward.

"Just like a dog, Leon knew his way. I forgave him for everything. I swore in my heart I'd never hold a harsh thought against him, not for anything in the past or anything he might do later on, because right there in that moment, he was saving our lives.

"When Mama wrapped my hands in warm rags and my daddy pulled off my boots to rub my toes as hard as he could, I knew that nothing, nothing in the world was ever going to matter so much again." She punched the clutch and shifted into fourth. "Do you know why I'm telling you this?" Willy nodded, but he didn't know; he didn't know at all.

It wasn't until Iona Moon eased into her driveway and shut off the engine that she remembered her mother's chocolate and the ragged dollar bill still crumpled in her pocket. *I think I've got to have some pleasure,* that was the last thing Mama said. She rested her head on the steering wheel. A single sob erupted, burst from between her ribs as if someone had pounded his fist against her chest. She fought her own cry, choked it dry, and was silent.

227

Bill Barich

HARD TO BE GOOD

Shane got arrested just before his sixteenth birthday. It was a dumb bust, out on a suburban street corner in Anaheim, California, on a warm spring night. A couple of cops were cruising through the haze and saw some kids passing around a joint, and they pulled over and did some unwarranted pushing and shoving, which resulted in a minor-league riot. Shane did not hit either of the cops, although they testified to the contrary in court, but he did break the antenna off their patrol car, so the judge was not entirely wrong to give him a suspended sentence and six months' probation. The whole affair was no big deal to Shane, since he didn't feel guilty about what he'd done—the cops had been *asking* for trouble—but it bothered his grandparents, with whom he'd been living for some time.

His grandfather, Charlie Harris, drove him home after the court appearance. Harris was a retired phone-company executive, stocky and white-haired, who had great respect for the institutions of the world. "I hope you know how lucky you are to get off easy," he said. "The judge could have thrown the book at you."

Shane was slumped in his seat, studying his fingernails. "It was a farce."

"You take that kind of attitude and you'll wind up in the penitentiary."

"I'm not going to wind up in any penitentiary. Anyhow, the cops didn't tell the truth."

"Then they must have had a reason," Harris said.

After this, Harris made several secretive phone calls to his daughter Susan, who was Shane's mother. She lived in the redwood country north of San Francisco with her third husband, Roy Bentley. Bentley was some kind of wealthy manufacturer. Shane heard only bits of the conversations, but he was still able to guess what they were about. His grandparents were fed up with him. They'd been on his case ever since his school grades had started to drop, and it did no good anymore for him to explain that his math teacher failed everybody who wasn't a jock, or that his chemistry teacher was notoriously unfair—to the Harrises, teachers were in the same unimpeachable category as judges, cops, and ministers.

So Shane was not surprised when his grandfather broke the bad news. This happened one night when they were watching the stock-car races out in Riverside. They both loved speed and machinery. After the next-to-last race, Harris put his arm around Shane and told him that Susan wanted him to spend a couple of months with her during the summer. He used a casual tone of voice, but Shane understood that something irreversible had been set in motion.

"It's because of the bust, isn't it?" he asked. "I said it wasn't my fault."

"Nobody's blaming you. Your mother just wants to see you. Things are going well for her now."

"You really think Susan wants to see me?"

"Of course I do," said Harris, giving Shane a squeeze. "Listen, this Bentley guy's loaded. He owns a whole ranch. Your mom says you can have a separate cabin all to yourself. You'll have a wonderful visit."

"Not when all my friends are here," Shane said. "What's there to do in Mendocino?"

"Same stuff you do here. Don't be a baby, Shane. Where's your spirit of adventure?"

"It dissolved."

Harris moved his arm. "If you're going to take that attitude," he said, "we won't discuss it any further."

"It's always *my* attitude, isn't it? Never anybody else's."

"Shane," said Harris, as calmly as he could, "you just simmer down. You're not always going to get your own way in life. That's the simple truth of the matter." He paused for a moment. "The important thing for you to remember is that we love you."

"Oh sure," said Shane. "Sure you do."

Right after school let out in June, Shane got a check in the mail from his mother. She sent enough for him to buy a first-class plane ticket, but he bought a regular ticket instead and spent the difference on some Quaaludes and a bunch of new tapes for his cassette player. The drive to the airport seemed endless. At the last minute, his grandmother had decided to come along, too, so he was forced to sit in the back seat, like a little kid. The space was too small for his body; he thought he might explode through the metal and glass, the way the Incredible Hulk exploded through clothes. He watched the passing landscape, with its giant neon figures, its many exaggerated hamburgers and hot dogs. It appeared to him now as a register of all the experiences he would be denied. He would have a summer without surf and beer, without friends, and possibly without sunshine.

The scene at the airport was as difficult as he feared it might be. His grandmother started sniffling, and then his grandfather went through a big hugging routine, and then Shane himself had to repress a terrible urge to cry. He was glad when the car pulled away, taking two white heads with it. In the coffee shop, he drank a Coke and swallowed a couple of 'ludes to calm his nerves. As the pills took hold, he began to be impressed by the interior of the terminal. It seemed very slick and shiny, hard-surfaced, with light bouncing around everywhere. The heels of people's shoes caused a lot of noise.

Susan had enclosed a snapshot with her check, and Shane removed it from his wallet to study it again. It showed his mother and Roy Bentley posed on the deck of their house. Bentley was skinny, sparsely bearded, with rotten teeth. He looked more like a dope dealer than a manufacturer. Shane figured that he probably farmed marijuana in Mendocino, where sinsemilla grew with such astounding energy that it made millionaires out of extremely improbable types. He hoped that Bentley would at least be easy to get along with; in the past, he'd suffered at the hands of Susan's men. She tended to fall for losers. Shane's father had deserted her when Shane was ten months old, vanishing into Canada to avoid both his new family and the demands of his draft board. Her second husband, a frustrated drummer for a rock band, had a violent temper. He'd punched Susan, and he'd punched Shane. Their flat in the Haight-Ashbury came to resemble a combat zone. It was the drummer's random attacks that had prompted Susan to send Shane to stay with her parents. He was supposed to be there for only a few months, but the arrangement continued for more than three years. Shane still hated the drummer. He had fantasies about meeting him someday and smashing his fingers one by one with a ball-peen hammer.

When Shane's flight was announced, he drifted down a polished corridor and gave his boarding pass to a stewardess whom he was sure he'd seen in an advertisement for shampoo. He had requested a seat over a wing, so he could watch the pilot work the flaps, and he had to slip by another young man to reach it. The young man smiled a sort of monkey smile at him. He was slightly older than Shane, maybe seventeen or eighteen, and dressed in a cheap department-store suit of Glen plaid.

Once the plane had taken off, Shane finagled a miniature bourbon from the shampoo lady and drank it in a gulp. The alcohol shot to his head. He felt exhilarated and drowsy, all at the same time. He glanced over at the young man next to him, who gave off a powerful aura of cleanliness, as though he'd been scoured with buckets and brushes, and said, without thinking much about it, "Hey, I'm really ripped."

The young man smiled his pleasant monkey smile. "It's okay," he said reassuringly. "Jesus loves you anyhow."

Shane thought the young man had missed the point. "I'm not talking bourbon," he whispered. "I'm talking drugs."

"I guess I must have done every drug there is," the young man said. He tugged on his right ear, which, like his left, was big. "I can understand the attraction."

The young man turned out to be Darren Grady. His parents were citrus growers. He was traveling to a seminary outside San Francisco.

"You're going to be a priest?" Shane asked.

Grady shook his head. "It's more in the nature of a brother-hood. Maybe you've seen those ads in magazines asking for new brothers?" Shane had not seen the ads. "I never noticed them, either," Grady went on, chewing a handful of peanuts, "until I got the call. You want to know how I got it? I was tripping on acid at Zuma Beach, and I saw this ball of fire over the ocean. Then I heard the ball speak. 'Judgment is near,' it said. I'm not kidding you. This really happened. At first, I thought I was hallucinating, but it wouldn't go away, even after I came down."

"So what'd you do?"

"Went and saw a doctor at the free clinic. He told me to lay off the dope. So I did. But I couldn't get rid of the ball."

"That's what made you want to be a priest?"

Grady frowned. "I can never tell it right," he said, picking through the peanut dust at the bottom of his little blue-and-silver bag.

Shane was moved by Grady's story. He'd had similar baffling trips, during which his mind had disgorged images of grievous importance, but he'd never put a religious meaning to any of them. He felt foolish for bragging about taking pills. In order to set the record straight, he explained to Grady that he'd been exposed to drugs very early in life, because his mother had been a hippie; she'd named him after her favorite movie.

"It's not as bad as some names," Grady said. "I had a guy

232

named Sunbeam in my class last year. Anyhow, you can go into court and get it changed."

Shane didn't want to see another judge, ever. "It doesn't bother me much now," he said, looking out at the sky. "When we lived in the Haight, Susan's husband, he was this drummer—he'd let me pass around joints during parties. Sometimes he'd let me have a hit. Susan knew, but I don't think she cared. I was so small, probably not much of it got into me. I don't know, though. I hate it when I see little kids smoking dope around school. You ought to be at least thirteen before you start."

"Maybe you should never start," Grady said.

"I wouldn't go that far. It helps to calm you."

Grady tapped his breastbone. "The calm should come from inside," he said.

It seemed to Shane that Grady was truly wise for his age, so he confided all his troubles. Grady listened patiently until he was done. "I don't want to downplay it, Shane," he said, "but I'm sure it'll be over soon. That's how it is with troubles. They float from one person to the next. It's bound to come clear for you real soon."

Shane's high had worn off by the time the plane landed. He and Grady took a bus into the city, and at the Greyhound station, off Market Street, they exchanged addresses and phone numbers. The light outside the station was intense, bathing bums and commuters. Shane was feeling relaxed, but he got anxious again when Grady left for the seminary. He was nervous about seeing Susan; their last visit, down in Anaheim at Christmas, had been marked by stupid quarrels. He tried talking to a soldier who was also waiting around, but it didn't work. The soldier was chewing about four sticks of gum. Shane asked him to buy a bottle of apple wine, so they could split it, and when the soldier did Shane drank most of it, washing down two more pills in the process. He was semiconscious on the bus ride up the coast. The town of Mendocino, arranged on a cliff overlooking the Pacific, struck him as a misinterpretation of New England. "It's cute," he said, to nobody in particular.

233

From the lobby of an inn on the main drag, he phoned his mother, and then he fell asleep in a chair. Later, he heard somebody (he thought it was Susan) say, "Aw, Roy, he's ruined," so he said a few words in return and walked wobbly-legged to a station wagon. The next thing he knew, somebody was handing him a sandwich. He took it apart, laying the various components—cheese, tomatoes, alfalfa sprouts, two slices of bread—on the table. It occurred to him that he wasn't hungry. He said something to that effect, and somebody said something back—Bentley, the guy from the photo. He followed Bentley into a black night. Moisture from redwood branches dripped onto his head. Bentley unlocked the door of a cabin that smelled of pitch and camphor, and said something about extra blankets. Then Shane was alone. The whirlies hit him, and he stumbled to a small unstable bed. After he was under the covers, the whirlies subsided, and he was able to assess his surroundings. He thought they were pretty nice. The only thing that concerned him was that there seemed to be animals in the cabin—they didn't scratch or howl, but he was aware of them anyway, lurking just beyond his line of vision.

The animals were ducks, two of them, with bulbs inside glowing like hearts. Shane saw them when he woke in the morning. Gradually, he remembered where he was, along with the details of his arrival, and he felt disgusted and ashamed and yanked the covers over his head.

For some reason, he started thinking about Darren Grady. He was certain that Grady had never pulled such a dumb stunt. He wondered if Grady had made it to the seminary and if the other priests had shaved off his hair; he wondered, too, if Grady would recall their meeting or if all such mundane occurrences would automatically vanish from his mind, to be replaced by a steady image of God. Fifteen minutes or so passed in this fashion, helping to temper Shane's guilt and instill in him a new commitment to righteous behavior. He didn't pretend that he could ever be as wise and good as Grady, but he considered it within his power to improve. He got out of bed, examined the ducks more closely—they were lamps—and then, outside the cabin, he dumped his remaining pills on the ground and crushed them to dust. The act was like drawing breath.

Bentley's place was indeed like a ranch, fenced-in and isolated

234

from any neighbors. There were a few outbuildings, including a chicken coop and a beat-up barn missing boards from its siding. Inside the barn, Shane found bird's nests, rusty tools, and a broken-down old Chrysler with fish fins. Parts from the Chrysler's carburetor were scattered on a shelf, leaking oil.

Shane expected to be jumped on as soon as he opened the door to the main house, but nobody seemed to be around. He had no memory of its interior, except as a series of difficult-to-negotiate planes and angles. In the kitchen, he poured himself a glass of orange juice and sat down to read the sports page of a day-old paper. He heard his mother call to him from upstairs. "Is that you, Shane?" she asked. "Come up here right now. I want to talk to you."

He poured more juice and went up. "Where are you, Susan?"

"In here. I'm taking a bath."

The bathroom door was ajar; steam escaped from within. Shane peeked and saw his mother in the tub, under a layer of froth and bubbles. Her hair was pinned up; it was thick, still mostly black, with a few gray strands. Shane thought she was immensely beautiful. He couldn't remember how old she was—maybe forty. The number was an ancient one, but he believed that it didn't really apply.

"Don't just stand there," she said. "It's drafty. Come in and shut the door." When he was inside, she said, "You look a little better today."

"Feel a little better," Shane said.

"How about a kiss for the old lady?"

He bent down, intending to kiss her on the cheek, but she lifted her arms from the water and hugged him. The sudden movement lifted her out of the soapsuds, so that her breasts were briefly visible. Shane had seen her naked before, countless times—in bathtubs and at nude beaches—but the quality of her flesh seemed different now, echoing as it did the flesh in the porn magazines that he hid in his room in Anaheim.

"Oh, Shane," she said, pushing him away, "you were such a mess last night. What happened to you?"

Shane put his hands in his pockets. "Me and this friend of mine, Grady, we bought a bottle of apple wine and drank it at the

235

bus station." He was quiet for a second or two. "I'm sorry I did it."

"Well, you *should* be sorry. You gave us a real scare. When you behave like that, it makes me think you want me to feel guilty. I know I shouldn't have left you with Grandma and Grandpa for so long. You're my responsibility, and I've done a poor job of raising you."

Shane recognized this as therapist talk; Susan was always seeing one kind of counsellor or another. Left to her own devices, she would have sputtered and thrown something at him. Once, she'd almost beaned him with a ladle; another time, an entire needlepoint kit had whistled by his ear. "You can't *raise* me, Susan," he said. "I'm not spinach."

She laughed and looked directly at him. "No, you're not spinach. But you'd better be telling me the truth about last night. It better not be pills again."

"It's not pills."

"It better not be, because if you get caught fooling with them you could go to jail, you know. It's a violation of your probation. I don't understand how you got arrested in the first place. Who were those kids you were hanging around with?"

"There's nothing wrong with the kids," Shane said heatedly. "The cops started it. Anyway, Susan, since when are you so much against drugs? You used to smoke a joint every morning."

"I haven't smoked marijuana in years."

"Sure, Susan."

"Don't you dare talk to me like that, Shane," she said. "I'm your mother."

"I know."

"I'm not trying to be moralistic or anything. I just want you to keep out of trouble." She stood up in the tub; water dripped down her breasts, all down her body. "Give me that towel, will you, honey?"

He grabbed a towel from the rack and threw it at her, much too hard.

She pressed the towel against her chest. *"Now* what is it?"

"What do you *think* it is? Christ, Susan, don't you have any modesty?"

"I'm sorry," she said, suddenly embarrassed. "I forgot how

old you are." She wrapped herself tightly in a terry-cloth robe. "Go downstairs and I'll make us some breakfast."

The eggs she fried were brown and fertile, with brilliant orange yolks. She served them on red ceramic plates from Mexico. The colors made Shane's head swim, but he still ate with appetite. He was glad the confrontation with Susan was over. Their future together no longer seemed littered with obstacles. As she moved about the kitchen, banging pots and pans in that careless way she had, he felt a deep and abiding fondness for her, even though he knew that she had presented him with a complicated life by refusing to simplify her own. Charlie Harris called her a "nonconformist," and Shane supposed that he was right. He respected her independent streak, because he had a similar streak in him; they were joined in a bond forged of trial and error.

After Susan cleared the table, she gave him some towels to put in the cabin and told him that she was going into town. He wanted to go with her, but she wouldn't let him.

"I don't mind errands," he said. He wanted to see what Mendocino looked like when it wasn't scrambled. "I could help you carry bags and stuff."

"We'll go tomorrow," Susan said firmly. "I'll have more time then. Today I've got my yoga class and a doctor's appointment." She came up behind him and hugged him again. Her breasts pressed against his backbone. "I love you very, very much," she said. "Now go get yourself clean."

Shane went dutifully out of the house, but he was worried a little. The word "doctor" had an awful connotation, like "teacher" or "cop." He had a terrible feeling that Susan might be sick. So a new thing began to haunt him—he ought to have been a better son. He remembered how in March his grandmother had reminded him to mail a birthday card to Susan, and how he had gone to the pharmacy and bought himself a candy bar instead. What possible use would candy be when Susan was in her grave? "You're so selfish," he said to himself, kicking at a pinecone. Every problem in the world, he saw, had its roots in some falling away from goodness.

That afternoon, around lunchtime, Shane was in the old barn, sitting behind the wheel of the Chrysler and staring at the bird-peopled rafters, when Bentley wandered in and interrupted his daydream, which had to do with driving at great speeds over the surface of the moon. In person, Bentley looked even more disreputable than he had in the photograph. He could have been a bow-legged prospector who'd spent the last thirty or forty years eating nothing but desert grit. His rotten teeth were like bits of sandstone hammered into his gums. "How's the boy?" he asked in a twangy, agreeable voice, leaning his elbows on the car door.

"The boy's fine," Shane said. "He's just fine."

"Well, I'm happy about that. I'd like to have the boy step from behind the steering wheel of the car so that I can have a chat with him."

Reluctantly, Shane got out of the car. His hands were balled into fists. Down in Anaheim, he'd decided that if Bentley was a puncher, he'd punch first.

"Take it easy," Bentley said. "I'm not going to hit you."

"Wouldn't put it past you to try," Shane muttered.

Bentley lifted an expensive lizard-skin cowboy boot and ground out the cigarette he'd been smoking against the sole. "I lost my taste for violence a long time ago," he said. "Course, if I needed to, I could still fold you up and put you in my pocket with the Marlboros."

"I'm warning you," Shane said, backing off.

"The trouble is, Shane," said Bentley, following him, "your mother and I got a good thing going, and I don't want some wise-ass punk from surfer land to come around and spoil it. You pull the kind of crap you pulled last night one more time, and I'll stick you into a Jiffy bag and mail you home to the old folks."

"You can't boss me around."

At this, Bentley chuckled a bit, revealing the stumps in his mouth. "Sure I can," he said. "So long as you're on my property, and living off my kindness, I am most assuredly your boss. And here's some more news, my friend—I'm putting you to work." When Shane protested, Bentley cut him short by jabbing him in the sternum. "I'm giving you two choices. Either you can work by yourself at the ranch, and do some painting and cleaning, or you can work with me at the factory."

"What's your business?"

"I'm a manufacturer."

"Yeah, but what do you manufacture?"

"What I manufacture," said Bentley, "is ducks."

They went to visit the factory in Bentley's station wagon, which smelled of stale tobacco and leather. "See that rise?" Bentley asked Shane, as they passed a sloping hillside off to the right. "If you were to walk to the top of it and then down into the gully, you'd come to another twenty-acre parcel I own."

"Do you have another house there?"

Bentley gave him a peculiar look. "No house, no nothing," he said. "It just sits. It's appreciating in value. We'll have a picnic there someday."

"My grandfather," said Shane, "he loves to barbecue."

"We don't barbecue," Bentley said. "What we do is eat that organic food that Susan cooks. The woman has a fear of meat." He turned on the radio; a country singer was singing about beer and divorce. "Listen here, boy," Bentley continued, "I want you to have a good time this summer. I'm not naïve about dope. I've done my share of it. But you have to learn yourself some moderation. Moderation is the key. You keep on abusing yourself the way you're going, you'll wind up in a pine box."

"My grandfather said I'd wind up in the penitentiary."

"That, too," Bentley said.

The factory was situated at the edge of town, in a concrete building that might once have been a machine shop. Inside, ten or twelve young longhairs, both men and women, formed an assembly line at long wooden tables. As Bentley had said, they were making ducks—or duck lamps—by gluing two pieces of heavy-duty celluloid around a metal stand that had a socket at the top for a bulb. Once the duck halves were glued together, they were secured with rubber bands and left to dry for a day or two. The excess glue was later wiped from the ducks with solvent, and they were put in cardboard boxes and cradled in excelsior. The wholesale price was twelve dollars a duck, but they were sold in trendy stores for as much as forty apiece. The materials came from Hong Kong.

239

Shane was shocked. His mind boggled at the notion that somebody could earn a fortune on celluloid ducks. The arithmetic didn't seem right. Forty dollars? Who'd pay forty dollars? A movie star? Were there enough duck-loving movie stars to provide Bentley with the capital to own a ranch and forty-odd acres? Apparently so. But Shane remained suspicious—the scam was too good to be true. He wished that Harris, who was always harping on the importance of hard work, could be there to watch Bentley as he lounged around the shop, smoking cigarettes and joking with his crew. Harris would go right through the roof; he'd say the whole shebang was un-American. Shane liked the atmosphere, though. Nobody treated the craft of duck making very seriously. Besides, a tall blond girl with ironed hair kept glancing at him from across the room; he fell into an immediate fantasy about her. He told Bentley he'd prefer to work at the factory instead of at the ranch.

"I'll start you in the morning," Bentley said. "You'll be a duck-packer. You'll pack so many damn ducks, you'll be quacking in your sleep."

They locked up after everybody had quit for the day. On the ride home, Shane's thoughts drifted back to Susan, and he asked Bentley if anything was wrong with her.

"No way," Bentley said. "She's a fine, fine lady. Absolutely perfect."

"I mean, is she sick or anything?"

"Sick? No, she's not sick. She's just got some female trouble. When you get older, you'll learn that every woman has it sooner or later. They can't avoid it, and you can't help 'em with it. It's just something they have to go through on their own," Bentley said with a sigh. "We'll talk about it more when we get to the ranch."

But Shane didn't bring up the subject again (he was afraid of what he might hear), and Bentley volunteered no further information. Instead, they returned to the barn and played with the Chrysler until they were both covered with oil. They cleaned the points and plugs and reinstalled the carburetor. Bentley showed Shane how the engine had been modified to make it operate at maximum efficiency. "Let's fire up the sumbitch," he said, wiping his face on a polka-dotted bandanna. He let Shane sit in the driver's seat and try the ignition, but the engine wouldn't turn over. "Pump the pedal," he said. Shane pumped it and tried the ignition again. The engine roared. It sounded big in the barn, scattering robins and swallows into the dusk. Shane floored the pedal briefly and felt himself transported; energy ran through him as though he were a sieve.

After Shane had been at the factory for three weeks, he sent a postcard to his Anaheim pal Burt, the kid who'd actually hit a cop during the bust. He described his cabin, the redwoods, and the factory. "If you want to come up here," he wrote, "I can squeeze in another bed easy. And don't worry about me doing any you-know-what. I'm off that stuff for good."

Twice his grandparents called to see how he was getting along. He still felt estranged from them, and this was compounded when they told him they'd bought a camper and were going to Joshua Tree National Monument until mid-August unless Shane planned to come back before then.

"Me?" he asked, sounding wounded. "Since when do I have plans?"

For the next twenty-four hours, he was sullen and depressed, but he had to work at it, because he was having so much fun on the job. Every morning at eight, he and Bentley headed off together into a coastal fogbank that was always just beginning to disperse. They drank coffee from Styrofoam cups and told each other duck jokes while they watched the sky separate into a confetti mist under which the town of Mendocino stood exposed, back from wherever it went at night. Shane packed boxes with a ponytailed guy who was known as Eager on account of his last name, Beaver. Eager was anything but—he had a meticulous nature, and he took pains to be sure that each duck was nestled as comfortably as possible in its excelsior. He could have been packing eggs or glass-ware. "C'mon, Eager," Shane said to him one afternoon. "They're not alive, you know."

The tall blond girl was Emma King. She was nineteen, a college student. Shane followed her around like a dog. When the weather was hot, Emma came to the factory in white shorts and a red halter top, and Shane would monitor her every movement from his packing station, waiting for her to reach down for a tube of glue or bend low for the X-Acto knife she kept dropping on the floor.

241

She had a boyfriend she saw on weekends, but she told Shane that she'd go to the movies with him before he returned to Anaheim. "I'm in love with this heavy girl, she's *nineteen!!!*" he wrote on another postcard to Burt. "We go drinking together after work." This was almost true, or at least on the outer fringe of validity. One Friday, Eager *had* invited him to go to a tavern in the woods where anybody could get served, but he'd decided against it to avoid trouble. Later, he heard that Emma had been there, so in his mind they were linked.

He asked her for a photo, but she didn't have any, so he borrowed Susan's camera and snapped her in different poses, while she pretended to complain. The cutest shot was one of Emma kissing a duck on its beak. Shane taped it to the dashboard of the Chrysler. He thought of it as his car now. Bentley had promised it to him in lieu of wages if he could pass his driver's test. Already, he was practicing. He did Y-turns and parallel parking. Some evenings, he and Bentley took a ride to the ocean, steaming down dirt roads that were dotted with Scotch broom and beach poppies. Once, Bentley let him go by himself, without any adult supervision, and he handled the Chrysler with such authority and skill that he developed a stitch in his side from excitement. It was a mystery to him how things kept changing.

Another mystery was his mother. He'd never seen her so happy. He could not reconcile so much happiness, in fact, with scraggly, bowlegged, rotten-toothed Bentley. Here was a man who could walk around for days with egg in his beard and never even notice. The scent of nicotine was embedded in his clothes and maybe in his skin. Could it be that love had nothing to do with beauty? If Bentley could provoke love, then so could a stone or a twig. So could a garbage can.

But there was no denying Susan's contentment. She thrived on Bentley's generosity. She seemed to float around the house, gliding barefoot an inch or two above the floor, dressed in blouses and peasant skirts that showed off her bosomy fullness. She baked bread, hummed romantic tunes, and filled all her vases with flowers. She was constantly hugging her egg-stained lover, patting him on his flat little prospector's ass. The affection spilled over to Shane. Susan's arms were always grasping for him, making up for lost time. She drew him to her for purposes of both measurement and embrace. The very size of him seemed to thrill her—he'd grown from almost nothing! "Oh, Shane," she'd say in a husky voice, holding a hunk of his cheek between her thumb and index finger. "You're such a dear boy."

If Shane hadn't known better, he would have sworn that she was stoned all the time, but he'd never seen any dope in the house. As far as he could tell, the Bentleys had adopted a much more civilized vice. They drank wine—a bottle every evening, with Bentley leading the way. The wine burnished their faces. It made them talkative, sentimental, occasionally teary-eyed. After dinner, if the fog wasn't too thick, they'd put on sweaters and sit on the deck and speak in conspiratorial tones about the day's events, while bats sailed overhead, like punctuation. When there was nothing on TV, Shane sat with them, shivering no matter how many layers of clothing he wore.

"Thin blood," Bentley would say to him. "Goddam thin Southern California surfer's blood."

"My blood's fine."

"It's *thin*, Shane. It takes six months for blood to adapt to a new climate."

Blood was yet another mystery. Sometimes Shame thought that he understood Susan better than Bentley did, simply because they were related by blood instead of marriage. Although he and Susan had often lived apart, had quarreled and made mistakes, she was still his mother, and he was able, in a curious way, to anticipate her moods and know when something was bothering her. One night, as they sat outside, he saw that she was unusually quiet, removed from the conversation, and when Bentley went into the house he asked her if she'd got bad news at the doctor's office— she'd had another in her ongoing series of appointments that afternoon. The question made him tremble. Suppose she confessed something awful to him? Ignorance was a kind of protection. But she only smiled wistfully and patted his hand and said no, nothing very serious was wrong. It was just that the doctor had told her that she might need an operation—minor corrective surgery. She started to explain the problem to him in clinical terms, but it sounded indecent somehow to hear her describe her body as though it were an engine in need of repair, so he interrupted. "I know," he said, mimicking Bentley's sad resignation. "Female trouble." He put an arm around her, wanting to say more, but by then Bentley was back with full wineglasses and a word about the rising moon.

Shane's driving test was scheduled for a Thursday afternoon. Bentley gave him permission to come home early from work to practice. He backed the Chrysler into the barn several times without scratching it, and then he walked over to the house, hoping that Susan would make him a snack, but she'd gone to town for her yoga class. The phone rang while he was eating a boiled hot dog. Darren Grady was on the line, calling from Elk, a town south of Mendocino. Grady was upset, distressed, talking a mile a minute. He'd run away from the seminary and he was stranded, broke. Shane couldn't believe it. Where had Grady's wisdom gone? "Take it easy, Darren," he said. "Everything's going to be all right."

But Grady was blubbering. "I was trying to hitch to your place," he said, "but this highway patrol, he kicked me off the road. I cooled it in the bushes for a while and tried again, but here comes old highway patrol with his flasher on. I gave him the finger and split for town. I'm like a hunted criminal, Shane. You got to help me."

Shane glanced at the kitchen clock. He figured that he could get to Elk and back before he and Bentley were scheduled to meet the state examiner, so he told Grady to sit tight. The drive over there took about twenty minutes and gave him a severe case of paranoia. Every car that approached him seemed from a distance to be black and ominous and full of cops.

Grady was where he said he'd be, in front of a restaurant. He was sitting on the curb and eating a hamburger—some ketchup was on his chin—and drinking a can of beer. When he saw Shane, he waved wildly and let loose his monkey smile. Shane was surprised that Grady still had hair—there was no bald spot or anything. The only truly abused part of him was his Glen-plaid suit. All its department-store slickness had been rubbed away; there were holes in the knees of his trousers, as if he'd been on a long pilgrimage over concrete. Also, he'd lost his socks. The confidence he'd had on the plane was gone; now he was nothing but fidget. "I'll never forget you for this, Shane," he said, getting to his feet. "Is this yours?" he asked in wonderment, touching the Chrysler's fins. "It's a mean machine."

Shane eyed the half-demolished burger. "I thought you were broke," he said.

"I am, but I talked up the waitress in there"—Grady jerked his streaked face in the direction of the restaurant—"and traded her my Bible."

"She gave you beer for a Bible?"

"Just the hamburger. The beer I found."

This sounded fishy to Shane. "Where'd you find it?" he asked.

"Some guy left it on the seat of his car." Grady climbed into the Chrysler. For a moment, he seemed collected, drawn virtuously into himself, but then he fell apart and started bawling. "You're the only damn friend I've got," he said, blowing his nose in the hamburger wrapper.

Grady told Shane that he'd been on the road for three days. The first night, after he'd snuck out of the seminary, he hitched to San Francisco and slept in the Greyhound station, thinking he would catch a bus to Anaheim in the morning, but when he woke he realized that he'd have to confront his parents with the sorry evidence of his failure, so, instead of phoning them, he walked all the way to Fisherman's Wharf and ate a breakfast of crab and shrimp, and then spent twenty-two bucks playing video games at an arcade. This left him with just one dollar to his name—his emergency dollar, which he kept folded in sixteenths and hidden in the secret compartment of his wallet. When he pulled it out, the slip of paper on which Shane had written Susan's address and phone number fell to the floor.

"You get it?" Grady asked, turning toward Shane, who was paying only a little attention, since he had to watch for cops. "It was a *sign!*"

"What about the ball?" Shane asked. His forehead was wrinkled in concentration.

"Ball? What ball?"

"The ball from Zuma Beach. Did it come back while you were with the priests?"

"It never did."

"Then why'd you leave?"

Grady shrugged. His fidgety fingers picked at his knees through the holes in his pants. "It's hard to be good," he said. From the pockets of his suit coat he took two fresh cans of beer and—before Shane could protest—popped the tops. Shane accepted a can and stuck it between his thighs. He hit a bump and got doused.

On the second day, Grady said, he'd reached the town of Healdsburg. He said it was the hottest place he'd ever been to—hotter than Hell, frankly. In the evening, when it got too dark to hitch anymore, he wandered to the town square, where there were palm trees and flowers and benches, and he took off his shoes and socks and dunked his feet in a fountain. The water felt soothing as it swirled between his toes, but a bunch of Mexicans who were hanging around the square kept watching him, and he thought they might knife him or otherwise do him harm. He knew this was a silly fear, but it was fear nonetheless, so he gathered himself together in a hurry, slipped his wet feet into his shoes, and walked briskly down a side street that led him to a vineyard, where he curled up on the warm ground and slept the night away under cover of grape leaves. A flaming sun woke him at dawn. He couldn't find his socks. Their absence seemed to hurt him more than anything else. "Everybody knows you're running away from something if you don't have socks on," he said, biting his lower lip. "Who's going to stop for a person with bare ankles?" With this, he finished his beer in a gulp and threw the empty can out the window. The can rattled over the macadam, bounced two or three times, and rolled past the nose of a highway-patrol car that was parked in the bushes, waiting for speeders.

"Aw, Grady," Shane said.

Grady swiveled around to look back. "That's the guy I gave the finger to," he said.

Shane felt as though his body had been stripped of a dimension and then spliced into a deadly, predictable horror movie. He tried to imagine that the cop hadn't seen the can—or, better, that the cop had decided to overlook it—but this didn't work, since the cop had left his hiding place and was approaching the Chrysler at a steady clip. Shane gave Grady the half-full beer he had between his thighs, and Grady dropped down in the seat and drank it off, then shoved the empty into the glove compartment. The cop came closer. Grady looked again, and, panicked, said, "He's going to bust us, Shane. I know by his face."

"You don't know for sure."

The cop's flasher went on.

Grady sank lower in the seat. "I'm holding, Shane," he said morosely.

Shane didn't want to take his eyes from the road. "You're *what?*"

"I'm holding some speed. I bought it at that arcade." He showed Shane four pills. "Should I throw them out the window?"

The pills got swallowed—Shane couldn't think of any other way to dispose of them. He and Grady ate two apiece, which lent a hallucinatory edge to subsequent events. The cop was wearing reflector sunglasses, for instance, so that Shane was able to watch himself react to the words that bubbled from between the cop's lips when the cop pulled them over. The cop spoke of littering, of underage drinking, of operating a motor vehicle without a license and without what he called a vehicular-registration slip. Eyeless, he led Shane and Grady to his car and locked them in the back seat behind a mesh screen. The pills really took hold on the ride to the police station, and Shane was possessed by a powerful sense of urgency and he couldn't stop talking. He believed that he had an important message to deliver about the nature of goodness, and he delivered it ceaselessly—to the cop, to the officer who booked him, to the ink of the fingerprint pad, and to the cold iron bars of his cell.

Roy Bentley bailed out the boys. He came to the station with his attorney, a fashionably dressed man whose hair was all gray curls. The attorney seemed to know everybody around, and after a brief back-room conversation he reported to Bentley that the charges, except for littering, had been dropped. Bentley paid a stiff fine, then put the boys in his wagon and drove them to the ranch. They were amazed to be let go so quickly. "You must be important, Mr. Bentley," Grady said.

"You two are just lucky I've got some clout," Bentley told them. "A successful businessman is not a nobody up here. I'm a Democrat and I belong to the Rotary. But don't think it's over yet. You still got Shane's mother to face."

Susan exploded. There was no therapist talk this time. When Shane came through the door, slinking like an animal, she yelled and threw a pot holder at him, and then, so as not to be discriminatory, she threw one at Grady, too. She grabbed Shane by the hair and held him in place while she lectured him. She said he was an ungrateful little bastard, spoiled, indifferent, snotty, rotten to the core. He refused to argue, but in the morning, when she was almost rational again, he explained to her exactly why he had done what he'd done, so that she would understand that he hadn't been frivolous or irresponsible. "It was circumstances, see?" he said, sitting forward in his chair and kneading his hands. "I couldn't just leave him in Elk, could I? How would you feel if you called some friend of yours for help and the friend said no?"

"What about Roy, Shane?" she asked. "You could have phoned him at the factory, and he would have gone for Darren."

"But it was an emergency, Susan."

"The only emergency was that you didn't think."

The next day she was more forgiving, taking into account his unblemished record, and also the fact that he had been (at least to some extent) a victim of fate. She also agreed that Grady could stay in the cabin for a few days, provided that he let his parents know where he was. This Grady did. "Hello, Dad?" he said to his father, while Shane listened in. "It's me, Darren, your son. Remember about the seminary? Well, you were right. It didn't work out."

In the cabin, Shane and Grady lay on their beds in the dark and had long philosophical discussions. Grady said that when he got home he was going to forget about religion and enroll in a junior college to study biology, so he'd have a grasp of how the universe was put together. "Science today," he said, "it has the answer to all the mysteries." Shane confessed that he was dreading his senior year in high school; he would be an entirely different person when he returned to that bleak, airless building, yet nobody would acknowledge it. "The system hates what's real," he said.

248

On more than one occasion, they talked about how strange it is that sometimes when you do everything right, everything comes out wrong. Grady had examples. "I gave my sister this kitten for her birthday," he said, "and she was allergic to it." Or, "Once when I was small, I washed my mom's car to surprise her, but I used steel wool and scratched up the paint."

Shane had other questions. "If it was me stranded in Elk," he asked, "would you have come and got me?"

"You know it," Grady said, with emotion crowding his throat.

Both of them took a solemn vow never to touch dope again, ever, in any form, no matter how tempted they might be.

Grady ended up staying for better than two weeks. Several important things happened while he was around.

First, Shane passed his rescheduled driver's test and celebrated by pinstriping the Chrysler and painting flames on both its doors. Then he asked Emma King to go to the drive-in with him. They went to a kung-fu double feature on a Friday night. She sat so far away from him that it seemed a deliberate attempt to deny his existence. He thought that maybe older women expected men to be bold, so after a while he walked his fingers across the seat and brushed them against Emma's thigh. She sneezed. He withdrew. Later, on the steps of her house, much to his surprise, she kissed him full on the lips and told him he was sweet. He knew it was the only kiss he'd ever get from her, so, driving home, he made a mental inventory of the moment and its various tactile sensations.

Next, on a Saturday afternoon, he and Grady took the Chrysler to the main beach, but it was crowded with townies throwing Frisbees to their dogs, and Shane suggested that they go instead to this great isolated spot even he had never been to before—Bentley's twenty undeveloped acres. They had to slide under a barbed-wire fence that had NO TRESPASSING and PRIVATE PROPERTY signs plastered all over it. The trail down into the gully was steep and overgrown; the gully, in fact, was more like a canyon, with a stream trickling through it, and vegetation sprouting from the soil. The vegetation was so thick and matted that it was almost impossible for them to distinguish individual plants, but one of the plants they *could* distinguish was marijuana. A few

stalky specimens were growing wild, like weeds. All Shane's suspi-
cions were confirmed—Bentley *was* a grower.

"That's why he had the attorney," he whispered to Grady.

"Are you going to say anything?"

"Uh-uh. No way."

But Shane's conscience bothered him. In the eyes of the law,
Bentley was a criminal. Did this put Susan in jeopardy, too?
Would she be considered an accessory to the crime? So Shane
spilled the beans to Bentley. He told him about the find and waited
for Bentley to react.

"Well, you got me, all right," Bentley said sheepishly. "I did
grow me a few crops of Colombian down there a while back, before
I met your mother, but the whole experience rubbed me wrong. I
had a couple of brushes with John Law, and they made me real
nervous. That's why I took my profits and went into ducks. Ducks
are as legal as it gets."

"What about the plants we saw?"

"Must be volunteers. That happens sometimes. Stuff grows
from old seeds, leftover seeds. We'll go pull 'em up."

They pulled up all the marijuana plants in the gully, arranged
them in a pyre, and burned them. "It's sad," said Bentley, leaning
on a pitchfork and wiping his brow. "But it has to be."

Next, Susan went into the hospital for her operation. The
surgery was performed in the afternoon, and Shane was allowed to
visit that evening. He was scared. Susan was in a private room. She
was still groggy from her anesthesia, and she had an I.V. tube in
her arm. He thought she was asleep, but she called to him in a
funny, childlike voice and asked him to sit in a chair by the bed.
"I'm in the clouds," she said, rubbing his hand.

"But are you okay?"

"I'm fine," she said. "The doctor fixed everything. He says I
can probably have a baby now."

"A *baby?*"

"You think I'm too old, don't you?"

"I don't know. How am I supposed to know about babies?"

"Lots of women have babies at my age," Susan said, rubbing
and rubbing. "Roy and I want to try. Oh, Shane honey, I made

things so tough on you, I want another chance. Don't I deserve another chance?"

"Sure," said Shane. "Of course you do."

But the potential baby confused him, and also depressed him a bit. In his mind, it was rotten-toothed, bearded, and smelling of tobacco. He wondered why Susan would want to introduce such a creature into the world. "I'm never going to understand anything," he complained to Grady that night. "Not anything."

"What's there to understand?" Grady asked.

"Maybe you are wise, Grady," said Shane.

Grady left at the end of the week. Shane dropped him at the Greyhound stop in Mendocino. They shook hands in a special way they'd devised, with plenty of interlocked fingers and thumbs.

"I never had a friend like you before," Grady said. "I'll never forget what you did for me."

"I'd do it again," said Shane. "Any time."

In late August there was an unseasonal thunderstorm. It rattled windowpanes and made chickens flap in their coops. When it was over, the morning sky was clear and absolutely free of fog. Shane got up early and changed the oil in the Chrysler. He packed the trunk with his belongings and put a pair of ducks for the Harrises on the back seat. Susan was not fully recovered from her surgery, so he had to say goodbye to her in her bedroom, where she was propped up against pillows. She asked him again if he didn't want to transfer to a school in Mendocino and stay on with them, but he told her that he missed his grandparents and his friends. "I might come back next summer," he said, kissing her on the cheek. "You'll probably have the baby by then." Bentley stuck fifty dollars in the pocket of his jeans. "You ain't such a bad apple, after all," said Bentley with a smile. Shane drove off quickly, without looking back. The highway was still slick and wet from the rain, and the scent of eucalyptus was in the air.

Joyce Carol Oates

BOY AND GIRL

The boy was loose and gangling and looked about fifteen instead of eighteen; it was embarrassing that his father was so handsome. The girl was slight and had the frail powdery look of a moth, a colorless fluttering insect of some sort. It was embarrassing that her mother was so solid and horsey; in fact the girl, Doris, called her mother "the horse" behind her back with a kind of smirking, satisfied affection. The boy, Alexander Jr., spoke of his father as "my father" and to his father's face he said, "Father. . . ."

They kept meeting all their lives, in and around Lakeshore Point. He went to a boys' school and she to a girls' school and their friends overlapped, though neither of them really had "friends"; they had new and old acquaintances. It was an achievement that they had both lived for so long in Lakeshore Point, because it was a suburb people moved in and out of constantly; it was a surprise, in April, how all the "For Sale" signs went up before houses, in time for a quick deft selling in a day or two, a few weeks of arrangements, and the move to the next city and the next suburb as soon as school ended. So, in the midst of all this coming and going, the loading and unloading of great Allied Vans that proudly conquered the continent, sooner or later Doris and Alex would have fixed upon each other, at least for a while. As Doris grew older—she was now sixteen—it occurred to her that the atmosphere of a typical school dance was the atmosphere of life itself. Partners went out to dance, the music changed, partners came back, switched around, danced again, and the gymnasium would be filled beneath its fluttering strips of crepe paper with the shuffling of legs and feet and the movements of arms: so many bodies. It was like this in Lakeshore Point itself, with strangers always moving in and strangers moving out.

They were different types: Doris was popular and had a nervous irritating laugh, the laugh of girls in crowds who are sure of being overheard. Alex was faintly stereotyped, liking chess and astronomy and complicated crossword puzzles his mother could not understand. Prepared for Harvard, he had been deeply wounded in his senior year at Lakepoint Boys' Academy when his application at Harvard had been rejected. He had the usual extraordinary grades, and his hobbies—chess and astronomy and, at an adviser's suggestion, ice hockey—had seemed good enough. It was a mystery, his rejection. So he would be going to the University of Michigan in the fall, and he walked about with his stoop more pronounced than usual, muttering in reply to greetings, casting away imagined slurs with a nervous wave of his hand. When the other boys bothered to think about him, they thought he was rather queer. Everyone had an opinion of Doris Moss, even at distant high schools, but Alex wasn't up on any recent news; he and Doris had gone to the same orthodontist several years before and he remembered her as a slight, shy child, perpetually twelve.

Alex had decided firmly to become a doctor and to go into medical research, and somehow his rejection from Harvard was not believable. He carried this rejection about with him everywhere, anxious to drag it out and admit it, humble, questioning, nervous

253

in the hope that it had all been a mistake and he was accepted after all. He was the kind of boy adults believed they could talk to, until they talked to him. His parents' friends approached him with stiff, helpful smiles.

He had decided to go into medical research because his father, a doctor, was in a kind of medical research himself. One evening when his parents were having a dinner party Alex had heard something that impressed him strangely and changed his life. He had come in from a movie—he always went alone—and used the downstairs guest bathroom, in the back of the house. There was something about this bathroom he liked. It was done in black and gold, with decanters of scented soap and lovely scented tissue and toilet paper, also gold, and small exquisite guest towels that were white linen with gold embroidering. On the dressing table was a delicate mirror, balanced for the fine-lashed eyes of his parents' lady guests; underfoot was a black, black rug. Alex liked to use this bathroom because he felt very special in it. He felt like one of his parents' guests. Before parties he cautiously checked this bathroom, by himself, since the maid was always harassed and could not be trusted to see whether the soap was clean or not. The special soap in this bathroom was ball-shaped, gold and white, and it gave off a lovely sweet scent. But sometimes the soap balls grew dusty because they were never used.

This feeling for the bathroom was important, because it might have had to do with Alex's decision. He was in there when he heard his father and another man come into the kitchen, and his father's grave words were somehow mixed in with the scent of the toilet paper and the soap. His father was saying, "It's a hell of a complex operation. You don't have a neat laboratory situation, of course. You must consider the environmental factors—the humidity, the wind, the area, the particle size, the amount of saturation, the method of ejaculation. You can imagine the variability there." The other man, unknown to Alex, said something about computers. "Yes, computers are certainly helpful," Alex's father said in his kind, serious voice, "but beyond a certain point only the existential fact is real. Nothing else is real. An event happens only once and that's the difficult thing about life—it isn't a laboratory experiment."

Alex was strangely agitated. He admired his father and feared him a little and it seemed that each of his father's words was valuable. His father worked for the government now on classified projects and it was sometimes necessary for him to be gone for weeks at a time. Perhaps these long trips or the isolation of the laboratory had made Alexa's father rather remote about most things, as if holding them out at arm's length; so it was intimate, hearing his father talk like this. Above the clinking of ice cubes his father said, "The biological cloud agent is a totally new frontier. It's fascinating work. You have to think of it as disease control in reverse, breeding pathogenic organisms that we've usually thought of in rather negative terms. And then, apart from the physical reality, there is a totally unexplored area of psychological reaction—what the bonus effect in terms of enemy panic might be, we don't know. We have some ideas, that's all."

Alex remained in the bathroom after they left. He kept hearing his father talk about "reality." His father's other words rose and circled in Alex's brain, and he could not quite understand them, but again and again the word "reality" returned to him. What was real? What was real? "Beyond a certain point only the existential fact is real," his father had said solemnly, and Alex tried to understand that concept. It was strange that he could be so quick at school and so slow, even dense, around the house. It was as if his father gave off a kind of glimmering cloud that fogged up Alex's glasses and also fogged up his brain.

Inspired, he wrote a theme for his English teacher, Mr. Godwin, called "Precisely What Is Real?" Mr. Godwin was very pleased with it and read it to the class, embarrassing Alex immensely. Mr. Godwin, though not so tall and handsome as Alex's father, was a minor, substantial hero in Alex's life. He was a raspy, enthusiastic man with nicotine-stained fingers.

Though Doris was younger, she was more experienced than Alex. For years she had been a child and she recalled those years with a kind of disbelief. Then, one summer, she had stayed with a girl friend at Cape Cod and met a boy who was supposed to be a television actor, or had hopes of being one. He told her about the television business and the people who ran it that you never saw and had no idea existed; they were the people who really counted,

255

he said. He had a narrow, darkly handsome face and might have been fifteen or twenty-three. There was something indeterminate about him, as if he were waiting to be instructed about himself. "The people that run things are off to the side. Hidden. You don't see them, you stupid guys at home," he said with a sneer. When they were together on the beach it was like a television scene. He was always close to her, with the head-on, slightly myopic look of actors on television; he seemed also to be saying words he had used before. Doris had a fragile, freckled look and a rather thin body. He had forced her to take an icy cold shower with him on the first night they met, and since then her body felt faintly unreal, tingling and numb at the same time. Her body held this sensation for some time. She could not get over it, her mind wanted to break free but couldn't, her body retained this daze—it was nothing she could explain. She didn't talk about it. What she remembered about the boy was his face and body and hands and especially his words, which were strange. "On television there's all these people running around you never see, and cameras and stuff. You stupid bastards at home don't know anything. You don't know how things really are and even the people on television, that work for it, they don't know either. It's too big."

Though what he did to her was no different from what other boys were to do to her when she returned to Lakeshore Point, she could not get over his words. There was something forlorn and angry in them, something violent. She kept hearing the violence in them, replaying the words in her head, and her body had that vague, suspended feeling about it, numb and excited at the same time.

Doris' mother insisted upon a Saturday-morning ritual of shopping. Doris shrank from anyone seeing her with her mother, and her small, closed, sleek face and her rather pigeon-toed, arrogant step quite clearly distinguished her from her mother. Her mother had a long, kindly face; it was unfortunate that her two front teeth were prominent. Doris' parents were both rather homely and sturdy; Doris was lithe and quite a surprise. While her mother chattered about nonsense in the stores, Doris dreamed of what he would be doing that evening on her date, and about whether she gave a damn if the boy called her again.

Alex's mother knew Doris' mother slightly. Both belonged to the Village Women's Club. Doris' mother had inherited quite a lot of money and seemed to apologize for it with her big, toothy, hesitant smile; Alex's mother, coming from a less wealthy background, was therefore sharper and knew whom to befriend and whom to slight; she always avoided Doris' mother. Sometimes she saw the mother and daughter out shopping on Saturday—the mother galloping along enthusiastically in short, squat, thick-heeled shoes, and the girl dressed like a little slut in a short skirt. At such times Alex's mother called out, "Why, hello, Edith!" and breezed on by.

Yes, she thought with an involuntary satisfaction, that girl what's-her-name did look like a slut.

She had her own problems with Alex. Though he was eighteen, his skin was still awful; it was a pity to look at him. Every Saturday she packed him in the car and drove him all the way into the city— and she hated the city—to a really superb dermatologist who played squash with her husband at the Athletic Club and who administered to poor Alex X-ray treatments, dried-ice treatments, a variety of pills and hormones, and numerous salves. Poor Alex had to wash his face with a white sponge and work the lather up and then rinse it away, using only lukewarm water. No hot water. Acne was caused by overexcitation of the oil glands, his mother had learned to her distaste, and so he must not make things worse. She thought the word acne was at least as ugly as the problem itself. It always startled her to see her own son—such a tall, gangling boy!—come out of the doctor's inner office and into the waiting room, with that apologetic stoop to his shoulders, that half-chagrined, half-challenging smirk, and that terrible bluish-violet acne all over his face—It fascinated her in a way. It was lumpy and flaky at once. Some pimples were very hard, like berries; others were ripe and soft and draining. Sometimes it was all she could do to keep her hands off his face, but no, no, one never squeezes these problems away; nothing so violent. After a good lathering and a good tepid rinsing, Alex applied a special ointment to his poor bumpy face, and it was also a shock to come upon him late in the evening—that tall, thin boy in his pajamas looking for food downstairs, his face covered with a ghostly white film of medicine that flaked off as he walked.

257

Poor Alex.

In the spring of his senior year in high school, something began to happen to him. He lost his appetite. He walked about mumbling to himself, arguing over something. His father was in Washington for most of April. His mother had a number of teas and luncheons; Alex felt vaguely protective, knowing that his mother dreaded to be alone and that loneliness was increased by this constant round of parties, and yet he was uneasy with such knowledge and did not know what to do with it. Should he have such an understanding of his own mother? Was it proper? Though he was forbidden by Dr. Lurch to eat chocolates, he ate them secretly, like a twelve-year-old. When his father called, every evening at eight, he made sure he was not around, though he would have liked nothing better than to talk to him. He felt dizzily as if he were becoming a child again. . . .

His mother began to plead with him. Wasn't he an intelligent boy, at the head of his class? Then what was wrong? Why was he so argumentative? Why did he so hate to change his clothes? His underwear? Ah, his mother pleaded with him! Alex knew that he was becoming strange but he did not understand it. He felt a peculiar resistance to taking showers or baths and he disliked brushing his teeth because . . . because in this way wasn't he stirring up germs . . . ? But he did not want to think about it.

"What will your father say about this?" his mother cried.

She was a pretty, dismayed woman. Every day she rose at seven-thirty and showered and put on excellent clothes, all the required paraphernalia of a woman, including high-heeled shoes; every day she went out at about noon or twelve-thirty to have luncheon somewhere or to play bridge or to do something, Alex wasn't sure what—she was tremendously and wonderfully busy. On the other days her friends visited her and she served luncheon— chicken or shrimp or crab in some kind of cream dish, usually, with a delicate icy fruit dessert—and Alex loved the very odor of such days, the rich promise of his mother's happy life. He did not want to disturb her. It would be a disgrace for any son to disturb so happy and busy a woman, and yet . . . he felt that there was indeed something wrong with him, some dissociation from his body, a fear and a distrust of his own skin.

For Mr. Godwin he wrote an unassigned essay called "The Limits of Reality." It was long, rambling, and feverish. He wrote it late at night and was quite proud of certain sentences: "The nature of disease may well be the ultimate reality, and the method of survival in adjustment. Isolation and adaptation. Living with disease. Nothing can be repeated. History comes and goes. There is nothing but the Existential Fact. My skin is a dense, swarming sea of maggots invisible to the eye. . . ."

He handed the essay in with great excitement on a Friday morning, and that evening he went to a party against his wishes, at his mother's wishes. She was concerned about his "social life." It was a party for high school kids at the big Payne house, and he was probably invited only because his mother played bridge with Mrs. Payne, no other reason. He spent most of his time eating, scooping up dip with his finger. He ate a lot of shrimp. In the recreation room—which was long, with a low, stucco ceiling and a great fireplace at one end, without a fire—couples were dancing in the darkness. Alex half-knew everyone there and disdained them. Betty Payne had been rude to him, which meant she had been forced to invite him. So he stayed by himself and his face was fixed with a knowing, philosophical smirk as he ate shrimp.

There was a commotion in the recreation room. One girl, dressed in white, stamped on the floor and threw herself about in what was either a new dance or a tantrum. She thrashed her body, flung her arms around violently, let her long hair fly out about her face—from the way others were watching her, Alex decided it must be a tantrum. The girl had a thin, delicate body and her legs were quite thin; it was Doris Moss. She was associated with a crowd Alex had been aware of for years, without taking any real interest, having heard of their perpetual adventures and daring every Monday throughout high school. He had heard a number of things about them but did not exactly believe everything he heard. The girl Doris continued stamping the floor in her shiny white low-heeled shoes, exactly like a child, and a boy shouted something in her face.

She whirled around and stalked out of the room and came right to Alex. "Hi, Alex, how are you," she said in a taunting voice. "Let's go for a ride and get out of here. Do you have a car?"

"I walked over."

"I've got a car. Come on."

Her face was wet with perspiration and strands of hair stuck to it. A few kids were watching her, but Alex ignored them. "Come on, come on," she said in a husky, flirtatious voice, tugging at Alex's hands. "Let's get out of this place before I suffocate."

He followed along with her, both surprised and pleased. She kept touching him with her small, darting, nervous hands and he wondered if perhaps a new self might rise out of him, a new Alex, popular and assured. But she said as they left the house, "Why don't you have a girl friend?" This hurt him a little and he did not reply. "Are you queer?" she said with a happy stamp of her foot. She leaned around and laughed up into his face. "There's my car. It's boxed in," she said, pulling at him. "No, don't look in that car, leave them alone! You really are queer, aren't you?"

They got into her car and she managed to get out by driving over the lawn. She had to back up and drive forward a few times, impatiently turning the wheel, and she finally managed to get out. Alex watched the doorway of the house for someone to appear and shout at them, but no one came.

"Why don't you have a car? Why don't you have a girl friend?"

"I don't know. Don't want them."

Her brisk, brassy manner was good because it expected nothing of him. She talked so fast and so loudly that she hardly listened to him. "No, really, tell the truth for once," she said, poking him in the ribs, "is it some religious thing or something? The way you act?"

He had been drinking at the party, but it had not released a freer, bolder Alex. Instead he felt hot and nervous. As Doris drove along the boulevard, she kept laughing in a strange, mocking way. "Alexander Junior!" she said with a snicker. Then her mockery changed to a kind of fake sugary concern. "Your father's kind of cute though. I like your father. Why didn't your father come to this lousy party tonight?"

She drove carelessly and kept jabbing at him and teasing him, and Alex wondered if this was the usual way for girls to behave with boys; he didn't know if he liked it or resented it. "Tell me what you're doing these days," Doris commanded. "Are the braces off your teeth? What's wrong with your skin? Tell me about your father. Tell me something, say something," she laughed. She let her head fall back and her mouth opened blankly. On her delicate ears tiny earrings glinted; Alex liked them. He was glad he had found something about her to like.

"My boyfriend pierced my ears for me. This was someone you don't know, some bastard. I don't go out with him any more. First you get it clean and then you put a piece of cotton behind the ear, you know, to protect that—you know—that vein or artery or something that's there—but anyway it bled a lot—My mother gave me these earrings for Christmas."

"They're very nice."

She reached over and seized his hand. "Do you like me, do you think I'm beautiful? What are you thinking right now?"

"I have sort of a headache. . . ."

"I've got this crazy idea, it's a great idea, there's this little kid I'm going to take for a ride. Let's take him for a ride. On Sundays people drive up and down the lake shore with kids on rides, looking at the lake, so let's go get him, all right?" There were flecks of saliva around her mouth. Alex, staring at her, felt his head begin to ache seriously and wondered how he would get out of this situation. She was driving fast and carelessly. She turned off onto a darker street and raced along it, not stopping at intersections, and after a while she braked the car to a fast stop before a ranch house. Alex sat in the car, bewildered, and she ran out.

A few minutes later she appeared at the door of the house, backing out, and then she turned and ran down the walk with something in her arms. It was a baby. "Look. This is my brother Dorsey's baby. Look at it. It's my nephew. What do you think, I'm an aunt. No, let me drive, I want to drive," she said rudely, though he had only slid over to look out at what she held. It was a baby, yes.

"What's that?"

"What's it look like?" she laughed. "I told the kid inside, she's in seventh grade at Cooley, I told her we'd be right back, we wanted to take the baby for a ride. It's sort of a nice baby. Here."

Alex did not want to hold the baby, thinking he was not good enough for it, wouldn't know how to hold it, would frighten it. But she thrust it at him and started the car again.

"But maybe we shouldn't—"

"Oh, shut up," she said. The baby began to whimper and Doris snapped on the radio. "This is a lousy car. This isn't my car. This is Fred's car, Fred Smith, do you know him? Of course you don't."

"Fred Smith?"

"You don't know him and you don't know anybody. Can't you stop that baby crying? What kind of a father are you?"

Alex rocked the baby experimentally and it did stop. He felt a kind of numbness move over him, as if he were indeed a father, and the frantic perspiring Doris who sat beside him were his wife, a mother. He stared down at the baby in awe. "Fred's this guy I have kind of a thing with, he's real wild. He's real strange, he's from Olcott. He doesn't hang around with any bunch. This is Fred's car that he lent me for tonight, I was at his place and drove it over, my mother thought I was at Toni Sargant's. There's a slumber party there tonight. She thinks I'm going there but I'm not."

"Where are you going, then?" Alex asked suspiciously.

He held the baby as if in accusation of her, rocking it gently. The girl cast a sideways glance at him. He could not figure out her wild chatter, and then he remembered suddenly talk at school about certain kids who took pills; Doris had been mentioned. He saw at once that of course she was high. She had a strange waxen look beneath the perspiration, a dummy's look. Seen in ordinary light, she would have been a girl of about sixteen with a slightly snubbed nose; in the changing, disruptive lights from the drive-in restaurants and gas stations they were passing she looked as if her skin had been painfully tightened around the blunt hollows and ridges of her face. "We'd better go back," Alex said.

"This Fred is awfully strange. He lives by himself," Doris went on. A car approaching them flicked its lights and finally blew its horn to urge her back onto her own side of the street. "I said I'd be back around twelve but I got hung up with someone, that Tommy, but he made me mad . . . and Fred will get mad, but . . . but I don't know if I'll go back to his place. . . . I don't know.

I should get his car back or he'll be mad. I took a bus over to his place but that was during the day . . . but if I go back he'll make me stay . . . he's sort of strange. . . . He's twenty-four.''

"Doris, we'd better go back. Let's take the baby back.''

He felt a little sick. Doris had driven out quite far and was in a dark, dinky suburb now, rushing along the main street. "I want to get to the country," she said angrily. "I'm so sick of all this, I could puke. We've got a cottage up north we could go to, nobody'd know. My brother Dorsey, he's a goddamn show-off, he's really my stepbrother and he's an awful lot older than I am. I don't remember him, really. That might not have been his house. I think it was. I told the babysitter my sister-in-law wanted the baby and she believed me, and I'm pretty sure it's the right baby, my nephew. His name should be Walter. . . . Isn't that a stupid name for a baby?" she said angrily.

The baby began to cry again, as if startled by her remark. Alex stared helplessly down at it and felt, once again, a magical sensation of being its father: the two of them besieged by the cruel, crazy words of its mother. He wondered suddenly if there might not be some danger of their infecting the baby. His hands were very large, holding it; his skin looked dangerous and flaky in the mottled light.

"I know what, let's play a trick on Dorsey. Let's fix him," Doris whispered.

"What?''

"Let's kill it.''

"What?''

"The baby here," Doris said. "Isn't that a wild idea? Huh? What do you think?''

She stopped the car. She leaned over to Alex and stared down at the baby's face; Alex leaned away from her. "We could let it drop out of the car by accident. We could say it got out by itself. Some other car would hit it, not us. We could watch. . . . We could stuff that blanket in its mouth, what do you think, isn't that wild? What do you think?''

Alex's head was pounding violently. "You're crazy," he said.

"Who's crazy?''

"You, you're crazy. Why do you want to do a thing like that?''

Doris laughed and laughed at him. Oh, he was absurdly intelli-

263

gent; he'd never get over it any more than he'd get over his acne. Doris lay back against the seat laughing until she began to sob angrily. Alex stared at her. "You want me to drive back?" he said cautiously.

"Stupid bastard like you don't know how to drive," she muttered.

She said nothing more. Her stare was fixed upon something before her, on the dashboard, maybe. Or on nothing. Her mouth opened upon rapid, jagged gasps. Once in a while she giggled convulsively and Alex waited, frightened, but she did not speak. He said shyly, "I'll drive back," and Doris made no resistance when he squeezed over her and got behind the wheel.

He drove back to the Payne's house and parked in the circle driveway and walked home by himself, terribly frightened. His fear was a kind of intoxication, and he could not think straight. Later he was to hear that the police had been called, that the baby did belong to Doris' brother, and that Doris had been found unconscious in the car; the baby was crying on the seat beside her.

And who was to know that Alex had been involved?

He told no one about it, no one. His father returned from Washington and had a talk with him. He was a serious, handsome, busy man and it was a serious matter that he take time to talk so lengthily with Alex. He talked about being normal. "Do you think it's normal," he said, "to hoard your dirty clothes? Not to change your socks, to wear them in bed?"

"I'm not bothering anybody," Alex muttered.

"Your mother says this is getting worse. It's getting worse. And what about this essay you wrote?"

Mr. Godwin had called Alex's father about the essay. It was no surprise; Alex should have known better than to write such a thing. *What is reality? Reality is germs and microbes and infectious scum. . . .*

As he listened to his father read these strange, angry words, he was torn between a knowledge of their insanity and a hope, a terrible hope, that his father would glance up at him with respect. But his father held the paper at some distance, reading, his mouth working the peculiar words as if they themselves were infectious. Finally he said, "Do you think this is the work of a *normal mind?*"

Alex broke down at that point. He confessed to his father about the terrible odor of his skin, the infection of his skin, the sensation of crawling and gnawing and fluttering. . . . Oh, it was terrible, it was terrible, and his voice rose to hysteria; he began to claw himself. "It's all over me, I tried to keep it secret but it got worse. I don't want it to fly off or anything . . . the X-ray treatments help, it isn't on my face . . . it needs to be burned off, not stirred up, that's the danger if I fool around, I don't want it to get stirred up and go off on other people. . . ."

"What's wrong with you? What are you talking about?" his father demanded. His father showed no fear; he was calm and logical, and Alex tried to imitate him, though his skin became cancerous with germs as he spoke; so active, so restless! His very skin crept upon his bones and his scalp moved of its own accord. "I think it could be treated but I don't want to miss school," he said sorrowfully. "I know something's wrong with me, I know it isn't normal, and I'm sorry. I'm sorry. Please don't tell Mother or she'll worry about it. . . ."

So he was taken by his father to Dr. Mate, a friend of his father's from Harvard Medical School. Dr. Mate was a psychiatrist whose practice consisted entirely of disturbed adolescent boys. Alex's problem was judged not a serious one because it did not threaten violence, and it was not even an uncommon one: a neurosis induced by feelings of Oedipal aggression further stimulated by a sense of inferiority and frustration. He clawed at himself, in the opinion of Dr. Mate, because he could not claw at his father. Still his "problem" did not go away. After many sessions with this doctor, who reminded Alex of his own father, Alex was made to understand that it was his mind that was sick and not his skin. They arranged for him to spend some time in a hospital called Oakridge Manor, about twenty miles from home, and he was cautioned not to tell the other patients his secret about his skin being infected and seething with germs. Oakridge Manor cost sixty dollars a day but was worth it, everyone said. After a while Alex's father transferred him to another private hospital, Foxridge Manor. He was allowed to come home on weekends. He liked these visits home but he was unable to relax; he carried himself about cautiously and stiffly through the familiar rooms, his own former

265

room, the lovely guest bathroom downstairs, and when he spoke, it was in a cautious, stiff voice. His mother talked to him about the way the living room was going to look when it was painted and the drapes changed.

"But why are you sitting like that? You can let your arms rest on the table, please, Alex, don't sit there like that—you know you're perfectly all right, please," his mother said.

"Yes, I know. That's right," Alex said.

"Then why are you sitting like that? You look so strange."

"I'm sorry. I know there's nothing wrong with me."

She rushed on to talk about the painters' union and the terrible fight a friend of hers had had with a painter. First he had painted her friend's dining-room walls white, and then apparently he had leaned on them with his dirty hands—and so the walls were blotched and smudged—and what did he think? What did Alex think happened next?

Alex said vaguely, "Out at the hospital the other day there was a girl I thought I knew. She was sitting in the reading room. She was leafing through magazines very fast. There were little scabs on her fingers, it looked like, as if she bit her fingernails, but . . . but maybe there weren't scabs, I didn't get that close. . . . I thought it might be Doris Moss."

"Was it?"

"I don't know."

His mother said slowly, avoiding his eyes, "Well, it was awfully sad about Doris. Of course I don't know anything about it. But some boy beat her up. Some man. He beat her up very badly a few weeks ago in some awful place downtown. It was such a shock."

"Then what happened?"

"To her, you mean? I don't know." She was staring at Alex with her blank, flattened-out look, a pretty, dismayed mother who had seen too much and thought about too much, who had been destined for a life of luncheons and dinners and the fulfillment of a good marriage and the enjoyment of a successful son . . . and instead, this had happened. She stared at him.

"She didn't die or anything?" Alex said.

"I don't think so, no, she didn't die. I don't know what happened to her," his mother said. The telephone began ringing in the next room. "That's the contractor with the estimate," she said apologetically and with a rush of mild enthusiasm; after a decent moment she rose and went to answer it and Alex heard her in the next room talking about the living-room walls. They were to be painted either white or oyster. That was the conclusion of their talk about Doris Moss, and the subject never came up again.

Alice Walker

▼

A SUDDEN TRIP HOME
IN THE SPRING

▼

For the Wellesley Class

1

Sarah walked slowly off the tennis court, fingering the back of her head, feeling the sturdy dark hair that grew there. She was popular. As she walked along the path toward Talfinger Hall, her friends fell into place around her. They formed a warm, jostling group of six. Sarah, because she was taller than the rest, saw the messenger first.

"Miss Davis," he said, standing still until the group came abreast of him, "I've got a telegram for ye." Brian was Irish and always quite respectful. He stood with his cap in his hand until Sarah took the telegram. Then he gave a nod that included all the young ladies before he turned away. He was young and good-looking, though annoyingly servile, and Sarah's friends twittered.

"Well, open it!" someone cried, for Sarah stood staring at the yellow envelope, turning it over and over in her hand.

"Look at her," said one of the girls, "isn't she beautiful! Such eyes, and hair, and *skin!*"

Sarah's tall, caplike hair framed a face of soft brown angles, high cheekbones, and large, dark eyes. Her eyes enchanted her friends because they always seemed to know more, and to find more of life amusing, or sad, than Sarah cared to tell.

Her friends often teased Sarah about her beauty; they loved dragging her out of her room so that their boy friends, naïve and worldly young men from Princeton and Yale, could see her. They never guessed she found this distasteful. She was gentle with her friends, and her outrage at their tactlessness did not show. She was most often inclined to pity them, though embarrassment sometimes drove her to fraudulent expressions. Now she smiled and raised eyes and arms to heaven. She acknowledged their unearned curiosity as a mother endures the prying impatience of a child. Her friends beamed love and envy upon her as she tore open the telegram.

"He's dead," she said.

Her friends reached out for the telegram, their eyes on Sarah.

"It's her father," one of them said softly. "He died yesterday. Oh, Sarah," the girl whimpered, "I'm so sorry!"

"Me too." "So am I." "Is there anything we can do?"

But Sarah had walked away, head high and neck stiff.

"So graceful!" one of her friends said.

"Like a proud gazelle," said another. Then they all trooped to their dormitories to change for supper.

Talfinger Hall was a pleasant dorm. The common room just off the entrance had been made into a small modern-art gallery with some very good original paintings, lithographs, and collages. Pieces were constantly being stolen. Some of the girls could not resist an honest-to-God Chagall, signed (in the plate) by his own hand, though they could have afforded to purchase one from the

269

gallery in town. Sarah Davis's room was next door to the gallery, but her walls were covered with inexpensive Gauguin reproductions, a Rubens ("The Head of a Negro"), a Modigliani, and a Picasso. There was a full wall of her own drawings, all of black women. She found black men impossible to draw or to paint; she could not bear to trace defeat onto blank pages. Her women figures were matronly, massive of arm, with a weary victory showing in their eyes. Surrounded by Sarah's drawings was a red SNCC poster of an old man holding a small girl whose face nestled in his shoulder. Sarah often felt she was the little girl whose face no one could see.

To leave Talfinger even for a few days filled Sarah with fear. Talfinger was her home now; it suited her better than any home she'd ever known. Perhaps she loved it because in winter there was a fragrant fireplace and snow outside her window. When hadn't she dreamed of fireplaces that really warmed, snow that almost pleasantly froze? Georgia seemed far away as she packed; she did not want to leave New York, where, her grandfather had liked to say, "the devil hangs out and catches young gals by the front of their dresses." He had always believed the South the best place to live on earth (never mind that certain people invariably marred the landscape), and swore he expected to die no more than a few miles from where he had been born. There was tenacity even in the gray frame house he lived in, and in scrawny animals on his farm who regularly reproduced. He was the first person Sarah wanted to see when she got home.

There was a knock on the door of the adjoining bathroom, and Sarah's suite mate entered, a loud Bach Concerto just finishing behind her. At first she stuck just her head into the room, but seeing Sarah fully dressed she trudged in and plopped down on the bed. She was a heavy blond girl with large, milk-white legs. Her eyes were small and her neck usually gray with grime.

"My, don't you look gorgeous," she said.

"Ah, Pam," said Sarah, waving her hand in disgust. In Georgia she knew that even to Pam she would be just another ordinarily attractive *colored* girl. In Georgia there were a million girls better looking. Pam wouldn't know that, of course, she'd never been to Georgia; she'd never even seen a black person to speak to—that is, before she met Sarah. One of her first poetic observations about Sarah was that she was "a poppy in a field of winter roses." She had found it weird that Sarah did not own more than one coat.

"Say, listen, Sarah," said Pam, "I heard about your father. I'm sorry. I really am."

"Thanks," said Sarah.

"Is there anything we can do? I thought, well, maybe you'd want my father to get somebody to fly you down. He'd go himself but he's taking mother to Madeira this week. You wouldn't have to worry about trains and things."

Pamela's father was one of the richest men in the world, though no one ever mentioned it. Pam only alluded to it at times of crisis, when a friend might benefit from the use of a private plane, train, or ship; or, if someone wanted to study the characteristics of a totally secluded village, island, or mountain, she might offer one of theirs. Sarah could not comprehend such wealth, and was always annoyed because Pam didn't look more like a billionaire's daughter. A billionaire's daughter, Sarah thought, should really be less horsy and brush her teeth more often.

"Gonna tell me what you're brooding about?" asked Pam.

Sarah stood in front of the radiator, her fingers resting on the window seat. Down below, girls were coming up the hill from supper.

"I'm thinking," she said, "of the child's duty to his parents after they are dead."

"Is that all?"

"Do you know," asked Sarah, "about Richard Wright and his father?"

Pamela frowned. Sarah looked down at her.

"Oh, I forgot," she said with a sigh, "they don't teach Wright here. The poshest school in the U.S. and the girls come out ignorant." She looked at her watch, saw she had twenty minutes before her train. "Really," she said almost inaudibly, "why Tears Eliot, Ezratic Pound, and even Sara Teacake, and no Wright?" She and Pamela thought e. e. cummings very clever with his perceptive spelling of great literary names.

"Is he a poet, then?" asked Pam. She adored poetry, all poetry. Half of America's poetry she had, of course, not read, for the simple reason that she had never heard of it.

"No," said Sarah, "he wasn't a poet." She felt weary. "He was a man who wrote, a man who had trouble with his father." She began to walk about the room, and came to stand below the picture of the old man and the little girl.

"When he was a child," she continued, "his father ran off with another woman, and one day when Richard and his mother went to ask him for money to buy food, he laughingly rejected them. Richard, being very young, thought his father Godlike—big, omnipotent, unpredictable, undependable, and cruel; entirely in control of his universe; just like God. But, many years later, after Wright had become a famous writer, he went down to Mississippi to visit his father. He found, instead of God, just an old, watery-eyed field hand, bent from plowing, his teeth gone, smelling of manure. Richard realized that the most daring thing his 'God' had done was run off with that other woman."

"So?" asked Pam. "What 'duty' did he feel he owed the old man?"

"So," said Sarah, "that's what Wright wondered as he peered into that old, shifty-eyed Mississippi Negro face. What was the duty of the son of a destroyed man? The son of a man whose vision had stopped at the edge of fields that weren't even his. Who was Wright without his father? Was he Wright the great writer? Wright the Communist? Wright the French farmer? Wright whose wife could never accompany him to Mississippi? Was he, in fact, still his father's son? Or was he freed by his father's desertion to be nobody's son, to be his own father? Could he disavow his father and live? And if so, live as what? As whom? And for what purpose?"

"Well," said Pam, swinging her hair over her shoulders and squinting her small eyes, "if his father rejected him I don't see why Wright even bothered to go see him again. From what you've said, Wright earned the freedom to be whoever he wanted to be. To a strong man a father is not essential."

"Maybe not," said Sarah, "but Wright's father was one faulty door in a house of many ancient rooms. Was that one faulty door to shut him off forever from the rest of the house? That was the question. And though he answered this question eloquently in his work, where it really counted, one can only wonder if he was able to answer it satisfactorily—or at all—in his life."

"You're thinking of his father more as a symbol of something, aren't you?" asked Pam.

"I suppose," said Sarah, taking a last look around her room. "I see him as a door that refused to open, a hand that was always closed. A fist."

Pamela walked with her to one of the college limousines, and in a few minutes she was at the station. The train to the city was just arriving.

"Have a nice trip," said the middle-aged driver courteously as she took her suitcase from him. But, for about the thousandth time since she'd seen him, he winked at her.

Once away from her friends, she did not miss them. The school was all they had in common. How could they ever know her if they were not allowed to know Wright? she wondered. She was interesting, "beautiful," only because they had no idea what made her, charming only because they had no idea from where she came. And where they came from, though she glimpsed it—in themselves and in F. Scott Fitzgerald—she was never to enter. She hadn't the inclination or the proper ticket.

2

Her father's body was in Sarah's old room. The bed had been taken down to make room for the flowers and chairs and casket. Sarah looked for a long time into the face, as if to find some answer to her questions written there. It was the same face, a dark, Shakespearean head framed by gray, woolly hair and split almost in half by a short, gray mustache. It was a completely silent face, a shut face. But her father's face also looked fat, stuffed, and ready to burst. He wore a navy-blue suit, white shirt, and black tie. Sarah bent and loosened the tie. Tears started behind her shoulder blades but did not reach her eyes.

"There's a rat here under the casket," she called to her brother, who apparently did not hear her, for he did not come in.

She was alone with her father, as she had rarely been when he was alive. When he was alive she had avoided him.

"Where's that girl at?" her father would ask. "Done closed herself up in her room again," he would answer himself.

For Sarah's mother had died in her sleep one night. Just gone to bed tired and never got up. And Sarah had blamed her father.

Stare the rat down, thought Sarah; surely that will help. *Perhaps it doesn't matter whether I misunderstood or never understood.*

"We moved so much, looking for crops, a place to *live*," her father had moaned, accompanied by Sarah's stony silence. "The moving killed her. And now we have a real house, with *four* rooms, and a mailbox on the *porch*, and it's too late. She gone. *She* ain't here to see it." On very bad days her father would not eat at all. At night he did not sleep.

Whatever had made her think she knew what love was or was not?

Here she was, Sarah Davis, immersed in Camusian philosophy, versed in many languages, a poppy, of all things, among winter roses. But before she became a poppy she was a native Georgian sunflower, but still had not spoken the language they both knew. Not to him.

Stare the rat down, she thought, and did. The rascal dropped his bold eyes and slunk away. Sarah felt she had, at least, accomplished something.

Why did she have to see the picture of her mother, the one on the mantel among all the religious doodads, come to life? Her mother had stood stout against the years, clean gray braids shining across the top of her head, her eyes snapping, protective. Talking to her father.

"He called you out your name, we'll leave this place today. Not tomorrow. That be too late. Today!" Her mother was magnificent in her quick decisions.

"But what about your garden, the children, the change of schools?" Her father would be holding, most likely, the wide brim of his hat in nervously twisting fingers.

"He called you out your name, we go!"

And go they would. Who knew exactly where, before they moved? Another soundless place, walls falling down, roofing gone; another face to please without leaving too much of her father's pride at his feet. But to Sarah then, no matter with what alacrity her father moved, foot-dragging alone was visible.

The moving killed her, her father had said, but the moving was also love.

Did it matter now that often he had threatened their lives with the rage of his despair? That once he had spanked the crying baby violently, who later died of something else altogether . . . and that the next day they moved?

"No," said Sarah aloud, "I don't think it does."

"Huh?" It was her brother, tall, wiry, black, deceptively calm. As a child he'd had an irrepressible temper. As a grown man he was tensely smooth, like a river that any day will overflow its bed.

He had chosen a dull gray casket. Sarah wished for red. Was it Dylan Thomas who had said something grand about the dead offering "deep, dark defiance"? It didn't matter; there were more ways to offer defiance than with a red casket.

"I was just thinking," said Sarah, "that with us Mama and Daddy were saying NO with capital letters."

"I don't follow you," said her brother. He had always been the activist in the family. He simply directed his calm rage against any obstacle that might exist, and awaited the consequences with the same serenity he awaited his sister's answer. Not for him the philosophical confusions and poetic observations that hung his sister up.

"That's because you're a radical preacher," said Sarah, smiling up at him. "You deliver your messages in person with your own body." It excited her that her brother had at last imbued their childhood Sunday sermons with the reality of fighting for change. And saddened her that no matter how she looked at it this seemed more important than Medieval Art, Course 201.

3

"Yes, Grandma," Sarah replied. "Cresselton is for girls only, and *no*, Grandma, I am not pregnant."

Her grandmother stood clutching the broad, wooden handle of her black bag, which she held, with elbows bent, in front of her stomach. Her eyes glinted through round, wire-framed glasses. She spat into the grass outside the privy. She had insisted that Sarah accompany her to the toilet while the body was being taken into the church. She had leaned heavily on Sarah's arm, her own arm thin and the flesh like crepe.

"I guess they teach you how to really handle the world," she said. "And who knows, the Lord is everywhere. I would like a whole lot to see a great-grand. You don't specially have to be married, you know. That's why I felt free to ask." She reached into her bag and took out a Three Sixes bottle, which she proceeded to drink from, taking deep, swift swallows with her head thrown back.

"There are very few black boys near Cresselton," Sarah explained, watching the corn liquor leave the bottle in spurts and bubbles. "Besides, I'm really caught up now in my painting and sculpturing . . ." Should she mention how much she admired Giacometti's work? No, she decided. Even if her grandmother had heard of him, and Sarah was positive she had not, she would surely think his statues much too thin. This made Sarah smile and remember how difficult it had been to convince her grandmother that even if Cresselton had not given her a scholarship she would have managed to go there anyway. Why? Because she wanted somebody to teach her to paint and to sculpture, and Cresselton had the best teachers. Her grandmother's notion of a successful granddaughter was a married one, pregnant the first year.

"Well," said her grandmother, placing the bottle with dignity back into her purse and gazing pleadingly into Sarah's face, "I sure would 'preshate a great-grand." Seeing her granddaughter's smile, she heaved a great sigh, and, walking rather haughtily over the stones and grass, made her way to the church steps.

As they walked down the aisle, Sarah's eyes rested on the back of her grandfather's head. He was sitting on the front middle bench in front of the casket, his hair extravagantly long and white and softly kinked. When she sat down beside him, her grandmother sitting next to him on the other side, he turned toward her and gently took her hand in his. Sarah briefly leaned her cheek against his shoulder and felt like a child again.

4

They had come twenty miles from town, on a dirt road, and the hot spring sun had drawn a steady rich scent from the honeysuckle vines along the way. The church was a bare, weatherbeaten ghost of a building with hollow windows and a sagging door. Arsonists had once burned it to the ground, lighting the dry wood of the walls with the flames from the crosses they carried. The tall, spreading red-oak tree under which Sarah had played as a child still dominated the churchyard, stretching its branches widely from the roof of the church to the other side of the road.

After a short and eminently dignified service, during which Sarah and her grandfather alone did not cry, her father's casket was slid into the waiting hearse and taken the short distance to the cemetery, an overgrown wilderness whose stark white stones appeared to be the small ruins of an ancient civilization. There Sarah watched her grandfather from the corner of her eye. He did not seem to bend under the grief of burying a son. His back was straight, his eyes dry and clear. He was simply and solemnly heroic, a man who kept with pride his family's trust and his own grief. *It is strange,* Sarah thought, *that I never thought to paint him like this, simply as he stands; without anonymous, meaningless people hovering beyond his profile; his face turned proud and brownly against the light.* The defeat that had frightened her in the faces of black men was the defeat of black forever defined by white. But that defeat was nowhere on her grandfather's face. He stood like a rock, outwardly calm, the grand patriarch of the Davis family. The family alone defined him, and he was not about to let them down.

"One day I will paint you, Grandpa," she said as they turned to go. "Just as you stand here now, with just," she moved closer and touched his face with her hand, "just the right stubborn tenseness of your cheek. Just that look of Yes and No in your eyes."

"You wouldn't want to paint an old man like me," he said, looking deep into her eyes from wherever his mind had been. "If you want to make me, make me up in stone."

The completed grave was plump and red. The wreaths of flowers were arranged all on one side, so that from the road there appeared to be only a large mass of flowers. But already the wind

277

was tugging at the rose petals and the rain was making dabs of faded color all over the greenfoam frames. In a week, the displaced honeysuckle vines, the wild roses, the grapevines, the grass, would be back. Nothing would seem to have changed.

5

"What do you mean, come *home?*" Her brother seemed genuinely amused. "We're all proud of you. How many black girls are at that school? Just *you?* Well, just one more besides you, and she's from the North. That's really something!"

"I'm glad you're pleased," said Sarah.

"Pleased! Why, it's what Mama would have wanted, a good education for little Sarah; and what Dad would have wanted too, if he could have wanted anything after Mama died. You were always smart. When you were two and I was five you showed me how to eat ice cream without getting it all over me. First, you said, nip off the bottom of the cone with your teeth, and suck the ice cream down. I never knew *how* you were supposed to eat the stuff once it began to melt."

"I don't know," she said; "sometimes you can want something a whole lot, only to find out later that it wasn't what you *needed* at all."

Sarah shook her head, a frown coming between her eyes. "I sometimes spend *weeks*," she said, "trying to sketch or paint a face that is unlike every other face around me, except, vaguely, for one. Can I help but wonder if I'm in the right place?"

Her brother smiled. "You mean to tell me you spend *weeks* trying to draw one face, and you still wonder whether you're in the right place? You must be kidding!" He chucked her under the chin and laughed out loud. "You learn how to draw the face," he said, "then you learn how to paint me and how to make Grandpa up in stone. Then you can come home or go live in Paris, France. It'll be the same thing."

It was the unpreacher-like gaiety of his affection that made her cry. She leaned peacefully into her brother's arms. She wondered if Richard Wright had had a brother.

"You are my door to all the rooms," she said; "don't ever close."
And he said, "I won't," as if he understood what she meant.

6

"When will we see you again, young woman?" he asked later as he
drove her to the bus stop.

"I'll sneak up one day and surprise you," she said.

At the bus stop, in front of a tiny service station, Sarah hugged
her brother with all her strength. The white station attendant
stopped his work to leer at them, his eyes bold and careless.

"Did you ever think," said Sarah, "that we are a very old
people in a very young place?"

She watched her brother from a window on the bus; her eyes
did not leave his face until the little station was out of sight and the
big Greyhound lurched on its way toward Atlanta. She would fly
from there to New York.

7

She took the train to the campus.

"My," said one of her friends, "you look wonderful! Home
sure must agree with you!"

"Sarah was home?" someone who didn't know asked. "Oh,
great, how was it?"

Well, how was it? went an echo in Sarah's head. The noise of
the echo almost made her dizzy.

"How was it?" she asked aloud, searching for, and regaining,
her balance.

"How was it?" She watched her reflection in a pair of smiling
hazel eyes.

"It was fine," she said slowly, returning the smile, thinking of
her grandfather. "Just fine."

The girl's smile deepened. Sarah watched her swinging along
toward the back tennis courts, hair blowing in the wind.

279

Stare the rat down, thought Sarah; *and whether it disappears or
not, I am a woman in the world. I have buried my father, and shall
soon know how to make my grandpa up in stone.*

Ethan Canin

LIES

What my father said was, "You pays your dime, you takes your choice," which, if you don't understand it, boils down to him saying one thing to me: Get out. He had a right to say it, though. I had it coming and he's not a man who says excuse me and pardon me. He's a man who tells the truth. Some guys my age are kids, but I'm eighteen and getting married and that's a big difference. It's a tough thing to get squeezed from your own house, but my father's done all right because he's tough. He runs a steam press in Roxbury. When the deodorant commercials come on the set he turns the TV off. That's the way he is. There's no second chance with him. Anyway, I'll do all right. Getting out of the house is what I wanted, so it's no hair off my head. You can't get everything you want. This summer two things I wanted were to get out of the house finally and to go up to Fountain Lake with Katy, and I got both. You don't have that happen to you very often, so I'm not doing so bad.

It's summer and I'm out of High. That's a relief. Some guys don't make it through, but they're the ones I was talking about—the kids. Part of the reason I made it is that my folks pushed me. Until I was too old to believe it my mother used to tell me the lie that anybody can be what you want to. "Anybody can rise up to be President of the United States," she used to say. Somewhere along the line you find out that's not true and that you're either fixed from the start or fixed by something you do without really thinking about it. I guess I was fixed by both. My mother, though, she doesn't give up. She got up twenty minutes early to make me provolone on rye for four years solid and cried when I was handed my diploma.

After graduation is when I got the job at Able's. Able's is the movie theater—a two-hundred-fifty-seat, one-aisle house on South Huntington. *Able's, where the service is friendly and the popcorn is fresh.* The bathrooms are cold-water-only though, and Mr. Able spends Monday mornings sewing the ripped seat upholstery himself because he won't let loose a few grand to re-cover the loges, which for some reason are coming apart faster than the standard seats. I don't know why that is. I sell maybe one-third loge tickets and that clientele doesn't carry penknives to go at the fabric with. The ones who carry knives are the ones who hang out in front. They wouldn't cut anybody but they might take the sidewall off your tire. They're the ones who stopped at tenth grade, when the law says the state doesn't care anymore. They hang out in front, drinking usually, only they almost never actually come in to see the movie.

I work inside, half the time selling tickets and the other half as the projectionist. It's not a bad job. I memorize most movies. But one thing about a movie theater is that it's always dark inside, even in the lobby because of the tinted glass. (You've seen that, the way the light explodes in when someone opens the exit door.) But when you work in the ticket booth you're looking outside to where it's bright daylight, and you're looking through the metal bars, and sometimes that makes you think. On a hot afternoon when I see the

281

wives coming indoors for the matinee, I want to push their money back under the slot. I want to ask them what in the world are they doing that for, trading away the light and the space outside for a seat here.

The projectionist half of the job isn't so bad, even though most people don't even know what one is. They don't realize some clown is sitting up in the room where the projectors are and changing the reels when it's time. Actually, most of the time the guy's just smoking, which he's not supposed to do, or he has a girl in there, which is what I did sometimes with Katy. All there is to do is watch for the yellow dot that comes on in the corner of the screen when it's time to change the reel. When I see that yellow dot there's five seconds before I have to have the other projector running. It's not hard, and after you do it a while you develop a sense. You get good enough so you can walk out to the lobby, maybe have popcorn or a medium drink, then sit on the stairs for a while before you go back to the booth, perfectly timed to catch the yellow spot and get the next reel going.

Anyway, it's pretty easy. But once I was in the booth with Katy when she told me something that made me forget to change the reel. The movie stopped and the theater was dark, and then everybody starts to boo and I hear Mr. Able's voice right up next to the wall. "Get on the ball, Jack," he says, and I have the other projector on before he even has time to open the door. If he knew Katy was in there he'd have canned me. Later he tells me it's my last warning.

What Katy told me was that she loved me. Nobody ever told me they loved me before except my mother, which is obvious, and I remember it exactly because suddenly I knew how old I was and how old I was getting. After she said that, getting older wasn't what I wanted so much. It's the way you feel after you get your first job. I remember exactly what she said. She said, "I love you, Jack. I thought about it and I know what I mean. I'm in love with you."

At the time the thing to do was kiss her, which I did. I wanted to tell her that I loved her too, but I couldn't say it. I don't mind lying, but not about that. Anyway, we're up there in the booth together, and it's while we have our tongues in each other's mouths that the reel runs out.

The first time I met Katy was at the theater. She's a pretty girl, all eyes, hair that's not quite blond. It falls a certain way. It was the thing I noticed first, the way it sat there on her shoulders. But it more than just sat; it touched her shoulders like a pair of hands, went in around the collar of her shirt and touched her neck. She was three rows in front. I wasn't working at the theater yet. It was end of senior year and I was sitting in two seats and had a box of popcorn in my lap. My friend LeFranc was next to me. We both saw Katy when she came in. LeFranc lit a match. "Put me out," he said, "before we all burn." LeFranc plays trumpet. He doesn't know what to say to a girl.

During the bright parts of the movie I kept looking at her neck. She's with three other girls we don't recognize. It turns out they go to Catholic school, which is why we don't know them. Then about halfway through she gets up by herself and heads back up the aisle. LeFranc breathes out and lights another match. I smile and think about following her back to the candy counter, where I might say something, but there's always the chance that she's gone out to the ladies' room instead and then where would I be? Time is on my side, so I decide to wait. The movie is *The Right Stuff*. They're taking up the supersonic planes when this is happening. They're talking about the envelope, and I don't know what that means, and then suddenly Katy's sitting next to me. I don't know where she came from. "Can I have some popcorn?" she says.

"You can have the whole box," I answer. I don't know where this comes from either, but it's the perfect thing to say and I feel a little bit of my life happening. On the other side LeFranc is still as an Indian. I push the bucket toward Katy. Her hands are milk.

She takes a few pieces and holds them with her palm flat up. Already I'm thinking, That's something I would never do—the way she holds the little popped kernels like that. Then she chews them slowly, one by one, while I pretend to watch the movie. Things come into my head.

After the movie I talk to her a little and so we go on a few dates. In the meantime I get the theater job and in August she invites me to her sister's wedding. Her sister's marrying a guy twenty years older named Hank. It's at a big church in Saugus. By this time Katy and I've kissed maybe two hours total. She always bites a piece of Juicy Fruit in two when we're done and gives me half.

Anyway, at the wedding I walk in wearing a coat and tie and have to meet her parents. Her father's got something wrong with one of his eyes. I'm not sure which one's the bad one, and I'm worried he's thinking I'm shifty because I'm not sure which one to look at. We shake hands and he doesn't say anything. We put our hands down and he still doesn't say anything.

"I've been at work," I say. It's a line I've thought about.

"I don't know what the hell you kids want," he says then. That's exactly what he says. I look at him. I realize he's drunk or been drinking, and then in a second Katy's mother's all over him. At practically the same time she's also kissing me on the cheek and telling me I look good in my suit and pulling Katy over from where she's talking with a couple of her girlfriends.

For the ceremony we sit in the pews. I'm on the aisle, with her mother one row in front and a couple of seats over so that I can see all the pleats and hems and miniature flowers sewn into her dress. I can hear her breathing. The father, who's paid for the whole bagful, is pacing behind the nave door waiting to give away the bride. Katy's back there too, with the other maids. They're wearing these dresses that stay up without straps. The wedding starts and the maids come up the aisle finally, ahead of the bride, in those dresses that remind you all the time. Katy's at the front, and when they pass me, stepping slowly, she leans over and gives me half a piece of Juicy Fruit.

So anyway, we've already been to a wedding together and maybe thanks to that I'm not so scared of our own, which is coming up. It's going to be in November. A fall wedding. Though actually it's not going to be a wedding at all but just something done by a justice of the peace. It's better that way. I had enough the first time, seeing Katy's father pace. He had loose skin on his face and a tired look and I don't want that at our wedding.

And besides, things are changing. I'm not sure who I'd want to come to a big wedding. I'm eighteen in two months and so is Katy, and to tell the truth I'm starting to get tired of my friends. It's another phase I'm coming into, probably. My friends are Hadley and Mike and LeFranc. LeFranc is my best friend. Katy doesn't like Hadley or Mike and she thinks LeFranc is okay mostly because he was there when we met. But LeFranc plays amazing trumpet, and if there's a way for him to play at the justice-of-the-peace wedding I'm going to get him to do it. I want him to play because sometimes I think about how this bit with Katy started and how fast it's gone, and it kind of stuns me that this is what happened, that of all the ways a life can turn out this is the way mine is going to.

We didn't get up to Fountain Lake until a couple of months after her sister's wedding. It's a Sunday and I'm sitting on the red-and-black carpet of Able's lobby steps eating a medium popcorn and waiting for the reel change to come. Able himself is upstairs in the office, so I'm just sitting there, watching the sun outside through the ticket window, thinking this is the kind of day I'd rather be doing something else. The clowns out front have their shirts off. They're hanging around out there and I'm sitting in the lobby when a car honks and then honks again. I look over and I'm so surprised I think the sun's doing something to my eyes. It's Katy in a red Cadillac. It's got whitewalls and chrome and she's honking at me. I don't even know where she learned to drive. But she honks again and the guys out front start to laugh and point inside the theater. What's funny is that I know they can't see inside because of the tint, but they're pointing right at me anyway.

There's certain times in your life when you do things and then have to stick to them later, and nobody likes to do that. But this was one of them, and Katy was going to honk again if I didn't do something. My father has a saying about it being like getting caught between two rocks, but if you knew Mr. Able and you knew Katy, you'd know it wasn't really like two rocks. It was more like one rock, and then Katy sitting in a Cadillac. So I get up and set the popcorn down on the snack bar, then walk over and look through the door. I stand there maybe half a minute. All the while I'm counting off the time in my head until I've got to be back in to change the reel. I think of my father. He's worked every day of his life. I think of Mr. Able, sewing on the loge upholstery with fishing line. They're banking on me, and I know it, and I start to feel kind of bad, but outside there's Katy in a red Fleetwood. "King of the Cadillac line," I say to myself. It's a blazing afternoon, and as soon as I open the door and step outside I know I'm not coming back.

On the street the sun's thrashing around off the fenders and the white shirts, and it's like walking into a wall. But I cross the street without really knowing what I'm doing and get into the car on the driver's side. All the time I'm crossing the street I know everybody's looking, but nobody says anything. When I get into the car I slip the seat back a little.

"How'd you get this?"

"It's Hank's," she says. "It's new. Where should we go?"

I don't know what she's doing with Hank's car, but my foot's pushing up and down on the gas and the clowns out front are looking, so I have to do something and I say, "The lake, let's go up to Fountain Lake." I put it in drive and the tires squeal a second before we're gone.

The windows are up and I swear the car's so quiet I'm not sure there's an engine. I push the gas and don't hear anything but just feel the leather seats pushing up under our backs. The leather's cool and has this buttered look. The windshield is tinted at the top. After about three blocks I start thinking to myself, I'm out, and I wheel the Cadillac out Jamaicaway toward the river. I really don't know the way up to Fountain Lake. Katy doesn't either, though, so I don't ask her.

We cross over the river at BU and head up Memorial Drive, past all the college students on the lawns throwing Frisbees and plastic footballs. Over by Harvard they're pulling rowing sculls out of the water. They're all wearing their red jackets and holding big glasses of beer while they work. The grass is so green it hurts my eyes.

On the long stretch past Boylston I put down the electric window and hold my arm out so that the air picks it up like a wing when we speed up, and then, just before we get out to the highway, something clicks in my head and I know it's time to change the reel. I touch the brakes for a second. I count to five and imagine the theater going dark, then one of the wives in the audience saying something out loud, real irate. I see Mr. Able opening the door to the projection booth, the expression on his face just like one my father has. It's a certain look, half like he's hit somebody and half like somebody's hit him. But then as we come out onto Route 2 and I hit the gas hard one of my father's sayings comes to me, that it's all water over the bridge, and it's like inside my head another reel suddenly runs out. Just like that, that part of my life is gone.

By the time we're out past Lincoln I'm really not thinking anything except Wow, we're out of here. The car feels good. You get a feeling sometimes right after you do something. Katy's next to me with her real tight body and the soft way girls look, and I'm no kid anymore. I think about how nice it would be to be able to take the car whenever you want and go up to the lake. I'm thinking all this and floating the car around big wide turns, and I can see the hills now way up the road in front of us. I look over at Katy, and then at the long yellow line sliding under the front of the car, and it seems to me that I'm doing something big. All the time Katy's just sitting there. Then she says, "I can't believe it."

She's right. I'm on the way to Fountain Lake, going fast in a car, the red arrow shivering around seventy-five in the dial, a girl next to me, pretty, smelling the nice way girls do. And I turn to her and I don't know why except you get a feeling when you finally bust out, and I say, "I love you, Katy," in a certain kind of voice, my foot crushing the accelerator and the car booming along the straightaways like it's some kind of rocket.

BIOGRAPHICAL NOTES

BILL BARICH is the author of two novels, *Laughing in the Hills* and *Traveling Light*. His fiction regularly appears in *The New Yorker*. "Hard to Be Good" is the title story of Barich's first collection of short fiction, published in 1987.

TONI CADE BAMBARA, a former Rutgers University professor, lives in Atlanta. A frequent lecturer, she is the author of *The Black Woman; Tales and Short Stories for Black Folks; Gorilla, My Love;* and the highly acclaimed novel, *The Salt Eaters.*

GINA BERRIAULT has written three novels, *The Descent, Conference of Victims*, and *The Son*. Her short fiction has appeared in *Esquire, Harper's Bazaar*, and *The Paris Review*. "The

Stone Boy" is taken from her collection, *The Infinite Passion of Expectation.*

ETHAN CANIN is a recent medical-school graduate who grew up in California, where many of his stories are set. The winner of a Houghton Mifflin Literary Fellowship and the James Michener Award, he recently published a novel entitled *Blue River*. "Lies" is from his first book, *Emperor of the Air*.

MICHAEL CHABON established himself as a noteworthy writer shortly after graduation from college with the publication of his bestselling novel, *The Mysteries of Pittsburgh*. He is also the author of *A Model World*, a collection of stories. He lives in Seattle and publishes regularly in *The New Yorker*.

ERNEST J. GAINES was born on a Louisiana plantation where, as a child, he worked the fields with his family. A winner of the Wallace Stegner Creative Writing Fellowship to Stanford, he has since established himself as one of America's most respected short story writers. He has also written several novels, including *The Autobiography of Miss Jane Pittman*.

GENARO GONZALEZ, the son of migrant workers, attended school erratically as his family traveled across the country. In 1968 he earned a scholarship to what is now the University of Texas at Pan American. His highly praised novel, *Rainbow's End*, was nominated for an American Book Award in 1988. Gonzalez now teaches in the Psychology department at the University of Texas at Pan American.

GISH JEN lives in Massachusetts. The family of the main character in "What Means Switch" is the subject of her first novel, *Typical American*, and several of her short stories. She has received grants from the National Endowment for the Arts and the James Michener/Copernicus Society.

BARBARA KINGSOLVER is the author of the novel *The Bean Trees* and a contributor to many periodicals and journals, including the travel section of the *New York Times*. She grew up in eastern Kentucky and now lives in Arizona. "Rose-Johnny" is from her collection *Homeland and Other Stories*.

RICHARD McCANN is co-director of the MFA Program in Creative Writing at the American University in Washington, D.C. McCann has served as a Fulbright Senior Lecturer in American Studies in Europe and has been the recipient of several awards. His short stories have appeared in *The Atlantic, Esquire, Ploughshares,* and numerous anthologies.

CARSON McCULLERS published "Wunderkind" in *Story* magazine in 1936 when she was nineteen years old. She went on to have a career as one of the most prominent American writers of her generation. Her best-known works are *The Member of the Wedding, The Heart Is a Lonely Hunter,* and *The Ballad of the Sad Café.* McCullers died in 1967.

REGINALD McKNIGHT is a teacher at Carnegie-Mellon University in Pittsburgh. His story "The Kind of Light That Shines on Texas" won an O. Henry Award and the Kenyon Review New Fiction Prize. McKnight has published one novel, *I Get on the Bus,* and one collection of short stories.

JOYCE CAROL OATES is the author of twenty novels and many books of short stories, poems, essays, and plays. Three times she has won the Continuing Achievement Award in the O. Henry Prize Stories Series. Her 1970 novel *them* won the National Book Award for Fiction. A resident of Princeton, Oates is the Roger S. Berlind Distinguished Professor in the Humanities at Princeton University.

PHILIP ROTH published *Goodbye, Columbus,* from which the story "The Conversion of the Jews" is taken, in 1959. Since then, he has written fourteen novels, including the controversial *Portnoy's Complaint, The Great American Novel, Our Gang,* the Zuckerman trilogy, and *Deception.*

LYNNE SHARON SCHWARTZ, who lives in New York City, is the author of four novels and two collections of short stories. "Over the Hill" is taken from her first book of short fiction, *Acquainted with the Night.*

MELANIE RAE THON is the author of a novel, *Meteors in August,* and a collection of short fiction, *Girls in the Grass.* Born in Montana, she now lives in Massachusetts and teaches at Harvard. "Iona Moon" was first published in *The Hudson Review* and is the basis for Thon's second novel, *Iona Moon.*

JOHN UPDIKE has been publishing short stories since his debut in *The New Yorker* in 1955. *Rabbit at Rest,* Updike's fourteenth novel, brought to a conclusion in 1990 his four-book series on the life of Rabbit Angstrom, one of the more famous characters in postwar American fiction. During the last twenty years Updike has won the Pulitzer Prize, the National Book Award, the American Book Award, and the National Book Critics Circle Award.

HELENA MARÍA VIRAMONTES was born in East Los Angeles in 1954 to a family of eleven. She has been writing about Chicano life and promoting Chicano literature in America since 1975. The author of *The Moth and Other Stories,* Viramontes lives and teaches in Irvine, California and is the coordinator of the Los Angeles Latino Writers Association.

ALICE WALKER is best known for her Pulitzer Prize-winning novel, *The Color Purple.* Her other novels include *Meridian, The Third Life of Grange Copeland,* and *The Temple of My Familiar.* She has also been a prolific short story writer examining the lives of black women in America.

JOY WILLIAMS has written three novels, *States of Grace* (which was nominated for a National Book Award in 1974), *The Changeling,* and *Breaking and Entering.* In 1989 she was the recipient of a Writing Award from the American Academy of Arts and Letters. Williams lives in Arizona.

by Gina Berriault. First published in *Mademoiselle*. Reprinted by permission of the Wallace Literary Agency, Inc.

ETHAN CANIN: "Lies," from *Emperor of the Air* by Ethan Canin, copyright © 1988 by Ethan Canin. Reprinted by permission of Houghton Mifflin Company. All rights reserved.

MICHAEL CHABON: "The Little Knife," from *A Model World and Other Stories* by Michael Chabon, copyright © 1991 by Michael Chabon. Reprinted by permission of William Morrow and Company, Inc.

ERNEST J. GAINES: "The Sky Is Gray," from *Bloodline* by Ernest J. Gaines, copyright © 1963 by Ernest J. Gaines. Reprinted by permission of Doubleday, a division of Bantam Doubleday Dell Publishing Group, Inc.

GENARO GONZALEZ: "Too Much His Father's Son," from *Only Sons* by Genaro Gonzalez, copyright © 1991 by Genaro Gonzalez. Reprinted by permission of Arte Publico Press, University of Houston, Houston, Texas.

GISH JEN: "What Means Switch," copyright © 1990 by Gish Jen. First published in slightly different form in *The Atlantic*. Reprinted by permission of the author.

BARBARA KINGSOLVER: "Rose-Johnny," from *Homeland and Other Stories* by Barbara Kingsolver, copyright © 1989 by Barbara Kingsolver. Reprinted by permission of HarperCollins Publishers.

RICHARD MCCANN: "My Mother's Clothes: The School of Beauty and Shame," copyright © 1986 by Richard McCann. First published in *The Atlantic*. Reprinted by permission of Brandt & Brandt Literary Agents.

CARSON MCCULLERS: "Wunderkind," from *The Ballad of the Sad Café and Collected Short Stories* by Carson McCullers, copyright © 1936, 1941, 1942, 1950, 1955 by Carson McCullers, copyright © renewed 1979 by Floria V. Lasky. Reprinted by permission of Houghton Mifflin Company. All rights reserved.

REGINALD MCKNIGHT: "The Kind of Light That Shines on Texas," from *The Kind of Light That Shines on Texas* by Reginald McKnight, copyright © 1992 by Reginald McKnight. Reprinted by permission of Little, Brown and Company.